Praise for *Love, Just In*

'*Love, Just In* is catnip for friends-to-lovers fans. Natalie Murray imbues her characters with honesty, depth and an aching amount of heart as they navigate their changing relationship. Rich with sparkling banter and the kind of inside jokes that can only happen between the best of friends, *Love, Just In* is an irresistible slow burn that sizzles on every hastily turned page.' **Amy Hutton, author of** *Sit, Stay, Love*

'Natalie Murray has written a delightful and heartfelt romcom about career, friendship and confronting your deepest fears. Flirty, fun and realistic, *Love, Just In* is a sizzling story with real depth ... a page turning friends-to-lovers romance with a local setting which is an ideal summer read!' **Steph Vizard, author of** *The Love Contract*

'Clever, witty and the perfect amount of steamy, *Love Just In* is an addictive friends-to-lovers story, the ultimate summer read.' **Ali Berg and Michelle Kalus, authors of** *Fancy Meeting You Here*

'If you like your romance bubbly and believable, full of brewing chemistry and building to an epic pay off, Natalie Murray has go͏ of *Five Bush Weddings*

Love, Just In

A novel

Natalie Murray

ALLEN&UNWIN

SYDNEY·MELBOURNE·AUCKLAND·LONDON

First published in 2024

Allen & Unwin
Cammeraygal Country
83 Alexander Street
Crows Nest NSW 2065
Australia
Phone: (61 2) 8425 0100
Email: info@allenandunwin.com
Web: www.allenandunwin.com

*Allen & Unwin acknowledges the Traditional Owners of the Country on which we
live and work. We pay our respects to all Aboriginal and Torres Strait Islander
Elders, past and present.*

A catalogue record for this
book is available from the
National Library of Australia

ISBN 978 1 76147 063 9

Set in 11.25/16 pt Sabon LT Pro by Midland Typesetters, Australia
Printed and bound in Australia by the Opus Group

10 9 8 7 6 5 4 3 2 1

The paper in this book is FSC® certified.
FSC® promotes environmentally responsible,
socially beneficial and economically viable
management of the world's forests.

To Tania

For the impersonations, the inside jokes that are no longer inside because I put everything in books now (I'll decide, riiight?), and for Newcastle.

Also, for always going first because I'm the runt but never leaving me behind.

PROLOGUE

Fourteen years ago

*P*lease don't be dying.

Fear grips my chest as Zac blinks down at me with his long arms draped around the shoulders of his mates Cody and Hayden, his eyes glassy and wide and his skin the colour of spoiled milk. I can hear his shallow breaths from here—is he about to tell me he's got a terminal disease?

'Go on, bro,' Cody says.

'Just ask her,' chimes in Hayden.

My fingers tighten around the edge of the train-station bench. 'What's going on?' I ask Zac, the mid-afternoon sun scorching my trembling shoulders through my school dress.

Cody nudges Zac, who sways a little on his feet.

'Uh, Josie?' Zac begins, his voice thin and wobbly.

'Yes?' My stomach clenches. *Don't die, please. You're* not *allowed to.*

'Will you go out with me?' he asks.

My mouth falls open and I gape up at him.

Zac stares into my eyes while all the blood drains from my face and horror crashes into my stomach.

OMG, tell me this is a joke.

Zac and I are just friends. We're the best of friends—why would he do this to me, *and* in front of Cody and Hayden??

'Jose?' Zac presses, a deep blush climbing over his cheeks.

My gaze darts to the infuriatingly empty train tracks behind the trio of sweaty boys in their crumpled school shirts. Why does my train have to be late today of all days?

'So, will you be his girlfriend or not?' Cody pushes.

I am being suffocated. 'I don't . . . I don't think so.'

Zac's face falls. Cody narrows his eyes at me, and Hayden bursts out laughing.

'Why not?' Zac asks in a small voice.

I lift a shoulder, mortified at being put on the spot in front of Cody and Hayden, who constantly tease me about being 'Zac's secret girlfriend'. Imagine if I say yes—Zac and I will be taunted for life. Plus, I've had a huge crush on Damien Di Fiore since Monday, when he left a sweet note in my locker that said he likes my hair. Damien is the most popular guy in our year—I can't lose my chance with him because he thinks I'm dating Zac Jameson, who's got the wild, messy hair of a lunatic and is built like a beanpole.

Don't get me wrong, I *adore* Zac. But not like that.

'Sorry?' is all I manage.

I wish I could siphon out the hurt that's seeping into my best friend's hazel eyes. Blocking out Cody and Hayden's amused stares, I zero in on Zac and offer him a small, apologetic smile, testing the waters. Because the thought of losing him as a friend is as bad as if he had told me he was dying.

His arms slip off his mates' shoulders as he steps towards me, reaching down to gently brush his thumb over my jaw. 'It's OK, sunbeam. Don't be mad. I won't ask again.'

CHAPTER 1

One month ago

ME: Hi, I'm not sure if you'll answer this, but I have some news you might be interested in.

ZAC: Hey, I'm so sorry I haven't been in touch. I meant to reply to your messages a while ago, but things have been a bit full-on.
What's your news?

ME: I hope not bad-full-on?
The news is that I'm coming to Newcastle in a couple of weeks.

ZAC: Really? Cool.
How long will you be staying?

ME: Six months

ZAC: Seriously?

ME: I'm joining the Newcastle bureau (NRN News) for half a year to cover another reporter's leave. It would be nice to see you.

ME: Only if you want to, that is . . .

ZAC: Yeah, of course

ZAC: When do you arrive?

ME: 11th of Feb. I'll be coming up by train because NRN is giving me a car.

ZAC: Cool.

ME: Cool.

ZAC: Hey, are you still arriving on Friday?
I'm off-shift that day, so I could pick you up from the station if you like. Where are you staying?

ME: Yup, still coming. I'll be at the Quest Apartments for a couple of weeks. Thanks, but I can get an Uber.

ZAC: It's fine, I don't mind picking you up.

ME: I don't want you to put yourself out for me.

ZAC: That's not what I'm doing. I'd be happy to pick you up. Can you get off at Hamilton station?

ME: OK, as long as you don't mind. I just checked, and my train will get into Hamilton at 11:05 am.

ZAC: OK cool. I'll be there.

ME: Cool.

CHAPTER 2

Today

I set my suitcase on the dusty platform and scan the train station for a face I haven't laid eyes on in two years. But among the smattering of bystanders in cargo shorts and singlet tops, there's no sign of the tall guy with a mop of curly dark hair that used to stain my high school yearbook photos like an ink blot.

I double check that the tangerine-orange station sign says 'Hamilton' before rolling my suitcase over to an empty bench.

While blocking out the whiff of train fumes with one hand, I pull out my phone with the other and tap open my last message to Zac, my brow pinching when I find nothing to let me know he's going to be late. When we lived together while we were at university, Zac was always so punctual that I used to tease him about waking up his own alarm clock in the morning. Is this a Newcastle thing? He's on some kind of surfie-boy, beach-vibes timeline now?

My stomach rises into my throat again at the thought of seeing him.

Why so serious, Josie? This is Zac Jameson ... high school bestie, university roommate, inappropriate-humour brother-in-arms. Chill.

My phone pings with a message alert from Christina Rice, my Sydney colleague and dear friend. I inhale another jittery breath. I've been waiting for this text since yesterday.

> **CHRISTINA:** Sorry, darling. Justin said he's not looking to get involved with anyone right now.
> I think you're going to find a gorgeous man in Newcastle. Call me when you've settled in? x

The greasy meat pie I downed on the ride up here sours in my stomach as I stare at the screen. Wait ... what? Did I imagine the eye-sex I shared with Christina's urban-planner friend Justin at her birthday party last week? He'd flown in that morning from a conference in Amsterdam and had oozed smart and successful vibes in his tailored shirt and designer jeans. Even Christina had noticed our subtle flirting, and suggested connecting us for a possible date. But *he's not looking to get involved with anyone right now.* Me being the 'anyone'.

I swipe out of the message, swallowing the small sting of rejection. Maybe Justin thinks I'm too much of a flight risk, given I'm about to spend the next six months living a two-hour drive away. But perhaps this is the universe looking out for me. If I'm going to be stuck in this regional, beachside city for half a year, I should be channelling my energy into kicking butt at this TV reporting role so that I can impress the bigwigs down in Sydney. It seems counterproductive to leave town to get their attention, but the Newcastle news bureau is part of the same network, and Christina assures me it's a sort of sideways promotion. Sweet of her to say when we both know that's not really the case.

After my gaze makes another sweep for Zac, I take a moment to size up my new home. I've only been to Newcastle once: I was fourteen when my parents dragged me here for my older sister Ingrid's soccer game, which apparently required as much attention as a World Cup Final. I'd screamed in my poor mum's face for separating me from my boyfriend at the time, the blue-eyed, smooth-haired Damien Di Fiore, for yet another one of Ingrid's higher-priority activities. I'd had no idea that Damien would dump me the following Monday because Clara Ng blinked at him.

Whatever happened to our school's leading lady-killer? I'll have to ask Zac, if he ever shows up.

Five minutes crawl by, each one whipping up more unease in my gut.

What if something happened to Zac on the way here?

A memory of my phone blasting at three am pushes into my mind, and I hunch forward until my forehead is between my knees.

But lightning never strikes twice . . . does it?

A piercing yap shocks my face back up. A pair of tiny coal-black eyes are death-staring me from within a ball of honey-toned dreadlocks that wriggles against a muscular lower leg. I lift my gaze higher and higher until it lands on Zac's slightly flushed face. He must've rounded on me from the building behind us.

Oh my god, it's the real, in-the-flesh Zac Jameson. The brightness I thought he'd lost has returned to his hazel eyes, and his chest fills out his white T-shirt, which is marked with the slogan 'Shoot Hoops, Not People'.

Newcastle suits him.

The faintest trace of a smile edges his mouth as I climb to my feet. 'Hey.' His voice is deeper and huskier than I remember it.

'Hey.'

I have much more to say than a one-syllable greeting, but my throat locks as a memory interrupts my vision. It's of this exact face—younger, rounder, a touch spottier—standing over me on a train station bench beside our Sydney high school.

'Josie, will you go out with me?'

'I don't think so.'

The tiniest shake of my head releases the flashback. We both step forward, our arms lifting and our elbows knocking in a clumsy, barely-there hug before we shift back again.

'Hey,' he says again.

'Hey.'

God, does either of us want to say 'hey' for the fifth time? News just in: We're awkward now!

An uncomfortable feeling tugs in my stomach, but the dreadlocked dog yaps at me again, interrupting my thoughts.

'What the hell is that thing?' I blurt through a grin, nodding down at it.

Zac scoops up the pint-sized pooch and presses his smiling cheek against its muss of Rastafarian fluff. 'This is Trouble.'

'Are you sure it's not Bob Marley?'

I've forgotten that the cutest sound in the world is Zac Jameson's laugh. The first time I heard it was when I secretly mimicked our Year Eight science teacher, Mr Rosebottom, who spoke painfully quietly and had a twitchy eye. Not kind of me, but hysterical to thirteen-year-old Zac. He'd laughed so hard that I'd suffered a fierce attack of the giggles too, and Mr Rosebottom had banned us from being lab partners for the rest of the term. Banished to the opposite side of the room, Zac would toss scrunched-up notes at me that said things like: 'Dare you to twitch your eye every time Rosebottom looks your way,' and 'Do you think he speaks so softly so he can hear the voices in his head better?'

Now, Zac's standing a metre away from me, yet it feels like twelve thousand.

Trying to relax the atmosphere, I bring my nose close to the dog's and scrunch my face, imitating its expression. This earns another chuckle from Zac—OK, still the biggest fan of my impersonations—and when I straighten back up, a sort of dull ache eclipses my abdomen as I think of the last time I saw Zac in person. When his eyes were red-rimmed, his cheeks hollow, and he wouldn't even look at me. Kind of like he's only half looking at me now.

'How was the ride up?' he asks stiffly, setting Trouble back down and lifting my suitcase. The scuffed bag vibrates over the platform's grid of plastic bumps as we head towards the stairs leading to the pedestrian overpass.

'Long. Didn't have anyone there with me to play "Would You Rather".'

I cast Zac a sideways smirk, searching for evidence that he remembers playing endless rounds of 'Would You Rather' during our multiple train rides between Sydney and Bathurst when we both went to uni there. His lightning-fast smile comes off as more polite than genuine and sends a flash of worry through me. Is Zac only here, picking me up, because we used to be so close that it's the expected thing to do? That would make sense; he's the most courteous person I've ever met. The dull ache spreads further through my stomach.

As Zac gets a little ahead of me on the concrete steps, I steal a moment to size up my oldest friend. His unruly hair has been cropped razor-short at the back, but he's left it long on top in a twist of dark-chocolate curls. I should tell him never to change barbers. The haircut isn't only super cool, it's perfect for him. But he looks so different from the man I last saw almost two years ago, and my heart sinks at the realisation that it's probably more than his looks that have changed.

From the top of the station footbridge, Hamilton's strip of redbrick houses is joined by a pub and a couple of shops, and it looks alarmingly small and desolate— like a lonely outer suburb of Sydney. When we reach the street at the base of the staircase, Zac halts behind a gleaming black Subaru Forester and flips open the boot, sliding my suitcase inside.

OK, this is officially the longest Zac and I have been in each other's company without being such motor-mouths that we compete for airtime. My mum used to have to set a timer when Zac would call after dinner each night because neither of us ever wanted to hang up.

I snort a little laugh to fill the silence. 'Are you sure there's room in the car for me with that thing?' I nod at the miniature dog lounging in the back seat while Zac opens my car door. 'He's literally three seats across.'

'Trouble is a *she*,' he replies with mock offence, and our gazes catch as I brush past him. His tight smile draws out his dimples, and I mentally cling to this nano-second of warmth from him. Those dimples drove the girls in high school batty after they decided that the cutest guy in our year wasn't actually Damien Di Fiore but Zachary Jameson, who just took a little longer to grow into his features. But to me he was always daggy, class-clown Zac, with limbs too long for his body and uncontrollable curly hair that sprouted from his head like the fronds of a palm tree.

Zac slides into the driver's seat and taps on the GPS. 'The Quest Apartments, right?'

'Yup. It's just around the corner from my new work, apparently.'

My gaze skims over the length of his body as he pulls out of the parking space. OK, that's one tidbit about Zac's secret life up here revealed: he's been working out. *Not so daggy now.*

The GPS calculates it'll be a four-minute drive to the serviced apartments that the news channel has put me in for two weeks. Wow, I wouldn't make it to the end of my street in Sydney in four minutes during rush hour.

Zac lightly drums his fingers on the steering wheel like he's as low-grade nervous as I am. 'Sorry I was a bit late,' he says. 'I was on a work call about a new role that's come up.'

'Oh, really? That sounds exciting.' I brave a direct look at his profile. 'Got some details to share?' Now that I'm nearing thirty and feeling five years behind where I should be, career pathways have become an urgent theme in my life.

He runs a hand up the back of his neck. 'Well, it's a more specialised position—I guess you could say more senior—and one of my supervisors thinks I'd be good for it.'

'Hell yeah, you would.' I smile. For as long as I've known Zac, he's been universally adored by his employers—even the sour-faced dude who ran the butcher shop where he had his first job was obsessed with keeping him on staff.

Zac clears his throat. 'The new role is to become a critical care paramedic, so I'd be covering a wider area and going out in the helicopter a lot ... doing more complex procedures and dealing mostly with the high-trauma jobs and life-threatening stuff.'

The smile drops off my face. *Are you serious, Zac?*

Instead of asking that, though, I shoot for something simpler. 'Are you going to apply?'

He lets out a deep sigh. 'I don't know. I finished the training last month, and it all went fine. But I only just started doing the hands-on stuff again after nearly two years on the desk. Am I really ready to work only the tough cases?'

His fingers tighten around the steering wheel and his question hangs unanswered. The fact is, Zac deserves a medal just for staying on as a paramedic after everything he went through, without being asked to handle only the high-trauma jobs as well.

He makes a right turn and I'm still searching for words that won't form. I don't really feel like the person who should be giving Zac life advice right now—not five minutes after I've arrived in his brave new world that I know nothing about. If the roles were reversed, and he tried to tell me what to do, I'd probably make a joke about marking him absent from my life for the past two years and dial the discomfort between us up a notch.

Remembering that Zac has mostly ignored me for all that time burns my throat, and I turn to the window, focusing on what will be my new home for the next half-year. The city's a bit industrial-looking, but it's greener than the inner city of Sydney, and there are plenty of funky cafés and eateries wedged between vibrant murals and street art. I'm now getting more 'cool, edgy Melbourne' than 'outer Sydney suburb' vibes. My eyes trail after a two-storey op shop with colourful clothing racks in the front window that I make a note to come back to.

The car rolls to a stop at a set of traffic lights, and Zac glances at me. 'Tell me more about your new job at NRN News. It's pretty cool they're giving you a car.'

'Yeah, they don't normally do that, but I negotiated it into my contract because they want me to drive to Sydney regularly to cover shifts there as well.'

A trace of a line forms on his brow. 'They want you to drive to Sydney a lot?'

'Yeah, I'm still technically part of the Sydney news team. I mean, seriously, just hire me full-time down there already—why move me up here?' I throw my hands up in the air.

He nods. 'I actually know someone who works there. At NRN.'

'Really? Who?'

'A girl called Meghan Mackay. Do you know her?'

I shake my head. 'The name's not familiar. But I'm sure I'll meet her soon enough.'

He falls silent again, and my fingertips slip beneath the rips in my jeans that feel too tight in this sweltering heat. Beside me, Zac's tanned hand rests on his bare thigh as he uses his other to turn the wheel. Questions pile up in my head about his new life up here, but none make it to my lips. Seeing him so tense and distant with me at close range hurts more than I thought it would. Where is the guy who'd toss pillows at me during sleepovers because he wouldn't want me to go to sleep, then drag his blow-up mattress beside mine so he could talk my ear off until we eventually passed out?

Zac, it's me. *Why are you acting like I'm a stranger?*

We're on what appears to be a relatively busy street for this city when he leans in my direction, bringing a pleasant whiff of men's soap. 'There it is.'

The white letters spelling 'QUEST' are barely visible through a thick cluster of trees. There are empty parking spots everywhere—another thing I'm amazed about—and Zac pulls his car up right outside the front entrance.

I turn to him. 'This is me,' I say, trying to be cute to mask my disappointment at how out of reach he feels. When his golden-green eyes trap mine and hold on for a moment, my breath lodges in my chest and triggers a fit of coughing that's been plaguing me for weeks.

Zac frowns. 'Are you OK? Jeez, that cough doesn't sound good.'

My stomach plunges to the carpeted floor beneath my leather slides.

That cough doesn't sound good.

Bile rises up in my throat, and my heart begins pummelling my ribs.

That cough doesn't sound good.

That cough doesn't sound good.

Don't panic.

Don't panic.

I can't breathe.

'Do you want me to come and look at rentals with you tomorrow?' Zac offers lightly, like he hasn't just confirmed my worst fear—that I have cancer spreading through my body. I can barely hear him through the pounding in my ears.

That cough doesn't sound good.

'You said you have some appointments lined up?' he adds.

I cling to the distraction of his question. 'Yeah, I—I've got three possible roommates to meet.' My voice trembles, but my heartbeat's already slowing.

That cough doesn't sound good.

'So, would you like me to come along?' His eyes travel over my face, the direct contact making me feel even more exposed. But it diverts my mind from the dark place it just travelled to.

'Do you *want* to come?' I ask.

I want him to say yes, but I don't want it to be out of a sense of 'former best friend' duty. If that's the case, I'd rather go alone.

He shrugs a shoulder. 'I'm off-shift tomorrow, and there's not meant to be much swell, so I can't surf.'

'You *surf*?' I tilt back a little, one corner of my mouth lifting.

He blinks at me. 'This is a shock to you because?'

'It's not a *shock*'—Sydney is teeming with surfers—'I've just never known you to be a wax-head.'

Live music bar addict, whisky connoisseur, practically Michelin-starred chef, health and science geek—yes to all of those. I have discovered many sides of Zac Jameson over the years, but I have never seen him go anywhere near a surfboard.

He laughs lightly, looks away, and then back to me again, reminding me of when he used to flirt with girls at university. 'I guess you'll have to reserve your judgement, Ms Larsen,' he says. 'Clearly, there's a lot you still don't know about me.'

I snort-laugh to hide the bitter truth that comment draws to my mind.

Zac exhales, tapping the steering wheel. 'Well, I guess that's—'

The wail of a siren cuts between us as an ambulance rounds the corner, then rushes past Zac's window. A few hundred metres up the street, it veers onto the footpath and comes to a screeching halt.

'Shit, what happened?' I say, stretching my neck, but a line-up of cars is already building, and it's hard to see from this far back.

Zac swallows hard. 'Dunno.'

I glance at him. 'Do you think we should go check it out?'

By *we*, I mean *him*, because he's a paramedic, but he's off-shift and there are clearly first responders on the scene already.

'I'm sure they've got it handled,' he mumbles. 'You're not going to call the news channel about this, are you?' He shoots me a teasing look, but I don't miss the slight shake in his voice or the way his face has paled.

'If this is considered TV-worthy news around here, then I'm worried about keeping my job.'

'If it bleeds, it leads, right?'

He stares back at the activity up ahead, and my mind whirls between wanting to defend my job as a journalist and asking Zac how the hell he can still be around ambulances after what he lived through nearly two years ago. But then he clicks open his door and I follow him out onto the street.

He jerks his chin at the Quest Apartments. 'Should we go in?'

We? I stare at him for a moment. *Is that it—are we back to him lazing around my space, flipping through TV channels while I have a shower or check my emails, like we used to? Just like that?*

'Although, I've actually got to head off soon,' he adds with a glance at his watch.

OK, not like that, then.

'Sure,' I reply, a little too brightly to hide my let-down feeling, before barging over to the car to retrieve my suitcase like a mafia bomb is about to detonate in there. 'They probably don't allow dogs inside, anyway.' I peek at Trouble through the back window to make sure she's OK in this heat.

Zac steps behind me and reaches past my arm to take hold of the bag that I can easily manage myself.

'I've got it, thanks,' I say. I attempt to untangle my forearm from his inner bicep, which ends in me bashing my forehead into his chest wall when I turn around. 'Shit, sorry.' I back away, gripping my suitcase with both hands.

'So, tomorrow then?' he asks.

'Yes, sounds good, thank you.' *God, I sound like a stranger who's just been offered an appointment that suits my schedule. Is that what's happening here?*

Zac mirrors my cautious smile before turning towards his car.

I lurch forward with one last-ditch effort to break the ice. After all, I'm just as responsible for salvaging what's left of this friendship as he is. 'Want to go and grab a bite or something?' I offer. 'Sushi? Bubble tea? Vodka shots?'

He must know I'm not serious about the vodka. The last time we went shot-for-shot on the clear stuff in a live music bar in Bathurst, the escapade ended with Zac holding my hair back while I puked into the gutter on the walk home to our miniscule apartment.

But there's an 'I've missed you' gift sitting inside my suitcase . . . conversations to be had . . . questions to be answered . . . intolerable discomfort to be eased—all so the rock growing inside my stomach can shrink and go away.

Zac rakes a hand through his curls, his brow pinching. 'That *does* sound good, except for maybe the vodka shots because, you know, old man now'—he points at himself—'but I'm actually meeting up with someone this afternoon.'

The look on his face answers the question immediately. The 'someone' is a girl.

'Oh, cool, no worries.'

My smile isn't entirely forced. It doesn't matter to me that he's got a date. Zac and I are more-than-old friends who've been each other's sounding boards after countless hook-ups with other people. I even hosted his Great Gatsby–themed engagement party after his then-girlfriend Tara proposed to him in Peru. He and I are strictly platonic and always have been.

I've just never known him to be the person who would arrange to pick me up in a new city after not seeing each other for two years and plan a date for the same afternoon. I not only know nothing about his new life up here, but I've seriously dropped on his priority list, which sends a sharp blade into my chest.

'We'll catch up tomorrow, if you like,' he says, looking right at me like he's making a life-changing promise.

'We'll do that. Thanks so much for the ride.'

I adjust my grip on my suitcase and dart forward to press a lightning-fast kiss on Zac's cheek, catching another whiff of soap and a brief smell of mint chewing gum. His spine snaps straight like I've assaulted him, and I spin away from him and drag my suitcase towards the serviced apartments without a backward glance.

A note-to-self rings through my head.

Don't kiss his cheek again. He doesn't like that anymore. He doesn't like you anymore. He only picked you up today because he's the world's most decent guy and he felt obliged to, and now you've gone and moved into his city, intruded upon his space, and interrupted his beachy, surfie, I'm-meeting-up-with-someone new life. There's a reason he never once came down to Sydney to visit you.

He doesn't want you in his life anymore.

The problem is, now that I've been in Zac's company again, heard that ridiculously cute laugh, felt his eyes on me—his full attention—I've never been so sure of anything.

I miss Zac. And I need him to be my best friend again.

CHAPTER 3

Fifteen years ago

I loathed the oppressively strict St Teresa's Girls High even more than my liberal-minded parents did, but right now, deciding to move to the local high school feels like a colossal mistake.

As I clutch my shiny new schoolbag and sink further into a sea of gawking faces, I don't find anyone I recognise. The guy with slicked-back hair and piercing blue eyes keeps wolf-whistling whenever I walk past, making the other boys laugh. There are happy, chilled-out students *everywhere*, while I can't seem to catch my breath.

I hover near a group of girls on the benches beside the canteen who are having an intense discussion about the lead star of the superhero movie that just came out. But when they don't invite me over, my throat draws tight, and I get a thumping feeling of pressure behind my chest wall.

I scan the other half of the quadrangle for potential new friends and spot one of the boys watching me—the tall one with curly hair that's so dark it's almost black. I duck my head, then wander over to the empty benches facing the sports field and dig my iPod out of my bag. I press the earbuds into my ears and hit play on *The Best of Billy Joel*. He's my dad's favourite, so I've heard him a lot in the car, and I know all his songs. My favourite is 'Piano Man'.

A hand lightly taps my shoulder from behind, and I nearly jump out of my skin. I fish out an earbud and twist to find the curly-haired guy smiling down at me.

'What are you listening to?' he asks.

My throat closes up. 'Billy Joel.'

This is the part where kids my age usually scrunch their faces or laugh, but the guy just says, 'Cool,' and drops onto the bench beside me. His thighs look twice the length of mine.

'So, you're the new girl,' he says. '*Josephine*.'

I exaggerate a shudder. 'Please don't call me that. It's Josie.'

His smile is as warm as my cheeks feel. 'I'm Zac. Zachary, actually, but please don't call me that.'

'OK.'

He flops out an upturned palm. 'Can I share your earphones? Billy Joel's cool.'

'Yeah, sure.' I hand him the earbud I just pulled out of my ear, and he shifts closer to me so that it can reach.

'This song's my favourite,' he says over 'Piano Man' while we sit, joined by wires, like a two-headed space creature.

My lips split into a smile. 'Mine too.'

'What do you think it's about?'

'My dad said it's about loneliness.'

Zac squints up at the sky, thickly blanketed with clouds. 'Good call.'

After a couple of bars of the song, a chattering group of boys I saw Zac with earlier sidle up to our bench, surrounding us on all sides like a prison gang.

'What are you and the new girl listening to, Jameson?' one asks Zac, like I'm not even here. I think his name is Cody.

Zac holds a hand over his eyes because the sky is so glary. 'Billy Joel.'

Cody grimaces. 'That's old-people music.'

And there it is.

'Thank you,' Zac replies brightly like the comment was a compliment. And I guess maybe it could be? My dad always says the best era for music was the '60s and '70s. It seems a long time ago, but it might be true. Thankfully, Cody and his posse quickly get bored and wander off.

Zac nods to the music while the closing chorus of 'Piano Man' plays out.

'Loneliness . . .' he repeats. 'Yet, they're all people together in a bar, aren't they?'

'You can be with people and still feel alone,' I suggest.

He turns to set his mossy-green eyes on me. 'You're smart, Josie.'

I just laugh because compliments are weird. But it's the first time I've smiled all day. I wriggle a touch closer to Zac and press play on 'Just the Way You Are'.

CHAPTER 4

Today

With a steaming mug of coffee in my left hand and my phone in my right, I'm Facebook-stalking the three potential housemates I've lined up to meet today. The only criterion to make my shortlist was that they weren't put off by my staying only six months in Newcastle.

The guy in Cooks Hill is a social media ghost who I can't find online; the girl in New Lambton's profile pic is a close-up of a Rottweiler with foamy drool clinging to its jowls; and the girl in Wallsend is a tangerine-tanned brunette who can hold one leg vertically against her ear. *Impressive.*

The dancer has loose privacy settings, so I scroll down, creeping her page. The headline of a news article she recently shared fills the screen: 'Young Mother Warns Others About Shock Breast Cancer Diagnosis: "I'd been told I had nothing to worry about"'.

My stomach flies into my throat. I hurriedly scan the article, each sentence burning my eyes.

'. . . has stage 4 breast cancer that has spread to her spine and lungs . . .'

'. . . the twenty-nine-year-old had an intuition that something wasn't right . . .'

'. . . dry coughs coupled with a shortness of breath can be a sign of metastatic breast cancer . . .'

By the time I reach the young woman's GoFundMe link at the bottom, my palms are slick, my heart's a bass drum, and I'm coughing like an eighty-year-old chain smoker.

Zac's words replay in my mind. *That cough doesn't sound good.*

I beat my fist against my chest with a sort of panicked fury, which exacerbates the phlegm attack. When I finally catch my breath, my eyes are glazed with tears.

What if my cough means I have breast cancer that's spread to my lungs?

I'm not even thirty. I haven't met my dream man, haven't had kids, haven't read the news on TV. I've done nothing with my life.

I jump as my phone vibrates with a call from Christina, my Sydney bestie of the post-Zac years. We met nearly two years ago when I joined Channel One News as a junior reporter. Because she was the network's prime-time newsreader, I'd expected Christina to be intimidating and dismissive of my low-ranking status, but the first words she ever spoke to me were a warm compliment.

'You're a great writer, Josie,' she said after pre-reading the intro I'd just written for a feature story. The unexpected praise from someone so accomplished totally threw me. I scrambled for something nice to say back, and while there were countless things I could've mentioned about Christina's work, I blurted a compliment about her sixties-style sheath dress because it was honestly gorgeous. She brightened and leaned closer to me from her presenter's chair.

'Don't tell the wardrobe team, but I got it from an op shop,' she said with a wink. 'It cost less than a cup of coffee.'

We exchanged snickers, and I confessed that half my clothing came from Vinnies, including the plaid blazer I was wearing. Christina then asked if I'd been to the giant op shop that had recently opened in North Sydney, and I said I hadn't. She scribbled the address down on the blank side of a script.

Later that day, a funny meme about second-hand clothing hit my inbox, and I debated for ages whether I should forward it to Christina before I eventually clicked 'send'. She replied right away with three laughing emojis and an even funnier meme about creepy op-shop junk. I cracked up and rose in my seat, finding Christina sharing my smile from across the newsroom. We ended up sending each other different memes almost daily, and a few weeks later, we met up in North Sydney to visit the op shop she mentioned. We've been meeting for treasure-hunt browses most Saturday mornings ever since.

I cough out what's left of my hoarse breath and answer her call. 'Hey, lovely. Sorry, I forgot to reply to your message yesterday.'

'Oh yes, a shame about Justin, but hey—it's a win for the eligible bachelors of Newcastle.' A smile edges Christina's velvety, TV-trained voice. 'How are you finding it there so far?'

I flop back onto the mattress, fixing my gaze on the paint-chipped ceiling. 'Newcastle is . . . small. Quiet. And hot.'

'It's hot here, too,' she says, like Sydney's on the other side of the planet. 'And nothing sounds better to me than quiet.'

'I actually haven't seen any of the city yet,' I admit. 'And it's not *that* quiet now that I think of it. I can hear every car on Hunter Street right now outside the window.'

'Well, the good thing is you have *plenty* of time left to get to know the place.'

She's teasing me. When I was offered the transfer to this bureau to cover another reporter's six-month sabbatical, I leaned so hard into Christina for advice that I'm surprised she's still standing. I complained to her that six months was too long to be off the radar of Oliver Novak—the CEO of Channel One News in Sydney; that this job was too far away from my life, my apartment, my favourite cafés and op shops.

That coming to Newcastle meant facing Zac and the painful possibility that his abandonment of me two years ago is going to be permanent.

But Christina convinced me this was the right move. Up here, I'd be a bigger fish in a smaller pond with fewer reporters ready to scratch my eyes out to get ahead of me. She glossed over the fact that the regional posting is a kind of punishment for my epic screw-up during a live news cross in Sydney a few months ago. I still can't think about it without wanting to punch myself in the eye. And while I didn't strictly *have* to take the Newcastle position, I feared it was that or being let go.

'So, I'm actually calling with some news,' Christina dangles, her voice rising.

I sit up. 'Oh my god, what? CNN called begging to poach you, didn't they? No, wait . . . CNBC. BBC. Just tell me it's not Fox. And I'm totally coming to visit you in New York.'

'You're totally coming to visit me at the hospital. In about half a year's time.'

The thought slams into my head like a freight train. *Christina has cancer. And she knows she's only got five months left.*

'I'm pregnant!' she squeals.

After a split second to process, I scream into the phone before bursting into tears of relief and delight. Christina and her divine husband, Pete, have been trying to get pregnant for the past eight years, and even though we've only been friends for two of those, I know this means more to her than anything.

Her voice clogs with sniffles. 'It's been so hard not to tell you, especially when I knew you were leaving me.

But after everything, we just wanted to hit that first trimester milestone, you know?'

'I'm *so* happy for you.' I brush my cheeks with my knuckles. 'And Pete.'

A few puffs sound like she's pulling tissues from a box. 'Now, I've also had time to think about this, Josie. After waiting so long—and fingers crossed everything stays well—I'm going to want at least a year off to spend with my baby. I don't even care at this point if Oliver fires me over it. Either way, Sydney is going to need a new newsreader. And that should be you, darling. You *have* to go for this.'

The stark hotel room collapses around me into a dizzying spin.

'All you need to do is shine in this Newcastle role,' Christina continues. 'Push for the big stories, save the best bits for your showreel, and most importantly, get on that anchor desk up there. Be the person they go to when their presenters are off sick or unavailable.'

I can hardly catch my breath. 'But there are so many reporters in Sydney who'd want to fill in for you. People with way more experience.' Names are slapping me in the face already—those of seasoned reporters who *haven't* fallen apart on live television.

'Josie, this lack of confidence is what's going to hold you back.' Christina's tone is gentle but firm, like I'm the piece of news she's delivering. 'You know how good you are. *I* know how good you are. And I've been in this game a long time. Oliver Novak doesn't want the person who's been there the longest; he wants the person who'll be the best at the job—full stop.'

'He wants someone who can handle themselves on air,' I counter.

She tuts. 'It's time to put that behind you. I'm telling you—you can do this. Viewers love you; they always have. That means more than anything. And when I tell Oliver I'm planning to take a year off, I'm going to be personally pushing for you.'

My heart swells in my chest. Only someone as kind and supportive as Christina would advocate for a younger, cheaper stand-in who could possibly swallow her job forever. But she's told me on numerous occasions that I remind her of herself when she was my age, and given how brutal network news can be, she wishes she'd had someone looking out for her back then. She also knows that if I were lucky enough to become her temporary replacement, I would *never* try to steal that position from her permanently, and I wouldn't need to. Channel One News has bulletins running all day. I could use the on-air experience to spring into a different timeslot once she returned to work.

Oh my god, is she right? Could I actually win this job? After that, all I would need would be to fall in love with an incredible man, get married on the beach in Hawaii, and be pregnant. All my ambitions achieved before I'm thirty—*tick, tick, tick.*

My phone pings against my ear. I jump up to peer

through the window, my heart skipping a beat when I spot Zac's Subaru idling outside.

I remind Christina how much I adore her, how utterly thrilled I am for her news, and how much I miss her already, before hanging up and grabbing my bag.

If yesterday was hot, today is a firepit, and Zac spends most of the short drive to his place apologising for it like he's a celestial being who oversees the weather.

Before we head out to my housemate interviews, he's offered to make me lunch, which is not an invitation a sane person would turn down. Zac is universally acknowledged as a *kick-ass* cook. He once made a French degustation dinner for ten of us from uni that was so jaw-droppingly good, we all begged him to switch from paramedicine to culinary school. But he's always maintained that if cooking became his job, he'd lose interest in it, and my stomach couldn't take that.

Two years ago, a lunch invite from Zac would be as normal as breathing, but when I saw his text this morning, my first thought was: *He feels bad for ditching my catch-up offer to go on a date yesterday*. It wouldn't be the first time Zac's guilty conscience drove him to do something sweet to make up for a decision he feels bad about.

We pull up outside a small but pretty house in Hamilton, the light-grey siding and white trim unlocking a memory of the rustic little home he'd rented with

Tara in Sydney's inner west after the three of us graduated from uni. Tara had loved everything about the place except for its mustard-coloured walls, so Zac and I painted the entire interior pale blue one weekend while she was away visiting her parents. Tara was so chuffed that she took us both to one of the fanciest restaurants in the city for dinner, ordering three courses each and several bottles of champagne. When the bill arrived and we figured out that the dinner cost more than a house painter would have done, we laughed our drunk asses off and caught a whole bunch of side-eyes from posh patrons at the surrounding tables.

Zac and I step out of the car and stroll up his short path, and he shifts a surfboard out of my way before holding the front door open for me.

Inside, my eyes dart between off-white walls that stretch to a surprisingly lofty ceiling, a navy couch set with latte-coloured throw pillows, and a trio of cushioned barstools with iron legs facing a marbled kitchen island.

Holy sophistication.

'I like what you've done with the place,' I say jokingly because, of course, I've never set foot in here before.

Zac breathes a light chuckle as he kicks off his shoes beside a gym bag and heads into the open-plan kitchen, where he's already set out a large bowl, a chopping board strewn with apple slices, a plate of bacon rashers, and a couple of other jugs and bowls.

I'm used to seeing Zac in charge behind a kitchen bench, but everything else requires processing. What happened to the decaying shacks with bad paint jobs? I inch closer to the large abstract painting of cobalt blue slashes positioned above the couch, the raised brush-strokes confirming it's an original artwork. I cringe internally at the thought of him being inside my studio apartment in Sydney with its IKEA wall art and op-shop furniture.

Zac gives his giant mixing bowl a stir. 'Want something to drink?'

'A water would be great, thanks.' I drag out one of the barstools, nearly tripping over a distressed-leather dog bed.

'I can't believe you bought a dog,' I add as he pours me a glass from the fridge dispenser.

'I didn't; I rescued her.' He scoops up Trouble and runs his fingers through her matted fur. 'As if you could have resisted this beast.'

I smile over my water as he sets her down on the dog bed. Even though Zac looks like the kind of guy who'd own a husky or a German Shepherd, he's always had a soft spot for tiny dogs. My shoulders lighten a little at the discovery that there are still parts of him that feel familiar.

I rest my chin in my palm and watch him pour batter into a special pan filled with little round moulds. This, too, feels more like the Zac I know. He heats up the frypan and uses a spatula to smooth out a few scoops of what I think is grated potato.

I give the air a cartoon-style sniff. 'What are you making? It smells amazing.'

'It's a Romanian dish called creier pane.' He shoots me a glance over his shoulder. 'Lamb's brains.'

I don't even try to hide my grimace. 'Oh, Jesus.'

Rude, but I can still be brutally honest in front of him. Can't I?

Zac laughs, tossing a kitchen towel over his shoulder. 'I'm kidding. It's aebleskiver. Danish pancakes.'

I let out a breath. 'Thank god. I don't want to eat someone's thoughts.'

That earns me another chuckle. 'I'm not sure how much deep thinking lambs do.'

He leans against the counter and crosses his arms at me, his white T-shirt printed with the words 'Sold Out' stretching across his broad chest.

'It's really good to see you, Josie.' The words come out soft and sudden, and I have no idea what to do with myself at this juncture.

'You too,' I blurt out, my cheeks pinking. I hide this by slipping off the stool to fumble through my bag. 'I actually brought something for you.'

I pull out the glossy cookbook and slide it towards him.

He spins the book to face him, gasping with amusement. 'What the hell is that?'

I snort-laugh as he takes in the cover of *Recipes from Iceland*—an image of a cooked animal skull resting beside a pile of mashed potato. 'It's pickled sheep's head,' I reply with a frown like I'm defending it. 'I was kind of hoping you were going to make it for me today.'

It's totally a gag gift—not that I want to offend Icelandic culture—but knowing Zac, he'll cook every recipe in this book.

'I got something for you, too.' He crouches to flip open a lower cupboard while one of his hands stays braced against the counter.

'What is it?' I say. 'One of those inflatable tube men from those car dealerships? A really, really tiny violin? No, wait—a monster-sized dildo with realistic vein detailing?'

Eeek, too far.

Zac reappears, and I'm kind of proud of the full-face flush I've induced. But I miss being silly and inappropriate with him.

He pushes a box towards me that's neatly wrapped in pearl-pink paper. I hadn't even thought to wrap the cookbook. I carefully unstick the paper, uncovering a one-thousand-piece puzzle of the gigantic words 'JIGSAW PUZZLES ARE FOR NERDS'.

I practically cackle, not because the gift is that funny, but because it propels me back to when Zac and I would argue over my half-finished puzzles of seascapes that would hijack our dining table at uni, thwarting his plans to host more international-themed dinner parties. Warmth spreads through my chest when I realise that both gifts prove we haven't forgotten each other just yet.

'Thank you,' I say. 'I feel so seen.'

I'm still a little buzzy over the whole thing when we sit down to eat his Danish masterpiece; the golden-brown spheres lie somewhere between a pancake and a doughnut. After I've downed three of them through borderline erotic moans of satisfaction, I sprinkle a rain of salt over the homemade hash browns and slice into one.

'Still do that?' Zac says, nodding at the salt storm.

'Still do that.'

'You'd better watch your blood pressure.' He brings his fork to his lips with his brows raised.

'Such a medical man,' I rag, but my gut twists tight. The gentle sound of Zac chewing envelopes the room before I collect enough courage to speak again. 'Can it cause cancer?'

'Too much salt?' He holds the back of his hand to his mouth while chewing. 'Possibly a loose link to stomach cancer.'

My chest clamps up and I do a mental sweep of my stomach for strange symptoms before pushing for a subject change. 'Any news on that accident from yesterday?' I nudge the salty hash browns to the side with my fork.

He shakes his head. 'My ambo mate told me a cyclist got hit by a car, but his injuries weren't too bad. I'm not sure what happened after that. They never tell us after we take them to the hospital.'

'Really?'

'It's not our business, I suppose. But for some of the bigger jobs—where you don't know if you've actually helped save someone's life or not—some closure might be nice.'

Some of the bigger jobs.

I watch him cut into a crispy rasher of bacon, questioning the timeline of when I became such a wimp and why I can't bring myself to just ask how he's been since everything happened. We used to be able to ask each other anything. I remember Zac once quizzing me over what it feels like to get a period, and I've probed him before about the finer details of having a male body. I think we both secretly loved these insights into the opposite sex, this all-access pass to insider information. Now, that secret door we once slipped through with ease feels bolted shut.

'How's it been going down in Sydney?' Zac says, making direct eye contact with me for short bursts at a time. 'Are you reading the news yet?'

My gaze falls to my plate. He has no idea that I recently proved incapable of handling myself on air because I'm so stupidly terrified of dying. I guess he's not the only one holding back key news updates.

'Not yet. But just this morning, I found out that one of the main newsreaders down there, who's a really good friend of mine, is going to be taking maternity leave in five months. She thinks I should apply to be her replacement while she's away.'

He drapes an arm over the back of his chair. 'Wow. What are the chances of that happening?'

'Who knows? To be honest, the head of news doesn't really like me, so, as my dad would say, I probably need to get my "head read" for even thinking about it.'

A small smile finds Zac's lips. 'I miss your dad.' He doesn't look away this time and his gaze entangles with mine. 'And what do you mean, the head of news doesn't like you? There's no one on this planet who wouldn't like you.'

A warm blush whips across my skin, and for the first time since I got here, I glimpse the old Zac—the one who cares about me deeply. 'Thank you, that's sweet, but I think my boss actually wants to kill me. He has very specific ideas about who he wants on air, and I can't seem to figure out what those are or why I'm never those things. I might be too blonde, not blonde enough, too old, too young, too bubbly, too serious—god only knows.'

When Oliver Novak hired me after my several years of reporting for a small online news channel, he was full of smiles and compliments. But I was young and nervous, and I made a couple of rookie screw-ups— like accidentally calling a newly elected politician the wrong name on air. After that, Oliver stopped saying hello when he walked past my desk, glazed over when I spoke in meetings, and all these years later, I still haven't managed to win him back. 'He kind of lost faith in me early on, when I was a junior and still learning,' I continue, 'but I've learned *a lot* since then. So, I have these next few months to nail it up here and prove to him that I'm not only good at my job, but that I'm exactly what he wants.'

I then leap into a caricature of a news reporter, all silky-edged and serious-browed. 'I'm Josie Larsen, and you're watching *60 Minutes*.' I add the tick-tocking of the *60 Minutes* clock to complete the scene.

Zac watches me with one side of his mouth turned up before he suddenly leans across the table and brings his hand to my face. My shoulders lock, and blood rushes to my cheeks as the pad of his thumb makes a slow, firm brush across my jaw. He pulls away, looking at the glob of syrup he's caught with his thumb.

'I was saving that for my waffles later,' I joke softly, and he hums a light laugh. I wrap my hand around my water glass and blurt out the first question that pops into my head. 'Enough about me. How was your *date* yesterday?'

Zac blushes like a schoolboy. 'Uh, the date was good.' He scratches the back of his neck, his T-shirt riding up to expose a stretch of toned stomach. 'I took her to a dumpling restaurant, but it wasn't great. One thing I miss about Sydney is the Chinese food.'

One thing I miss.

Dumplings, I guess, but not me.

He says no more, so I force a smile. 'It's good to hear you're dating again. Meanwhile, I'm going to be the last single person left on earth, so . . .'

His eyes flicker to mine. 'You are? And why is that?'

'Oh, I don't know. I've been to five weddings in the past two years. Multiple christenings. All the eligible bachelors have dried up in Sydney, except for a couple of stragglers—none of whom have asked me out, so I guess I'm undateable now.' I gulp water, pitying my own self-pity.

Instead of telling me what I want to hear—*You're more than dateable, Josie*—Zac's gaze falls back to his glass, his finger drawing a slow circle around the rim.

'Let me guess: you've been beating them off with a stick since you got here,' I joke. 'While us girls are saving up for Botox, you men are getting more attractive as you get older. Yes, it's a thing.'

A laugh pushes through his lips. 'I've got no interest in finding a girlfriend. But I'm more than OK with playing the field.'

His mouth hints at a playful smile, but his tone is no-nonsense. If his intention was to shock me, it's paid off. To my knowledge, Zac does not, and has never, played the field. He bounced from one girlfriend to the next before he met Tara, which turned into an engagement when he was twenty-five. He's one of those unicorn men who's attractive enough to be a player but is bafflingly honourable and nice. And committed.

I add this revelation to the growing list of Zac Jameson changes.

He jumps up and grabs my empty plate, resting it over his. 'We should get going,' he says, heading into the kitchen with a trace of tension in his gait.

My repeated offers to help him clean up are shut down, and I promise to cook for him next. We both know that would be like writing a poem for Shakespeare, but after today's peek into Zac's living space, I'm determined to get my shit together and be more of a grown-up. No wonder I can't land a decent guy in Sydney. While Zac's evidently been blossoming into a mature home-owner here in Newcastle, I've been frozen in time.

We're halfway out the door when I nearly collide with a man on the front step whose beefy body is barely contained by his white linen shirt.

'Whoa, hello,' he says, stepping backwards with his palms in the air, his gold watch catching the sunlight.

'Oh, hey, man,' Zac cuts in flatly, kicking the front door open again. 'We were just heading out. Josie, meet Lindsay. Lindsay: Josie. Josie's an old friend from Sydney, and Lindsay's my housemate for exactly six more days.'

'Six more days and how many minutes?' the guy quips with an empty smile. 'Didn't realise you were keeping time, bro.'

'You want to know the seconds too, *bro*?' Zac throws him an intense look.

At first, I think they're joking, but that quickly transitions to feeling like I'm caught between two griz-zlies about to charge each other. Lindsay pushes his frameless glasses up his nose, his startlingly blue eyes staring Zac down before his gaze shifts to mine and clings there.

'It's nice to meet you, Josie from Sydney,' he says, and a little spark of chemistry zings between us.

I feel rude leaving without more of a chat, but Zac's already waiting for me on the footpath with his brow tensing, and my brain fights to catch up as I chase after him.

I hadn't even known Zac had a housemate up here. He never mentioned it. The housemate, the dog, the haircut, the surfing ... my chest tightens with a pang of sadness that's becoming all too familiar. I used to know everything about this man. *Everything*. Now, I feel like I've been sent back to square one, as if I landed on the wrong square in a game of Snakes and Ladders.

While Zac gets inside his car, Lindsay flashes me a smile that's plastered with the message: *You're cute*. The distraction feels perfectly timed.

I pass Lindsay a shy smile back, ignoring the strange, disloyal feeling that washes over me.

The first house we visit is dog-girl's, who turns out to be the owner of not one but six drooly Rottweilers. They bark so viciously upon my arrival that I don't even make it through the front door without Zac tugging me back outside. No wonder her ad has been up for four months.

House two is the domain of flexible-leg-girl, who fails to answer my knocks on her coral-pink door. Zac cups his hands against the front window, scouring for signs of life, while I dial her number. She doesn't pick up, but less than a minute later, she texts me.

UNKNOWN: Who is tis?

> **ME:** Hi, it's Josie, we have an appointment to talk about the room for rent. I'm outside your house. 😊

> **UNKNOWN:** Duck sorry I'm not home can do later or just leave it – larry

'*Larry?*'

Zac leans over my shoulder. 'I think she means "sorry", and it got autocorrected. I also think she's on the juice.'

'Shit.'

'I don't think you want to live this far out of town, anyway, do you?' He offers me a hopeful smile, sliding his hand inside the back pocket of his shorts.

He's right; I could be a lot closer to work than this, but I'm deflating fast. 'The network's only paying for my apartment for two weeks. And the movers in Sydney are waiting for my address to deliver my stuff.'

'The next one will be the one,' he reassures me while opening my passenger door. 'And it's in Cooks Hill—we like that.'

I just smile uncertainly, like I have any idea where Cooks Hill is or why it's Zac-approved.

'What happened with *your* housemate?' I ask a little tightly as he steers us back towards the coastal suburbs. 'You said he's moving out?'

He frowns at the road, taking a moment to reply. 'I think he's moving into his parents' place near the beach.'

'So . . . you need a housemate.' I steal a peek at him, but he doesn't look at me.

'Not really. I can afford the place on my own, and to be honest, Lindsay kind of scared me off housemates for life.'

I turn my gaze to the run of car dealerships unfurling through the window. 'Leaves out his junkie needles, does he?'

Zac goes to reply but then pauses before muttering, 'More like he's a nudist who thinks every night's a Saturday night and still needs to be potty trained.'

'Christ.'

The topic falls away, but disappointment seeps into my chest. If things between Zac and me hadn't changed so much, surely I could have just moved in with him. We were awesome roommates throughout university who shared the housework without argument. Zac would cook and clean up afterwards, and I'd vacuum, dust and take out the rubbish. We'd alternate the bathrooms and the mopping . . . we even had the same taste in TV shows. The only big fight we had was when I was dating this older MBA student named Felix, who was a strict vegan and couldn't even stand the sight of meat. I had been trying so hard to impress the guy that I foolishly asked Zac if he wouldn't mind scheduling his cooking with meat products around Felix's visits. Zac is such a sweet-natured guy that he obliged without protest, until Felix turned up unannounced one evening while Zac was in the middle of making pork souvlaki. Felix physically gagged, aggressively lectured Zac in his own home, then asked me in front of Zac if we could 'please go fuck' because he was feeling stressed. It's one of the only times I've seen Zac lose his shit. He snatched Felix's shirt with both hands and physically shoved him out of the apartment. Zac and I had a massive blow-up over it and Felix dumped me the next day, but truthfully, losing Felix didn't exactly break my heart.

All these years later, though, Zac makes no offer for me to move in with him. He just scopes out the letter-boxes dotting a quiet tree-lined street before pulling over outside number 28.

I step out of the car and wince at the crumbling two-storey terrace that looks like it wouldn't stand up on its own if it weren't for the houses holding it up on either side.

'It looks nice,' Zac tries, and I shoot him a look.

'It looks like a murder sce—hello!' I say as the front door swings open. A petite, slender guy peeks out, his shoulder-length hair brushing the shoulders of his tie-dyed T-shirt.

This is the man I couldn't find on social media. He invites us inside, where it's so dark I can barely make out his features, and introduces himself as Davide (pronounced Dah-vid). The smell of burning Nag Champa wafts through the living room, and I turn on my feet to take in the altar of crystals, the fireplace crowded with cascading ferns, and the velvet couch draped with a crocheted rainbow blanket. I'm pretty sure I'm being the definition of a snob when I consider running screaming from this ramshackle share house that smells like feet. But beggars can't be choosers—I can tough it out for half a year.

Davide is softly spoken and doesn't look me in the eye when he explains that he works as a reiki therapist. Still, the upstairs room for rent is relatively clean and positioned at the back of the house, away from the street noise. Most importantly, he's not bothered that I'm only going to be a tenant for six months.

My potential new housemate gives me a few minutes to think it over and squeaks back down the thousand-year-old staircase.

Just as Zac's giving me a hesitant nod of approval, the question I wish I could ask becomes trapped in my throat. *'Are you sure you don't want me to move in with you?'*

But I can't say that, not with all this weird distance between us. I remind myself that he only cooked me lunch today and came to my housemate appointments because we have history together, and Zac Jameson is nothing if not polite.

Overcompensating for the downheartedness that I don't want Zac to sense, I give the rigid muscle in his arm a playful whack. 'What do you think?' I ask.

He runs his eyes over my face, looking unsure. 'What do *you* think?'

'Well, I need a place to live for six months only, and that's not easy to find. Davide seems all right, even if he's possibly stoned off his head right now, and you said the location's good. I think this place is perfect.'

It's our friendship that's broken.

'Then it sounds like you're moving in.'

Zac slips through the door with no further comment, leaving my heart sinking into my stomach. In twenty-two months, I feel like we've lost fourteen years of friendship.

I'm just not sure that Zac even cares.

CHAPTER 5

Eight years ago

I rest my rusty bike against the hallway wall, then wedge my key into the apartment door lock and summon the strength of a hammer-throw champion to twist it open.

Zac glances up from the kitchen table, his pile of open textbooks competing for space with my half-finished, jewel-toned puzzle of a coral reef.

'Don't break the door. We can't afford a new one,' he says.

'I think you mean: *I heard you out there, and I'm sorry I didn't come and help you*,' I reply, dumping my satchel stuffed with textbooks on the slightly slanted floor. 'Plus, if the door breaks, it's the landlord who has to fix it.'

'Not if it's our fault.' Zac smirks, tapping his chewed pen against his lips. 'And I'm sorry I didn't come and help you.'

'You busy?' I cross the living room in five steps and fling open the fridge door, finding the shelves mostly empty, barring Zac's random jars of Chinese chilli paste and tamarind purée.

'Yeah,' he mumbles. 'I've got an anatomy and physiology test tomorrow.' He clasps his arms over his head in a stretch, which is when my gaze snags on his bottle-green T-shirt. The white lettering printed across the front says 'I Hate Everyone'.

I shut the fridge door. 'What is that shirt?'

Zac glances at his chest. 'I bought it at that op shop you kept bugging me to go to. Thought it was funny.'

I lean my forearms against the counter. 'Zac, you know I love you, so I can be brutally honest, right?'

'Oh god. When you frame it like that, I'm not sure.'

'That T-shirt is not you. It would work on someone who's grumpy or frowny or generally an asshole, but you are *way* too nice to pull that off.'

His brows draw together, but he must know I'm right. Zac Jameson is the furthest thing from a misanthrope. He likes almost *everyone*—unless it's Felix, the MBA student I'm seeing.

'Maybe I got it because it's ironic,' he offers, folding his arms. 'A bit of T-shirt humour to lighten these dark-as-hell exam days.'

'Ah, OK.' I push off the counter and fish a chipped water glass from the drying rack. 'In that case, remind me to buy you a T-shirt for Christmas that says "Pay Me In Mushrooms".'

His lips kick up. 'Or how about "This Shirt Is Not Humerus", but on it is a drawing of a humerus bone?'

I chuckle against the rim of my glass. 'You should become a writer. We can swap; I'll change to paramedicine.'

He groans and slides his fingers into his thick mound of curly hair while frowning at his notes. 'Don't tempt me.'

I gulp the last of my water. 'Want me to test you? OK—what's a gluteus maximus?'

Zac slumps onto the table until his chest is flush with his notebook. 'The largest muscle in the body,' he says tiredly.

I make a game show fail buzzer sound. 'It's an ass.'

'No, that's a donkey.'

'Oh, Zac, you're so sheltered.'

With his cheek pressed to the Formica tabletop, he peeks at me with one green-gold eye. 'Then test me properly, sunbeam. Bring that *ass* of yours over here.'

A strange sensation of warmth ripples lightly up my back. I quickly shake it off, perform an exaggerated huff like I'm put out, and scamper towards his mound of textbooks.

CHAPTER 6

Today

NRN News sits facing the industrial shoreline of Newcastle Harbour in the prettily named suburb of Honeysuckle, which—at first glance—appears to be a hotspot for new, sterile-looking apartment buildings.

I catch the lift to the building's third floor and press the security buzzer three times before an irritated voice picks up. 'Yes?'

'Hi, I'm Josephine Larsen; I have an appointment this morning with Natasha Harrington?'

The door clicks open without a reply.

I step inside an open-plan newsroom that's a quarter of the size of the one I'm used to in Sydney. I'm met by the backs of a handful of producers tapping away at computer stations while a laser printer spits out scripts beside me. There's no indication of who buzzed me in—not even a cursory glance in my direction. Still, it feels strangely quiet in here compared with the ulcer-causing stress of the Sydney newsroom.

I approach the person nearest me, a girl with a neat blonde ponytail and a face that says *please just fuck off*.

After a gentle apology for bothering her, I ask where I might find the news director.

'I'll go and tell her you're here,' she huffs, rolling her chair back and leaving me feeling like the self-conscious new kid at school again. Except, this time, there's no Zac Jameson to shyly ask to share my earphones.

Everyone tenses up—including me—as a woman bounds across the carpet like a Hollywood showrunner entering a writers' room in which her entire team has been goofing off.

'Josephine Larsen?' she says to me. Her high-pitched voice is a comical contrast against her towering frame, expensive-facial skin and razor-sharp stare. I could do an epic impersonation of this woman.

'I usually go by Josie.' We shake hands, and I follow her down a short hallway and into a corner office. Through the floor-to-ceiling windows, a glistening ribbon of water unfurls across the industrial landscape, partially obscured by the new apartment building going up across the road.

Natasha flops into her plush leather chair and digs through a mound of papers on her desk. 'So, you've had around two years in the Sydney newsroom, correct?'

'That's right. I started there as a junior reporter after four years at an internet news channel.'

'What sort of reporting have you done at Channel One?'

'General news . . . environmental, court rounds, some health, politics, a bit of entertainment . . . basically everything other than sport.'

She leans back in her chair, and I wonder if her lashes are fake or just spectacular. 'Good. You'll be a jack-of-all-trades up here, too, and with less hand-holding than you're probably used to. We've already got politics well covered, and there's not a great deal of entertainment up here, so I'll keep you on general news, environmental and health. We recently picked up the John Hunter Hospital as a sponsor, and as a result, we've become quite heavy on health content lately. We're in the middle of a series with the hospital's new cancer centre, so please familiarise yourself with what we've done there so far.'

I nod and say all the right things, but my clammy fingers slide down my second-hand pencil skirt, gripping my thighs like a lifeline.

I am not going to mess up again.

I am going to walk through that cancer centre like a boss and uncover the compelling stories with truth and sensitivity, and I. Am. Not. Going. To. Screw. It. Up.

Natasha mutters something about a meeting and guides me into the office beside hers like she can't get rid of me fast enough. I'm introduced to Isabella, the operations manager, who greets me warmly and escorts me around the newsroom on a road trip of introductions.

While most of the reporters are out shooting stories, I meet a few of the producers and the chief of staff— a guy named Colin, with a man-bun, who looks about eighteen—before Isabella leads me to the attractive blonde I interrupted earlier.

My eyes catch on the sentence she's just typed about a shark sighting at Bar Beach: *The area is known to be popular with sharks.*

'Popular with sharks'? It's not a nightclub, I think meanly.

'Hi, sweetheart. I wanted to introduce our new reporter, Josie Larsen,' Isabella says to her.

A smile graces the girl's lips, but her ice-blue eyes size me up as potential competition. I'm not sure why. She's younger than me, blonder than me, and—I learn as she stands up—taller than me.

'Hi, I'm Meghan.'

My lips part. 'Meghan Mackay?'

She laughs musically. 'You're Zac's friend.'

She says his name like she owns it, and a territorial feeling sweeps through me.

'He's the sweetest, honestly,' she says, blushing. 'I can't fault him—you'll have to tell me what he's hiding.' She glows at Isabella. 'I don't think I told you yet that I have a new boyfriend.' They share a quiet squeal.

Isabella speeds up our tour, which we're apparently now behind on, but I'm having trouble focusing on anything but Meghan calling Zac her boyfriend. After what happened with Tara, this feels like earth-shaking information. And why did he tell me just yesterday that he doesn't have a girlfriend?

I trail Isabella into the studio, excitement firing in my chest at the sight of the news-presenting desk sitting empty behind four robotic cameras. I'm already aware that the main presenting duo here, Yvette Sinclair and Robert Knight, will need to be wheeled out in coffins before ever quitting their jobs. But the weekend news-readers feel closer to my age and level—Genevieve Meleska and Richard Cross, who double as sports and weather reporters on weekdays.

I spend the rest of the day shadowing a friendly reporter named Lola, and we head to a courthouse in Belmont, where a guy accused of selling drugs on the dark web is attending a bail hearing. Lola is one of those approachable, bubbly people who I click with instantly, and after learning I'm new in town, she suggests we get together for drinks one evening after work. She's also impressively patient with her camera-person, Gus, who doesn't appear to want to shoot anything. Instead, he huffs around, muttering, 'We've got gobs of archival footage of that at the station,' and 'The editors will never use that shot,' and 'You've already got way more vision than you need.' At first, I think he's insecure about his abilities, but when he films Lola's piece to camera like a seasoned pro, I cotton on that Gus is just lazy.

The bail hearing runs late, and when we get back to the station, poor Lola bolts to the voiceover booth because the deadline for her news package is looming. Still, compared with the panic-stricken Sydney newsroom, today's atmosphere bordered on a Zen meditation session. Maybe Christina is right. There's less competition up here, and if I knuckle down and avoid distractions, I could end up covering the region's leading stories and prove to Oliver Novak that Christina's unwavering belief in me is justified.

The rest of the week goes smoothly, and as I drive out of Honeysuckle on Friday evening in my gleaming new work car, I give my parents a call in Koh Samui.

'Hello, darling, how are you coping?' Mum asks right off the bat, like I've checked in to prison instead of Newcastle.

'I'm going well,' I reply truthfully. 'I just finished up my first week at work, and it was all very calm and easy compared with Sydney. I think the news director here likes me, *and* I made a new friend called Lola.'

'Well, that's wonderful.'

Mum pauses so she can relay all this to Dad before she comes back on the line.

'What do you think of the city itself?' she asks. 'It was quite small when we were there all those years ago.'

I flip on the indicator to make a left turn onto Hunter Street. 'I'm still getting to know it, but I like it so far. It feels like a cool mix of beachy and quirky, like someone combined the best of Sydney and Melbourne.

I also can't believe how much cheaper everything is here.'

'Sounds like you might actually enjoy the next six months in the boondocks,' Mum jokes.

I breathe a light laugh. 'I wouldn't go that far.'

Mum pauses. 'Have you seen Zac?'

My throat draws tight. 'Yeah.'

'How is he?'

My teeth dig into my bottom lip. 'I don't know yet. I'm still trying to figure that out.'

There's not much either of us can say on that complicated topic right now, so the conversation shifts to Mum and Dad's latest adventures in Thailand, which included a visit to the jungles of Chang Mai. Throughout our catch-up, I say nothing about the panic attacks I've been having over my health. It took incredible courage and planning for my parents to chase their retirement dream in Thailand, and I don't want to be the one who sticks a pin into their happy bubble and makes them feel bad for being far away. It doesn't help that my sister has a fantastic life and career in London as the communications director for a British politician, and is the living definition of having one's shit together. I love Ingrid to death and want only the best for her, but I'm determined not to be the sibling who can't keep up.

After I finish the call with Mum, I make an unplanned turn towards Hamilton. I haven't spoken to Zac all week, and showing off my new set of wheels is a good excuse to make contact. Plus, Fridays used to be our favourite night to hang out when we were living in Bathurst. We'd usually start with a game of pool at our local, then hunt out some live music—even if it was a crappy soloist—and end up stumbling home while making each other laugh with retellings of the night's events . . . odd people we got chatting to, singers who'd screwed up the lyrics, my weird dance moves if it had been a particularly rowdy one.

My car slows outside Zac's place, where a massive moving van sits blocking his house. There's no sign of Zac's black Subaru. I pull over behind the van and decide to text him when a shadow falls over my passenger-side window.

Zac's housemate, Lindsay, is standing on the footpath clutching a cardboard box. He spotted me right away—this guy should be a reporter.

I reach across the car seat and push the button to open the window. 'Hey there.'

His smile crinkles his eyes behind his glasses. 'I thought that was you. Zac's friend, Josie, right?'

'Definitely Josie. But Zac's friend?' I shake my hand like it's touch-and-go.

I have no idea why I even said that, but Lindsay chuckles, his eyes gleaming. 'Zac's not here right now.'

'Ah, OK. I was just driving past.' I rest my hand on the gearstick, but Lindsay shows no indication of leaving.

'You're moving out today,' I observe. I don't know why I'm continuing this conversation, but the thought of heading back to my dingy house with Davide and his clouds of incense sends a swell of loneliness through me. I already suggested to Lola that we go for those cocktails she mentioned, but she's got a date night planned with her live-in boyfriend, Nathan.

'Yeah, we're obviously running late,' Lindsay replies. He plonks down the box he's holding while two guys in orange hi-vis shirts heft a bedframe in the background. Lindsay thumb-points at them. 'Those dickheads booked two jobs in one day and didn't get here until an hour ago.'

Silently, I note that Lindsay's not exactly hurrying either.

'Zac's an all-right guy deep down; that's not why I'm moving out,' he adds randomly, like I know nothing about my oldest friend. 'We just didn't see eye to eye on a few things. Plus, my folks have an awesome pad over in Merewether that they're not using, so they're letting me move in. Rent-free.'

'Sounds like an offer too good to refuse.'

I'm trying not to think about Zac's description of Lindsay as a nudist who can't aim his pee. With his rimless glasses, white polo-neck shirt and blingy watch, Lindsay comes off as more of a weekend golfer with a corporate desk job. And I can't deny that his boastful smile looks good on his face.

I hold his gaze for a few jittery heartbeats before switching on the engine. 'Will you tell Zac I stopped by?'

Lindsay leans closer to the window. 'You know, Zac's been holding out on me. He never told me he had a stunning friend called Josie.'

Zac never told him about me. That little nugget of information unlocks a desolate feeling in my chest that I push away.

'That's probably because I'm from Sydney, and I only just moved up here recently.'

'Ah, so you'll need a tour guide then.' Lindsay stares at me with a question in his eyes. 'Can I show you around? You tell me what you like doing, and I'll show you where to find it in Newy.'

My cheeks flush, and I fumble for what to say before Lindsay flops out an upturned hand. 'May I please borrow your phone, Miss Josie from Sydney?' This guy is all confidence, which I certainly don't hate.

'My phone?' I parrot, even though I know where this is going. My heart steps up its pace as I give Lindsay the handset and watch him tap his number into it. When he passes the phone back to me, he grazes his fingers over mine.

'If Zac's cool with it, give me a call.' He cocks his head, his eyes making a deliberate slide down and up my body. Sleazy or sexy? I can't decide. All I know is that I seem to have scored myself a date. I've got zero plans to stick around this city once my contract ends, but who knows, if things went well between us, maybe Lindsay would move to Sydney for me. He's got 'city slicker' written all over him.

I bite down a smile all the way home, but when I push through the front door, I nearly stumble backwards. *What the . . .*

I blink hard at the two white globes of Davide's bare ass, unsure if I'm seeing right. He spins to face me, holding a lighter against the tip of a smudge stick of white sage. *Yup, he's definitely naked.*

'God, sorry!' I splutter, squeezing my eyes shut. When I open them again, Davide's casually flicking the sage smoke into the room's corners while his hairy bits swing in my vision. Our gazes catch again, and something suggestive sparks in his eyes. I race past him and dash up the stairs before shutting my bedroom door and pressing my back to it. My gut twists as I pull out my phone, figuring out what to type to Zac. I don't want to launch straight into: *Davide's a nudist, and I think he wants to hook up with me.*

> **ME:** Hey favourite, I swung past your place today, but you weren't home. Hope you've been having a lovely day.

Using a nickname that I haven't given Zac for two years makes my breaths quicken. It's not like he calls me 'sunbeam' anymore. But when three dots appear immediately, my shoulders loosen a little.

> **ZAC:** What time was that? I was at the gym, then took the dog to the groomer.

> **ME:** Oh no, you didn't shave Bob Marley, did you??

He replies with a photo of himself holding Trouble, whose ratty dreads have been clipped into something only marginally more presentable. Zac's amber-green eyes sparkle through the screen as he presses his smiling lips to her fur.

> **ME:** Both looking gorgeous

Eeek, was that too much?

Zac begins typing something before the speech bubble disappears. It reappears then vanishes again, twice. I decide to rescue both him and me in one move.

> **ME:** Do you have dinner plans? Want to come over?
> I'm going to make that sheep head thing from Iceland.

> **ZAC:** Sounds good, as long as you absolutely do not make that thing from Iceland.
> Is it OK if I bring Trouble? She's feeling needy with her new coif.

> **ME:** Zac, trouble follows you wherever you go. Of course you can. Come in an hour or so?
> And can I pls ask a favour? 🙏

ZAC: I'm sorry, I can't babysit your kids. They are truly terribly behaved, and you should be ashamed of yourself for raising such brats.

ME: 😩 My new housemate's being weird (already).
While you're here, do you think you could pretend to be my boyfriend?
It can just be a verbal thing.
I promise you don't have to kiss me. 🤢

I already regret the puke-face emoji, but it's too late. Zac's typing.

ZAC: No problem. What's that tree-hugger done? Is he chanting at the full moon? Burning all the gluten? Making you crochet him a poncho?

ME: Haha, it's all good, he just insists on walking around naked, no biggie.
(And really, I mean no biggie)

ZAC: You're kidding, right?

ME: Wish I was. But don't worry,
I think he thought I wasn't coming home.
Are all the men in Newcastle nudists?

ZAC: Apparently it's a requirement. I'm so sorry. 🙈

> **ME:** Not your fault! Plus, I know there are at least two decent men left in Newcastle. Did your housemate Lindsay tell you he gave me his number today?

My finger hovers over the 'send' arrow before I chicken out and delete the message. Zac didn't seem to think much of Lindsay, and right now, our friendship feels fragile enough.

> **ME:** Better run and get ingredients. See you soon, my sexy-a-f boyfriend. 😊

This is exactly what I would have said to old-Zac, but this is new-Zac now, and the words I've already sent make me grimace at my phone screen. When he doesn't reply, I fast-type another message.

> **ME:** I was obviously joking . . . see you soon.

> **ZAC:** As long as you don't puke if I kiss you. 😉

My stomach does a funny dip and doesn't seem to right itself until I get to the grocery store.

CHAPTER 7

Eleven years ago

My lips detach from Damien Di Fiori's. His eyes glaze over as they blink into mine before I hurriedly shift backwards, realising we're being stared at by, like, *everyone* in this circle.

'I thought the rule was to kiss, not eat each other's faces off,' Cody teases with a snort, and my cheeks redden as I ease back into my spot beside Amy. I cast Zac a sidelong glance, but his gaze is fixed on his lap.

'Sorry,' Damien says with a wink. 'Got a bit carried away there.'

He's absolutely right—Damien is the one who attempted to turn that kiss into a tongue battle, not me. It's been two years since he first slipped his tongue inside my mouth behind the science building at school, which nearly made me puke, and while his kisses did get better after that, it's been a long time since I've wanted to make out with him.

Emily takes her turn to spin the bottle, and cheers break out when the glass tip halts at Hayden. Hayden used to date Bianca, Emily's best friend, so I cringe internally when they both shuffle forward on their knees and press their mouths together. Zac and I exchange a look that says, *Eeek*.

'Next up—Zachary!' Cody shouts, and a few guys make drum rolls on the carpet with their palms.

Zac chugs a third of his beer like he's preparing for an intense moment, then leans forward and whips the glass bottle into a fierce spin. It takes a few seconds for it to slow, and slow, and slow, until it lands on . . .

Me.

My stomach pitches, and the background music is instantly swallowed up by the whoops and cheers and sarcastic comments about Zac and me pretending to be 'just good friends'.

But we are just good friends. We're the best of friends, and best friends *don't kiss*.

I glance over at Zac, whose cheeks have turned crimson, and steal a quick look at his lips. They don't look like they'd be *bad* to kiss. They're plump and pink, and . . . my heart begins to gallop in my chest.

My gaze drifts back up to meet Zac's, and through the noise and excitement around us, a question forms in his eyes, reaching into my mind.

Am I OK with this?

My brow tightens because I don't know the answer to that, but Zac instantly registers my hesitation and climbs to his feet, clutching an empty beer bottle. 'This game's stupid,' he says, giving the boys all the ammunition they need.

Phrases like 'Zac's too scared to kiss Josie' and 'Zac doesn't want Josie to see how much he likes her' are sung in taunting tones by people I'm too scared to look at. Instead, I watch Zac stalk off towards Cody's rumpus-room bar fridge in the hunt for another drink. An urge to get up and follow him rolls through me, but I ignore it. That'll get us even more teased.

Instead, I cross my legs and watch the game bottle pass to Lucas. There must be a dip in the carpet or something because when Lucas spins the bottle, it stops at me again. *For crying out loud.* Fearful of another round of ridicule, I quickly crawl forward and tug Lucas towards me by his scrawny shoulders, planting a kiss on his trembling lips. The circle erupts in wolf whistles and cheers.

When I shift back to my spot, Amy high-fives me, and my gaze snags on Zac's as he watches from the bar fridge. He offers me a cool, detached smile, but an empty feeling overcomes my stomach, like I've rejected him or something, when it shouldn't be like that between us in the first place.

Josie, it's just Zac. You should have given him one measly kiss.

What the hell are you so afraid of?

CHAPTER 8

Today

I'm arms-deep in garlic, mince and breadcrumbs, attempting to roll meatballs that aren't shaped like ball sacks, when Zac steps through the beaded curtain draped across the kitchen doorway. A bottle of shiraz dangles from one hand while his other clutches a leather strap leading to the cutest dog on earth.

Before I can utter a word, Davide snatches the wine from Zac and deposits a kiss on both his cheeks, French-style, before making little high-pitched barking calls at Trouble. Zac just stares at me over Davide's head, and I nearly choke on my snicker. When Davide turns his back, I do a little impersonation of a moustache-twirling Frenchman and immediately feel guilty, even as Zac is shuddering with silent laughter.

'Thanks for coming, baby,' I say for Davide's benefit as Zac strolls over to me.

'Any chance to see you, gorgeous.'

OK, these words sound even weirder coming out of our mouths than I would've thought. But I need Davide to see this so he doesn't get the wrong idea about our living arrangement.

Zac steps close behind me, bracing his palms against the counter on either side of my arms. 'What are we making?' he asks. Speaking near my ear, his rich voice vibrates through me.

'Spaghetti with Italian meatballs,' I reply, trying not to tremble. What is with me tonight? I couldn't count how many times I've hugged Zac or given him a shoulder massage. We've been physically close countless times over the years, but I've never reacted this way. It must be another unfortunate symptom of having spent so much time apart.

Davide twists open Zac's shiraz without asking, and the bottle glugs as he fills three comically large glasses to the rim, draining the bottle.

'Yeah, sure, you can open that. Why not,' Zac says with a sarcastic smile while Davide hands us each a glass.

Just as Zac taps his glass with mine in a 'cheers' gesture, Davide gives his Tibetan singing bowl a strike with a mallet to balance the energy in the room. The shock of the hollow clang makes me jerk my backside into Zac's crotch, my wine nearly spilling as I flinch away. *Jesus Christ.*

Zac sets down his glass and brings his lips close to my ear. 'Stop bouncing.'

He scoops out a chunk of mince and cups it between his deft fingers, rolling it into a tight ball in front of me.

Davide sits at the dining table and points his gaze in our direction, so Zac dials our little performance up a notch.

'You're so sweet to cook for me, beautiful.' He lightly nuzzles his nose into my hair, his breath tickling my neck and making goosebumps explode over my skin. I tilt my face away while giving myself a silent lecture to stop being so skittish and childish. This is *Zac*.

A recording of wind chimes tingles from Davide's back pocket. He grunts an apology and pads upstairs to answer his phone, carrying his cauldron of wine.

Cold, empty air blasts me from all directions when Zac instantly drops away now that Davide's not present.

'Thanks for that,' I say a little throatily as Zac moves to stand beside me, still expertly rolling meatballs while Trouble pushes between his ankles.

'Anytime. Although I'm a bit worried this was even necessary. What actually happened—was Davide just roaming around upstairs with his kit off, or is it a full-blown nudist colony around here?'

'Full-blown, full-frontal nudist colony. He was parading around the house without a stitch on, and at one point, I'm pretty sure he made eyes at me while his junk was blowin' in the wind.'

When the frown deepens in Zac's brow, flashing me back to the time he physically threw Felix out of our apartment, I steer the conversation towards work. As we continue rolling meatballs, I fill him in on my first week at NRN News and how I've made quick friends with my colleague Lola.

'I also met *Meghan*,' I say, dramatically drawing out the name.

Instead of replying, Zac attempts a sip from his over-filled wine glass, trying not to spill it down his black T-shirt, which, I notice, is stamped with the words 'Kill Them With Kindness'.

'She's very pretty,' I add, refraining from doing an impersonation of Meghan.

He returns to his line-up of perfectly shaped meatballs. 'She is certainly pretty.'

Then, for reasons I can't explain, I don't want to talk about Meghan anymore.

'How was *your* work this week?' I divert, firing up the centuries-old stove and tipping a lug of oil into the pan. 'Any news on that job?'

'Not yet. The last few days were quite hectic, actually. We had six deaths in two days.'

'Oh god, that's terrible. And you only just started back doing on-road duties.' My lips turn down as I unstick a knife from the magnetic rack to slice up some basil.

'Yeah. All of them were cancer patients.'

The knife slips in my fingers.

'*Six* cancer deaths in two days?' I sound like I'm being choked.

'Yep. They were all getting end-of-life care already and were at home with their families, so there's that.'

I can't feel my face. I can't feel my hands. I can't feel my breath. All I can feel is my heart beating a hole through my chest.

'Are you OK?' Zac's palm lightly lands on my upper back, a crease forming between his eyes.

'Yeah, 'course.' I slice into the basil, nearly nicking my finger. 'What sort of cancer did they have?'

'By this point, who even knows where it started. One woman was only thirty-two. So sad.'

The knife slides out of my hand and bounces across the linoleum floor.

Zac gasps. 'Shit, are you OK?'

'I'm fine,' I mutter as he picks up the knife, angling myself away from the eyes of the one person who used to know me better than I know myself.

I snatch up my phone and escape into the downstairs bathroom, locking the door and running the tap. I sit on the toilet and google '32-year-old woman cancer death Newcastle', but no related articles spring up. Instead, millions of stories flood the screen about other thirty-two-year-old women who've died of cancer.

Tears burn the backs of my eyes as I frantically read through them, searching for positive outcomes.

'Josie? You OK?' The door muffles Zac's soft voice. I've been in the bathroom for nearly ten minutes. God, he must think I have diarrhoea.

'Coming!' I sing out and swipe away my mascara

stains with my thumbs before opening the door with a smile that's totally overcooked.

'I don't have diarrhoea,' I say for the record, but make a show of washing my hands anyway. 'I just checked some work emails and got stuck.'

He lets out an unsure chuckle. 'I'm happy to hear that. Do you want me to turn the meatballs over?' He leads me back to the kitchen and points at the smoking pan.

'Oh, for the love of—' I dash to the stove and thrust a wooden spoon beneath a meatball, but it's glued to the pan and crumbles apart.

'Let me do it,' Zac offers gently, reaching over my shoulder with a slotted turner. He finishes off the meatballs and pasta sauce while I'm relegated to boiling the spaghetti—doing whatever it takes to shove those cancer articles out of my head.

'Davide left while you were in the loo,' Zac says as he fossicks around for plates and cutlery. 'He mentioned something about a full moon party and said he won't be back until tomorrow. Actually, he invited us to come too, but I said no. Is that OK? Did you want to go?'

A tentative look finds its way into Zac's eyes. He clearly has no idea that the thought of having him all to myself in a quiet house—like we've done a thousand times before, but not for a painfully long time—has every cell in my body somersaulting. I couldn't think of a better way to keep my anxious mind occupied.

'Hell no; we're staying here for my meatballs masterpiece,' I say firmly. 'And given that Davide's out for the night, I totally think that you and Trouble should crash over.'

Zac slides his hand into the back pocket of his athletic shorts and bites down on his bottom lip. 'Do you think Davide would mind?'

I lift a brow. 'The guy who walks around with his ass out and leaves his trimmed pubes in the toilet? Yeah, I really think we need that guy's opinion.'

He breathes a laugh, still thinking it over. I get the hesitation—we're a long way from our teenage sleepover days. There's still a wall of ice between us, but this is our opportunity to break it down.

Please stay. Please.

'Fine, but I'm not sleeping in that wingnut's bed,' Zac says with a playful gleam in his eye.

I excitedly gulp back a gargantuan sip of wine to make the point that tonight's going to be a Zac–Josie reunion party. Happiness wells up inside me, but self-preservation kicks it back down. There's no doubt that Zac and I have grown apart, and it's going take more than one evening to get back to where we once were. But it's a start.

After I've made up a bed for Trouble with cushions and a towel, we set our steaming plates on the turquoise dining table and dig into our spaghetti and meatballs.

'How are Lizzie and Stefan?' Zac asks between chews.

'The parentals are good. Living their best lives in Koh Samui.' My parents would be delighted to hear who I'm with right now. Zac was always their favourite.

He lifts his wine glass to his lips. 'They do love their Thai holidays.'

'No, they actually live there now.'

His eyes expand. 'They *moved* to Thailand?'

I nod, twirling my fork in my spaghetti. 'Just over a year ago, for their retirement. They're living the dream: eating out every night, sunbaking, and their live-in helper does all the housework. Australia's really just an afterthought now.'

A slight line forms on his brow as he searches my face. 'And Ingrid's still in London?'

'Yup. I'm literally the only Larsen left in Australia.'

The *tsk* sound that escapes his lips makes me want to crawl into his lap and wrap my arms around him. I've always believed that when you survive high school with someone, you'll always share a bit of the same blood, but Zac and I became even more like family over our uni years. He knows right away that Australia hasn't been the only afterthought in all this. While I encouraged Mum and Dad to follow their dreams, when your entire family makes a permanent move overseas, it's hard not to take it a little bit personally.

A gust of loneliness blows through me, and I push it aside.

'Want to take a road trip this weekend?' I ask on a whim. 'You're not on shift, right? Port Stephens or the Hunter Valley? We can drink *all* the shiraz and the sav blanc.'

'The Hunter Valley's not really known for its sauvignon blanc,' Zac replies with a cocky glint in his eye. 'It prefers a cooler climate. The resident reporter should probably know that.'

I make a face at him. 'Ah, I see. You're a wax-head *and* a wine expert now.'

He pushes his fork through his pasta. 'This weekend's supposed to be sunny, so I need to mow the lawn.'

I sit back in my chair and stare at him for a good five seconds. 'Oh. My. God. Who chooses mowing over a holiday?'

He sighs, his eyes darting away. 'I'm not really that into road trips these days,' he mumbles, and my throat contracts.

Of course.

I have no idea how to get out of this hole I've just dug, so I default to my comfort zone of teasing the crap out of him. 'You're so *domesticated* now,' I say with an accusing smirk. The wine is making everything soft, including my restraint. 'Is this a Newcastle thing? No one has any fun around here? It's all lawnmowers and play dates?'

'I happen to enjoy mowing the lawn,' Zac says matter-of-factly.

I exaggerate my snort-laugh. 'Of course you do. At heart, Zachary has always been a *country boy*.' I fake my best American cowboy accent on that phrase, even though I know Newcastle is hardly the countryside.

Zac's forearms flex as he crosses his arms at me. 'Oh, yes, the girl with big-city dreams,' he retorts. 'And what do your weekends look like? Sunday brunch in Bronte? Speculating on the housing market? Putting the kids you haven't yet had on waiting lists for private school?'

My lips purse over a smile I can't help. It's not just *my* inhibitions being swallowed up by shiraz, and I love it.

I exaggerate my frown. 'Don't tease me about kids. At the rate I'm going, there aren't going to be any. Which is fine: I've got "big-city dreams" to be a barren old spinster. With twelve cats.'

'At the rate you're going?'

I toss back another gulp of red. 'I'm twenty-seven. And single. And poor.'

His eyes move over my face before returning to mine. 'Josie, you do know that women can get pregnant into their mid-forties, right?'

My stomach caves inward.

But I'm going to be gone by then, like those women in the articles.

Like Aunt Susie, whose life was snatched away by breast cancer when she was only twenty-nine. My grandma was older when she succumbed to it, but she was first diagnosed in her twenties.

'Don't get medical on me,' I say gruffly, which wins me a cute chuckle and distracts me from my thoughts.

Zac's fingers stroke up and down the stem of his wine glass.

'How did you meet Meghan?' I ask, having now shaken off whatever reservations kept me silent earlier.

I genuinely want to like the girl Zac's seeing, even though her vibe towards me at work has been arctic. 'Wait, let me guess. You go to the same gym, thought her ass looked good in yoga pants, and so you slid onto the treadmill beside hers, and *boom*—cue candy-eyes and sweaty hot bodies. Must be love.'

His lips curl up. 'I think that's your fantasy porn scenario, not mine. I met Meg at the beach and asked for her number. Don't you know I'm a wax-head now?'

I lean back in my chair and give an impressed nod. But at this point, I'm having trouble focusing because all my attention has travelled to where Zac's ankle is resting lightly against mine beneath the table.

'Meghan thinks she's your girlfriend,' I say.

His brow pinches. 'She said that?'

'Yup.' My lips pop on the word, and I make a dramatic, you're-in-trouble-now grimace.

'I should probably have a talk to her about that.'

I find myself forcing a smile off my face. 'Well, she does have the kind of alliterative name that makes a woman instantly hot. You know, Marilyn Monroe . . . Bridget Bardot . . . Meghan Mackay.'

Josie Jameson pops into my head unsolicited, and I stuff that one back in the box. I must be tipsier than I thought.

A noncommittal smile passes over Zac's lips, and I wonder why he hasn't moved his leg yet. It tingles against mine, heavy and warm. I was already feeling his cold distance from me beginning to thaw, but this return to physical contact is another level entirely. It makes my heart beat a little harder against my ribs.

'So, it's just a casual thing with Meghan, then?' I clarify, refocusing. 'Because now that we're almost twenty-eight, I feel like I need to know if you intend to activate The Back-Up Plan or not.'

Holy shit, I really have had too much of the red stuff.

I search Zac's face for signs he remembers the deal we made over a Friday night beer-clink when we were in second-year uni. With slightly breathless voices, we agreed that if we hit the age of twenty-eight and were still single, we'd marry each other. He'd wanted to go with thirty, but I'd argued that we'd need to be married for two years before having a baby, and I wasn't having my first baby any later than thirty. It was the first time I genuinely imagined—and in some detail—what it would be like to taste Zac's watermelon-pink lips. Two days after that, he met Tara Amiri.

'Ah, yes, I forgot . . . I'm your fallback guy.' His cheeks ignite. 'Although you're going to be a big-time news-reader down in Sydney, aren't you? So, it'll never work.'

'I can't have both?' My stomach tenses as his brows lift.

'What, you're going to move up here permanently?'

I can't believe we're even having this conversation. It's entirely the fault of whoever invented shiraz. I need to change the subject.

'There's always *Dah-viiide*,' I say in a mock-serious tone. 'He seems keen.'

'Now, now, Josephine, you can't have all the boys.' Zac's lower leg nudges mine where they're still touching before he suddenly shifts away.

'What about Lindsay?' I suppress the awkwardness of the question by jumping up to dig out another bottle of shiraz, since Davide drank a third of this one.

'My housemate Lindsay?' Zac asks, looking confused.

'He gave me his number today. When I came by your house.'

I brave a glance back at Zac, finding his lips parted. 'That guy is un-fucking-believable.'

'What?' My voice is all high as I slide back into my chair and top up our glasses. 'Is it weird if he calls me?'

Zac tosses back a large swig of wine. 'Why would it be weird if he called you?'

'Well, you did say he's a nudist who can't aim at the toilet.'

He sets his glass down. 'You can go out with whoever you want. And he *is* your type.'

Oh, this is going to be good.

I lean back in my seat. 'And what exactly is my type? Come on, give it to me.' I curl my fingers at him.

Zac doesn't even take a beat. 'Sydney stockbroker who pops the collar up on his polo-neck shirts and posts pics of his business-class boarding passes on social media, or pics when he's on a boat—literally anytime, anywhere. Oh, and when he orders his oat milk lattes with a dash of Madagascar cinnamon, he feels compelled to speak at ten thousand decibels into his earpiece about cryptocurrency.'

I bite away a smile. 'I don't know Lindsay, but I doubt he's any of those things.'

He makes a pretend laugh. 'He's a business analyst for a software company, and his parents are loaded. Very rich, very boring, and very much your type.' He lifts his glass in a 'cheers' before taking another sip.

I paint my face with a mask of amusement to hide my offence. Even though Zac's words aren't exactly off the mark, I don't like the way they feel in my head.

'I'm like you, Zac. I just want to "play the field" since I'm not staying up here in Newcastle,' I joke to get him back. 'Someone with a cute smile, a hot body, and a big bank account—they're my priorities. Like Lindsay.' I mimic his 'cheers' gesture to the air.

Even as I smirk, though, I can't help thinking that none of those characteristics sound too bad. *Bloody hell, am I as superficial as he thinks I am?*

Zac just shrugs and looks away like he has nothing more to say about this. There's a hint of tension seeping into the room, but I need this topic clarified.

'So, just to be clear,' I say slowly, twirling the base of my wine glass back and forth. 'You don't mind if I go out on a date with Lindsay.'

'Jeez, Josie, if you want to go out with him that badly, just do it. Fuck, what do I care?'

'OK.' My lips tighten, and I look away, but I feel his eyes on me.

'Sorry, I didn't mean it like that.'

'No, it's all good.'

Zac gets up and paces towards the sink, where he flings open the lower cabinet. 'Where's your washing-up liquid?'

'Oh no, you're not doing that.' I get up and dart over to him, giving him a little shove back towards the table. 'Sit and drink like a good boy.'

After a couple of protests that I rebuff, he settles back at the dining table, and I turn on the tap to fill the sink.

'Did you see me on the news this week?' I ask, like the world's biggest egocentric.

'Sure did. You look good on TV. Although you pronounced one of the suburb names wrong.'

I twist around. 'I did?'

'Minmi. You said it as Min-mee, but it's Min-mih.'

'Oh, shit.' Those small details don't go unnoticed in regional communities.

'I thought pronouncing names correctly was Journalism 101,' he teases. 'Did you do any actual studying at uni, or were you too busy chasing after those MBA tosspots to learn how to do your job properly?'

The fact that he's finally comfortable enough to take the piss out of me fills me with a delight that's more powerful than my slightly wounded feelings. But I have to get him back, so I grab a pen off the counter and lightly fling it in his direction.

Zac ducks, but the plastic lid connects with his hair.

'What the?' he says, tugging at the pen clinging to his muss of dark curls.

I clap a hand over my mouth to hide my laugh. 'Oh, dear. What's going on here?' I bark like a school principal, heading over to him.

'What's going on is that my oldest friend in the world just assaulted me.' He carefully lifts his wine glass to his lips while I work to unclip the trapped pen.

'Your hair really is incredible,' I say, playing with a baby-soft spiral. 'Do you even know the actual length of your hair if you straightened it?' I drag my fingers through the curls like a child who's discovered a new plush toy. When my fingertips brush against his scalp, his head tilts back, inviting me to keep going.

'I need a massage so bad,' he moans, his eyes sinking shut. From this angle, his long lashes rest like little black fans over his skin. Feeling my years of affection for him reignite, I dig a little harder with my fingers, releasing a faint waft of mint-scented shampoo. His lips part, all pink and full, as I keep working his scalp like my hairdresser does. It's been a long time since I've stared at Zac quite this closely, and I'm a little whiplashed by how handsome he is.

Bloody hell, Josie, what are you even doing?

His ringtone blasts from the table, and I jerk backwards.

'Sorry,' he says, reaching for his phone. 'It's Ross.'

'Oh, say hi from me,' I blurt and retreat to the kitchen, clutching the pen in my slightly clammy fingers. Ross is

Zac's cousin; he lives locally and is undoubtedly one of the biggest reasons Zac moved to Newcastle.

Zac fiddles with his hair, restyling it, as he slips outside onto the patio with his phone at his ear. Our gazes catch through the glass, and I turn away, wondering why my stomach feels so whipped up.

When Zac resurfaces, the dishes are dry, and I'm wiping the last section of countertop.

'Ross wants to see you,' he says with a half-smile, dropping his phone onto the table.

'Absolutely, I'd love to see him.'

'You know he's engaged, right? They're getting married in a few months. I'm the best man.'

'Yeah, I saw it on Facebook.'

He nods once, and our gazes drift apart. It should've been Zac who told me about his cousin's engagement, not a dumb social media page.

'I'll set up drinks so you can meet his fiancée, Holly,' he murmurs. 'She's awesome.'

'Sounds good.'

I refill our glasses, and we head outside to the patio so we can gawk through the trees at what feels like the darkest, deadest street on earth.

'Is Newcastle always this quiet?' I ask as I light a citronella candle.

'Isn't it the best?' Zac smiles through the flickering glow as I drop into the plastic chair beside his.

'Mmm, not sure yet,' I reply diplomatically. I can't say I hate the tranquil mood of this place, but I feel a pang for the familiar buzz of traffic and the steady hum of voices outside my city apartment.

'Do you miss Sydney?' I ask.

'Not even one iota.'

'Oh god, that bad? OK.' I pin my gaze to the knobbly tree roots erupting through the footpath beyond the patio.

'I don't mean you,' he says quickly. 'Of course I miss *you*.'

A lump grows in my throat. 'I miss you too.'

We both stare straight ahead, like the cloud-shaped silhouette of the rustling tree is the most interesting sight known to humankind.

'You never came down to visit me,' I say carefully.

Zac's breathing slows, and he takes a moment to answer. 'You never came up here, either.'

'I wasn't sure if you wanted me to.'

For what feels like a full minute, we remain in a stand-off of uneasy silence.

I'm sorry I never came up here to see you after what happened. I'm so sorry. I wanted to, but it was so hard to reach you. Why wouldn't you talk to me?

Even thinking the words sends the pressure of tears to my eyes, so I blurt the plainest, dumbest thought in my mind.

'Hey, do you know whatever happened to Damien Di Fiore from high school? He popped into my head recently, and I don't think I've ever seen him on Facebook.'

Zac lets out a breath like he's relieved I changed the subject. 'Oh, man, must you? I'd forgotten about that poser. Do you remember when he tried to get people to call him "Gunner", but everyone just continued to call him Damien?'

For some reason that may be wine-related, I find this comment hysterical. When I finally stop giggling, Zac's looking at me like I need a check-up.

'You right there?' he asks. 'Do I need to unglue that glass from your hand?'

I clutch the wine closely like it's my newborn. 'You're not getting anywhere near my child.'

He rests back in his chair and links his fingers behind his head. 'Do you remember Damien leaving a love note in your locker once?'

I grunt a laugh. 'Of course. It said he wanted to "kiss and smell my beautiful hair". It's what triggered my crush on him. Wait—he told you about that?'

'I wrote that note.'

I sit forward and gape at him. 'You *what*?'

He nods without looking at me. 'Damien wanted to write you a love letter, and he couldn't think of what to say, so he asked me to do it for him.' He clasps his forehead, grimacing. 'But it's not like I was any better. "I want to kiss and smell your beautiful hair"? And then what—put the lotion on its skin or else it gets the hose again?'

I chuckle at the reference to the creepy serial killer from *The Silence of the Lambs*, but Zac just cringes into his glass. It's not the point, though, that the note he wrote wasn't exactly Shakespeare. It's more that it had made me smile from the inside out and look at Damien Di Fiore in an entirely new way. Learning it was Zac who penned those words is a head-trip.

'I can't believe it was you!' I reach out and give him a gentle shove.

'You still have gorgeous hair, by the way.' His gaze snags on the wild clump of honey-blonde strands twirling in my fingers.

I hold out a lock. 'You want to kiss and smell it?'

He laughs, and my mind shifts to another memory from the same year as the locker note. 'Oh my god!' I spring to my feet. 'I just remembered something that's going to Freak. You. The. Hell. Out.'

'OK?'

He blinks nervously as I duck inside and run upstairs to my bedroom, sliding open the wardrobe and digging out a shoebox stuffed with old jewellery. I untangle the silver charm bracelet and clip it to my wrist.

When I return to Zac's curious stare, I sit back down and lift my wine glass to my lips, ensuring the bracelet falls into his view.

'Well?' he says, on the verge of laughing even though he has no idea what's happening.

'Well, what?' I tap my fingers against my lips like I'm thinking, my wrist on display.

He catches my arm in his hand. 'Oh my god—is that . . . ?' He draws my wrist closer to the candlelight. 'Josie!'

My smile deepens. 'You know I never throw anything out.'

His fingertips brush the two charms dangling from the chain. One is shaped like a sun, which was the bracelet's inaugural charm when he gave it to me for my fourteenth birthday. When we first became friends, he nicknamed me 'sunbeam' because he said I was always so bright and sunny. The second charm is a tiny stack of three books he gave me on my fifteenth birthday, which fell during my bookish phase.

'There are only two charms on there,' he says, releasing my wrist with a pout.

'You totally let me down. You said you would give me one every year for my birthday.' I impersonate the saddest face I can think of, even though I've only ever adored his attempt at a birthday tradition that lasted all of two years.

'That's because you started dating *Damien*,' he scoffs like the name itself is gross.

'Yeah, but the bracelet was just a friend thing.'

''Course it was.' He runs his palm down his thick thigh, a trace of a frown creasing his brow.

Silence slides between us and hovers there for a moment.

'That's very sweet that you kept that,' Zac eventually says.

I give a dismissive grunt. 'You'll probably notice it at the op shop next week. I'm gonna trade it in for a used pair of old man's shoes.'

His chuckle turns into a yawn. I have no idea what time it is, but the last thing I want is for Zac to fade off to sleep and this night to be over.

I sit up higher, waking him up with my voice. 'So, given all the reminiscing, I think we should play an old high school game.'

He shoots me a look.

'"Two Truths, One Lie?"' I suggest in a sweet voice.

His mouth pulls up into a smile. 'Remember the last time we tried to play that game? We guessed the lie every time. We know too much about each other.'

'OK then, "Two Truths, One Lie" based on the last two years only?'

He clutches the side of his face. 'That sounds like too much effort right now.'

'What about "Spin the Bottle"?'

I'm not being serious, but Zac stills and his eyes graze over my lips for a split second that I don't miss. I need to show him I'm joking, so I let the laughter tear from my throat, even though I'd love to have teased him with that one a little longer. 'Just kidding.' I slap my knee, and he jumps. 'What about "Would You Rather"? Oh no, wait— I have it! "Best and Worst Features". We *have* to play that.'

He rests his chin in his palm. '"Best and Worst Features?"'

'Don't you remember that game? I tell you what I think your best and worst feature is, both physically and personality-wise, and you do the same for me.'

'That sounds totally juvenile.'

'Exactly! Which is why I love it.' I grin against the rim of my glass.

Compliments from Zac have always lit sparks in my chest, even though I'd never admit that to him. I can handle him telling me my two worst features in exchange for two things he loves about me.

Zac looks unconvinced.

'I'll start,' I press.

My gaze begins a slow trail over his body, assessing the ruffled curls that sit up over his forehead, the curves of his biceps that stretch the sleeves of his T-shirt, and the tanned forearms that bulge in all the right places. I glance down, taking in the length of his defined calves. I might have to make up a 'worst' physical feature.

'I think your best physical feature is ... ahh,' I grumble, 'I can't choose between your eyes and your hair.'

'My *hair*?'

'You have no idea how good your hair looks right now. That haircut is seriously hot.'

'Wow, OK.' He runs his palm up the shaved back of his neck before tugging at a couple of curls springing from the top.

'Now for your worst physical feature.' I clap a hand over my giggle. 'I feel so mean.'

'Let's not do worst features,' he says. 'At least, I'm not going to tell you anything bad about yourself.'

God, I could hug him.

'Fine, agreed,' I sigh like I'm giving in. 'Just best features, then. So, for your best personality feature, there are honestly so many, but I would have to say your sweetheart nature. You're always so kind and thoughtful.'

The corner of his mouth lifts, and suddenly I'm on my first day as the new kid at school, looking at thirteen-year-old Zac who's making me feel like less of a nerd over my geriatric taste in music. I don't think he realises that he's been making me feel less alone ever since.

'Thank you,' he says, his eyes glittering in the low light.

I angle myself towards him, ready to suck up all the praise, which I'm eighty per cent sure is to do with living in my over-achieving sister's shadow for half my life. 'So, what about me?' I ask, like a fully diagnosed narcissist.

Zac laces his fingers behind his head as he runs his eyes over me, and I suddenly think I should have said 'arms' instead of 'hair'.

'Give me a few days to answer,' he finally says.

My lips fall open. 'You can't come up with *one* thing you like about my body or my personality?'

'I can come up with many. But if I can only say one of each, then I want to make sure it's the right one.'

A bemused chuckle leaves my throat. 'Zac, it's not a school project. You don't have to come up with "the right answer".'

He sinks his teeth into his bottom lip as his gaze rakes over me again. 'Fine. I was thinking to maybe go with your ass,' he says like he's still thinking it over. 'Or your eyes.'

Holy shit, I've totally fed Reserved Zac Jameson too much wine.

He drains the last of the red in his glass. 'Given I've somewhat regrettably never really seen your ass, I'm probably going to say eyes. But, like I said, let me think about it. For personality, too.'

My body temperature has risen to a thousand degrees, and words are having trouble forming in my mouth.

Zac stands up, catching the table with his palm. I can't remember the last time I saw him tipsy like this. Because there's no way in hell he'd have said those words to me if he were sober.

'Is it OK if we call it a night?' he asks, covering another yawn with his fist. 'I'm slammed from this week.'

'Yeah, of course.'

I scoop up my wine glass and trail him inside, hiding my disappointment that this night has already come to an end.

I fish out a couple of clean blankets from the cupboard before grabbing the nicest pillow off my bed and setting Zac up on the downstairs couch beside Trouble's make-shift dog bed.

After leaving him in the bathroom with a spare tooth-brush from my bulk pack, I head back upstairs and shut the door to my bedroom, his comment doing circles in my head.

I've somewhat regrettably never really seen your ass.

What the hell? Is this just a guy thing? Guys like asses in general, don't they?

As I crawl beneath the sheets, an image invades my mind of Zac strolling around in the room beneath mine wearing nothing but his T-shirt and boxer briefs.

Jesus, Josie. I scrunch my face into the pillow, hunting for the source of these weird thoughts so that I can annihilate them.

Zac and I have had our chances to turn our effortless intimacy into something more. We even floated the idea of going to the high school formal together over blushy giggles, but when Emily Weston asked Zac to go with her, he didn't want to hurt her feelings, so he said yes. I ended up going with Lucas Pallas, who was so timid that he barely said two words to me the entire night.

Zac's never been anything more than my favourite friend and sidekick. But it's been an ice age since I've seen him, and he looks undeniably *good* right now, and that's thrown me off balance.

The desolate silence floating through the open window shakes me straight. We're not in Sydney anymore, we're in Newcastle, and this isn't where my life is.

Zac and I live in two different worlds now, and he is not and has never been part of my hopes, my dreams, or my plans. Not in *that* way.

CHAPTER 9

Sixteen years ago

My fingers pick at the St Teresa's Girls High logo embroidered into my tartan kilt, my eyes braving a quick glance at the hospital bed.

Aunt Susie sits propped against a pillow with her lips curled up at the edges, gazing at me. I blink away, then to the empty doorway. *Where's Mum with her takeaway coffee? I want to go home.*

I regret that thought instantly because I love Aunt Susie. I love how she calls me 'Jojo' and lets me try on her make-up and sparkly shoes, even though they're so big that when I take a step, my foot comes right out. She never says no when I ask if she can braid my hair or if we can play another round of Uno. But right now, she looks so . . . different.

'Your mum told me you're changing schools next year,' she says, sounding even more breathless than she did last week.

I nod, wanting to tell her how worried I am that I'll miss my friends at St Teresa's, even though that super-strict school never felt like me and I'm glad to be getting out of there. But the words cling to my throat. The unexplained beeps of the hospital machines, the sickly smell of disinfectant, the freezing temperature and bright ceiling lights—nothing in this room feels like my aunt.

'Do you know anyone at your new school?' she continues croakily.

I shake my head. 'Maybe I'll see someone who went to my primary school.'

'Maybe you'll meet some cute boys there,' she counters with a smile.

I embellish a grossed-out look, but when I think about going to a school with boys at it, my face turns weirdly hot.

Silence slips into the room, and Aunt Susie's stare drifts to the drawn window blinds before her eyelids sink shut.

Her little sleeps are my opportunities to look at her without worrying I'll burst into tears and make her feel even worse. With my stomach in knots, I trace my gaze over her dark-rimmed eyes, the thin tube poking from her nose and stretching across her hollow cheeks, and the flowery scarf wrapped around her bald skull. Every visible part of her is tinged with yellow—even her eyes, I noticed earlier.

Aunt Susie blinks awake, and I glance down.

'Do you think you could pass me some water?' she asks, fluttering her fingers tipped with coral-pink polish at the table beside the bed.

'Sure.' I get up to reach for the plastic cup, ensuring the lid is on properly before carefully bringing the straw to her cracked lips. Her face strains as she takes a small sip, but when the water seeps into her mouth, she relaxes. When she lifts her hand to gently pat my wrist, my fingers fold around hers.

'Don't be afraid, Jojo,' she whispers.

At first, I think she means to not be afraid of her . . . of how unwell she looks, of how painfully obvious it is that she's going to die soon.

But she holds my hand a little tighter and says, 'I know you'll miss your friends at your old school, even though you didn't like it so much there. But you keep looking forward, OK? Not back. Because, my baby girl, take it from me . . . when we become very afraid of something ending, nothing else can really begin.'

CHAPTER 10

Today

Over the next week, my phone fills with texts from Lindsay that become increasingly flirtatious with each day that passes. We end up agreeing to a Thursday night date, and I suggest a cool bar in Honeysuckle that Lola took me to a few nights ago with Isabella, the operations manager.

On Thursday morning, after a sunrise FaceTime with my sister in London, I stroll into work early, ready to make a start on a feature story about flood prevention that I hope will shine up my showreel.

The newsroom's already throbbing with energy, and thirty seconds after I plonk down at my desk, Man-Bun-Colin waves me over and hands me a police statement. Late yesterday afternoon, a mother from West Wallsend was charged with murdering her five-month-old baby and released on bail. Lola does most of the court and police rounds, but she's off today for her nan's funeral.

When Colin suggests I drive out to West Wallsend with a cameraperson, my pulse quickens. It'll likely be the biggest local news story of the day, and with Meghan Mackay eyeing us off from her computer, I need this to go well. Last week, while I covered a public spat over bicycle lanes in Minmi, Meghan reported on a record-breaking march against domestic violence and the new state budget.

I tell myself that no part of the thrill I feel about winning the story over her is down to her gushing to me all week about her dates with Zac. There was the dinner at the authentic Vietnamese restaurant, the cocktails at the live music bar, and the big-hit comedy movie.

Yes, I get it, Meghan. He really likes you. You don't have to tattoo it on your forehead.

I reset my focus on the news story and wince when I'm paired with Gus, who never wants to shoot anything. He drives at a snail's pace towards West Wallsend while I scroll through articles on my phone about the accused woman. I keep asking myself if I'm game enough to knock on her door, or if I should play it safe and only approach the neighbours. Christina would tell me to go for gold, and I bet neither Lola or Meghan would hesitate either.

'Let's try the accused woman's house first,' I say to Gus. 'Just stay close to me in case she starts losing it.'

He blanches at that possibility and pulls over outside a decaying fibro shack with a lawn that looks like it's never met the sharp end of a mower.

'You ready?' I ask over my shoulder as we pace up the footpath.

'Rolling,' he says behind me. *For once.*

I knock three times with progressively more force, but there's either no one home or the woman's hiding inside. A voice yells, 'Fucking vultures!' from a passing car before it screeches up the street.

Zac's words crash into my mind. *If it bleeds, it leads.*

I know he was just teasing, but it's enough to tip me off balance. I'm generally thick-skinned when it comes to criticisms of my job, but anything remotely negative from Zac and I turn into a wounded bird.

Why do you still care so much what he thinks, Josie? Think only of that newsreading desk in Sydney.

Gus and I move on to try several neighbours' houses with no luck before an elderly woman agrees to speak with us. Her bewildered expression and unfiltered comments make it obvious this is her first time being interviewed by the media. When she spends five minutes unloading about how aggressive the accused woman is, and how she once witnessed her wrenching another child out of a car, I know I have everything I need.

Gus and I are two minutes from Honeysuckle when Colin calls. He wants us to head over to the John Hunter Hospital to cover some interviews Meghan lined up for today about their new cancer centre. My stomach plummets.

Not me. Please.

'Is Meghan sick?' I mumble with full knowledge that, in TV news, you do what you're told, no questions asked.

'Yvette's got the flu, and Genevieve's away, so Meghan's reading tonight,' Colin rattles off, like I'm wasting his time.

My jaw drops. 'Meghan's reading the news?'

'Gotta go, Josie, too much to do,' Colin barks before hanging up.

My chest sinks into my gut. NRN News needed a back-up newsreader for tonight, and they picked Meghan Mackay instead of me. Lola already told me she's not interested in presenting and much prefers 'being amongst it', as she put it, but I've dropped several hints to Natasha that I would love to be considered.

I tell myself that Meghan was probably picked because she was sitting in the newsroom when this all went down, right in Natasha Harrington's sight line.

I tell myself it's because Meghan has worked there longer than I have.

Then I tell myself it's because she's better than me, and Christina is on crack for thinking I could ever find myself on the Sydney presenting desk.

'Two stories in one day,' Gus grumbles as he pulls into the hospital carpark. 'That place runs on the fucking smell of an oily rag.' I resist the urge to break it to him that, down in Sydney, we often cover three news stories at once, trying desperately not to let our frantic timetables cause us to make mistakes and report something inaccurate that gets the network sued.

Gus continues to whinge all the way to the gleaming new cancer centre on the hospital's third floor.

The head of oncology has clearly been media trained, and the interview goes smoothly until she warns me that the patient I'm set to interview is 'having a bit of a bad day'.

The cheese scroll I demolished on the way here rises in my throat as I trail the doctor into a single-bed room that feels cold enough to store ice inside. I'm introduced to Margie, a forty-five-year-old woman with terminal ovarian cancer who was once considered cured, until the cancer returned nine years later.

Everything in this room sends me right back to my aunt's and my grandma's dismal final days, but I find my focus and fire off questions like: *What were the first symptoms you noticed? What's a typical day like for you at the moment? What more do you think can be done to support women with ovarian cancer?* But then my questions succumb to what's really on my mind: *Are you in a lot of pain? What was it like to be told the cancer was back after you thought you'd beaten it? How do you hope you will be remembered?*

Someone gasps behind me at that last question, either Gus or the oncology doc—I can't tell. The room has spun into a whirlpool of sallow skin, sunken eyes and a hairless scalp.

'I'm not sure . . . I don't know if I . . .' poor Margie splutters before I retract my question and apologise. Stammering an excuse that we need to get back to the station, I push Gus and his bulky camera out into the hallway, wanting to fall into a hole where I can punch myself in the face.

I'm not the sort of reporter to ask such an insensitive question, but I know it had nothing to do with the patient. It was brought on by the same runaway train of terror that turned me into a choking mess two months ago during my live TV cross on Pink Ribbon Day.

Tears sting my eyes, and I clench them away as I send Gus to the car, lying about needing a couple of minutes to make a phone call.

The moment he's gone, I double over outside the emergency department entrance, gulping air.

'Josie?'

My head snaps up, meeting Zac's surprised face. I haven't seen him in his short-sleeved navy paramedic uniform in years. Behind him, an ambulance sits quietly in one of the waiting bays.

'Is everything OK?' He darts towards me, his eyes sweeping up and down, scanning me for injuries.

'I'm here for work.' My heart has pounded away all my breath. 'I just did some interviews about the new cancer centre.'

I should explain why he just caught me in a full-blown panic attack, but my lips won't open. Zac used to be the one person I could say anything to with zero embarrassment, but not having heard a peep from him since he crashed over at my place last week has left a sting in my side.

'What are you doing here?' I ask instead. *He's a paramedic, for god's sake.*

'We're just waiting for our patient to get a bed. The usual story.' He rolls his eyes.

'I heard that your girlfriend's reading the news tonight.'

It's my antsy mood that made me throw that in—a secret little test of loyalty that I hope Zac passes. It'll make me feel better.

He smiles, blushing. 'Yeah, she's over the moon.'

I wait for more, but this time, there's no *she's not my girlfriend* rebuttal, and no hint of sympathy for me—even though he must know how much I would have loved to have been chosen.

'I've gotta go,' I mutter, turning away from him. 'I'll see you later.'

'Wait.' Zac steps forward, his silver badge glinting in a patch of afternoon sunlight peeking through the trees. 'Want to grab dinner tonight? There's a new Sri Lankan place I want to try.'

Disappointment surges through me over having already made plans. 'That would've been great, but I've got something on tonight. I have a date. With Lindsay.'

His smile vanishes, and his throat flexes. 'Oh, cool. Say hi from me.'

'Will do.' My phone pings from my handbag. It's Gus asking where I am. *The nerve!*

After I farewell Zac and drag my feet towards the crosswalk, he calls out after me.

'Jose?' His gaze rests on mine for a moment. 'Safe drive back to work.'

'OK,' I mumble.

He then unclips the radio mic from his shoulder and speaks into it as he strides back to the ambulance.

The Honeysuckle bar where I'm meeting Lindsay is only a five-minute walk from the news station, so I decide to leave my car at work overnight and Uber home. I have no intention of getting sloshed, but first dates make me nervous, and a bit of lubrication might help me relax. Plus, my mind is still unsettled after today's hospital visit.

As I stroll along the windy street towards the muffled music and twinkling lights of the harbourside bar strip, I shrink internally at the offhand comment Natasha Harrington made in the lift as we were leaving.

'There was a big death focus in that cancer story,' she said while straightening her silk scarf.

'Oh, you thought so? I think those were just the best grabs,' I explained dumbly.

'Getting the right grabs comes down to asking the right questions,' she countered while setting her gaze on me through the mirror. 'I'd like to see a bit more optimism next time.'

In a terminal cancer story? I thought as I escaped out to the ground floor ahead of her. Though I only half meant it. I'm not so dark a soul that I have no faith in hope.

Keep telling yourself that, Josie. How's that persistent cancerous cough that you're pretending isn't there coming along? Storm clouds of panic begin to form inside my chest, but I force them away and up my pace, looking forward to relaxing my mind with a drink.

By the time I reach the buzzy outdoor bar that sits beneath a canopy of fairy lights, I've convinced myself of two things: (1) if I make an appointment to get my lungs checked, they could find suspicious spots on the X-ray, and I won't be able to handle that, so it's better if I don't go, and (2) Natasha Harrington hates my guts and I've got a higher chance of finding out I'm a gnome than ever being put on that news desk by her.

Lindsay waves me over from a bar stool, looking eye-catchingly handsome in a striped button-down shirt and distressed jeans. He's nursing what might be a bourbon and Coke, and pulls off his glasses as he gets up to hug me. He's warm and smells freshly showered, but when his fingertips trace a line down my arm, I get a slightly strange shiver.

'You look stunning,' he says, dragging out a bar stool for me.

'Thank you. I did a bunch of running around today for work, so I'm surprised to hear you say that.' I give my messy ponytail a flick.

'You're a TV reporter, right?' He slides me the drinks menu. I nod and order a glass of rosé. 'You have a hot voice for TV,' he adds with a smirk, lifting his bourbon to his lips.

'And a face for radio, right?' I deadpan.

He laughs. 'Hardly.'

The first wave of awkward silence crashes over us.

'So, how's the new beach pad?' I ask, sipping my wine and letting it soothe my frayed nerves a little.

'Oh, fuck, it's awesome,' he says, loudly enough for the bartender to turn his head, which is when I cotton on that Lindsay's bourbon isn't his first of the night.

'I love having my own place,' he continues. 'No one in my personal space, criticising me about stuff and wanting me to be quiet because they're on night shift, so apparently that means we all are. To be honest, I don't even know what I was thinking, moving in with a housemate. I thought I might want the company, but in reality? Shit no.'

'Zac says hi, by the way.' I smile over my glass.

'Oh, yeah, you guys are buds.' Lindsay grins like he's got amnesia about how he and I met.

'And Zac says you work for a software company?'

He tilts his head. 'Been asking about me, huh?'

A blush tints my cheeks, and he shifts his stool a little closer to mine. 'I don't really need to work, but I like what I do. Basically, I look after the strategic vision of the business and make sure that our software aligns with it. I set up the benchmarks, the customer acquisition strategies, the value propositions, the KPIs. I also manage the implementation, the stakeholders, the development life cycle . . . and many more cool things like that.'

My eyes are glazing over, so I divert the topic to some of the day's news stories until it becomes apparent that Lindsay is as uninterested in news and politics as I am in software.

'How are you enjoying Newcastle? Zac taken you anywhere good yet?' he asks with a hint of competition in his tone.

'Um, we've both been busy, but we're going to a Sri Lankan place soon,' I reply, weirdly defensive.

Lindsay snaps his fingers at the bartender for another bourbon. 'How long have you been friends with Zac?' he asks as I unfold the dinner menu.

I blurt half a laugh. 'I think since the Cretaceous Period.'

'The what?'

'We've been friends a long time,' I explain. 'High school. We also went to uni together.'

Lindsay studies my face, a strange smile dancing around his lips. 'Have you ever been a couple?'

'Nope. I might get the salt and pepper squid. It looks good.'

'Oh, *come on*.' Lindsay blocks the menu with his shoulder, peering into my face. 'You and Jaymo never dated?'

'*Jaymo?*'

'Jaymo as in Jameson. Zac Jameson.' His chin jerks back. 'You went to school together and don't know his last name?'

'I know his last name, and I also know that no one has ever called him "Jaymo". That's a terrible nickname.' I push the menu towards him. 'What do you think you'll have?'

Lindsay's playful gaze refuses to part with my face, like he's waiting for some big reveal. 'You never answered my question.'

What is this guy's deal? 'I just told you. Zac and I have never dated.'

'Why not? He's a good-looking guy. And you're obviously gorgeous.'

I breathe a chuckle into my rosé. 'Thank you,' is all I can think to reply.

'Guess I read the signals wrong then,' Lindsay mutters, flipping the menu over. 'I'm gonna have a schnitty.'

Signals?

'Actually, Zac did have a blonde chick coming over recently who was pretty sizzling,' he adds, and that territorial feeling eclipses my chest again. 'Maybe they're "just friends" too.'

Lindsay chuckles at his own joke, but it's obvious that he doesn't really like Zac, and I'm having trouble figuring out why. Did something happen between them? One thing I've picked up on is that they have wildly different energies. The Zac I know—or used to know— is chilled, low-key and comfortable in his own skin. Whereas Lindsay keeps fidgeting with his gold watch, gulping bourbon like it's water, and tapping one of his feet. I'd pegged Lindsay as Mr Confidence, but right now, he's coming off as the more insecure of the two. *Oh my god—why am I comparing them?* I kick Zac Jameson out of my head.

The food's greasy but good, and by our third round of drinks—which I'm pretty sure is Lindsay's fourth, fifth or even sixth—we've uncovered a similar taste in movies and dream holiday destinations, and he's looking more appealing with every sip of my wine.

It's a little after ten when the bartender calls for last orders. I'm tired after being up with the sparrows to chat to Ingrid this morning, but Lindsay gets one more bourbon for the road and suggests we move on to a pub in Hamilton. I shake my swimming head and remind him that I'm working tomorrow.

'So am I, you lightweight.' His cheeky smirk suits his face, and I reconsider his offer for a split second before deciding against it.

'I'm going to call an Uber home,' I say, catching a trace of a slur in my voice. Lindsay tosses back the last of his drink and chases me outside.

A gust of cool air whips my cheeks from the water's edge, and I cross my arms over myself, already dreading my inevitable headache tomorrow. Natasha was disappointed in me today, and while Meghan was reading the news tonight, I was out getting half-sozzled with a guy I barely know. A blade of self-loathing cuts into my chest, followed by a twist of regret that I didn't just go to the Sri Lankan restaurant with Zac. I'd be in bed by now, getting a good sleep before work tomorrow.

Two arms slide around my waist from behind, and I nearly shriek but then will myself to relax a little into Lindsay. It's been months since I've felt a man's touch, and at least he's keeping me warm.

'You want to come and check out Merewether?' he says into my ear. His breath smells like bourbon, which I don't hate, and the cold frame of his glasses skims my cheek.

I smile and shake my head. 'Not coming home with you tonight.'

'Meaning you will on another night?'

He guides me around to face him, but before I can find eye contact, his mouth has already landed on mine. *Ohh-kay, then.*

His lips are needy and a little too forceful for the sleepy mood the wine's left me in. But I let his tongue sink into my mouth while his palms glide down my lower back and settle on my backside, giving it a light squeeze. For half a minute, I lose myself in the kiss, considering whether I like the taste of him. I do, but when his hardening length makes itself known against my thigh, I detach from him and take a step back.

'Sorry,' he says, his cheeks pinking. He pulls off his foggy glasses and wipes them on his shirt.

'It's OK.' To reassure him, I stretch on my toes to press a short kiss to his lips. 'Car's here. Gotta go.'

'I'll call you, babe,' Lindsay says, looking a little glowy-eyed while his fingers cling to mine for as long as they can.

As the car pulls away, I relax into the seat and pull out my phone, finding a friend request from Meghan Mackay.

My gut tenses, but I tell myself not to be a competitive bitch and accept the request. Her profile unlocks, flooding my feed with images. The latest is a selfie of her sitting at the news desk with a smile wider than the circumference of the earth. Reminding myself that I should be happy for her rather than envious, I continue scrolling.

Her previous post is a string of images filled with my best friend's face. Meghan and Zac are sitting on one side of a restaurant table, and I can tell she's forced him to be in these pics, which draws an affectionate chuckle to my throat. I swipe left—god, how many did she take?—until I reach the last photo. It's a selfie of Meghan burrowed into Zac's chest as they cuddle up on a leather couch. The band posters on the wall behind them have me guessing it's the live music bar they went to the other night. Zac's arm is draped around Meghan's shoulder, his fingers threaded with hers, his hazel eyes shining.

I back out of the app entirely.

The Uber drops me off, and I fumble to connect my front door key with the lock while I sway on my feet, praying that the dull bass reverberating through my skull isn't coming from our house.

I step inside, and for half a second, I think I've stumbled onto a porn film set. A woman is lying spread-eagled on our couch with a guy's head buried between her thighs while Davide stands watching, butt-naked, with his dick in his hand.

Oh. My. God.

The house music's too loud for any of them to have heard me come in, and I silently back out the door until I'm left shivering on the footpath. Tears rise in my eyes, and my phone shakes in my hand.

What do I do? What the hell do I do!

My fingers quiver against my ear as I call Zac, but his phone rings out.

Shit.

I can't call Lola this late on a weeknight when I'm still getting to know her, especially on the day she buried her grandmother. I consider ringing Lindsay, but the thought of his hands on me after what I've just seen makes me want to retch.

After trying Zac again, I book another Uber to take me to the nearest roadside motel.

A moment later, rosé shoots up into my throat and spills into the gutter.

CHAPTER 11

Thirteen years ago

'I kissed Damien.'

The whites of Zac's eyes expand in the darkness, the moonlight casting stripes of silvery blue light over our blankets as it shines through the window blinds.

I wait for the questions from my best friend.

What was it like?

Was he a good kisser?

Would you do it again?

Zac's mouth opens, but then shuts again. He rolls onto his back and silently stares up at his living-room ceiling, the line in his brow setting off an alarm bell in my head.

'Are you mad?' I say, my stomach shrinking with a pang that reminds me of that time when he asked me out at the train station. To be honest, I'm still mad at him for risking this friendship by doing that.

He scrunches his face. 'No. Why would I be?' The edges of our blow-up mattresses squeak together when he shifts around to face me. 'So, *you* kissed Damien?'

'Yeah. I just said that.'

'I mean, you put your lips on his first?'

'Zac.' I pull a face like he's being weird. 'Why does that matter? We *kissed*. With tongue.'

He almost gags, like I just suggested he eat mushroom soup. Except I know that Zac made out with Clara Ng last month at the train station for ten whole minutes, and now he's acting as if this topic is grossing him out.

'*He* kissed *me*,' I elaborate, a little irked by his reaction. 'We were behind the science building.'

'*Everyone* kisses there,' Zac mumbles. Why is he being a brat? This was my first kiss, and it's kind of a big deal.

'I liked it a lot,' I lie, turning onto my back and flopping an arm behind my head.

Zac says nothing.

Whatever. I've waited an absolute eternity of a day to tell Zac this because I wanted it to be when we were alone, face to face, and his mum and dad have only just gone to bed. I pictured a proud grin, maybe a congratulatory jab on the shoulder, an interrogation for all the details. That's how Amy reacted when I blabbed to her about it during our free period together this morning because I *had* to tell someone.

But Zac doesn't seem to want to know.

After a long time, he asks, 'Are you his girlfriend now?'

I'm almost asleep, but I peel my eyes open and blink hazily at the miniature mountain range of Zac's silhouette. He's facing me, sitting up on one elbow.

'I think I am,' I reply.

His swallow is audible. 'Cool. I'm gonna go to sleep now.'

''Kay. Have a good sleep, favourite.'

''Night, Josie.'

CHAPTER 12

Today

I'm mid-pee and smiling at Lindsay's text praising my news report on solar panel recycling last night, when a message from Zac flashes at the top of the screen. Mr Punctuality is waiting outside—my ride for today's pub lunch with Zac's cousin Ross and Ross's fiancée, Holly.

I set my phone on the vanity and hurriedly wipe before my gaze stills on a splotch of red blooming across the toilet paper.

My stomach hits the floor. *What the hell? My period finished ten days ago!*

The crepe-thin paper shakes in my fingers as I bring it closer to my face.

I flush away the offending tissue like it's diseased, then dig out an emergency pad from my bag in case there's any further flow.

Once I've buttoned up my jeans with shaky fingers, I gape at my stunned reflection in the mirror. A series of images steamroll into my head: breaking it to everyone that I have cancer . . . being told it's now spread throughout my body . . . my family weeping at my funeral. Actually, my parents are in tears while stoic Ingrid's solemnly flicking through the funeral booklet.

The hollow chime of the downstairs doorbell shocks me back into my skin.

I quickly erase my smudged mascara with my fingers and suck back my tears.

When I dash downstairs and fling open the door, Zac's face drops.

'Are you OK?' he says. 'What's wrong?'

'Nothing!' *Way too perky, Josie.* 'I might have a bit of a cold,' I lie, pinching my throat.

He frowns. 'Do you still have that cough?'

The question hits like a gut punch right now. 'No, that's gone,' I mumble as we get inside his car, forcing all thoughts of bloodied toilet paper and metastatic cancer out of my head.

Tension begins to leak out of my bones the moment we pull away from the house. I haven't told Zac yet about Davide's public three-way or the fact that I spent the night in a hotel. It's not the sort of thing I wanted to mention over text.

Zac's gaze flickers to mine for a moment. His olive-coloured T-shirt that says 'Stop Making Stupid People Famous' matches his eye colour to an almost farcical degree.

'You're quiet today,' he observes.

I expel a heavy sigh. 'It's been a week.'

'Oh yeah? Work kicking your ass again?'

I'm grateful to have a distraction from what's going on inside my body, and we share a few stories about our work weeks until I rip the bandaid off and tell Zac all about Davide's living-room threesome.

His fingers tighten around the steering wheel. 'Are you joking with me right now?'

'I wish. I slept in a motel that night. I was actually scared.'

'Josie.' His brows come together. 'Why didn't you call me?'

'I did. You didn't answer.'

With one hand on the wheel, his other grips his hair, mocha curls sprouting through his fingers. 'Shit. I'm so sorry. That was a Thursday, right? I had an early shift on Friday. I texted you in the morning, but—'

'It's fine. It's old news now.'

We stop at a set of traffic lights, and Zac looks at me, his jaw set. 'I don't like that guy. At all.'

'Why would you? He's an A-grade weirdo. But he apologised, and I've hardly seen him since, thank goodness. He's started up his late-night reiki sessions again, and I'm usually gone before he gets up in the morning.' I shrug a shoulder.

Zac watches me for a moment before the light changes. He makes another left, then reverse parks opposite a sprawling corner pub that looks newly renovated. As we climb out of the car, I register how close we are to Zac's house—he could have just walked here. I hope Meghan knows how lucky she is. Lindsay didn't even ask me how I'd be getting to our date.

'How come Meghan's not coming today?' I ask, aware of the hesitation in my voice as we cross the road to the pub.

'Does she have to come everywhere?' he replies lightly, the sun setting his caramel eyes alight. When I don't answer, he elaborates. 'She's had a big work week, so she's taking some chill time today.'

'Oh, right.'

No, Josie, they haven't broken up. Stop being horribly selfish and also weird.

I'm probably only grumpy over Meghan because she presented the news four nights in a row this week. Christina's been texting me for days now, and I've been replying with hilarious memes about small-town life, but I haven't been able to break it to her yet that I'm not exactly kicking butt up here at NRN News.

Inside the pub, Ross waves us over from a high table in a beer garden surrounded by potted palms and string lights. I dart towards his infectious smile. Few people in this universe can make you feel as instantly at ease as Ross Jameson.

'Josie-girl,' he says through a grin, standing to engulf me in a bear hug. Over his shoulder, a petite woman with black hair styled into a fifties-look quiff offers me a shy smile.

I step towards her. 'Hey, I'm Josie.'

'The girl I've heard so much about,' she replies warmly, her brief hug smelling like hairspray.

Zac buys a round of beers, and we all catch up, tossing in explanations to Holly so she doesn't get lost when we begin reminiscing about our younger years. Ross also grew up in Sydney but moved to Newcastle when he started university and quickly fell in love with the smaller, sleepier city. He asks about my family and gives me a sad smile when I explain that they've all deserted me for the excitement of living abroad.

Half a beer in, Ross is telling Holly about the time Zac brought him to school with him for an entire day, and none of the teachers noticed that Ross wasn't an actual student until the very last period. It still makes me cry with laughter. When my elbow accidentally grazes the soft plane of Zac's forearm, my attention zeroes in on that one spot.

Zac's eyes flash to mine just as my phone lights up with a text from Lindsay.

> **LINDSAY:** Hey, stunner. Didn't hear back from you after my message about the news report! I went to such trouble to watch that, lol.
> What time are we meeting tonight?
> I really can't wait to see you. x

Holy shit, I completely forgot.

Zac's gaze sweeps over the handset as I type out a reply that I should be home no later than five. I'd better go easy on the beers.

124

I spend the next ten minutes half-contributing to the casual conversation and half-reconsidering this date tonight. Even though Lindsay is a handsome, ambitious go-getter—exactly the sort of man I've been trying to attract—I can't honestly say I've missed him this past week.

Zac's warm hand covers my bare thigh beneath the table, and all the blood in the world rushes there. His palm disappears as fast as it arrived, and he's looking right at me.

'Ross just asked if you want to come to the wedding.'

My eyes widen at Ross. 'Really?'

He rolls his eyes. 'Of course, Jose. I would've invited you sooner had I known you'd be up here.'

'I'd love to.'

I push away the thought that he wouldn't have thought to invite me if I'd still been living in Sydney—only a two-hour drive from here. I guess my time apart from Zac has also affected my friendship with Ross.

The wedding is only six weeks away, and I make a mental note to buy a dress while I pepper Ross and Holly with questions about the ceremony and reception.

After we drain our beers, we agree to order lunch, and Zac slides me a menu. 'Surprise swap?' he asks under his breath, his eyes lit up.

I grin. 'Hell, yes.'

I love this game. We used to play it at uni, ordering each other's meals in secret back in our local pub in Bathurst. Sometimes my ideal lunch would come sailing out of the kitchen, and other times it would be something vile like broccoli and lentil soup that would launch one of Zac's cute-laugh attacks. Shovelling the offending dish down my throat would be worth it just for that.

My fingertip traces the menu. He'd love any of the pizzas, but that feels a bit boring. I could also see him appreciating the peri-peri chicken, but I pause at the smoked mushroom burger. Zac isn't allergic to mushrooms, but he despises them. I only know of him eating them once—when he started dating Tara, and she baked him mushroom pie before learning about his aversion. Because Zac's a sweetheart, he ate half the pie, then threw up in our bathroom three hours later.

Mushroom burger it is, I decide and cackle internally.

I don't want to make the poor boy ill, but I'm gunning to see the look on his face when the burger lands in front of him. It's even worth me paying for a second meal afterwards—I'd never expect him to eat something he hates.

After Holly and I place our orders at the bar, Zac jumps up to join the queue with Ross, shooting me a glance from the line. He'd better not be ordering me the cauliflower salad, *puke*.

'He looks at you a lot,' Holly says, and my eyes snap to hers. She smiles coyly over her beer glass like she knows something I don't.

'What do you mean?'

She just tilts her head at me, and I make little rips in the beer-soaked coaster, my heart skipping. 'We're just friends.'

'Only ever just friends?'

Jeez, first Lindsay, and now Holly?

I nod, guessing that Zac and I didn't get this question nearly as much in the past—at least, not once school was over—because he was always with Tara.

'He's such a beautiful soul,' Holly adds, her eyes warming.

My gaze drifts to where Zac's saying something in Ross's ear that's making Ross shudder with laughter. Zac's got his hand in his back pocket again, cupping the perfectly rounded curve of his—

'He's definitely a sweetheart,' I blurt, spinning back to Holly and resetting my head. 'But we've been really close friends since we were thirteen. If something was going to happen between us, it would have by now.'

She seems content with my answer, and the conversation shifts to her work as an art therapist. The nosy reporter in me grills her about it until the boys return with another round of beers.

Zac plonks one down in front of me. 'Oh, thank you, but I'd better be careful,' I say. 'I've got a date tonight with Lindsay.'

His brow pinches. 'You do?'

'Yeah, I totally forgot; is that bad?' I make a face.

'Well, I'm not sure it's *good*.' He slides back onto the stool beside me.

A waiter swoops in, dumping a plate in front of Zac that steams with the ammonia-tinged smell of cooked mushrooms. He pokes his fork at the stack of creamy-brown flesh stuffed inside the burger, taking a second to figure out what it is.

'Oh my fucking god,' he says under his breath.

I fight laughter as the waiter plonks down my plate. My eye fillet steak bulges like it's cooked to perfection and sits beside a small Caesar salad and a wire basket of fries caked in salt.

Zac's staring at his meal like it just screwed his girl-friend.

'I'm sorry, it's just a joke,' I utter, still wanting to crack up, but also totally heartsore. Zac ordered my favourite meal—even swapped out the garden salad for my beloved Caesar.

I push my plate towards him. 'You have mine. I'm going to order you something else.'

'No way.' He slides the steak back to me and grips his burger with both hands. A slimy glob of mushroom drops onto his plate as he takes a bite.

'You can't eat that!' I latch on to his forearm. 'You'll be sick later.'

He continues chewing with a look of defiance before he drops the burger and gags into his serviette. 'You're right. I can't eat this; I'm so sorry.'

'Don't be. It's my fault.' I saw my knife through the steak like solving this issue is the most urgent thing on earth, and point a piece of meat at his mouth. 'Eat this while I get another menu. I'll order you whatever you want.'

Zac's fingers wind around mine, taking hold of the fork. He feeds the steak into his mouth, and a moan of pleasure rumbles out of his throat.

'Fuck, that's good,' he says, releasing my hand, and I realise I'm staring.

'Then that's what you're getting.' I stand up.

'No, it's too expensive,' he protests. 'You can't order a burger *and* a steak. I'll get it.'

He rises beside me, but I cup my hands around the firm ridges of his shoulders, pushing him back down.

I catch Ross and Holly watching us with interest as they nibble on their shared pizza before I escape to the bar and sheepishly order a forty-five-dollar steak.

An hour later, Zac and I reluctantly say goodbye to Ross and Holly so I can get home in time to change for my date with Lindsay. After two beers and a steak, all I want to do is watch mindless TV in bed with my laptop, and I make a silent pledge to be more organised so that I don't double-book myself next time.

Rather than dropping me off outside my house, Zac insists on parking and walking me to my door. I'm not sure he'd do that if I hadn't told him about Davide's ménage à trois, but when I step inside the house, I'm so grateful he's here.

'What the fuck?' Zac hisses behind me.

David's bare ass freezes mid-thrust, and his face jerks towards us from where he's hunched over his massage table. A pair of naked, feminine legs are locked tightly around his sweaty hips.

'Oh, shit. I thought you were out today,' Davide says as he pulls back from the woman he was just ramming into.

'I was,' I breathe, trying not to look . . . *down*.

Zac lurches towards Davide. 'What the hell do you think you're doing? You realise you don't live alone, right? Have you never heard of something called *consideration* for other people?'

The poor woman rolls off the table and yanks a towel over herself, muttering an apology.

'Don't *you* be sorry,' Zac says to her. 'It's this pervert's house. Don't you have a fucking bedroom?' he snaps at Davide, who cowers a little.

I'm struggling for breath like I've been punched in the throat. I don't want any more of this. Davide's shoulder-length mane of hair and crazy eyes are beginning to resemble Charles Manson's.

Zac twists to look at me, his brow creased. 'You can't stay here.'

It sounds more like a plea than an order, but I nod. *No, I can't stay here.*

He returns his gaze to the wide-eyed woman. 'Do you want to leave with us?'

She shares a glance with Davide, who's put the massage table between himself and Zac. 'I'm OK,' she murmurs, swiping a matted strand of hair from her eyes. 'We were in the middle of a reiki session, and I'm paying by the hour.'

Zac shakes his head and reaches for my hand. My fingers curl into his, gripping tightly.

'Do you need to pack some stuff?' he asks me softly. 'I can bring you back tomorrow when he's not here to get whatever you need.'

Right now, I just want to be out of here. My faded jeans and op-shop cami top are going to have to be good enough for Lindsay.

Am I seriously still going on that date? My stomach is as tight as a fist.

Davide's intense gaze burns a hole in my back as Zac follows me outside. Zac stops to mutter something sharply to Davide that I can't make out, but I'm sure it's nothing good.

Because I'm shaken up, Zac offers to drive and bring me back to pick up my car tomorrow. He sits and looks at me before he switches on the engine, his lips turned down.

'You can't live there anymore, Jose.'

I nod, blinking away tears. 'I know.'

'You can stay with me, OK? Until you find a new place.'

Something I hadn't realised was trapped bursts free inside me, and I tilt forward, reaching for his shoulders. He *tsks* and folds himself around me, smelling like soap and something indescribably *Zac*. His heart beats hard against mine, and I turn my face into his neck, my breath fluttering warm air over the strip of skin beneath his hairline. His arms tighten around me, and I think he breathes a sigh, but I'm not sure.

My phone pings, and we both jolt backwards like a parent just walked in on us making out on the bed.

It's a message from Lindsay, letting me know he'll be fifteen minutes late. Zac kicks the car into gear, and I type out a reply saying I'm unexpectedly staying at Zac's house and without a car. I can't help but hope it ends the date, but Lindsay offers to pick me up, which makes Zac go oddly quiet.

The moment we're inside his house, Zac falls into his classic protective mode, bringing me water and making up a couch bed because he hasn't refurnished the spare room yet. He promises to buy me a toothbrush and anything else I need while I'm out with Lindsay.

'Stop being so nice,' I say through a pouty smile, clearly not meaning that at all, as I curl up on the adjacent couch.

He tosses a pillow onto the couch bed. 'You know you don't have to go out tonight. I'm sure Lindsay will survive.'

I force a smile. 'I only walked in on Davide giving his reiki client the full-service package. I'm not suffering from war wounds.'

'Well, I am.' He grimaces at the memory.

As much as I want to be excited about seeing Lindsay, all I feel like doing is hanging out in this comfortable living room with my oldest friend who I've missed so much, but it feels too late to cancel the date.

Zac rests against the arm of the couch and thumbs through his phone. 'I'm going to crash at Meghan's tonight. I'll give you a spare key to get back in.'

'OK, sure,' I say in a rush and lurch to my feet.

I slip into the bathroom to fix my hair and apply the mascara I found in my handbag, suppressing the little twist of jealousy in my chest that's all kinds of stupid. I'm going out tonight, so why shouldn't he?

I stare myself down in the mirror. *Get your shit together, Josie. You're just crashing over. It's not a Zac–Josie reunion party.*

The date with Lindsay at an American-style burger bar goes surprisingly well, and even though I fight off his pleas for me to come back to his place, I let his mouth devour mine in his car for a good thirty minutes outside Zac's house. It's just after eleven when I finally unlock my mouth and head inside, my lips raw and tingling.

A blue light glows from the couch bed where Zac's laid out, staring at his phone.

'I thought you were staying at Meghan's,' I say with surprise.

He folds an arm behind his head, and I register that he's shirtless beneath the quilt. 'Decided to come home. I've got the early shift tomorrow.'

'Ah.' I hover silently for a few heartbeats before pointing my phone at him accusingly. 'You're in my bed.'

He makes a *pffsh* sound. 'No way in hell am I making you sleep on the couch. I changed the sheets in my room. Go for it.'

'Zac.'

He gives me a resolute headshake without looking at me.

'Thank you,' I mumble after a yawn. 'But this conversation is to be continued.'

His gaze finally lifts to mine. 'You were outside for a while.'

My cheeks colour. 'Stalker, much?'

'Your lips are all swollen. That good, huh?'

'Zac!'

He chuckles noncommittally and switches off his phone, casting the room into darkness. 'I should probably warn you,' he says sleepily, 'you're going to hear every car driving past tonight. These walls may look pretty, but they're paper thin.'

'Hmm, I'll have to remember that for when I bring Lindsay *inside* next time,' I reply pointedly, trying to get him back for the lips comment. But a sharp silence chews up the air and an uncomfortable feeling washes over me.

Why did I just say that? Why?

Zac expels a deep breath and rolls away from me. 'Well, if you're going to fuck Lindsay in my bed, Josie, at least give me a heads-up, so I can head over to Meghan's. Then both you and Meg can scream as loud as you want to.'

'Zac.' My mouth falls open.

When he says nothing more, I stalk off to bed with a gaping hole growing in my stomach.

I feel like my best friend and I just swung bloody swords at each other on a battlefield. And I'm not sure I understand why.

CHAPTER 13

Seven years ago

'Hey, Willy Wonkaaaa,' drawls a second-year science student dressed as Austin Powers. He tips his beer bottle against Zac's tumbler, which is housing the bar's cheapest whisky.

Zac cuts me a sidelong scowl as I stifle a laugh, my fingers sweeping the gold beads of my crooked Cleopatra headpiece out of my face. 'That's *three* dinners you owe me, Willy,' I gloat under my breath while tugging Zac away. Every time someone erroneously guesses Zac's Mad Hatter costume to be Willy Wonka, he has to take over one of my scheduled cooking nights.

'You know that making dinner is not a punishment for me,' Zac scoffs. 'You should've picked something else.'

'Sexual favours?'

He squints a 'very funny' look at me and begins fidgeting with the spotty satin bow tied around his neck.

I don't know if it's the gigantic bow, the frizzy orange wig, or the bright-red lipstick making me snicker every time I look at him.

'Come on, let's go see if there's anyone we know here,' I say, looping my arm through Zac's and pulling him deeper into the swarm of university students adorned in fancy dress. 'Oh, shit,' I blurt.

I spin away from Felix, the MBA student that Zac manhandled out of our apartment.

When Zac catches sight of Felix preaching to some first-years while sporting a glittery angel costume, complete with gold wings and a toga, he groans. 'What a fucking dick.'

'Said the guy wearing cherry-red lipstick.'

Zac goes to give me a pretend shove, but when I giggle and duck out of the way, he accidentally collides with a black-haired girl wrapped in a cute blue dress with a white apron. Her sheet of straight, shiny hair is pushed off her face with a bowed headband, and she's trying to balance a margarita glass that's on the brink of spilling.

'*Shit*, sorry,' Zac says, steadying her shoulders with both hands. He lets go right away.

'It's all good, Hatter,' the girl replies, her pretty smile moving from him to me.

'You know who I am?' Zac says. The curls in his wig bounce when he smacks his palm to his chest.

'They all think he's Willy Wonka,' I explain to the girl.

She laughs. 'Ah, OK. Well, everyone keeps calling me Dorothy from *The Wizard of Oz*.'

'As if, *Alice*,' Zac replies, his lips curling up at the Alice in Wonderland costume that complements his Mad Hatter outfit. Anyone who didn't know them would guess they came here as a couple.

They exchange shy smiles, and I swear I can see Zac's schoolboy blush burning through his white face paint.

I step forward and stretch out a hand to the girl, the white cape clipped to my wrists moving with it. 'I'm Josie, by the way. Second-year comms.'

Her fingers lightly shake mine. 'Lovely to meet you; I'm Tara. I'm a second-year too. Nursing.' Her dark eyes skip to Zac. 'And you?'

'Zac. Second-year paramedicine.'

Her smile expands. 'Really? I can't believe we haven't met before; we're travelling on the same wavelength. Similar courses, similar costumes.' Her eyes slide to me. 'You two are together?'

'No,' Zac answers right away.

'*Nooo*,' I reinforce for his benefit. 'Are you here with friends?' I ask Tara.

'Yes, I was just coming back from the bar. You want to join us?' She tips her head at a small group of students lazing on some rustic leather lounges in a low-lit corner.

'Sure,' Zac replies without even looking at me. His scuffed leather brogues trail after Tara like a beagle on a scent trail.

137

Ohh-kay, this is going to be one of those times where Zac becomes uber-focused on a girl, and I lose his attention for the entire evening. But Tara seems friendly and approachable, unlike the arts student Zac was dating recently, who hated him having a female best friend. I guess I don't mind being relegated to wingwoman, even though I was hoping to revisit our mischievous conversation from the other night about The Back-Up Plan.

Zac squeezes in beside Tara on one of the couches, and I drop onto the adjacent couch between two girls in matching creepy twin costumes. A guy in a Jack Sparrow outfit jumps up to exclaim over Zac's Willy Wonka costume, then offers him a fist bump because they're both 'Johnny Depp characters'.

When Zac passes me a subtle headshake over the guy's shoulder, I smile and hold up four fingers at him. Warmth sparks in his eyes as they linger on mine before he turns to Tara.

CHAPTER 14

Today

Zac's buttery-soft linen sheets envelop me like a cloud, and his pillows must have been stolen off a bed from heaven. He wasn't wrong about the street noise, but last night still delivered my soundest sleep in weeks.

A yearning for coffee eventually kicks me out of bed, and I wrap the king-sized quilt around my shoulders and stumble towards the coffee machine, scooping up Trouble and holding her twitchy body against my chest. Zac's left out a mug for me, the sugar jar, and handwritten instructions on how to use the machine that are borderline formal. My smile travels from my heart to my face.

After a gloriously strong coffee and a bowl of toasted muesli, I reluctantly return Zac's comfy quilt to his bed and venture into his bathroom on the hunt for a clean towel.

A strange excitement tingles through me as I poke through his things, sniffing his woody aftershave balm and sweeping the feathery bristles of his shaving brush across my jaw.

I slip into the spare-bathroom shower, and when I re-emerge with a fluffy white towel wrapped around my wet hair, my phone pings.

ZAC: Hope you slept OK? I don't finish until 7, but after that, I'm happy to take you to pick up your car and stuff from asshat's place if you like?

ME: That would be great, thank you. Sweet of you after such a long shift!

ZAC: Happy to

ME: Do you think I should ask Davide if he can be out at that time?
Would really rather not see him. 😬

ZAC: Want me to? If you give me his number, I'll also happily send him a fake text congratulating him on winning a lifetime supply of tie-dyed T-shirts.

ME: Haha, thanks so much, Dad, but I can do it. 😊

ZAC: You never told me your dad is such a hottie. 😁

ME: You want his number?

ZAC: Hell no. Have you met his daughter? 😨

ME: I know! She has the absolute worst taste in friends. 👎

ZAC: Exactly! They can't stand her but are too scared to tell her that.

ME: 🔪💔

ZAC: Naw, I'm kidding, nutjob. *hugs*

My cheeks glow, and I have no idea why Zac and I can chat this way over text, but in real life, feel like the Great Wall of China is still standing between us.

I suck in a bracing breath of air and text Davide that I'm moving out and coming to get some stuff tonight, adding that I'd prefer it if he wasn't there.

He replies an hour later with nothing but a sad-face emoji. I ignore it and continue reading the report I discovered on Zac's desk while I was in fully-fledged snoop mode. It's directed to the commissioner and chief executive of NSW Ambulance and essentially makes the case that more empathy is needed in paramedic practice. *Oh, Zac.* My chest twists up as I read through the well-written report, which argues that educators should study empathy to reduce paramedic burnout and increase patient satisfaction. When Zac delves into the suggestion that little empathy is typically shown for physically unharmed survivors at scenes of trauma, I close the report with a pained sigh. I'm still in two minds about whether his history makes him the best person for this critical care job that he's going for, or the worst.

Liquid trickles into my underpants, and I freeze on the spot like I've just been caught shoplifting.

No.

A second trickle chases it, and I bolt into the bathroom, unbuttoning my jeans and yanking them down. A spot of blood deepens on the pad I put in this morning, and I hunch forward on the toilet seat, wrapping my arms around my head.

No, no, no. Please no.

When my phone pings from the kitchen, I change the pad and wash my quivering hands, trying to refill my lungs with air.

The text is from Christina, who's sent a meme depicting someone turning into a skeleton while waiting for a phone call. Desperate to wrench my mind off the bleeding, I inhale four steadying breaths and tap her number.

'Is that really you?' she says in lieu of a hello.

'I'm so sorry, I've been meaning to call you, but things have been a bit manic here.'

'Manic?'

Leaving out my crippling fears about my weird health symptoms, I fill her in on Davide and his home brothel, and the fact that I'm dating 'nudist Lindsay'— who's actually turned out to be way less of a nudist than Davide.

'It feels like you only got there five minutes ago,' she exclaims, like I've done well on the drama.

'Newcastle's way more interesting than I thought.'

She chuckles, and I relax my mind by probing her for baby updates. Her voice trembles a touch when she tells me she's planning to inform the network heads about the pregnancy next week.

'You'll be fine,' I encourage. 'You have every right to have a baby. Those bigwigs will be thrilled for you.'

'OK, what drugs are they giving you in Newcastle?'

I laugh. We both know that pregnant female anchors are seen as a headache in network television, but Christina is as adored by her bosses as she is by her audience. When she launches into another speech about me becoming her replacement, I break it to her that NRN News's resident favourite up here isn't me but Meghan Mackay.

'She's also dating my friend Zac, if you can believe that,' I add. 'She seems totally smitten, so with any luck, she'll have no interest in a Sydney job because he's never, ever leaving Newcastle, apparently.'

'Wait, back up. You mean your best friend, Zac?'

'The very same. They met before I even got up here. Small world, hey.'

Christina pauses. 'Are you OK with them dating?'

The question catches me off guard. 'Why wouldn't I be?'

'No reason. It just seems a little like muddying the waters or something. Your best friend dating your colleague.'

'Well, how's this for muddying the waters? I'm *living* with Zac at the moment. But it's just temporary; he basically rescued me from dirtbag Davide. At one point, I was worried that Zac was going to deck him.'

Christina makes a half-amused, half-horrified sound. 'It sounds like I really need to come up there. I'm missing way too much.'

'No, you sit tight and rest up. I'll be down there soon enough for some shifts.'

'That would be great, but I'd still love to meet this friend I've heard so much about but have never set eyes on. Are you sure he's not a hallucination?'

I breathe a laugh. 'Yeah, he's been kind of elusive in recent years.' My gaze skims over the stylishly decorated yet manly living space. 'He's not really the same guy I knew before,' I admit. 'He's quieter now, more mature . . . I don't know. Sadder, I think.'

Christina goes quiet.

'It's good for him to be dating someone,' I decide. 'Before he moved up here, he was engaged.'

She gives a sympathetic murmur. 'Let me guess: she broke his heart?'

My chest contracts. 'She died.'

'Oh,' Christina says, genuinely stricken. 'Shit.'

'Yeah, that pretty much covers it.' Talking about this turns my skin cold, like I'm betraying Zac or something. He's said so little about it to me, which is why I don't generally bring it up with other people—not even Christina. But her gentle, compassionate breaths make me want to continue.

'She died in a car accident. Zac was in the car with her.'

'Oh no.'

My mind tears back to the phone call he made to me from the hospital that night, hyperventilating with so much panic and distress that he couldn't speak properly.

'What happened?' Christina asks in a breath.

My voice pulls tight. 'They were driving from Sydney down to Mittagong to spend the weekend at her parents' place. She was driving, it was late, and they were on a dark highway. A car came flying around a blind corner from the opposite direction and crashed straight into them. Tara—that was her name—took the brunt of the impact, but Zac barely had a scratch. I've probably mentioned that he's a paramedic?'

'You have.'

'So, he obviously didn't have any equipment with him, but he would have tried *so* hard to save her.' My voice cracks.

'Oh, darling. I'm so sorry.'

I nod silently, trying to suck back tears that I feel like I've been holding in forever.

'The other awful thing is that no one saw the accident,' I continue shakily, 'and because they were on a country road, there was no phone reception. So, Zac was trapped in that car with Tara for a couple of hours before anyone came to help them. He held her while she died.' Tears slide down my cheeks as I press my eyes shut.

'Josie,' Christina says painfully, but it's not me she should be worried about. I can't even think about what that night must have done to Zac without my chest cleaving open.

I was there the moment he met Tara at that start-of-semester costume party.

I was at the student bar crawl the following week when he worked up the courage to guide a giggling Tara around the back of a building so he could kiss her.

I was at their Glebe housewarming party when they moved in together after uni, and I planned their engagement celebration three years later.

I was at Tara's funeral, when the only person in the church who wasn't crying was Zac, his cheeks hardened to two blocks of white marble, his eyes like sheets of glass.

And I was there when, a week after the funeral, he packed up and moved to Newcastle, disappearing off social media and barely returning my messages. Hurt grips my heart when I think that if I hadn't moved up here this year for work, he'd still be a stranger to me.

I know it was Zac who survived something unimaginable, not me. I should have been there for *him,* not the other way around. But I can't help feeling like Zac decided I wasn't really worth continuing a friendship with after he lost the only girl who actually mattered.

'Josie? Are you OK?' Christina's tender voice brings me back.

'Yeah.' I brush the heel of my hand beneath my eyes. 'Sorry, this convo took a dark turn quickly.'

'Gosh, don't apologise. Did they charge the driver who hit them?'

'Shit, yes. The bastard was drunk—five times over the legal limit. He's in jail now, where he belongs.' My throat feels lined with lead. It's been so long since I've really thought about this. About how I woke up every morning in the weeks following the accident with hideous flashes of both Tara and Zac being dead. About how, ever since, I've developed an obsessive fear of dying young . . . convincing myself that my life will be the next to be snatched away. *Except my family history points towards cancer as the culprit,* I think, as memories of Aunt Susie's rattling breaths and my grandma's mottled skin roll through my head.

Before we hang up, Christina says the loveliest things about how lucky Zac is to have me in his life, but our conversation has left a dead weight in my chest.

When Lindsay sends a text inviting me on a spontaneous date day because he misses me, I grab the opportunity to shake off my spell of dark thoughts and ask if he can pick me up.

Lindsay and I stand gazing at the waves crashing wildly over the rocks beyond the breakwall at Nobbys Beach.

'What do you think, princess?' he asks. 'Sydney's got nothing on Newy, right?'

I smile and lean into him, needing comfort today. 'It's beautiful up here.'

It's not like Sydney's beaches aren't spectacular, but I can't deny the appeal of Newcastle's fierce, free coast-line compared with Sydney's neatly landscaped beach zones where you have to fight tooth and nail for a parking spot. While I expected to feel a bit bored in Newcastle, the city's relaxed, low-pressure lifestyle has been a literal breath of fresh air.

After our stroll, Lindsay takes me for fresh prawns and calamari at a nearby seafood co-op, which escalates into beers at the brewery next door. After two rounds, I assume we're going to leave, but he orders a third and drags my stool closer to his while I'm still parked on it.

I jerk to steady myself, and a laugh tumbles out of me. 'Aren't you driving?' I ask, tilting my head like he's being naughty.

'What are you, the cops?' He tugs me against him and seals his mouth over mine.

OK, I guess we're tongue-kissing in the middle of a craft beer pub.

The taste of beer on his lips hits me in all the right places, and the words *screw it* fly through my head as I deepen the kiss, chasing something other than anxiety and loneliness.

The bartender grumbles a request for us to tone it down, and my cheeks flame as I hide my forehead in Lindsay's chest.

'Do you like fairs?' he asks, and I giggle at the random question.

'Um, I guess?'

He combs his fingers through the loose waves of my hair. 'The Newcastle Show's on next weekend, and while it's totally daggy, I usually go because it takes me back to being a kid.'

'Aww.' I give his jaw a little pat.

'I figure it could be a fun place to take my girl.' He smirks over the lip of his beer.

I lift a brow. 'Your girl?'

I'm not sure yet that I want that label, but it's hard not to smile when someone as attractive and successful as Lindsay is chasing me. Lately, it's felt like it's always me doing the chasing while almost everyone I remotely care about runs in the opposite direction.

He takes a swig and blinks at me. 'What do you say, Josephine? Would you like to go to the Newcastle Show with me?'

I teasingly roll my eyes so hard they just about fall out of my head. 'If I must.'

My phone pings, and I immediately swipe open the message from Zac.

> **ZAC:** Just leaving work now, sorry I'm a bit late.
> I'll take you to Davide's as soon as I get back. There in 10.

'*Shit.*'

'What is it?' Lindsay asks, and I hope the slight slur in his voice is because he's alarmed rather than over the limit.

'I have to go home right now.'

'*Now?*' He grips his beer like it's superglued to his hand.

I stand up, throwing my bag strap over my shoulder. 'Are you OK to drive?'

He makes an 'of course' face. 'These are light beers.'

We make it home in ten minutes, and Lindsay insists on walking me to the front door like a prom date, where he tugs me to his mouth just as the door swings open.

'Oh, shit, sorry,' I hear Zac mutter as I twist out of Lindsay's grip.

Zac's staring at the phone in his hand. 'I was just texting you, then I heard you outside, so—'

'Hey, dude,' Lindsay says to him with an exaggerated wave. 'Nice to see you too.' He grabs me by the waist and yanks me backwards against his chest, wrapping his arms around me and nuzzling my neck. 'My girl smells *good* today.'

Zac's jaw turns rigid as he looks down to where Trouble's licking his ankle.

This is the slightly unhinged side of Lindsay that makes me want to be anything but his girl. Zac would never be this handsy if he was the one dropping Meghan home; he's way too polite.

'See you on the weekend,' I say to Lindsay, shrinking out of his embrace. Zac doesn't budge as I brush past his shoulder and head inside.

I hear them talking in low, slightly terse voices before Zac kicks the door shut and paces towards me.

'How much has he had to drink? Did he drive you home?'

'He had three light beers,' I reply, a little aghast at his tone.

His brow furrows. 'Do you feel like you need to get wasted to enjoy that guy's company—is that it?'

'What's that supposed to mean?'

'Why doesn't he take you for a walk or to a movie or something? Why does it always have to be a bar with that guy?'

'Excuse me, *grandpa*,' I say a little meanly—judgement from Zac never fails to hit where it hurts. 'For your information, Lindsay did take me for a walk at the beach today. So don't be so quick to judge. You obviously don't know what you're talking about.' My defensive tone booms through my ears, and I know I'm trying to convince myself just as much as him.

Zac's troubled gaze sweeps away, then back to me again like he's got something more to say. But rather than reveal it, he mumbles that we should get going to Davide's.

On the drive over, he lets out a long exhale like he's been holding air in all this time. 'So, things are getting more serious with Lindsay, huh?'

I glance at him, but he stays focused on the road, the passing streetlights flashing in his tiger-coloured eyes.

'Not serious yet,' I admit. 'But he's fun ... most of the time. We're going to the Newcastle Show next week.' A spontaneous question bursts through my lips. 'Want to come with us?'

Zac's instant frown isn't a shock. Why would he want to come on a date with me and the housemate he didn't get along with? But Zac and I used to go to fairs together all the time when we were teenagers. I'll look forward to it more if he's coming.

'Sure, why not,' he eventually mumbles. 'If Lindsay's OK with that. I'll ask Meghan if she wants to come, too.'

'Cool.' I shrink into my seat and turn my eyes to the passenger window.

I feel Zac's gaze brush the side of my face. 'You're not going to get all doe-eyed with him around me, are you? Because I might need a warning shot if that's the case.'

My heart picks up its pace. 'Who's doe-eyed? I don't get doe-eyed.'

I reach across and playfully squeeze his arm, the mound of his bicep tensing beneath my fingers. My hand falls away, my cheeks igniting.

The rest of the way there, one thought obliterates all others in my mind.

If Zac doesn't really care who I date, why would he need a warning shot about that?

CHAPTER 15

Six years ago

Zac gazes at the email on my phone with a grin of pride to rival my parents'. 'Jose, this is fucking amazing.'

'Shucks, thanks. It's just an internet news channel.'

He slides the phone back to me. 'It's a reporting job based in Sydney. It's *amazing*. I wish someone would hire me before I even graduate,' he adds, sliding a forkful of puttanesca pasta into his mouth.

'You'll have no trouble. Employers everywhere worship at the altar of Zac Jameson. Plus, paramedics are always in demand.'

'Yeah, but not necessarily in the area I want.'

'Which is where?' I twirl my fork in my pasta.

He pauses. 'The inner west.'

'Really?' I cover my mouth with the back of my hand while my chewing slows. 'You don't want to go back to the north side?'

He makes a face. 'Too quiet. Plus, Tara has her heart set on Glebe, so . . .'

I freeze, taking a moment to process the bombshell Zac just shoehorned into this conversation. 'You guys are moving in together?' I say, staring at his slightly darkening cheeks. While Tara has been his longest relationship by far, moving in together feels *huge*.

'Yeah,' he replies, his lips tugging up at the corners. 'Tara suggested it, and it makes sense. We're both moving back to Sydney; we both need a place.'

I try to focus on the chuffed blush surrounding Zac's smile instead of the ungracious thumping in my chest. I'm not jealous of this new arrangement—Zac and Tara are adorable together, and she's become a really good friend of mine too. It's more that I can't help but feel a little . . . overlooked? After all, Zac and I have been spectacular housemates for nearly three years.

Josie, Zac and Tara are a couple. *You're the third wheel now.*

Zac tugs the neck of his T-shirt, the rouge-coloured fabric printed with the words 'I Look Good In Green'.

'What's going on in that head of yours, sunbeam?' he asks.

'Nothing. I guess maybe I'll miss this place.'

He baulks, then leans forward with a confused smile. 'Have you lost your mind? I can't wait to get out of this shithole and live somewhere where the door's not conspiring to trap us inside and the floor's not so slanted that I always feel half-plastered.'

My laugh is a little forced. 'I guess you're right.'

As we silently finish our pasta, the uncomfortable feeling in my stomach persists, but I refuse to acknowledge it. This is happy news for Zac, so I'm determined to love it too.

When he sets down his fork across his plate, I get up out of my chair. Zac's hazel eyes track me and widen a touch when I approach his seat and bend to wrap my arms around his upper back. He catches the space between my shoulder blades with his palm.

'I'm really happy for you both,' I say. When I pull back, his cheeks have tinted pink.

'Thank you,' he replies softly, his warm hand slowly gliding down and off me. 'Where do you think you'll live when you head back to Sydney?'

'Not sure. The east side would be closest to my new job, so probably around there if I can afford it.'

Smiling, I ruffle his curls, then scoop up our empty plates and carry them into the kitchen so he can't see the feeling of loss crawling into my heart and creasing my face.

CHAPTER 16

Today

In last night's long and playful text exchange with Lindsay, he didn't seem to take issue with Zac and Meghan joining our fair outing. But when Zac and I approach him outside the ticket window on Saturday morning, Lindsay tosses a look at Zac that says something like, *Thanks for screwing up my date, asshole.* They shake hands so tightly that I'm surprised one doesn't lose an arm.

I glide between them to kiss Lindsay's cheek, but he hooks an arm around my waist and bends to catch my lips with his instead.

'Hey, hot stuff,' he says after I've tasted his tongue a little too early in the morning.

When I glance back at Zac, he's studying the ticket prices like they're the most fascinating thing on earth.

'Where's Meghan?' I ask no one in particular, scrambling for something to say.

'She's here,' a silky voice behind me replies, and Zac's face lights up as Meghan strides into his arms like they haven't seen each other in weeks.

When they push through the turnstiles in front of us, I catch Lindsay's gaze latch on to Meghan's perky backside in cut-off jean shorts. But the little burn in my chest feels more like irritation than jealousy.

The fair circles around the muddy Newcastle Showground—a time warp to my childhood with rickety, rusting rides that look half-deadly; old-school carnival games like creepy laughing clown heads and magnetic fishing; and popcorn stands releasing wafts of nostalgic, buttery aromas.

Meghan wants to see the baby animals, so we follow the paper map to the animal nursery, which turns out to be nothing more than a mucky barn housing a few juvenile goats and a pen of fully grown chickens.

Hoping for something a bit more thrilling, we wander in the direction of the rides. When Zac laces his fingers with Meghan's ahead of us, I pull Lindsay's arm close to mine.

'What do you think, babe; should we go check out the beer tent?' he asks, giving my ass a light squeeze through the thin fabric of my sundress.

I glance at my watch. 'It's not even midday yet.'

'Ah, should've remembered; I'm dating a good girl. My bad.' He winks at me.

Up ahead, Zac turns around and tosses us a cheeky grin. 'Who's up for the bumper cars?'

'Me!' I call out with a shiver of excitement, which says something about the calibre of rides at this fair. But I haven't been on a bumper car track since high school, and Zac and I used to love that sadistic little ride.

'Not me,' Meghan says, running her fingers up and down Zac's arm. 'They make me feel sick. But you guys go, I'll watch.'

'Lindsay?' I smile up at him, but he's still eyeing off the beer tent.

'I think I'll skip it,' he replies, dropping a soft kiss on my lips. 'I'm gonna find a bathroom, but I'll be back.'

'OK.' I glide my palm down his cheek. When the light catches his face, he really is easy on the eyes.

'Looks like it's you and me, Jose,' Zac says, snaring my attention away.

I follow him over to the ticket booth, where he pays for us both to ride.

We climb onto the metal track blasting nineties dance music through tinny speakers, finding only one beaten-up car left.

'You drive,' I say to Zac, even though I could handle the savage little beast just as well as he. I decide that now isn't the time to ask why bumper cars aren't triggering for him after his car accident, but given he has to drive at high speeds for his job, I figure—I *hope*—he's had therapy somewhere along the line to help with that.

We squeeze inside the glittery blue vehicle, and I instantly turn fourteen years old again. The music turns up, the car jerks forward, and I'm already giggling my ass off.

Zac uses his paramedic driving skills to avoid every snotty-nosed kid attempting to bang into us. Rather than being bumped, we're flying around the track, jolting left and right out of people's way, which is its own brand of fun. Every time Zac turns the wheel left, he leans harder into me, his adorable laugh cutting through the blasting music.

His firm upper arm rubs against mine, and when we share a simultaneous glance, our gazes stick together. Half a breath later, I'm slammed forward so hard that my teeth chatter. Both my hands are gripping on to Zac's forearm, and I feel like a startled cat as the car lurches to a stop.

'You OK?' he asks, his brows high.

'Yeah. Ouch. I might need your ambo skills after this.'

He twists around and glares at the teen who just rammed us.

'Oh, that dude's fucking dead,' Zac says under his breath, but the sparkle in his eyes makes clear he has no intention of doing any real damage to the kid. He spins the wheel vigorously to back up.

It's only when we're chasing the kid's tail that I realise I'm still clutching Zac's arm. He makes no sign of wanting me to let go, and his body is angled slightly towards mine, but I release him from my grasp and rub my sore neck.

Our car flies towards the long-haired boy, who braces for impact, but Zac twists the wheel away at the last second, averting a crash and leaving the teenager panting.

We're still laughing like idiots when we climb out of the vehicle and stroll back to Meghan, who's staring at us like she's the one with whiplash.

'Where's Lindsay?' I ask her, feeling like I'm covering for something even though I'm not sure what.

'He hasn't come back yet.' She lifts her arms to Zac like a toddler looking for a cuddle, and he rocks back on his heels to catch her, his eyes flashing to mine over her shoulder.

We agree to head over to the Turkish gözleme truck for mince-stuffed flatbreads to fill our stomachs. I consider buying an extra one for Lindsay, but I'm too irked. While Zac's been nothing but attentive to Meghan all day, my date appears to have ditched me.

The three of us are finishing our plates beside the showbag tent when Lindsay rounds on me like a horror movie jump-scare.

'Shit,' I gasp. 'There you are.'

He's inexplicably bare-chested, his T-shirt swinging from his back pocket as he pulls me into a one-armed hug, the smell of beer and cigarettes coating his skin.

'Where did you go?' I ask suspiciously.

He grins like a naughty schoolboy and flips his baseball cap backwards on his head. 'Just the beer tent for one. Should we get something to eat, babe? I'm starved.'

I hold up my finished plate of gözleme crumbs.

'Oh shit. Guess it's beer for lunch, then. Full of carbs. You guys want to go and get drinks?' He finally twists to acknowledge Zac and Meghan.

'I can't, I'm working tonight,' Meghan replies.

'On a Saturday?' I cut in. The newsroom runs twenty-four seven, but the juniors usually work the weekend shifts.

'Yeah, I'm presenting again,' she says smugly.

'That's great,' I reply, wishing my smile was genuine. I don't want to compete with Meghan for work or anything else, but my instincts seem to have a different opinion.

'Cool, maybe we should split up, then,' Lindsay suggests. 'Enjoy the rest of your afternoon, guys.' He tugs me towards the beer tent, but I'm not really in the drinking mood.

Zac steps towards me, his palm landing on my lower back. 'How will you get home if we split up?' he asks softly, a line forming between his brows.

Lindsay pushes between us. 'Obviously I'll drive her, Daddy-o. Don't worry; she'll be home before midnight.'

'I wasn't speaking to you.' Zac's tone is steady, but there's a fire burning in his eyes.

'Dude, fuck off,' Lindsay says, tugging me away.

I gasp and jerk out of Lindsay's grip. 'Lindsay, please don't talk to him like that. Can you two not fight?' Something in my chest twists sharply.

Lindsay leads me a few steps away from Zac. 'We don't have to go to the beer tent. But let's go and do our own thing, OK?'

I look back at Zac.

'What do you want to do?' he asks me.

I lift a shoulder. 'I guess I'd like to walk around the fair a bit longer?'

'We'll do that then,' Lindsay replies, yanking my hand so hard that I bang into his bare chest.

'Cool, we'll join you,' Zac adds immediately, weaving his fingers through Meghan's. 'Should we go play some games?'

Before anyone can answer, he stalks ahead of us towards the carnival game strip, pulling Meghan with him.

The four of us gather beside a duck-shooting game like we're on a cute double date, none of us acknowledging the sharp tension in the air.

The moment Lindsay raises his plastic gun, I lose hope of him winning me a ratty stuffed toy. The only thing less steady than his hands are his feet. When his last shot lands wide, he spits the gum out of his mouth like it's responsible and sticks it to a metal pole.

Zac gapes at me with a *Did he really just do that?* look before he steps back from the group to answer a call on his phone.

I inch closer to Meghan, feeling bad for letting my professional envy overtake my support of her.

'You're really good at newsreading,' I say, and it's not a word of a lie.

She gives me an unsure glance. 'Thank you. I saw that story you did this week about the guy taste-testing all the pies in the region. It was really good.'

I snort a laugh. 'Thanks. Breaking news at its finest.'

A few metres ahead of us, Zac finishes up his call and joins Lindsay at the basketball game. When Lindsay says something to him, I tense up, but Zac barks a laugh and hands him his next ball.

'He's so hard to get to know,' Meghan says beside me.

'Who, Zac?'

'Yeah. I feel like he's a really closed book.' We watch the two of them shoot basket for basket. 'Like, we hang out together all the time,' Meghan continues, 'and he's super sweet, and funny, and sexy as hell.' My brow tightens. 'But I feel like he's holding back or hiding something, I don't know.' She stares at the side of my face like I'm supposed to reveal all of Zac's secrets to her. 'Has he had, like, some major heartbreak in his past or something?'

I stiffen, a little surprised that Zac hasn't told her yet about Tara.

'He's had some serious girlfriends,' I reply vaguely. 'But honestly, anything other than that, you'll have to ask him.'

Meghan looks away like she's annoyed I'm not giving her any more intel on Zac, but she has no idea how far back he and I go. If Zac isn't ready to share his past with her, there's zero chance of me doing it.

Lindsay swoops over empty-handed, wincing at me. 'Sorry, princess, came up short.'

Zac tosses Meghan a stuffed elephant, and she beams like he's presented her with something you can't get at the two-dollar shop for less than what he paid for the game.

'Who's up for ice cream?' Lindsay asks, jerking his chin at a truck painted with candy-cane stripes.

'Hell yes,' I reply, and the four of us wander over and order ice cream cones.

The blazing afternoon sun threatens to set my shoulders on fire, and I shrink into the truck's sliver of shadow while I work on my salted caramel. My eyes fall on Zac as he circles his tongue over the crest of his ice cream, sliding it back and forth across the icy peaks like he's making out with the damn thing. For a couple of seconds, I'm kind of hypnotised. When I catch myself staring, I give myself a mental slap and turn away. It's not like I haven't seen Zac eat ice cream before; it was basically our primary food group when we were seventeen. I don't know what's gotten into me.

Lindsay slides into my view, twirling the tip of his cone between his lips, having already demolished most of his cookies-and-cream.

'Whoa, slow down there, speedy,' I joke. 'You'll get a tummy ache.'

He finishes his last bite of cone. 'That's what happens when your date deserts you for lunch.'

'You get dessert when you get deserted?'

My play on words expands the smile on his face. 'Come here, gorgeous,' he growls, reaching for my waist and tugging me against him. 'Fuck, you smell good today.'

'Wait, I'm not done yet!' I squeal, holding up my half-eaten ice cream.

Lindsay buries his face in my neck, using his body to block mine from the view of the others. His palms make a brisk glide from my waist to my breasts, giving them a cheeky squeeze.

'Stop that,' I hiss through a chuckle, giving one of his hands a swat.

He pulls back, grinning. 'Sorry, sorry. You're just so tempting in that white dress. So fresh and innocent.'

I have to laugh at his ridiculousness, and my eyes catch on Zac's before I set my gaze back on Lindsay.

'Have you had kids or something?' he asks, smirking.

I laugh through my nose. 'What?'

He nods at my chest. 'One of those girls felt milkier.'

Milkier? What does he mean—one of my breasts is bigger than the other?

A second after that thought registers, my stomach plummets and then convulses into a painful twist. Is Lindsay saying that one of my breasts has a lump in it?

My throat fills with dust, and I spin around to face the ice cream truck, using my free hand to quickly cup one of my breasts and then the other, lifting and squeezing. I don't feel anything remotely like a lump, which relaxes the sudden spike of tension in my body. *Thank god.* Lindsay barely touched them *and* he's tipsy, so his perception must be off. Still, the comment has stolen the rest of my appetite.

I step towards the rubbish bin when a blast of cold liquid smacks me right in the chest, sending me stumbling back. My ice cream splatters at my feet, and I stare open-mouthed at my soaked dress. *What the hell?*

'Dude!' Zac snaps at a spotty-faced kid clutching a hose a few metres away. 'What did you just do?'

'Shiiiit, babe, your dress is see-through,' Lindsay says to me while the hose-kid stammers as he explains to Zac that he was just trying to wash the camel dung off the path.

Lindsay also caught some of the water, and he uses his T-shirt to wipe himself down rather than offering it to me to cover myself with.

Meghan gapes at my now-transparent dress and turns away from me with a huff like I did this on purpose. *Seriously, Meghan? You think I planned to have this sopping-wet material glued to my body so that everyone can see my underwear?*

The hose-kid paces towards me to apologise, with a frowning Zac chasing after him. I assure the poor kid I'm fine and cross my arms over myself, hovering in the direct sun so I can start to dry off. 'I think this is my cue to bail,' I say to our little group.

Zac's gaze flickers down and up my body for a split second. 'Come on, I'll take you home.'

The four of us begin a path towards the exit, passing a cluster of teenage boys whose wide eyes zero in on my visible nipples.

Zac glowers at them, then stops to pinch the neck of his T-shirt. He tugs it over his head and hands it to me. 'Here. Put this on.'

Feeling Meghan's stare, I thank him and pull the giant T-shirt over my head, closing my arms around it like it's the most comforting thing on earth. It's silky-soft and smells divine.

Lindsay rolls his eyes at Zac's chest. 'Oh, come on, man,' he scoffs like he hasn't spent the last hour shirtless himself.

'Every guy here is gawking at your girlfriend like she's their wet dream, so I decided to do something about it,' Zac says tersely before taking Meghan's hand.

I have no trouble believing Zac. He's never been the type to covet attention, no matter how good he looks. I'm more bothered by the fact that it was him who helped me out rather than the guy I'm dating.

Lindsay drapes an arm around me. 'Come to my place?'

Up ahead, Zac drops his lips into Meghan's neck while she squeezes him goodbye. When she heads off to her car, he calls out to me. 'Want a ride home, Jose?'

I look up at Lindsay, my reluctant expression mostly staged. 'I think I'm just going to go home. I need to get changed.'

His hands glide around my waist. 'I'll get you clean and dry, princess. Whatever you need. I've got you.'

I stretch on my toes to plant a kiss on his nose, making a vague promise to meet up with him this week.

*

After a takeaway dinner and a hot shower, I hover behind the couch, rubbing my hair dry with a towel. Zac's changed into a light-blue T-shirt and loose shorts and sits watching his beautiful girlfriend read the news like a seasoned pro while Trouble snoozes in his lap.

'She's really good,' I admit, and he lifts his head to look at me.

'So are you. That'll be you one day.'

'Thank you.' I return his soft smile.

I don't entirely believe him, but his support gives me the confidence to flop beside him and watch the remainder of the bulletin. When a closing story about the Newcastle Show appears, and the camera pans past the hose-kid watering the lawn, we share a look and crack up.

The credits roll, and I jiggle my fingers through my damp hair. 'Do you mind if I change the channel?'

'Sure. Or pull up something on Netflix if you want.' Zac holds out the remote, and when I reach for it, he whisks it behind his back.

'Oh, come on, what are you—seven?' I smirk and make a lunge for the remote, but he swaps hands and holds it high above his head. Trouble jumps up and scampers off to her bed.

'I bet you were cute when you were seven,' Zac says, his eyes dancing.

'That's kind of a creepy comment.'

I pause before lurching for the remote again, but he quickly shoves it down the front of his shorts, his cute Zac-laugh in full force.

'Are you kidding me?'

'What?' he says innocently. 'You want the remote; come and get it.' He folds his arms behind his head.

I attempt to pantomime shock and fury, but my smile won't fade. 'You realise this definitely counts as housemate sexual harassment. You're no better than Davide.'

Zac clutches his heart like that comment hurt, and in a flash of movement, I whip forward and push my hand inside his shorts.

He gasps as my fingers brush the cotton waistband of his boxer briefs before hitting something that I hope to god is the remote. I pull it out and give it a little victory wave over my head.

Zac scrapes a hand over his jaw. 'I can't believe you just felt me up. You think *I'm* as bad as Davide?'

'You loved it,' I toss back without looking at him. My cheeks flash hot as I flick the TV to Netflix, feeling Zac's gaze linger on me before he gets up.

'Want something to drink?' he asks from the fridge. 'I've got some sav blanc, a pinot grigio or beer. Oh, and shiraz, but shiraz makes you want to play extra-ordinarily childish games, so I think we should steer clear of that.'

'Childish games like hiding the TV remote down your pants?' I rib, clicking on a show about Thai street food. 'Actually, I wouldn't mind trying out some of your whisky collection.' I spotted his line-up of fancy whiskys during one of my snooping sessions.

'You like it hard, hey?' A cupboard opens, and glasses tinker behind me.

I curl my legs up, squeezing away my body's inappropriate response to those words.

You like it hard.

What the actual hell is wrong with me? Am I a pervert now?

Also, this is *Zac*. I should not be thinking about Zac giving it to me hard—or at all. I gulp, questioning whether he's switched on the heating without telling me.

He drops beside me and hands me a tumbler housing a few centimetres of bronze liquid.

We watch the presenter haggle for ingredients in a Bangkok market for a while, before Zac's gaze drifts to the side of my face. 'So, you turned down Lindsay today, I couldn't help but notice.'

A delicious whisky-burn coats my throat as I swallow. 'I have to work tomorrow.'

He nods back at the TV. 'Well, if I really liked someone, I wouldn't give a shit if I had to work tomorrow. I'm going home with them. Just sayin'.'

'It sounds like what you're *sayin'* is that you're kind of happy I didn't go home with Lindsay,' I retort bravely.

His throat bobs as his eyes stay glued to the screen. 'You're just catching on now that I don't have much time for that asshat, are you?'

A breath of laughter escapes me. 'He's not that bad.'

Zac grimaces. '*Not that bad?* Sounds like you can't wait to rip his clothes off with your teeth.'

'Shhhh,' I reply, watching him brush his full lips against the rim of his glass like he's in some pornographic ad for whisky. He finally takes a sip, and my mind drifts back to something Lindsay mentioned today.

'Can I ask you a favour?' I say, a combination of morbid curiosity and evil whisky spurring me on. I suck in a deep breath. 'Would you look at my boobs for me?'

Zac spurts whisky everywhere.

'Are you OK there?' I say with a laugh as Zac tugs up his T-shirt to dab his face, exposing a glimpse of the abs I gawked at earlier.

He turns and blinks at me. '*What* did you just ask me?'

To be honest, I'm still not that worried about Lindsay's fleeting, half-drunk comment, especially after I groped around my boobs and didn't feel any lumps. And I'm completely aware of how insane and improper this is, but the whisky keeps goading me on. Plus, this guy knew when I had my first kiss ... my first sexual encounter ... my first orgasm. And he's a medical man, isn't he? It wouldn't hurt to have some confirmation.

'Lindsay made a comment about one of my boobs being "milkier" than the other,' I explain, like saying these words to my best guy friend is totally normal. 'So, I'm wondering if that means they're uneven.' I glance down at my black singlet.

Zac's gaze travels to the same place and hovers there for a moment before our eyes reconnect. He sucks in a breath before looking away, and I have no idea what he's thinking.

'Well?' I find myself saying. 'I just want to know if something's not right with them.'

He chokes out a laugh and holds his head like he has no idea where to start with me right now. I do feel bad for him, but this runaway train has left the station, and I don't really feel like backing down. *Bad Josie.*

'First of all,' he says slowly, without looking at me, 'a lot of women have asymmetrical breasts. Not only is it normal, but if that's what that dude's thinking when he's looking at them, I'm seriously questioning his sexuality.'

'*Asymmetrical breasts?*' I parrot. 'You're such a medic. Just call them boobs. Or tits. Or knockers. Or melons.'

OK, I really need to stop talking now.

'Actually, the medical term would be mammary glands,' Zac counters before taking a large sip of whisky.

My heart is a thundering racehorse, but I fight to look relaxed. 'God, this is a hot conversation,' I tease. 'What do you call sex, then? *Coitus maximus?*'

He swirls his glass. 'No, that would be just coitus. Coitus maximus is a really long session of fucking.'

Blood rushes to my cheeks, and I have no hope of being articulate enough to say anything back.

'OK then,' is all I manage, gripping my tumbler tightly and refocusing on the TV. We sit and watch for a while, but there's so much tension in the room that it feels like it could catch fire at any moment.

'So that's a no, then?' I finally say, glancing back at him. I'm an absolute she-devil tonight. 'You're *so* grossed out at the thought of my possibly asymmetrical mammary glands that you won't even help me confirm whether they look normal?'

Zac levels a look at me, his cheeks crimson. 'It wouldn't be appropriate, and you know that.'

'Why? I'd show them to a doctor . . . a nurse . . . a massage therapist.'

'And I'm none of those things.'

I sit forward on the edge of the couch. 'What are you so afraid of? I'm giving you consent to look at my breasts like a medical person and tell me if they look even to you.'

'Why don't you just look yourself?' he splutters. 'Haven't you heard of a mirror?' He's all red and flustered again, and I'm the only one who can save this poor man from myself.

'*Fine*,' I concede dramatically and kick my legs off the couch. 'I'll go now and report back. Because I know you're dying for the answer to this.' I stalk towards the bathroom.

'Fuck it,' he blurts, jumping up and draining his glass. 'If you really want my opinion on this, as a friend and a somewhat medically trained person, I'm happy to give it to you.'

My heart threatens to beat out of my chest as he paces towards me, his cognac eyes dragging down my body before settling on my chest area.

I'm a really terrible person.

A terrible person who's enjoying this interaction way too much.

'Give me a look, then,' Zac demands, the muscles in his arms bunching as he crosses them. 'If there is some swelling, then it's probably not a bad thing to know about so you can get it checked out.'

My tongue locks to the roof of my mouth. I haven't even taken off my shirt and already he's talking about swelling? 'What do you mean? I thought you said asymmetry was normal.'

'Well it almost always is. But just to make sure everything's OK in there. That there's nothing sinister going on.'

Nothing sinister.

All the excitement that has been bubbling inside my body drains away, leaving behind an icy tremor. When Zac tilts into my sightline, I realise I'm staring off into the distance.

He genuinely thinks I might have breast cancer. And he's a medical professional, so he knows about this stuff.

With my heart crawling into my throat, I grab my phone and charge towards the bathroom, shutting the door and pressing my back to it. My palms are so clammy that I can barely type the words: 'Are asymmetrical breasts a sign of breast cancer?'

The first words I read allow me to catch my breath: '. . . usually no cause for concern.' But it's the word 'usually' that sends me scrolling for more evidence until

I'm slammed with the phrase: '. . . could be an indication of cancer.'

My vision wobbles with tears, but I keep reading, scanning medical websites for the one that will assure me there's no way I could have breast cancer.

'Josie?' Zac taps on the door, but I ignore him and click on a journal article that discusses breast volume and cancer. I have to open a second window to google terms like 'logistic regression', 'menarche', and 'fecundity' until the gist becomes clear: there is definitely an association between uneven breast volume and breast cancer.

I slide down the door until my butt hits the cold tiles, scanning articles on women diagnosed with breast cancer after finding a size difference in their breasts, reading right through to the GoFundMe links.

Zac knocks again as I drop my phone and clutch my breasts, frantically feeling them through my singlet, my throat poised to scream the moment I find the lump. The door opens behind me, and I tumble backwards.

'Shit, sorry,' Zac says, crouching beside me. 'I didn't know you were sitting there. What's going on?'

I can't bring myself to look at him.

His hand gently clasps the small of my back. 'Josie. What is it?'

When I don't reply, he picks up my phone and studies the last article I've been reading. 'You know this woman?'

'No,' I reply in a thick voice. 'It's me. That woman's going to be me.' The words sound so stupid coming out of my mouth, yet I believe them entirely.

A mixture of confusion and concern colours Zac's eyes.

'I'm scared I have cancer.' It's the first time I've ever said those words aloud, but it doesn't ease any of the anxiety tying me up inside.

He looks blown back. '*What?*'

'I haven't been diagnosed,' I clarify quickly. 'But I think it's cancer.'

He collapses onto his butt like he can't hold himself up anymore. 'What do you mean? What has the doctor said?'

'I'm too scared to see a doctor.'

His brows meet in the middle. 'So, you haven't been tested for anything?'

'No, but I have a cough that won't go away, bleeding between my periods and, apparently, uneven breasts. So, you tell me, Zac. Tell me those aren't all signs of cancer.'

His frown deepens. 'There are plenty of reasons for a persistent cough, cancer being the least likely. Bleeding between periods is also quite common and could be something to do with your hormones. And, like I said, having different-sized breasts is normal.' He sounds bewildered at how I've joined all the dots to cancer, skipping everything else. *Welcome to the shit show that is my mind.*

I rest against the door, feeling like I've run a million miles and I'm still going.

'I don't get it, Jose,' Zac presses gently. 'Why are you sure you have cancer?'

Fresh tears well in my eyes. 'You know about my aunt and my grandma.'

He grazes a knuckle across my wet cheek. 'I do. But that doesn't mean the same thing's going to happen to you.'

I close my eyes, soothed by the softness of his touch. 'I've never had a mammogram,' I admit. 'Even with my family history.'

'OK,' he says. 'So, we'll get you checked out.'

My lips press tightly together. Even though I've begun obsessing about my health in the last year or so, I'm not the sort of hypochondriac who's at the doctor's every two minutes asking to be examined. I'm the opposite: I'd rather stick pins in my eyes than get tested for anything. That's why I've never had a mammogram. There are no bad results if there are no tests in the first place.

Zac crosses his arms over his knees. 'I knew something wasn't right with you. I knew you were crying in the bathroom that night when we had dinner at your house.' My face crumples, and I can't bear to look at him. 'When did this start?' he asks.

I heave a sigh. 'The bleeding? The coughing? Which part?'

His eyes soften. 'The health anxiety.'

I angle my face away. 'I have real symptoms, Zac. This isn't in my head.'

He catches my jaw in his fingers and gently guides me to look at him. 'Do you know that severe anxiety can cause all sorts of physical symptoms? I think you should go and see a doctor about this. I know an amazing one up here; she's been brilliant for me and my shit. And *this*,' he adds, holding up my phone, 'is not a good idea. Misinformation is going to make your anxiety ten times worse. They're doing studies at the moment on Doctor Google and how bad it is.'

A wave of shame swells in my chest. Zac's fiancée died in his freaking arms, and he's having to counsel *me*.

That thought makes my eyes spill over again like a tap that won't switch off, and I bury my face in my knees.

His palm strokes up and down my spine. 'You don't have to hide from me, OK?' he says softly. 'If this is a part of you, then I want to know about it.'

I cry into my knees while his thumb gently rubs circles into my back. When I finally catch my breath, I scrub my hands down my face, certain that I look like Frankenstein's bride by this point.

My voice comes out strained. 'Around a year ago, I found a swollen lymph node in my armpit that my doctor wanted to keep an eye on. It went away in the end, but because of what happened to my aunt and my grandma, it scared the absolute shit out of me. Since then, every time my body does something weird, I become fixated on it. I google, I panic, and I convince myself I have cancer.'

I leave out a key part of this explanation—the part about how Tara's death has screwed me up too. It's made me terrified of dying young, and I'm pretty sure it triggered all this—even before the lymph node.

Zac's hand covers mine on my knee, the tips of our fingers threading together.

'It's ruining my life,' I admit. 'I think the reason I was sent up here from Sydney was because I screwed up on air while I was interviewing a breast cancer doctor. She said something that freaked me out, and I had a panic attack on live television. I'm surprised they didn't fire me.'

'Oh, sunbeam,' Zac says softly.

My eyes sink shut, and my chest wrenches with a vehement ache.

Sunbeam.

He has no idea how much I've needed to hear him call me that.

My shoulder wilts against his, and he wraps an arm around me, pulling me into the warm cradle of his chest. 'I'm sorry I wasn't there for you,' he says into my hair. 'When you were dealing with all this.'

I'm sorry I wasn't there for you, either. I'm so sorry.

My fears about my health begin to disappear as my focus shifts to all the places where Zac's body is touching mine. When he tilts his face towards me, his lips accidentally brush over my hairline, and I instinctively shift even closer until I'm practically hugging him. Zac stills as my mouth hovers close to his neck. His skin smells like the woody aftershave balm I found in his bathroom. I can't help but inhale, and neither of us moves as my exhale washes over his warm neck, my heart tripping over itself.

Is it normal to feel flutters in your stomach when your best friend's body is pressed against yours and your lips are almost touching their skin? To want to lean in even closer when you hear their soothing voice near your ear?

Zac suddenly detaches himself from me and climbs onto his feet, sending a blast of cold air over my body.

'You let me know anything you need from me, OK?' he says, his expression as tight as his voice. 'I'm here for you.'

I gaze up at him with a grateful smile, but my heart is jackhammering my chest.

If only I knew what it is that I need.

CHAPTER 17

Two years ago

'Zac. I'm so, *so* sorry.'

My useless words summon another surge of tears, and I slip my fingertips beneath my sunglasses to brush away those that spill.

Zac says nothing, his arms hanging by his sides, his empty gaze aimed somewhere in the direction of the solitary palm tree that's planted between two graves.

Behind his shoulder, those who were invited to the burial remain gathered, some quietly chatting, others crying or comforting Tara's poor parents, who haven't stopped weeping.

'It was a beautiful service,' I mumble to Zac again because what on earth else is there to say? I'm not going to ask if he's OK—*I'm* not OK, and I wasn't Tara's fiancé.

'It was,' I think he replies, but his tone is so muted that I can't be sure.

A violent gust of wind pastes my loose hair to my face, and I swipe away the strands while Zac continues to stand in silence.

A throb of pain reverberates in my chest. This is not how I expected today to go or how I imagined Zac to be. I thought he'd want comfort, but he hasn't let me, or anyone, hug him, and he's barely said a word. Instead, everything he's feeling is inscribed all over his hollow cheeks and lifeless eyes—he's frozen with grief. I've never seen Zac in mourning before, and I guess this is how he handles it. He completely shuts down, and I don't know how to help him.

'Do you want to go somewhere after this?' I offer gently. When I reach for his hand, his fingers echo every other part of him. They're stiff and cold.

'Thanks, but I'm just gonna go home,' he mumbles, his hand falling back to his side.

'Home as in your mum and dad's?'

He nods. 'I can't go back to the Glebe house.'

Another sharp ache takes hold of me. 'Of course. Do you want me to go there and get some of your things for you?'

He shakes his head, looking down. 'Thanks, but it's OK.'

'Are you sure? I don't mind at all.'

'I said I don't want you to.'

After a tense beat of silence, his gaze finally drags to mine, and I stare into his beautiful, tortured eyes, thrown by this tone that I've so rarely heard from Zac. But I get it—he's angry at the world for stealing away his future wife. He has every right to be furious.

Zac's chest expands with a long breath. 'Sorry,' he utters. 'It's not you. I promise.'

Before I can reply, his mum appears beside us, her brow lined and her movements tentative, but Zac immediately turns towards her.

'Can we go?' he asks her.

'Of course, darling.' She lays her fingers on his shirt sleeve and offers me a sympathetic smile. Mrs Jameson and I already said hello to each other before the service.

'Thanks for coming, Josie,' Zac says to me.

Then he's gone.

CHAPTER 18

Today

Sitting at my desk with a takeaway coffee, I stare at the number in my phone for an eternity before sucking in a harden-the-hell-up breath and calling the office of Zac's GP. Her books are full, but the softly spoken receptionist divulges that she's been specifically asked to squeeze me in. My chest heats and swells. Zac must've called earlier this week, undoubtedly combining his natural charisma and honeyed voice to propel me to the top of the waitlist. The same way he managed to convince me to make this appointment that I've been avoiding for months.

Given I have a few reporting shifts coming up in Sydney, I book in a time for next week, my blood turning to ice over the medical tests I know I'm going to have to face. I'm just thanking the receptionist when my phone pings with a text from Lindsay.

LINDSAY: When do I get to see you again, gorgeous? x

The fact that he still wants to spend time with me, despite me being a bit hot and cold lately, makes me wonder if there's something worth salvaging with Lindsay. I may not be madly in love with him just yet, but he's sent so many sweet messages since the Newcastle Show that I decide to give him another shot. Plus, I need to keep my mind occupied.

ME: Soon, I promise. Work's been kicking my ass lately, and I've been crashing out early, but it would be nice to see you.

LINDSAY: Poor thing. What's been going on at work that's got you so knackered? x

I reply by filling him in on how I'm trying to improve my showreel, which means working extra hours on voluntary feature stories like the one on flood prevention. Lola and I have also been putting together a feel-good feature about local kids writing personal ads for rescue dogs to help find them homes. I text Lindsay one of the adorable examples before he's called into a meeting, and I put my phone away and pour my focus into work.

I'm an hour from finishing up for the day when Man-Bun-Colin dials up the volume on the police radio. There's a house on fire in Mayfield with multiple units en route.

Meghan sits higher in her seat, but I'm the closest to Colin, and I want this story. My packages keep getting bumped to the bottom of the rundown, and something tells me this one's going to lead tonight's late news bulletin.

I rush at Colin like a bulldozer. 'I can go cover it.'

The stars must be aligned in my favour, because not only does he grant me the story, but lazy-ass Gus is off sick so I'm paired with Gemma, our newest camera recruit, who's still young enough that she's willing to please. Lola pokes her head up over her computer and offers me a subtle thumbs-up that makes me giggle. No one knows the punishment of working with whingey Gus more than she does.

Gemma and I follow the GPS towards Mayfield, but as soon as we turn onto the correct street, there's no more need for a map. A thick funnel of smoke twists up into the sky like a furious tornado over a house engulfed in lashing flames. We park near a gathering of onlookers, and the intense heat of the blaze stings my cheeks as we step over ash and rubble to reach the police crossing.

A cop directs us to a taped-off zone facing the burning house from across the road. Gemma clicks the camera into the tripod and begins filming the blazing building that cracks and pops, while police, firefighters and paramedics dash about in a race against the inferno.

'Why so many ambulances?' Gemma wonders, and my gut makes a sickening twist.

'There must be people inside the house.'

Just ahead of us, a reporter from the local newspaper is interviewing a police officer. I zip open my microphone bag and plug the cable into the camera. 'Let's go,' I instruct Gemma, and she hefts the camera over her shoulder and trails me over to them.

The reporter angles his back to me, trying to cut me out, while I hold out my microphone with Gemma filming behind me. This is the dog-eat-dog part of the media world: there really is no such thing as an exclusive.

The moment the irritated reporter wraps up his interview, I step through to the officer. 'Josie Larsen, NRN News. Are there any people inside the house?'

Her steady tone suggests she's done this multiple times before. 'Yes, there are, but I cannot confirm their number at this time.'

I shift on my feet. 'How many people have been evacuated? Have there been any fatalities?'

'There are no confirmed fatalities at this point, and I believe that three people have been evacuated so far and are on their way to hospital.'

'Do you know how the fire began, and do you expect any charges to be laid?'

'We will have to wait for the results of the investigation, which will take place in due course.'

Over her shoulder, two firefighters draped in protective gear dart out of the house with a stretcher holding a small body wrapped in a blanket. I thank the officer and direct Gemma to point the camera at the action. A paramedic rushes over to meet the stretcher, and I do a double take at the broad shoulders and familiar muss of dark curls. Zac, soaking wet from the water hoses, begins checking the vitals of the figure who looks no more than four feet tall.

'That's a kid,' I realise out loud, my throat clamping. A second later, I ask Gemma to aim the camera at something else.

Shit. Maybe it makes me a gutless news reporter, but I just can't film a child in these conditions.

I scan for someone else I can interview, but my eyes keep returning to Zac, who's still hunched over the small body. A second paramedic helps him heft the stretcher into the back of an ambulance.

'That might be family over there. Should we grab one of them?' Gemma says, pointing at a huddle of adults standing several metres away. Soot coats their tear-stained faces, and one man is convulsing into a woman's shoulder.

My chest clenches up. 'No, I'm going to try to talk to one of the ambos,' I decide, before asking a police officer if we can interview a paramedic.

'They're a little busy right now,' he snaps.

'I just need a couple of minutes as soon as one is available, OK?' The public has a right to know what's happening in their community, regardless of how the cop feels about it.

I write up a script in my head and ask Gemma to film my piece to camera with the burning house in the background. The moment I'm done, a hand taps my shoulder.

'Here you go,' the policeman grunts as Zac steps forward, his distressed eyes falling on mine.

'Hi,' I mumble, taken aback. 'I didn't expect you to—'

'The supervisor's busy, so . . . just talk to me,' he says in a rush. 'But I've only got a minute.'

His hazel eyes glitter against the black soot lining his skin, his expression bleaker than I've seen it in a long time.

Paramedics of Zac's ranking are discouraged from talking to the media—it's the onsite supervisor's job—which makes me think he's doing this for me. I want to reach out and pull him close, to ask if he's OK with all this trauma around him, but instead, I snap into reporter mode. I fire questions at him about the state of the victims while his colleagues exchange updates through the radio crackling from his belt.

'Sorry, but do you mind turning the radio down?' Gemma jumps in between questions. 'It's really loud through the mic.'

Zac wrinkles his brow at her. 'Well, given one child just died and there are more inside the house, I'd rather not miss anything for the sake of a bit of evening enter-tainment.'

My insides crush.

If it bleeds, it leads.

I know that Zac's under pressure and wouldn't intend to sound so harsh, but this is a constant battle between trauma response teams and the media. Of course, I know not everyone understands that we play our own integral role in these situations, but when it's Zac taking this view, it disorients me. I want his approval. I want him to love every part of me like I do every part of him.

'You go,' I say to him, even though I'm not done with my questions.

His eyes flicker back to mine, his brow lining. 'No, it's OK. I didn't mean—'

One of the other paramedics shouts for Zac, and he twists around. Another small body is being hefted out of the house on a stretcher, and I hear something about 'not breathing' before Zac dashes back over.

'Shit, sorry,' Gemma says to me, her eyes wide. 'I didn't mean to piss him off.'

'It's fine. I actually know that guy. In fact, he's my housemate.'

'Wow, really?'

I watch from afar as Zac looks closely into the child's face, checks their pulse and airway, then rushes them behind a privacy wall, possibly to begin CPR. Horror grips me everywhere—for the child, for their parents— and for Zac, who only recently felt ready to return to devastating scenes like these. A desperate need to go over to him and see if he's all right takes hold of me, but I shake it off, knowing I can't.

Overwhelmed and beginning to shiver, I tell Gemma that we should probably head back so an editor can cut the story in time for the late news.

*

I arrive home to an empty house, save for the sweet-faced dog wiggling her tail at me. I scoop up Trouble for a cuddle, letting her soothe my shaken nerves before I shower and change, a heaviness in every step I take. I heat up a plate of beef goulash that Zac made last night, leaving plenty for him. While I sit at the counter and attempt to eat, I search for the latest news on the house fire.

Mercifully, no more children have died since the one Zac mentioned, but two are in critical condition in hospital. The image of a tiny body lying motionless on a stretcher clings to my vision, and I blink away tears until a well-timed text from Lola diverts my attention.

> **LOLA:** I'm sure today was really hard, but every story like this raises important awareness about fire safety, and I think you told it just right. It was informative and empathetic. Inspired by you. Hope you're OK. ♡

I've only known Lola a short time, but I already feel so lucky to have met her. I type a reply right away.

> **ME:** Thank you so much. You're right, a hard day, but hearing this helps. I might need a hug tomorrow. ♡

> **LOLA:** You're on, lovely. x

I'm scraping most of my dinner into the bin when the front door pushes open.

'Hey,' Zac says, kicking off his shoes and crouching to give Trouble a scratch.

'Hey. Are you OK? Do you want some goulash?'

'No. And no. But thanks.' He strides past me to grab a beer from the fridge, a crease etched into his brow as he twists off the bottle cap.

'Oh my god, you're bleeding!' I dart towards the dried streak of red running down the back of his neck.

He presses a hand to it. 'Am I? No, that's not my blood.'

'Oh.' My gut hollows.

He downs a third of his beer in one gulp. 'I need a shower badly, sorry. It was late when I got back to the station from the hospital, and to be honest, I just wanted to get the hell out of there.'

'Don't apologise.' I give him a supportive look. 'Are you OK?'

He sighs. 'I'll be fine. But today was a hard one. No amount of training can prepare you for the jobs with little kids involved.'

'I know.'

He leans against the counter, his face torn up. 'We lost a little boy tonight.'

I gently squeeze his forearm through his uniform. 'You did everything you could. Everything. And I'm so sorry for that family. I cried all the way home.'

I wince internally. Zac was working to save lives tonight, and here I am, searching for sympathy. But he lays his hand over mine where I'm still holding his arm.

'I'm sorry,' he says, emotion filling his eyes. 'And I'm also fucking sorry about what I said tonight. I didn't mean that thing about evening entertainment. I can't tell you how stressed out I was at that moment.'

'It's OK. There's definitely an element of that. But it's also news, and I was just doing my job. I didn't film the children or the family, or try to interview them.'

His brows pull together. 'You don't have to justify anything to me. I think you're amazing at your job.'

His warm hand is still cupped over mine, and I note how his chest is rising and falling in tandem with my own.

'You did brilliantly tonight,' I reassure him right back, scared he'll pull away from me.

With that, he heaves a sigh and lets go of my hand, reaching for his beer. 'We did OK. Things could've been done better. The supervisor calling the shots tonight had no clue. He's all process this and process that, with no humanity whatsoever, no empathy.'

I rest my elbows against the counter, absorbing the download Zac clearly needs.

'I get that we need to go for the most salvageable person first,' he continues, 'but it's not always easy to tell who that is. There'll be a debrief next week for sure about this one and the shit that went wrong. To be honest, I can't wait to say my piece.' He downs what's left of his beer.

'You know, I never told you this,' I say, 'but I read some of the report you had on your desk about more empathy being needed in paramedic practice. I hope you don't mind. And while I'm no expert, you know I read medical stuff for work, and it made a lot of sense to me. It was really impressive.'

One side of his mouth quirks. 'I should've known that nothing's off-limits when you live with a reporter.'

I give him a half-hearted smile, and our gazes catch and hold.

'How did you really go tonight?' I probe gently. 'I know you only recently felt ready to go back out in the field, and this was . . .' I shake my head.

'Full-on, I know. But I actually feel good about how I handled it. I was really focused and calm for the most part.' He inhales deeply. 'I think I should apply for that critical care job. They haven't filled it yet, and after today, I feel like I really am ready.'

My lips pull up. 'That's great. I'm sure you'll get it.'

'Thanks, Jose. But if I do, it'll probably mean dealing with some pretty serious car accidents, and you know that's a whole 'nother story.'

My body stiffens as he looks at me, his eyes seeming to ask for help. Like I might have the answers on how to repair the damage to his soul after what happened with Tara.

'Oh, Zac,' is all I can get out as I place my hand over his. I can't seem to stop touching him tonight.

This time, he turns his hand and brings our palms together, a shiver of electricity rushing into my skin as I instinctively wrap my fingers around his. His gaze clings to mine before it slips down to my lips, and my heart rate triples in pace.

But then his hand parts from mine and he steps back, swallowing tightly.

'I'm going to have a shower,' he says, his eyes now everywhere but me.

It's certainly not an invitation to join him, and I can't believe that thought even occurred to me as I watch him disappear into the bathroom, a little lost as to what just happened.

I'm on the couch with a beer, surfing through channels, when Zac emerges in light-grey trackpants and a white T-shirt, his damp curls flopping over his head.

'What do you feel like watching?' I ask.

It takes him a moment to reply. 'Um, I told Meghan I'd go over to hers tonight. I want to go for a surf near her place in the morning.'

'Oh.' I pin my gaze to the TV, my heart sinking.

Josie, he has a girlfriend. And you know her. And he's your freaking best friend! If Zac wasn't standing in the room, I'd catch my face in my hands. I have no idea what's gotten into my head. I'm clearly emotional from the fire.

After a few minutes, he drops onto the couch beside me, gripping another beer. 'I just texted her and said I'm gonna stay home. I don't really feel like seeing anyone after today.'

'Do you want me to go out?' I offer. 'So that you can be alone?'

'You don't count,' he says with a sideways smirk like I should know that.

I choose to take that as a compliment and nestle into the cushions, flicking through TV channels before we settle on an Australian music marathon.

It's obvious that neither of us wants to talk anymore about the house fire, but images, sounds and smells hang heavy in the air between us ... bodies on stretchers, family members shuddering with sobs, the oppressive stench of smoke, and the horrific, relentless revving of the fire hose.

We silently sip our beers through 'Blow Up the Pokies' by The Whitlams, 'Ana's Song' by Silverchair, 'The Day You Come' by Powderfinger, and 'Hearts a Mess' by Gotye, when I steal a sideways look at Zac. His eyes have fallen shut, and his chest is rising and falling with the even rhythm of sleep. I get up and grab the quilt from the couch bed, carefully draping it over him.

'From the Sea' by Eskimo Joe cuts into the screen as I settle back into my spot. I should go to bed, but the nostalgic music videos feel more comforting than a dark room with nothing but memories of today to fill my head.

I tug one corner of the quilt over myself and watch four more songs play out before my eyes sink closed.

An imperceptible amount of time later, something solid and warm rubs up against me, bringing a waft of mint and body wash. My eyes flutter open, finding Zac's face so close to mine that our mouths are sharing the same patch of air. My lungs seize up as I shamelessly stare at him, my gaze tracing the soft pink of his lips, the delicate curve of his nose, and the little black fans of his eyelashes.

The sexy lyrics of 'Need You Tonight' by INXS burrow into my ears as I angle myself a little closer to him, hyper-aware that I can taste the sweet heat of his breath. If I lowered my lips just a fraction, our mouths would brush together, and maybe the confusing ache of want that's growing somewhere deep inside me would get some relief.

My mind wanders further, and I imagine what it would be like to wrap my hand around his muscular arm and pull him on top of me, to feel his weight pinning me down on the couch while I drag my pelvis up and down, feeling the full, hard length of him.

Good lord, Josie Larsen. What on earth has come over you?

Zac's breathing changes, and he makes the slightest shift before his eyes drift open. My heart rams my chest wall as I prepare for him to jerk away from my personal space invasion.

But he doesn't. He just blinks at me through sleepy eyes before his gaze suddenly sharpens, then floats down to my lips, resting there for a long moment before returning to my eyes.

My lungs can't find air as we silently gaze at each other, our faces so close that I can make out every ring of green and gold in his irises, my throat bobbing tightly. The air feels charged, and we've ended up on the edge of a ravine without warning. If one of us leans a fraction closer, we'll tip right into it.

After a few uneven breaths, Zac's eyes flicker away, and he rolls onto his other side, resettling himself back to sleep.

I stare blankly at the TV for a while with a thumping heart, waiting for Zac to move again. Waiting to see what he'll do. But when he doesn't stir, I push off the couch and turn down the volume before creeping off to bed.

After a restless sleep, I awaken just after five in the morning, and thirst drags me off the mattress.

Careful not to wake Zac, I quietly pad into the kitchen, frowning when I find the living room empty. I peel off the note taped to the coffee machine.

> *Ended up going to Meg's. Thanks for*
> *being a friend last night.*

I drop the note like it's diseased, heat flooding my cheeks.

What planet have I been on? Zac's not only dating someone he clearly likes—maybe even loves—but I'm so deep in the friend zone that I'd need a shovel to dig myself out.

Josie, you seem utterly determined to screw up every good thing in your life.

With a dull weight pressing against my sternum, I grab my laptop and settle onto a kitchen stool. I need to find a place to live. I can't spend many more nights keeping Zac from his own bed or thinking about him stretched out in the next room in a pair of boxer briefs, and pretending that's not what's getting me off when I bring myself to release.

My palms cover my eyes at this new horror. I've somehow developed a *thing* for Zac, and I don't know how to get rid of it. I need to focus on work, Lola, Lindsay—anything.

Because the idea of actually hitting on Zac isn't funny to me. I just got him back in my life, and I can't risk losing him again—especially now, when there might be something really wrong with my health. This friendship means more to me than anything, and my massively inappropriate feelings are screwing up my one chance at fixing it.

This ends now, I promise myself, before grabbing my phone to text Lindsay.

CHAPTER 19

One year ago

'Josie, it's Doctor Theodosi calling.'

My fingers stiffen around the handset. 'Hi.'

'I've got your ultrasound results. The lymph node appears to be benign, but because it is so enlarged, we'll need to keep an eye on it. Come back in about four weeks, and if it hasn't reduced in size, I will suggest we do a biopsy.'

My chest constricts. *Biopsy?*

My hand flies to my armpit, and I stroke my fingers over the walnut-sized lump, circling and squeezing it.

'When you say "biopsy",' I mumble into the phone, 'do you mean you're looking for . . . cancer?'

The line rustles like Doctor Theodosi's switching the receiver to her other ear. 'It's too early to have that conversation,' she replies a little impatiently. 'As I said, the lymph node *looks* benign, but we do need to watch closely anything that's over one-and-a-half centimetres.

Your lymph node is two centimetres. But if it's nothing to worry about, it should resolve on its own within a few weeks.'

I swallow through the cement lining my throat. 'OK. Thank you.'

After we hang up, I sit motionless on the edge of my bed with the doctor's no-nonsense words echoing inside my skull.

I will suggest we do a biopsy.

If it's nothing to worry about.

If.

With trembling fingers, I snatch my phone back up and type into Google: 'Swollen lymph node and cancer'.

Tens of millions of results overcome the screen and frighten my eyes.

Lymphoma.

Leukaemia.

Metastasized tumours.

Secondary breast cancer.

Breast cancer. The same cancer that stole away the lives of my aunt and my grandma.

My palms break into a sweat as I grab at my armpit again, searching for evidence that the lymph node has reduced since the last time I checked a minute ago.

It's still huge.

A monstrous feeling of dread takes root in the pit of my stomach.

No . . . please no.

My fingers sweep over the lymph node again before

moving to my left breast . . . my right breast . . . my right armpit . . . back to the swollen gland.

My mouth turns so dry that my lips clack as my lungs struggle to find oxygen.

My god, I'm going to be next.

Just like my aunt, my grandma . . . Tara . . .

I'm going to die.

CHAPTER 20

Today

Doctor Ellison is running nearly an hour behind, leaving me plenty of time to read and reread the cancer awareness posters taped to the wall until my palms are slick and my mouth has dried to a desert. By the time a gentle voice calls out my name, I'm considering making a run for it.

I buck up and stride towards the young doctor, who offers me a disarming smile as I step through to her consultation room.

'I'm Claudia,' she says with a mild Scandinavian accent, which I cling to as a source of comfort—my dad was born in Norway. 'How can I help you today?'

My gut clenches as I dig for courage, still contemplating fleeing.

'I think I have cancer,' I say in a small voice.

I expect a look of alarm, but Doctor Ellison doesn't flinch. 'Why do you think that?'

With a shuddery inhale, I unload to her about my symptoms. Lindsay's comment about my breasts, the bleeding between my periods, and the persistent cough.

Doctor Ellison squints at her computer. 'When was your last pap smear?'

My heart bunches in my throat. 'It was around two years ago. They said I didn't need to come back for five years.'

'That's good. And what makes you think these symptoms mean cancer?' She almost smiles when she asks the question, but it doesn't feel patronising. She actually has the same sort of calming aura as Christina.

My fingers twist in my lap. 'Both my aunt and my grandmother died of breast cancer.'

'I'm sorry to hear that. Why don't you come over here, and I'll have a look.'

My entire body stiffens before I drag myself over to the examination table, struggling for breath as the doctor feels around both breasts with her gloved hands. When she gently presses over my lymph nodes, I tense up even more, but it's been a year since the overly swollen gland reduced back to normal by itself.

When Doctor Ellison says, 'I don't feel anything out of the ordinary,' relief streams into my chest with such speed that I could almost pass out.

Thank god.

'Do you know if your aunt or grandmother had the BRCA gene?' she then asks from her computer as I tug my shirt back down.

'I'm pretty sure they didn't.' I settle back into the chair beside her.

'Great. Well, given there's no indication of the BRCA gene in your family, and you don't have multiple first-degree relatives with breast cancer, the truth is that you're really at no higher risk than the average woman. You're still very young, and your breasts feel completely normal to me.'

'First-degree relatives?' I repeat faintly.

'Let's say you have a mother and two sisters who have had breast cancer. That would put you in a much higher risk category than having an aunt or a grand-mother with breast cancer.'

I nod blankly. Every time she says 'breast cancer', my tongue feels coated in sand.

'You know, it's a common misconception that family history is a prime factor in breast cancer diagnosis, but in ninety-five per cent of cases, it's just bad luck,' Dr Ellison explains. 'One in eight women in Australia will be diagnosed with breast cancer at some point in their lives, and the reality is that we're all at equal risk simply by being female.'

Her words sound right, but my brain spits them back out, telling me that I'm the exception, that I'll be the one in eight.

I must look petrified, because she quickly shifts tone. 'It's no reason for panic, though. There are many treat-ments available these days, and with early screening, we're seeing far more positive outcomes. But I feel like we're jumping much too far ahead with this conversation. I've heard nothing today that makes me feel worried. But if you are concerned, I could send you for an ultrasound just to reassure—'

'No, no, that's OK,' I cut in. 'Thank you.'

There are no bad results if there are no tests in the first place.

Doctor Ellison leans forward and studies me, resting her elbows on her knees. 'There is clearly some anxiety over your health here, too, which is much more common than you think. Anxiety is a truly horrible thing to live with, but it is treatable. There are a number of things we can do to help you overcome it.'

'But I have other symptoms,' I protest. 'The cough, the bleeding . . .'

'And we're going to look at those,' she assures me. 'The intermenstrual bleeding could be fibroids, it could be hormonal, it could be that your cervix bleeds more easily than others. Are you on any oral contraception?'

When I shake my head and then confirm that I couldn't be pregnant, she rolls her chair closer to her computer. 'If it's OK, I'd like to take some swabs and blood. Just in case you have an infection you're not aware of. We should do another pap smear, too, just to cover all our bases.'

'OK.' A pit opens up in my stomach. *Here we go. Just because she can't feel a lump, it doesn't mean I'm OK.*

After she's taken the swabs, the conversation shifts to my coughing. Within minutes, Doctor Ellison has convinced me to have a chest X-ray and a pelvic ultrasound, making it clear that she's looking for things like infections and fibroids rather than cancer. Whether she's telling me the truth or not, my gaze slips to the white wall behind her shoulder, seeing all the possibilities, and her gentle, lightly accented voice returns me to the room.

'I think you're going to feel a *lot* better when all this is over. And then we can treat what's causing these symptoms and maybe talk a bit more about your health anxiety. It's also smart to be vigilant about any changes in your breasts, so keep doing regular self-exams, and be sure to come in if you notice anything out of the ordinary.'

Her smile is reassuring as she hands me the referrals, a prescription for the pill to consider, and a script for Valium that I can take on the day of my tests if I need to.

'Thank you,' I manage, fighting an urge to hug her.

As soon as I'm safely outside, I hover in a street alcove out of the wind and text Zac.

> **ME:** You were right. Dr Ellison is amazing. Thank you so much for recommending her. x

He's on shift, so I don't expect a reply, but his message appears right away.

> **ZAC:** I'm so happy to hear that. U OK?

> **ME:** Yeah, I'm good. I'm getting a couple of scary tests done, but at least I got Valium for those. 😼 😂

> **ZAC:** Haha, trust you to get the good stuff.
> Want me to come to the tests with you?
> As long as I'm not on shift, I will.
> You know I'm always here for you.

I stare at his message, reading it several times, while a boulder forms inside my chest. Zac's note this morning made clear that he's here for me as a friend but nothing more.

Just as it should be.

Instead of replying, I 'like' the message and slide my phone into my bag.

Surprisingly, given that I'm still shaken up after this morning *and* saddled with Gus for the day, the news story I cover about a new luxury hotel opening goes well—aside from when I lose Gus while the hotel manager's waiting to be interviewed before eventually finding him checking out the restaurant menu.

My and Lola's story about the personal ads for dogs also aired today and was so well received that Sydney ran it in their evening news bulletin. Lola and I promise each other dinner at a tapas bar on King Street soon to celebrate.

After I've hugged her goodbye in the carpark, I race home. I can think of nothing I want more than a quiet night on the couch with my best friend. Meghan's away this week covering a surfing championship at Port Macquarie, so Zac and I have planned a lazy evening making dinner and watching a documentary about the history of Japanese food. I'm determined not to ruin it by staring at him like a creep.

Zac's still out when I arrive, so I rinse off in the shower and change into trackpants and a comfy hoodie. I'm halfway through finishing the puzzle Zac bought me when my phone lights up with a FaceTime call from my parents in Thailand.

I grin at the screen. 'Hey, strangers.'

They're sitting on their poolside patio, looking sun-kissed and relaxed. 'How are you, champ?' Dad asks me, giving Mum a nudge so he can see me properly.

The question jabs a pin into my chest.

Anxious, terrified, lonely, ashamed.

Swallowing every critical word I toss at myself, I reset my smile and catch them up on life in Newcastle and my role at NRN News.

'I've scored some good stories lately, one of which made the national bulletin. I've also been doing heaps of outdoor stuff on the weekends, like exploring the beaches, which are all so close, and there are lots of nice walks in the national park. And I'm slowly making my way through all the op shops and markets, too.'

When I slip in that I'm currently living with Zac, Mum squeals over me before I can finish talking. Dad's smile is so big it needs its own postcode.

'Relax, relax, I'm looking for my own place,' I say, even though I haven't technically done more than browse a few housemate ads. Alarm ripples through me at the idea that I might have overstayed my welcome. For all I know, Zac's itching for me to be gone and has been too polite to say anything. That would be very him.

The front door bangs shut, and three seconds later, Zac's smiling face appears behind mine. Mum and Dad just about lose it. It's beyond embarrassing, but I tilt out of the screen so the son they never had can take centre stage. He braces a hand on the table in front of me, leaning over my shoulder and answering their nosy questions with an effortless charm that appears made purely to delight my parents. When he holds up Trouble and nuzzles his nose into her fur, Mum and Dad exclaim so loudly it distorts their microphone.

'OK, give the poor man and his dog some space,' I whine. Zac chuckles and pulls away, taking his heat and scent with him.

I chat with Mum and Dad a little longer while Zac fumbles around the kitchen, my gaze snagging on his as I exaggerate to my parents again about how well I'm doing up here. I get a little carried away, even telling them that I'm being considered for a prime-time news-reading role, and that I've been browsing possible investment properties. *Absolute bollocks.*

After we say goodbye, I wander over to where Zac's chopping carrots into tiny cubes, the look in his eye telling me he knows exactly what game I'm playing.

'What's with the face?' I imitate his scrutinising expression while I pull out a stool.

'Why do you do that?' he asks quietly.

'Do what?'

'Lie to your parents.'

A little thrill of relief ripples through me as I watch him toss the cut carrots into a bowl. If Zac's being this direct with me, he's definitely comfortable in my company again.

I set my gaze on the dog, who's licking her paws near my feet. 'It's just easier. It's what they want to hear. I try not to stress them out or make them feel bad about being over there. It was a big decision for them to make that move, and I know they wrestled with leaving me behind. I don't want them to think they made a mistake.'

Zac's eyes cling to mine. 'I've known your mum and dad a long time, Jose, and I think they'd much rather know what's really going on in your life.'

I press my lips together and shrug a shoulder. I don't tell him that part of the reason I put this show on for my family is because it almost makes me believe that my life really is going spectacularly. That I'm not slowly dying of fear and loneliness—tirelessly chasing after ideas and dreams that are only making me feel emptier, while convincing myself I'm filled with tumours. Maybe if I say I'm OK enough times, it'll become true.

I slump on my stool.

Zac tosses a tea towel over his shoulder. 'You know you never have to make shit up to me, right? I want *real* Josie. Always.'

'Don't worry, you're stuck with her,' I grumble, but the comment lights up his eyes, and I can't quite look away.

On Tuesday, I'm typing up a script at work when my phone blows up with texts from Lindsay asking to meet up tonight. *Hell, yes.* This is exactly what I need to turn my focus off things I shouldn't be thinking about.

I've got a craving for sushi, but the local football team is playing, so Lindsay talks me into meeting him at a sports bar in Wickham—a quirky inner suburb of the city that feels like it's on the cusp of becoming super trendy.

When I arrive, Lindsay's sitting at a high table facing a wall of TV screens blasting different codes of sports. We order cheeseburgers and beers and chat about some new software his company is launching, and I tell him about the insanely busy Sydney newsroom I was in before moving here, remembering the ruthless deadlines and how every toilet break felt like a race against time.

Lindsay drops a run of kisses on my neck and gets up to order a third round, but I swipe a hand across my throat. 'I'm driving.'

He hovers there, glancing between the bar and me. 'It's OK; I'll drive you home, babe.'

Zac's repeated warnings ring in my head, and a confused chuckle leaves my throat. 'You shouldn't be driving either if you're going to keep drinking.'

'Don't worry, I've *got you*,' he says dramatically, wrapping an arm around me and kissing my cheek. 'I'm drinking light beer. We can have one or two more, then I'll drive us home. I'll even bring you back in the morning to pick up your car. How's that for five-star service? Only the best for my girl.' He bends to stamp his lips on mine.

When he pulls back, I raise an eyebrow at him, but he darts off to the bar with an almost childlike eagerness. My shoulders tense as I watch him, everything inside me saying *no*. No, I don't want to sit here and drink late on a weeknight. No, I don't want to leave my car overnight somewhere it might be broken into. No, I don't want to get up any earlier than I have to tomorrow so that I can collect my car before work. And no, as much as I wish I did, I don't want to go home with Lindsay and have sex with him.

My gaze travels down and up his nice body as he hunches over the bar, a hollow feeling expanding through my abdomen.

As hard as I've tried, I'm just not that into him.

There's so much about Lindsay that fits the description of what I thought I wanted. He's handsome, he's career-oriented and, crucially, he seems crazy about me. But when something important happens to me, he's not someone I think to text. When I'm in one of my panic spirals, he's not who I want to confide in. He doesn't make me so giddy that I never want our time together to end. There's nothing about him that compels me to strive to be a better version of myself. Dating him hasn't filled the hole left by whatever's missing in my life that's made me feel so lonely. He's just a set of ticked boxes that's come to feel shallow and meaningless.

But when he strides back to me with two overflowing beers and a cheeky grin, I know I should at least see this night out, even though it's probably going to be our last.

After my third beer, my body is gently buzzing like someone has spiked my blood with lemonade, and Lindsay whoops happily when his team wins. Before the staff can change the channel, the late news fills the screen, and I watch a few seconds of the newsreaders' bobbing heads before the frame cuts to my story about flood prevention.

'Hey, that's me!' I say, sounding like I'm eight years old. Lindsay smirks up at the screen while my four-minute package plays out. When my phone pings with a text from Natasha Harrington saying 'Good job', I feel like high-fiving every fuzzy-eyed bar fly in the place.

'My girl, the TV star,' Lindsay sings, dragging my stool closer to him until our knees scrape. 'Come home with me,' he begs, nibbling my ear. His palm glides down my lower back, his fingers making seductive little flexes into my skin.

I rest my chin in my palm. 'I think I'd rather go home tonight.'

'All right. I'll drive you back, then.' Lindsay lets out a deep sigh, and I don't blame him. That's multiple dates now where I've insisted we part ways at the end of the night. It's becoming pretty clear to us both that this isn't working for me.

'But I had a fun night,' I add to make him feel better, lightly rubbing his knee.

He just pouts before chugging the last of his beer. On the way out, he ducks into the men's room, and I pull out my phone, finding a text from Zac.

ZAC: Music channel isn't the same without you.
You'd better be out having the time of your life because Trouble and I miss you.

My cheeks flush warm as I type out my reply.

ME: If I told you who I was with, you probably wouldn't let me in the door tonight.
But please do, I'll be home soon.

ZAC: If you're with Davide, I'll break his balls that he insists on showing everyone.

A laugh flies through my lips.

ME: Did you have to remind me about Davide's balls? I just ate.

ZAC: Not meatballs, I hope. Or sausages.
OK, next guess is Lindsay.

ME: 🎯

ZAC: Now I'm the one wishing I hadn't
just eaten.

My stomach flips strangely, but before I can type anything,
another message appears.

ZAC: Sorry, bit harsh.
If you guys are drinking, do you need a
ride home?

ME: Thanks, but I'm good.
I'm a big girl these days. :D

ZAC: Fake news.
You're still a little baby sunbeam. ☼

A stupid smile eclipses my face as I type my reply.

ME: Just about to leave. Will be home
soon. x

ZAC: Would be lying if I said I wasn't
happy to hear that. x

The way I stare at Zac's message for far too long sends the unsettling truth crashing into me. Spending the evening with Lindsay hasn't fixed anything. In fact, it's made everything worse.

Because figuring out what I don't want has made what I do want even clearer.

And as much as I wish I could hack into my own brain and delete the feelings I'd give anything to change, Mission: Get Romantic Thoughts About Zac Jameson Out Of My Head is officially failing.

Lindsay stumbles on the footpath on the way to his car, and when I chuckle, he grabs my waist and tugs me hard against him, closing his mouth over mine. I let him kiss me for a few seconds as a sort of consolation prize for not going home with him before gently untying his hands from my waist.

We climb into his Tesla, and he cranks up the volume on a retro rap hit.

When he tailgates the white Honda in front of us that's driving a little slowly, I give his arm a light whack. 'You're not one of those road-ragers, are you?'

He scowls at the yellow sign stuck to the car's rear window. 'I fucking hate those Baby On Board signs.'

I lift a brow. 'You hate Baby On Board signs.'

'Why is a baby's life more valuable than mine?' His tongue gets caught on the word 'valuable'.

I just stare at his profile.

Do I even bother explaining that babies are much more likely to be seriously hurt in an accident?

Lindsay makes an irritated grunt and turns his wheel to overtake the car, flying past it on the wrong side of the road. Half a second later, the world whirls around me in a fierce spin, and my neck snaps painfully to the left. My palms slam against the glove box and cling on to stop myself from falling, like I'm on a rollercoaster without a seatbelt. Tyres squeal in my ears, and the window beside me explodes. I swing my head towards it, but a loud bang hits my ears, chased by a hissing sound. Two heartbeats pass before a thunderous noise clangs in my skull from behind, and everything collapses into blackness.

CHAPTER 21

Two years ago

I answer my phone with a croaky whisper. 'Hello.'

Heavy breaths shudder on the other end of the line.

I sit up in bed with a start, blinking hazily at the pitch-black bedroom, my mind a jumble of sleep fog. My dry mouth clacks when I speak. 'Zac? What's wrong?'

He lets out a choked sob, and instantly, I'm awake. 'Zac?'

The heartbreaking sound of him crying sends a rush of tears to my eyes.

'Zac, what is it? Where are you?' I lower the phone for half a second to glance at the time. It's three o'clock in the morning.

He breathes out hard in my ear. 'I'm at the hospital.'

My palm flies to my chest. 'Why?'

'I was . . . in . . . a car accident.' He can barely get the words out.

'Oh my god, are you OK? Which hospital? I'm coming.' I fumble to switch on my bedside table lamp, then jump out of bed, so disoriented that I bang into the dresser.

'She's gone, Josie,' Zac sobs into my ear.

The painting on the wall of a windswept beach becomes a wobbly blur of blue and grey, and a sharp pain clamps around my torso.

'Who's gone?' I whisper, even though I already know.

'Tara.'

CHAPTER 22

Today

I struggle to peel open my eyelids, my tongue refuses to detach from the roof of my mouth, and my legs kick at scratchy, bunched-up sheets.

'Josie?' breathes a familiar voice that soothes me for half a second before a wave of nausea shoots up my throat. I groan, and a hand catches my upper back, encouraging me to tilt forward. A metal bowl appears beneath my chin.

'Be sick in this,' the voice says, and the acidic taste of vomit splashes over my tongue and into the bowl.

Oh god. I feel terrible.

His palm gently rubs my back. 'It's OK. It's probably just the pain medication.'

I flop against the pillow that rustles like it's made from plastic and blink dazedly at Zac. He looks as unwell as I feel: his cheeks are ashen, his eyes are shadowed, and his messy curls are twisting up out of control. He hands me a tissue with a sympathetic look before slipping through a curtain with my puke bowl, leaving me to figure out my surroundings.

I'm in a hospital bed. A thin tube runs from my hand to a gently beeping monitor, and a blue curtain forms a privacy wall around me. Above my head, a small TV is playing a daytime talk show with the volume turned down, and an impressive bouquet of colourful flowers bursts from a table on wheels beside me.

My head swims, and I gulp a panicky breath as images swipe through my memory: a close set of taillights . . . a white hatchback screeching past the window . . . flashing blue and red lights . . . a paramedic with a pixie haircut peering into my face.

Zac steps back through the curtain.

'Was I in a car accident?' I blurt, my voice raspy like I've smoked a hundred cigarettes.

He nods, his eyes wrung with distress. 'Lindsay was driving you home last night, and the cops said he was on the wrong side of the road. He hit a car, and another one smashed into you from behind. He had a blood alcohol reading of 0.145.'

'Is Lindsay OK?'

Zac's brows jam together as he drops into the plastic chair beside the bed. 'He's fine. Not a scratch.'

Relief seeps through me before I frantically wriggle my legs and curl my fingers. 'Why am I in here? What's wrong with me?'

'You're OK. You hit your head and lost consciousness, so they did a CT scan. Thank god it was fine, but because you were so groggy and couldn't walk, they decided to keep you in overnight.'

I gape at him. 'I don't remember any of that.'

My stomach swoops at the seriousness of being sent for a CT scan. And what if they missed something? I once read a report about misdiagnosis and CT scans. My mind continues to wrestle through my foggy thoughts while Zac runs me through what else he knows. The driver of the car that Lindsay hit broke two ribs and the third driver got whiplash. It was a miracle that Lindsay didn't kill someone. He was taken to the police station and charged with drink driving and dangerous driving before being released on bail.

Zac turns silent and crosses his arms with a sullen expression.

I lie back and close my eyes, caught between wanting to process this and wishing I hadn't heard any of it. When I glance back at Zac, he's clutching his head in his hands. That's when my sluggish brain catches up: Zac Jameson and car accidents.

I sit up on my elbows. 'I'm so sorry, Zac.'

His face flies up, his lips parting. 'Don't *you* be sorry. That fucking asshole could have killed you.' A film of tears coats his eyes, making my heart twist.

'I didn't know he'd had that much to drink,' I say, even though the statement feels a little false. 'He said they were light beers.'

Zac bites down on his bottom lip. 'It's OK. You need to rest.'

But lying in this bed is making me feel the opposite of relaxed. The beeping machine, the tube dangling from my hand, the smell of disinfectant—they're all a time warp to when I visited my aunt and my grandma during their last days of cancer treatment.

Agitation prickles up my spine, and I push at the sheets with my feet. 'I want to go home.'

Zac leans forward, his fingers slipping around my forearm. 'It's OK, Jose. You'll get to go home soon. We can ask the nurse when she comes back.'

'I'm sorry,' I say again, my face scrunching up. 'I'm so sorry.'

He turns his head, blinking fast. Then his forehead drops. 'Last night scared me so fucking much. I don't know, I . . .' His voice trails off, and a yearning to touch him—to wind my fingers through his—surges up through my chest and into my throat, but he's already moved his hand away.

My head falls back against the crinkly pillow, my eyes squeezing shut.

So, I guess even a concussion isn't enough to kill these unwanted feelings.

The curtain twitches as someone tries to find the gap. I sit up with the hope that I'm about to be told I can go home, but it's Lindsay who appears, clutching a bunch of pale-yellow roses.

Zac lurches to his feet. 'You get the fuck out of here.'

Whoa.

Lindsay holds up his free hand. 'Calm down, dude. I'm just here to see how she is.'

Zac turns to look at me, his mouth tight.

'I'm OK,' I say to Lindsay. I have no idea how to deal with any of this right now.

Lindsay steps past Zac to approach me, resting his flowers on the table. I was picturing him in jail or at least in a pair of handcuffs, but here he is, looking sheepish as hell.

'I'm so sorry, babe,' he says, and Zac makes a sound of irritation. Lindsay looks over his shoulder at him. 'Do you mind giving us a minute alone?'

'Yes, I do, actually.' Zac folds his thick arms, his feet rooted to the spot. As a paramedic, he's good at staying calm in stressful situations, and I've never seen him like this. The veins in his neck are pulsing.

'It's OK,' I urge Zac gently, more out of concern for him than in defence of Lindsay. But that's not how Zac takes it.

His face crumples. 'Fine. If you'd rather this piece of shit be in here, then go ahead. I'm heading outside for some air.'

'We might need more than a minute,' Lindsay says when Zac's halfway through the curtain. 'So, take a few deep breaths, all right? It sounds like you need them.'

Zac spins around and jerks right up into Lindsay's face, seeming three feet taller, even though he's only got a few inches on him.

'Don't fuck with me,' Zac snaps. 'You could have killed her last night. And you're very lucky you didn't, because if you had? It would be me killing you next.'

Zac's blazing eyes flash over mine before he pushes through the curtain.

Lindsay gives me a look like Zac's gone off the deep end; obviously he has no idea how triggering this accident would have been for him.

'He's just upset,' I mumble. 'You got behind the wheel of a car when you were drunk, and things could have ended a lot worse.'

Lindsay flops into the chair. 'Yeah, I don't think that's all he's upset about.'

I frown. 'What do you mean?'

He just rests his chin in his palm and stares at me. 'I'm really so sorry. I honestly thought I was fine to drive. If it's any consolation, I've lost my licence, and I have to go to court. I might not be able to drive again for a fucking *year*.'

I just stare at him, too appalled to reply to that.

He drags the chair closer and sets his hand over mine. An uncomfortable shiver spreads across my skin, and I pull my fingers away.

Lindsay's lips tilt down. 'Are you going to forgive me?'

I grit my teeth at the swell of nausea rippling through my stomach.

'I forgive you,' I decide. 'I know you didn't intend for this to happen. And I'm extremely relieved that no one

227

lost their life. But Lindsay, this is the end of the road for me.'

His brow pulls tight. 'Please don't say that. Please, Josie, I really like you.'

'I'm sorry. I wish I felt differently, but that's just the way it is. And you know I'm leaving town in a few months, anyway.'

He releases my hand, his lips pursing. 'You're not gonna hook up with that dickhead, are you?'

My lips fall open. 'What?'

He shakes his head and blinks away. 'That guy thinks he's top shit, I tell you, but I wouldn't piss on him if he was on fire.'

'Lindsay!'

'Sorry, I know he's your *friend*,' he mumbles. 'But you just wait until you do something that's not up to his standard, and he kicks you out onto the street. He thinks he knows everything about fucking everything.'

'What are you talking about?'

'He evicted me from the Hamilton house! That's why I moved out. He kept banging on about me driving when I went out for drinks, and I admit, I did hit his letterbox once with my car when I'd had a few too many, but I apologised for it *and* offered to get it fixed. But no, it wasn't good enough for Zac. I mean, who does he think he is—my fucking dad? What a self-righteous prick.'

'You need to leave,' I say firmly.

He leans forward. 'Oh, come on, babe.'

'Get out, Lindsay.'

He expels a huff and stands up so fast that the chair scrapes. 'Whatever. Best of luck to you. You'll need it with that loser by your side.'

I clutch my head, trying to figure out how I feel about the fact that Zac didn't tell me the reason he kicked Lindsay out. But it's hardly Zac's fault I'm in hospital right now—I saw Lindsay drinking alcohol and still got in the car with him. Still, though, why wouldn't Zac tell me? He's dropped a few hints, but that's not the same thing.

A nurse bursts through the curtain. 'How's the patient feeling this morning?' she booms with a smile, shuffling past a seething Lindsay to inspect the monitor.

'It's OK; I was just leaving,' Lindsay grunts before shoving through the curtain without a backwards glance.

Still reeling from his visit, I answer the nurse's questions about vision and numbness before mentioning the nausea. She promises some medication to help, but is otherwise happy with my progress. Once the doctor's been in to see me, I'll likely be discharged so they can free up the bed. I want to get out of here more than anything, but the idea of leaving also makes me uneasy: what if they missed something on the scan and I've got some sort of brain bleed I don't know about?

After the nurse leaves, I thumb through a string of frantic messages from Mum, Dad and Ingrid, who want me to call them as soon as I can talk. Zac must've let them know what happened. Mum and Dad are looking into flying home, but I send a text assuring them I'm doing OK and will call soon.

Natasha Harrington's also sent a kind message offering me as much time off as I need. I thank her for the flowers and tell her I'll be back as soon as the doctor gives me the all-clear. I can't afford to be off her radar for too long.

Zac steps back through the curtain, looking red-faced and adorable.

'Hey, bodyguard,' I say weakly.

He slumps into the chair. 'I'm sorry. Not about the sentiment, but I'm sorry about the tone. And the bad language.'

I smile. 'You kiss your mama with that mouth?'

He taps his fingers on the armrests. 'I see that he's gone,' he says pointedly.

'He's gone. And he won't be back.'

He sits a little higher in his seat, and I watch that information sink in.

'You broke up with him?' he asks.

'Well, that implies we were a couple in the first place. But yes, I ended it. It's not even so much about last night, to be honest. I'd already decided I wasn't into it. And now he's well and truly in the Insect Category.'

Zac raises a brow. 'The *Insect Category*?'

'Yup. It's when you're dating someone, but then you suddenly go off them and don't even want them to touch you. Because when they do, it feels like an insect is crawling over your skin. It's a very bad sign. Because once you're in the Insect Category, you never come out.'

He scrubs a hand down his face. 'Oh, Josie. Josie, Josie, Josie.'

I smile at him, a touch blown back by how handsome he looks in his navy T-shirt, which is printed with the words 'I'm Not Angry. This Is Just My Face'.

The perfectly ironic shirt for today.

'Hey, the nurse thinks I can go home,' I say. 'But the doctor still has to OK it.'

'That's great.' Zac's cheeks lift, and a little river of warmth rises up in my chest. I don't know if it's the painkillers making me soft, or the way the muscles in his arms flex as he rests his elbows on his knees, but I'm having all sorts of inappropriate thoughts. Again.

Zac insists on staying, and we eat bad hospital food together and watch mindless afternoon TV until he can't linger another minute without being late for work.

'Are you sure you don't want me to try to get out of it?' he asks for the third time. 'You know I'm a non-existent person when I'm on a shift. It'll be harder for me to help you out.'

'I'll be fine. It's just a bit of brain trauma,' I tease. 'It'll be good for me to have some quiet time to rest so I can get back to work. Can't have Meghan getting Christina's Sydney job instead of me,' I add with a smirk.

It occurs to me that Zac hasn't mentioned Meghan for a few days, but he doesn't react. He just offers me a contained smile and reluctantly heads off.

I finally call Mum and Dad, and we chat for more than an hour before the doctor clears me to go home.

After texting Ingrid because it's the early hours of the morning in London, I order an Uber, which I know Zac will feel terrible about, but I'm so relieved to be on my way back to his place that I couldn't care less how I get there.

As the car rumbles past the football stadium on the way to Hamilton, I let out a long sigh and file this accident as a wake-up call of epic proportions. I came to Newcastle to kick butt at NRN News and prove to my bosses that they need me on the news desk down in Sydney—not to act like a teenager who's just discovered boys and alcohol.

It's time that I grew the hell up and figured out my life.

CHAPTER 23

One year ago

My ballet flats scuff against the concrete driveway leading to my car while Mum and Dad's words bounce around my head, still trying to fall into place.

'We're moving to Koh Samui. We've found an agent there, a lovely lady named Win who's going to help us sort out our visas and find a beach house . . .'

They practically tripped over each other to go on about the low cost of living, the gorgeous beaches and jungles, the incredible food, and the fun British couple they met on their last trip there, who are already Thai residents.

Holy shit. My parents are moving to another country, and with my sister on the other side of the world, I'm going to be all alone in Australia.

Mum and Dad's round-eyed regret over that fact filtered through their otherwise palpable excitement today, but my sparkling smile of encouragement seemed to keep their parental guilt from overwhelming their decision. I'm twenty-six years old; my parents have spent decades putting me and Ingrid first. Moving to Koh Samui is clearly their retirement dream, and I won't stand in the way of that. If there's anything remotely positive to come out of Tara's tragic death, it's the knowledge that life is too short to tuck dreams away into a 'one day' folder.

Still, when I glance through my car window at my tan-brick childhood home that will soon be going on the market, my eyes begin to burn. I angle away from the window so Mum and Dad can't see my face, and press my fingertips to the corners of my eyes.

It's gonna be OK, Josie.

Everything's going to be fine.

The dread that's been festering in my stomach since I spoke to my doctor on Monday sends my hand back to my underarm. I stroke my fingers over the bulging lymph node through my shirt. When I register that it hasn't reduced in size since I last felt it in Mum and Dad's bathroom five minutes ago, I drop my hand and flex my fingers open and shut a few times, resisting the urge to keep touching it.

A thrumming need pushes against my ribs, and I clutch the steering wheel and rest my forehead against it.

God, I still ache for him. For his comfort, his warmth, his smile. Learning to live without Zac has been one of the hardest things I've ever had to do, but I have to try to understand why he's stopped responding to my messages and phone calls.

But Zac.

I need you.

I promised myself I wouldn't keep trying. Not when he clearly doesn't want me around anymore. But like I've lost control of my own body, I snatch up the phone and frantically tap through to his number, holding the cold handset to my ear.

Please answer.

Please answer.

Please answer.

The call rings out.

CHAPTER 24

Today

The first few nights after my discharge from hospital, I hardly sleep a wink. Every hint of a dizzy spell or twinge of a headache makes me worry that my brain is haemorrhaging from the concussion. What if I fall asleep and don't wake up? Fortunately for Zac, being on night shift means he's not home to bear witness to this neurotic behaviour. I'm fully aware it would seem extreme to him—to anyone, really—yet I can't seem to make it stop.

When I finally accept that I'm probably not going to die of an undiagnosed brain bleed, I begin to relax. I spend my recovery days solving puzzles on the dining table, reading dog-eared historical novels in the bath, strolling around Hamilton with Trouble at my heels and chatting with Christina on the phone. I hardly even see Zac, who's either sleeping the day away or out somewhere. When I text him to ask if he's with Meghan or if I need to send out a search party, all I get back is a one-word 'no', and zero explanation as to which question he's even answering. Regardless, I feel guilty about commandeering his heavenly bed for so long, so I wash all the sheets and make myself a new spot on the couch. I expect a bit of pushback for that, but Zac barely says a word about it.

On day six, I realise that he's being more than quiet. He's avoiding me. When I'm in the living room, he disappears into his bedroom. When we cross paths in the kitchen, he keeps our conversations short. After Lola visits with a bunch of native flowers the size of Antarctica, I bring them to Zac and do the old 'you shouldn't have' joke, but he barely cracks a smile.

Chatty, smiley, doting Zac has evaporated. And if there's something worse in the world than Zac Jameson being upset with me, I haven't found it. I'll never forget the time he stopped talking to me for two weeks in high school when I continued to date an older uni student who felt me up after I'd asked him to stop. It took the agony of Zac's silent treatment to scare me into action and dump the guy.

I watch Zac toss back his morning coffee, observing how he refuses to meet my eyes.

'Can I come grocery shopping with you this morning?' I ask, swallowing nervously. 'I want to practise being around people again before I go back to work tomorrow.'

Dumbest excuse ever, but I need the face time with Zac to feel out this mood he's in.

'If you want,' he replies, bending to stack the dish-washer without another word.

By the time we get to the supermarket, my gut is being slowly eaten alive by how little Zac's saying to me—or even looking at me. I have to resolve this the only way I know how: by being an absolute child.

'Look out!' I cry, pushing past him to leap onto the back of the shopping trolley and ride it down the cereal aisle.

'Jesus, Josie,' he huffs as the trolley sails towards an elderly woman inspecting a packet of sliced bread. I leap off the trolley and jerk it away from her just in time.

Zac's hand lands beside mine on the handle. 'Are you high on painkillers or what?' He carefully guides me and the trolley away from the lady.

I pout. 'Don't you remember doing that when we were kids? We always laughed ourselves stupid.'

'You're recovering from a concussion.' He tosses a packet of dark-roasted coffee beans into the trolley.

'Meh, a king hit to the head was probably just what I needed.'

He shoots me a disapproving glance, confirming he's lost all sense of humour in the past few days.

Before he can blink, I duck under his arm and climb onto the bottom rail of the trolley, facing away from him. I'm caged between his forearms, and I expect him to let go or at least pull me off, but he doesn't move.

'Get down,' he grumbles near my ear.

My ass brushes against the crotch of his jeans and heat streaks up my back, but I hold my nerve. 'No. I have a concussion, remember? It hurts to walk.'

He just blows through his lips and shoves the trolley forward, making me jerk to find my balance. *Little shit*. He makes a fast wheel-around to the next aisle, evidently no longer concerned about my recovering head injury.

I'm not backing down either. I hold on tight and call out things I want him to add to the trolley, my heart pounding out of rhythm every time his pelvis knocks against my backside.

By the time Zac wheels me to the check-out, I'm giggling like an idiot at this silly situation, but when I twist to steal a glance at him, he's still got that same distant look slapped on his face. My smile fades as I climb down and help him load up the conveyor belt.

When he begins hefting shopping bags into the back of his car without a single word to me, I snap.

'Are you pissed off with me about something?' I ask, immediately flushing pink.

He stills before he looks at me, the burning autumn sun beating down on our heads.

'No, I'm not angry,' he finally replies, but his voice carries a tremble.

'Then what's wrong? You've been acting really weird for the past few days.'

Emotion wells up in his eyes before they dart away. 'I'm sorry I haven't said anything. I've been wondering how to.'

My chest makes a horrible flip-flop. 'Say anything about what?'

He glances around, his jaw working. 'Can we not do this here?'

'Do *what* here? Zac, what's going on?'

'Nothing. I just . . .' The words come out slowly, like he's hesitant to say them. 'I think I need you to find another place to live. I'm so sorry.'

I gape at him, embarrassment twisting around my spine. 'Oh, I know. I've stayed too long. It was just meant to be a few days. I'm so sorry.'

'No, it's not that. I've loved having you there with me.' Something about his tone makes my breath seize up as he continues in a rush. 'It's just that I've worked really hard to get to where I am in my head. And—well, if you're going to keep doing stupid things like you did with Lindsay, then I don't think I can have you in my life. At least not in my house. I'm sorry.'

My face crumples up, and a flare of remorse deepens in his eyes.

'What stupid things?' I ask. 'You said the accident wasn't my fault.'

'It wasn't. But you got into a car with a man who you'd been drinking with all night. And it wasn't the first time, was it?'

I blink at him, gobsmacked. 'And I said I was sorry. But it's what happened, and I don't understand what you expect me to do about it now.'

'Nothing. But like I said, if you're going to get in

cars with drunk assholes, then I can't have you in my life, OK?'

His distressed face blurs as my eyes fill up. 'Wow. Well, I'm sorry you feel that way, Zac, I really am. It's not like we haven't known each other since we were thirteen.'

His brow creases as he flattens a hand over his chest. 'Josie, you know my history. You know I lost the woman I was supposed to marry to a drunk driver. Right?'

A tear spills from my eye, and I drop my chin to hide it. 'You make me sound like a walking liability. Have you never made a mistake, Zac? Do you ever get tired of being such a good person all the time? Of being five hundred levels above everybody else?'

'Do you ever get tired of thinking you need to be *bad*?' he counters. 'It's not cancer that's going to kill you, Josie; it's this shit. Going out every night of the week with fuckwits who aren't mature enough to know when enough's enough.'

'Well, I might not have done that if you'd had the courtesy of telling me that Lindsay has a habit of driving when he's over the limit!'

Zac's chin jerks back. 'What?'

My hand tightens to a fist at my side. 'At the hospital, Lindsay told me the reason he moved out of your house was because you kicked him out after he drove home drunk and hit your letterbox. So, why the hell didn't you tell me that? If you had, maybe we wouldn't be in this situation!'

'I didn't think I would have to tell you that, Josie!' Zac practically shouts. 'I would've thought that you, of all people, wouldn't take the risk!'

A young couple beside us share an uncomfortable glance as they toss their grocery bags into their car. After they quickly drive away, I feel Zac's eyes burning a hole in my cheek as I stare at the street.

'I'm sorry about the cancer thing I said,' he mumbles. 'I want you to know that I'm still happy to come with you to your tests.'

'Oh, whatever, Zac.' I wave a hand in his direction. 'You do you.'

I hate that we're having what feels like a couple's fight in the middle of a carpark, but the thought of going back to his lovely home to feel unwanted there fills my stomach with lead.

'Spoiler alert, this is a *friendship*, Zac,' I add, those words sending a jolt of nerves through me. 'We're not a couple. You don't get to have deal-breakers and ice me out. Friendship is unconditional.' I hear how ridiculous that sounds as soon as I say it. Friends are allowed to have boundaries too, I know, but I'm too damn upset to correct myself.

Zac looks a little taken aback before he steels his face at me. 'I'm sorry, but getting in cars with drunk drivers *is* a deal-breaker for me.'

Tears build on my eyelashes, and I rapidly blink them away. This painful avoidance of me is feeling a little too familiar.

'Got it,' I say thickly. 'Well, come on then. Let's go, so I can grab my stuff and get out of your life like you want me to. I'm sorry I didn't pick up on it this time. I should've read the room better.' I circle two fingers in the air.

He just stands there. 'What do you mean, *this time*?'

'Oh, come on, Zac. This isn't really our first goodbye, is it.'

The look on his face says he truly wants me to believe he has no idea what I'm talking about.

I fold my arms at him. 'How have you been for the last *two years*? Because I wouldn't have a clue. And I know what you went through was awful. It was one of the worst things anyone could ever imagine. But you didn't let me be there for you. A week after the funeral, you just took off, and you never once came back.'

Zac's eyes gleam with tears. It's so hard to talk to him about this stuff without feeling like a selfish prick, but if this is the last conversation we're going to have, I'm going to drop some ugly truth bombs.

'I didn't move to the moon, Josie,' he protests. 'You could have visited me up here anytime.'

My voice turns high. 'Why would I when you wouldn't return my phone calls and barely replied to my messages? You cut me out of your life; you shut me out of your pain entirely.'

'I was traumatised!' He steps forward, his watery eyes blazing into mine. 'My fiancée *died in my fucking arms*. Not a day has gone by since then that I haven't thought about it. About how I tried everything to keep her alive, and nothing worked. Imagine how utterly hopeless I felt. Three years of training, learning how to save lives, and it all meant jack shit in that moment. I couldn't do anything to help her. And it should have been *me* driving that car. I wanted to, but she kept insisting, and I should've—'

'Shut up!' I rush forward to clamp my hand over his lips. 'Don't you dare stand here and tell me you were supposed to die in that car. Because if you do, I will never fucking speak to you again. Do you hear me?'

His eyes shine with tears, and I pace backwards, heaving breaths.

For what feels like an eternity, we stand in a deadlock of silence while my heart slowly disintegrates at the thought of Zac blaming himself for Tara's death.

'Zac, you need to stop guilt-tripping yourself over this,' I say, my voice fighting for breath. When he doesn't reply, I wrap my hands around his wrists and guide him to look at me. 'You did everything you could to save Tara. Everything. This is not your fault. *Please*, Zac. Forgive yourself.'

His face twists up, and I reach around his back, pulling him close. The unexpected proximity of him sends me into a dizzying spin, and all I can do is clutch on tightly. He buries his face in my neck, a deep sigh shuddering through him as I run my palm up and down his spine.

I whisper how sorry I am, over and over, while his tears dampen the nape of my neck, my heart sore to bursting.

'How could I have just gone on with my life down there?' he chokes out. 'How could I get up each day . . . eat breakfast . . . brush my teeth . . . walk around Sydney with the sun on my face . . . when she was never going to do any of those things again?' His arms tighten around me. 'It was too much to live with, Josie.'

Tears drip down my cheeks, and my palms keep scoring lines up and down his back as I savour the frantic beats of his heart against mine. *I nearly lost you, too.*

'I'm sorry,' I tell him for the millionth time. 'I'm sorry I couldn't be there for you. I understand that you needed to leave every part of your life down there. I get it now. I'm sorry.'

He pulls away from me, leaving me cold and empty, but there's some relief when his fingers slip around my wrists, his glistening eyes holding mine.

'No, you don't understand,' he says, a deep blush overcoming his face. 'You don't understand all of it.'

I wait for more, but he looks away and wipes his eyes with the heel of his hand. '*Fuck*, sorry,' he says. 'I clearly needed to let some shit out.'

'Have you spoken to someone about all this?' I ask gently. 'A counsellor?'

He nods. 'It's helped with things like being able to get behind the wheel of a car without falling apart, but I honestly just need to keep toughing it out and putting my big-boy pants on.' His expression hardens with the same look I saw on his face at the funeral.

'You know it's just as brave to say you're not OK, right?'

He looks down and releases a long breath.

God, I was an idiot to get into that car with Lindsay after he'd been drinking. I hadn't realised how much pain Zac was still in over the accident. I screwed everything up between us again, and now I have to live with it.

'We should get going,' I say, my voice fading. 'I'll stay in a motel until I find someone who doesn't mind a temporary housemate.'

I turn for the car, but Zac catches my forearm. 'I don't want you to do that.' Regret burns in his eyes. 'I overreacted. I'm sorry. You know that drunk drivers are a seriously sore point for me, and when I saw you lying in that hospital bed, I just . . . fuck.' He inhales a throttled breath. 'I was living my worst nightmare. I'm so sorry, Jose.'

I clasp my hand over his, and his palm turns upward, pressing into mine. I give his hand a light squeeze and let go, but he holds on. My breath stalls as he gazes down at me, the spot where his fingers are gently kneading mine now the focal point of the entire world.

I need to say something, but no words form. I just stare up at him as his eyes flicker back and forth between my own before his gaze begins to travel over my face, finishing with a very clear drop to my mouth.

What is happening right now?

A blush creeps up my neck and across my cheeks.

'Are we OK?' Zac asks softly.

I assume he's talking about our friendship, which throws me, so I force out a smile and nod, which is pure performance.

Because the thing is, I want him to kiss me. Right now.

I want him to kiss me stupid.

I want him to press me up against the car and kiss me until there's no breath left in my body.

Even though he's dating someone, and we have fourteen years of friendship to lose.

I just can't keep trying to fight against it anymore. I won't.

But as those thoughts settle in my head with perfect clarity, Zac's fingers let go of mine, and he turns away from me.

CHAPTER 25

Nine years ago

Zac twists the heel of his shoe back and forth through the wood chips, digging a little trench.

'So, who do you wanna go to the formal with?' he asks.

I run my palms up and down the park swing's ice-cold chain and push my tongue into my cheek. 'Who do *you* wanna go with?'

'No way.' He hunches forward on his swing seat to pin me in his stare, his dark-chocolate curls flopping everywhere like a rag doll's. 'I asked you first, sunbeam.'

I stare at the playground's rickety old seesaw and shrug. 'There's really no one I want to go with,' I admit. Objectively, Damien Di Fiori is still probably the hottest guy in our year—although Zac won the poll some of the girls did recently—but I lost interest in Damien years ago. Plus, he's been with Amy for weeks now.

'I don't want to go with anyone either,' Zac mumbles, swaying back and forth a little as he keeps his huge feet planted on the ground. Given that Zac's dated different girls at school for most of the year, it's pretty unlucky timing that he's ended up single a month before the graduation formal. But because we both just got into the same university and will be moving to Bathurst for three years, he said he 'doesn't want any attachments', which I guess is a wise call.

'I might go on my own,' I decide. 'Go stag.'

'I think only boys can go stag. That's why it's "stag", like a male deer.'

'Really? What about girls, then? Does that mean girls go "doe"?'

Zac frowns. 'Maybe hen. You'd go "hen", I think.'

For no real reason other than he's fun to tease, I jerk my trainer towards his, kicking up wood chips that land over his shoe.

'Hey,' he grumbles, shaking them off.

'Just let me go stag, science nerd.' After a moment, I suggest, 'Or we could go together.'

Zac turns still except for his throat, which rises and falls.

'Just as friends, *obviously*,' I clarify. 'So we don't have to turn up like two dateless dweebs.' The guys in our year stopped teasing Zac and me for our friendship years ago, thank heavens, so that's a non-issue.

Zac tilts his head at me, a hesitant smile inching along his lips. 'You're really serious?'

'We're gonna end up hanging out together the whole night anyway.'

'True.'

Our gazes bind together, our cheeks flushing in unison before we burst out laughing, even though this isn't exactly a comedy-gold moment. But it's a bit weird, so I guess laughing is the only way to make it less so.

'Would I get you a corsage?' Zac teases, his brows lifting up and down.

'And a limo.'

'A *limo*? How rich do you think I am? My dad's an electrician.'

'My dad says electricians are the new millionaires.'

Zac grunts a laugh. 'I better ask Dad where he's hiding all our millions, then.'

The conversation falls away without a clear resolution about whether we're going to be each other's formal dates, and I consider bringing it up again while Zac fishes his phone out of his back pocket.

'Ooh, I got a Facebook message from Emily Weston,' he announces.

I roll my eyes. 'She's got *such* a crush on you.'

I eye his phone as he taps into it, but I'm too far away to read the message. 'She asked if we could talk at school tomorrow about something,' Zac says.

'Really?' My brow scrunches. 'That's kind of dramatic, isn't it?'

'*Dramatic?*' he echoes.

'Why doesn't she just bring up whatever it is at school tomorrow? Why the big lead-up?'

Zac doesn't reply, too busy furiously typing with both his thumbs, and I set my gaze on the rusted-up soccer goals, a hint of annoyance pinching my throat.

I'll bet the sixty-four dollars in my bank account right now that Emily's planning to ask Zac to the formal. She wants to do it face to face, obviously, and Zac will say yes because he can never handle disappointing anyone.

A tiny huff slips out of me that's much too quiet for him to notice. It's not like I wanted to go with Zac as his *date*-date, but that doesn't mean I love the idea of him bumping me for Emily-freaking-Weston.

CHAPTER 26

Today

When Zac and I went to school camp in the Snowy Mountains, we got lost on a trail and had such an explosive argument over how to get back—spurred on by fifteen-year-old hormones—that Zac spent the remainder of the trip pouring me bottomless cups of hot chocolate and saving my favourite seat by the fireplace, repeatedly making up for having flown off the handle even worse than I had.

This sweet, atoning behaviour returns in the week following our supermarket clash. Zac cooks me everything from French crepes to sushi rolls, records my favourite TV shows when I have to work late, and even throws in a few pranks to make me smile—one morning handing me a bowl of steaming-hot coffee and a mug stuffed with buttered toast.

It's all helped take my mind off my looming X-ray and ultrasound, but when test-day Friday rolls around,

252

my eyes are bugging out of my head and my hands are quivering.

Zac takes one look at me and calls in sick, insisting that he will accompany me to the clinic. We don't speak much—that would require more breath in my lungs than I have to give—but his comforting presence gets me through both tests without falling apart.

Doctor Ellison promises to call as soon as she has the results, but given that won't happen until at least Monday, I can enjoy a couple more days of ignorant bliss. *No news is good news.*

The silky, open-backed dress I picked out for Ross's wedding clings to me like a second skin, rippling when I walk and making me appreciate all my recent toning efforts at the women's gym Lola told me about near work.

I planned to wear my hair out and sleeked down, but my damn straightener has chosen today of all days not to heat up. I fidget with it for a bit before unplugging it with a huff and carrying it into Zac's bathroom.

'Do you have time to see why this might not be working?' I ask him.

He spins around with his tie half-fastened, and my breath snags in my throat. My eyes plummet to the navy-blue slacks hugging his muscular legs before gliding up to take in his crisp white shirt, and landing on the dark hair he's swept up into a stylish wave of curls.

It's not fair. He looks too good.

Heat fizzes in my chest as I feel his eyes slide over me the same way before his brow pinches as he reaches for the hair straightener. 'What's wrong with it?'

'It won't heat up.'

He spins around to plug it into the wall socket, and *oh my god, that ass in those pants is positively lethal.*

'It's probably the wiring,' he mutters after clicking the device a few times. I snap myself out of my stupor and trail him into the kitchen. A couple of minutes later, he's got the hair straightener pulled apart on the counter and is fiddling with the wires like a sexy bomb disposal expert in a three-piece suit. He must've learned how to do this from his dad.

'You look nice,' Zac says without looking at me.

'Thank you.' I shamelessly lean over the counter until my dress drapes slightly lower. 'So do you. I love your suit.'

'Thanks.' His eyes find mine and linger there for several breath-stealing seconds before he screws the straightener back together and hands it to me. 'Try that.'

His fingertips graze mine, and my heart rate doubles. For the zillionth time, I remind myself that not only is Zac my *best friend*, but as far as I know he's still dating Meghan, although she's evidently not coming to the wedding. I want to ask him why, but the thought of a giddy look overcoming his face at the mention of her name scares me off the idea.

Ross and Holly have booked out a French-inspired vineyard in the Hunter Valley wine region, and because

Zac's got a poorly timed shift tomorrow, he's decided to drive. At first, I was disappointed that we couldn't get tipsy and giggly together, but now that he's wrapped up like a birthday present in that fancy suit, and my silky dress is making me feel more naked than if I was actually wearing nothing at all, I decide it's safer if we both stay somewhat sober.

An hour after leaving Hamilton, we're standing beneath a rustic, lavender-lined terrace that leads to a walkway of olive trees, where an elegant woman clutching a clipboard is directing wedding guests. She sends Zac off to join the wedding party for pre-ceremony photos, and I meander into a courtyard garden dotted with urns and fountains. I sip on a flute of champagne and introduce myself to a few of Ross's extended family members, who kindly invite me to sit with them for the ceremony.

Clipboard-woman asks us to take our seats, and we all shuffle over to a cluster of white chairs facing a sunlit field of grapevines. Zac and Ross stand murmuring to each other beside a cedar arbour draped in chiffon that dances lightly on the breeze. When Zac's eyes move to mine and his chin dips like a question, I pass him a look that says *I'm doing fine* and press my hand to my chest to add *Isn't this all so beautiful?*

He smiles, his eyes sparkling warmly, and my heart trips over itself.

The ceremony is brief but lovely, and an outdoor reception follows beneath a canopy of vintage lightbulbs, with plenty of standing gas heaters to stave off the evening chill. With Zac seated up at the head table, I've been put beside Holly's hilarious high school friends, who crack me up while we devour shared plates of barbecued king prawns, Moroccan-style chicken and slow-roasted lamb.

I dig my fork into a cube of Belgian dark chocolate cake while Zac has the whole room in stitches with his best man speech, his tie loosened and his shirtsleeves rolled up. He sits back down at the wedding party table, and I catch myself in a doting stare, before replacing it with something a little less *I'm imagining my best friend naked right now*.

After the dessert plates are cleared, the song 'Can't Take My Eyes Off You' by Frankie Valli seeps into the air as Ross and Holly saunter onto the dance floor to cheers and whistles. They fold their arms around each other, and I turn a little misty-eyed as the beautiful lyrics curl up in my ears.

Holly stumbles over Ross's feet and he steadies her, sending a ripple of adoring laughter through the crowd. My eyes flicker to Zac, whose gaze catches mine and holds on. My cheeks burn as he glances away then back at me, his eyes glimmering in the low light.

The song speeds up and Ross and Holly detach and scatter to grab their parents, opening up the dance floor. The girls I'm sitting with jump up and tug at my fingers, but I tell them I'm good. *My heart's beating fast enough as it is.*

The seat beside mine is empty for all of ten seconds before a tall body slides into it. 'Having fun?' Zac asks me, his dimpled smile setting my heart on fire.

I gulp rosé. 'So much it should be illegal. Ross and Holly are the cutest. And your speech was hysterical.'

A contrary chuckle flees his throat. 'Thank you.'

His fingertips make little drum rolls on the table as we watch the guests dance, my body acutely aware of how closely his arm is resting to mine.

The sexy opening melody of 'Cream' by Prince kicks in, and I almost jump out of my seat. 'Oh my god, I *love* this song.'

'It's so underrated,' Zac agrees. He gets up and stretches out a hand, his brows raised.

Do I want to dance to one of the raunchiest songs in the world with Zac Jameson? I sure as hell do.

'Yes!' I shout to the DJ as I slide my palm into Zac's, all my senses sharpening to that point of contact. I follow him into the middle of the dance floor, where he turns around and begins moving to the music, our bodies centimetres apart but not touching. I look up, and his gaze locks on mine, making me glance down shyly. I shift my focus to keeping up with his moves, memories of other kids circling around him at our Year Twelve formal reminding me that this boy can *dance*.

By the time the song finishes, we're giggling like idiots. We hover in wait for the next track, cheering when we realise it's another one of our high school favourites: 'I Gotta Feeling' by The Black-Eyed Peas. We've shifted even closer together, the bodies around us disappearing as I shut my eyes and lose myself in this moment, almost hip-to-hip with Zac.

I'm ready for a break, but when the DJ launches into 'One More Time' by Daft Punk, Zac and I share a look that agrees we can't miss this one. We jump and sway and go full freak until I'm nearly crying with laughter. Halfway through the track, the song slows to a soft trance. When the couple beside us wrap their arms around each other, Zac blinks at me, a decision forming in his eyes, before he reaches an arm around my waist and drags me against him.

A gasp flees my throat as his face falls into my neck, and I close my arms around his soft shirt, my fingertips brushing the muscles in his back as the line between us blurs.

Holy shit.

I'm wrapped up in Zac's arms, his heart thumping hard against my chest. He flattens his palm against the patch of bare skin between my shoulder blades, kicking all the air out of my lungs. When his soft lips make the lightest graze over my neck, my grip on him tightens.

The slow part of the song is over, and we should be back to jumping around and being idiots, but Zac hasn't loosened his hold on me. Instead, his hand is making a slow, purposeful glide down my back, leaving a trail of sparks. Just as I want to get closer, he suddenly pulls away, and I mourn the loss of contact. His fingertips trace a line from my bare shoulder down my arm, and his eyes demand me to look at him.

I'm staring into the most gorgeous shade of honey, his gaze searching mine.

Why can't he just be a cute guy I met at a wedding? Why does he have to be my most treasured friend?

My sightline drops to a safer zone, but as I focus on how his body fills up his shirt, all I can think about is unbuttoning the fabric, one charcoal stud at a time.

The velvety richness of his voice shocks me back into myself. 'You know, I was happy that we were friends again until I remembered how you dance. I'm not sure I can be seen with you after tonight.'

I breathe half a laugh. 'Why do you always have to tease me?' I challenge.

'Because it riles you up,' he replies with amusement. 'Kind of like how you keep riling *me* up by flirting with me.'

My eyes snap to his. 'What?'

He levels a look at me. 'Come on, sunbeam. You've been baiting me since you got to this town. Don't even try to deny it.'

'I have not!' I poke his rib, which lands me one of those cute laughs.

'*How about spin the bottle?*' he mimics, recalling my suggestion on that first night we spent at Davide's place. '*Hey Zac, lie on the couch beside me so that I can stare into your eyes. Oh, and can you please look at my boobs and tell me if they look right?*'

I'm barely moving to the music now as I stare at him open-mouthed, wondering why I feel so delighted with the direction this conversation has taken.

'And what about you, *Zachary*, gluing the TV remote to your junk?' I retort. It's my turn to mock, and I'm the impersonation queen. The moment I morph into him, the smile expands on his face. '*Come and get it, Josie . . . Come and stick your hand down my pants. Do you like it "hard"?*'

He blurts a laugh. 'I never said that!'

I can feel the heat between us building, our bodies back to being centimetres apart, those incredible eyes burning into mine again.

Just stare down at the buttons. The buttons are safe.

'And now you're refusing to look at me,' Zac quips. 'That's curious.'

I scramble for a response. 'Well, you can blame your stupidly attractive colour-changing eyes for that.'

His chuckle lifts an octave. 'My what?'

'One minute, your eyes are brown; the next, they're green. I wish they'd bloody decide.' *Josie, shut your trap this instant.*

When I lift my gaze again, he's looking at me in a way that fills me with the urge to speak so I don't do something else with my mouth that I can't take back.

'Why isn't Meghan here with you?'

His smile disappears and his expression clouds. 'I'm not with Meghan anymore. I ended that weeks ago.'

My brows fly up. 'You never told me that.' With a

thud, I realise she's been avoiding me at work. 'Why'd you break up?'

He goes to reply but decides against it, his jaw tensing as his gaze slips to his feet. The music's now no more than a faint echo in my ears, drowned out by my pounding heart.

The question hesitates on my tongue before it bursts free. 'Was it because of me?' I breathe.

Zac's lips part with surprise. He stares down at me before his brow puckers with confusion. 'Why would it have anything to do with you?'

I blink at him for a dumbstruck moment until my chest makes a sharp twist.

Why did I just ask him that? I could die of embarrassment!

Panic clogs my throat, and I pace backwards, colliding with a woman dancing. I mumble an apology to both her and Zac, and turn away, worming my way through the huddle of moving bodies.

I head for my table, but tears are threatening my eyes, and I can't let Zac see me cry over this. It would be too humiliating.

I cross an empty courtyard glittering with fairy lights and stop where a sandstone wall faces a silent orchard of fruit trees, the moonlight washing their leaves in silver.

'Josie?'

Shit.

'I just need a minute,' I say, angling my face away from Zac.

He comes right up to me, the glow of the overhanging lights making my tears impossible to hide. His brows pull together as he brushes his knuckles over my cheeks.

'I didn't mean what I said back there,' he says with a tremble. 'You just . . . you make me so nervous.'

Nervous? My lungs jam up while his chest lifts and falls with heavy breaths.

A small smile finds his face, loosening some of the tension in the air. 'You know, I've finally decided on my favourite features of yours. Remember that game?'

A choked laugh slips through my lips. 'How could I forget?'

'For best personality feature, I'd have to say your forgiveness. No matter what I do and how much I screw up, Josie, you always look at me with *that* face.' He catches my jaw between his fingers, giving it an affectionate squeeze.

'What are you talking about?' I ask softly. 'You've never done anything to me that requires forgiveness.'

His hand drops back down, but he doesn't move away from me. 'Are you kidding? What about that time I said I'd drive you home from school, but because I'd only just got my licence, I wanted to go driving around the national park, and you couldn't, so I asked you to get the bus home?'

A smile tugs at the corners of my mouth. 'Can you believe I survived that?'

'What about the time I nearly killed you in the snow when we got lost? Or when you were dating that uni prick, and I stopped talking to you—not just because he was an asshole, but because I was so sick with jealousy over it?'

Heat blooms in my stomach.

Zac shifts on his feet. 'Then there was the time I met Tara and decided to ask her out, even though you and I were finally just starting to spark.'

A blush spreads across his cheeks, and I fight for what to say to that, but he keeps going. 'So that's the personality one. Want to hear the physical one?'

I have never wanted anything more in my life.

'Go on then,' I say in an effort to play it cool. 'Ass or eyes? What's it to be?'

He bites down on his bottom lip like he has no idea how sexy that is. 'Your mouth.'

'My *mouth*?' I give him an unsure smile. 'Is this a trap?'

'Your mouth.' His gaze falls to the subject in question and clings there.

I snort a little. 'That's a bit weird. You mean my lips?'

'Your lips, the way you speak, the way you smile—everything. Every part of your mouth makes me fucking crazy.'

With a deep breath, he steps forward and braces his hands against the wall on either side of me, locking me inside his cage.

Fuuuck, just kiss me.

Kiss me this instant, or I'm going to grab that tie around your neck and yank your mouth to mine, putting it where it belongs.

I clasp my hands behind my back and rest against them, blinking up at him through my lashes, making what I want clear. But instead of sealing his lips to mine, Zac brings his mouth close to my ear, his breath peppering my skin with goosebumps. 'Do you know I must have thought a thousand times in the past week about what it would be like to kiss you? I haven't been able to think about anything else.'

It takes everything I have not to turn my head and bring our mouths together, but I'm determined not to be the one to make the first move.

His soft lips graze my ear. 'If I kiss you right now, am I going to need to ask forgiveness?'

'I forgive you,' I say breathlessly.

He makes a sound like he can't hold back anymore and grasps my jaw, pulling my mouth to his. My heart detonates as his lips cover mine before our tongues collide and sweep together with a desperate, aching hunger. He tastes incredible, and my hands clasp the back of his neck, pulling him closer, kissing him deeper, the burning relief of it setting fire to my soul. He knots his fingers in my hair, angling my mouth where he wants it before grunting out a sound that I could record and sell to women to help them get off. His hips pin me tightly against the wall as he rasps another moan into my mouth, kissing me like it's the last thing he'll ever do in this life. I writhe against him, grasping at his shirt, his face, his hair—amazed that I can feel this turned on by my best friend. I feel like I'm tasting a secret, something just for me.

I know that what we're doing is dangerous, but the last thing I want to do is stop. I want to ravage his mouth, tangle our tongues, kiss him filthily, and suck on his bottom lip. *I. Never. Want. This. To. Stop.*

Still kissing me into a stupor, Zac grips my thigh and lifts my leg, hooking it around his hip. It opens up a point of contact that makes a moan rise up in my throat as he rubs against me.

'*Fuck*,' I whisper, rolling myself against him and getting off on the way it makes him groan.

'Why haven't we done this before?' he says hotly, capturing my breasts in his hands over my silky dress. 'Why haven't we been doing this the entire time?'

'It's *your* fault,' I tease into his glazed eyes. 'You always had a girlfriend.'

His brow creases with arousal as he strokes the peaks of my breasts over the fabric. My hands reach around to palm the tight globes of his ass that I've been dying to touch for weeks. *So perfect.*

'Why *did* you hook up with Tara when you and I were just starting to spark?' I ask in a breath, and Zac's fingers still. An alarm bell rings in my head that says I should shut up right now, but I've never been much good at that.

A second later, the worst question I could ask leaves my lips, spurred on by a jealous streak I didn't know I had until now.

'I felt something back then,' I admit. 'We'd just had that conversation about getting married when we were twenty-eight, and . . .' I pin my gaze to his, insecurity gripping me everywhere. 'Why *didn't* you choose me?'

Zac's hands fall to his sides, and a weighty exhale blows through his lips as he takes a step back.

Oh no.

'Sorry, I shouldn't have asked that,' I add quickly.

'No, it's OK,' he says, his cheeks flushed, his lips swollen, and his hair mussed from where I've clawed at it. I just stare at him like a crushing schoolgirl while he brushes a hand over his jaw in a way that frightens me.

'Talk to me, Zac.'

The chill in the air finally finds my skin as he looks away, then back at me with a sea of emotions swirling in his eyes. 'Fuck, Josie, I just . . . I don't know . . . Maybe we shouldn't . . . I'm not sure . . .'

'It's fine; let's go back to the wedding,' I say in a hollow tone. Because there's no way I'm going to try to convince this guy to stay here and make out with me if he's not sure it's what he wants.

He doesn't protest, which jabs a needle into my heart, and I flip up the strap of my dress and head back towards the music, Zac falling into step behind me.

'I don't know . . .'

'Maybe we shouldn't . . .'

'I'm not sure . . .'

My stomach churns all the way back to my chair, where I sit and wrap my cashmere shawl around myself like a safety blanket.

Zac drops into the seat beside me and gently sets his hand over mine. I feel like pulling away, but I don't.

What am I even thinking?

Zac *didn't* choose me when he sensed the option was there. If Tara hadn't died, they'd be married now, and she'd be the one here as his wedding date.

I'm just the back-up plan.

He may be your best friend, but he's still a guy. He already told you that he only wants to play the field, and you're a hook-up in a pretty dress who's basically been throwing yourself at him. That's what this is.

I feel his eyes on me, but I slide my fingers away from his. I sense him stiffen as he drops his hand into his lap, the message received. We both stare silently at the dance floor, the truth growing over us like a storm cloud.

We should never have kissed.

Because how are we supposed to hang out together now with this strange, unbearable new tension between us?

Ross waves Zac over for something and he gets up with a sigh, assuring me he'll be back. His palm sweeps over my shoulder as he leaves, but it only makes me feel worse.

'I'm not sure . . .'

With my chest stinging, I pull out my phone and message Natasha Harrington. She's been especially kind to me since the accident, and I make up a story about an urgent appointment in Sydney tomorrow, asking if I can please work from there for a couple of days. It's a bold and risky move, but it's one worth taking.

Because I just can't be around Zac right now.

I'd thought it would be me, but we *both* messed up. We shouldn't have given in and crossed that forbidden line.

Even though it was the most heart-melting kiss of my entire life.

With my stomach tying itself in knots, I call an Uber.

CHAPTER 27

Seven years ago

'I'm never getting married.'

My statement sends a stunned stare to Zac's face, his skin bronzed and glowing from the Bathurst summer sun. 'Since when are you against marriage?' he asks.

The bartender hands us our beers, and I bend forward to slurp up a bit of the froth that's bulging from my glass. Zac wrinkles his brow at this behaviour.

'I'm not *against* marriage,' I clarify as we carry our drinks over to an outdoor table that's built into a tree tangled with fairy lights. 'I just don't see it ever happening. I haven't met anyone around here who's decent, apart from Felix.'

Zac scoffs. 'That fucking poser was the antithesis of decent. Plus, you don't want to meet someone in Bathurst, do you? What happens after you graduate?'

'The guy chases me to Sydney because he can't live without me?' I grin over the rim of my glass.

Zac's chuckle sounds mildly irritated. 'Whatever.'

'What about you?' I ask. 'This could be the longest I've seen you go without a girlfriend. Are we finally having a drink named "loneliness" at the same time?' I tease, referencing our favourite 'Piano Man' lyric.

'How could I ever be lonely when I have you, sunbeam?' he quips, tossing me a smug smile.

Zac sits back and runs his fingers through his Shawn Mendes–style curls, and I register that he looks pretty undeniably handsome tonight. His blue T-shirt that says 'Don't Meth With Me' looks like it was made for his chest to model, and his sun-kissed skin is making the green flecks in his eyes take centre stage. I have no doubt that he could pick up any girl tonight without even needing to speak, but I don't voice that because I'm greedy and don't want to share him.

'Is there an ideal time you would like to get married?' I ask, continuing our conversation.

A bemused line hits Zac's forehead. 'Uh, when I meet the right person?'

'That could be when you're eighty.'

'And?'

'*And?* What about having kids?'

He raises a brow. 'So, having children out of wedlock is unacceptable now? Have you joined a church group and not told me?'

'Has anyone ever found God and not told everyone within a ten-kilometre radius?'

Zac chuckles and stretches a leg out beneath the table, his calf resting against mine. 'What about you, then?' he asks as our legs swing lightly back and forth together. 'Assuming you change your mind on the no-marriage policy, when would you like to do it?'

'To be honest, if I'm not married by the time I'm thirty, I'm gonna consider myself a failure.'

'Jeez.' The glint of the overhanging fairy lights dances in his eyes. 'No pressure.'

'I'm serious. I want kids, and there's a cut-off time for that. You're a guy, you're lucky, you don't have to worry about biological clocks.'

'You're *twenty-one*, you nutjob.' He knocks my leg with his.

'Yeah, well, that's less than ten years until my cut-off, and in case you haven't noticed, I don't exactly attract boyfriends easily.'

'Oh, you attract them,' Zac counters right away. 'You just don't want any of them, but trust me, they're interested.'

His gaze falls to his beer, and a faint spiral of warmth coils up my spine.

'I'm sure *someone* will marry you when you're thirty if you're that desperate,' he eventually mumbles.

An idea crashes into my head, propelling me to sit forward. 'Would you?'

Zac's eyes jump to mine, expanding.

'What I mean is,' I continue quickly, 'if you're still single when you turn thirty, and so am I, would you marry me?'

Our gazes fuse tightly together, and a strange thickness invades my stomach. 'If you really want me to,' Zac replies, sounding a little hoarse.

'Really?'

His throat flexes. 'Why not? We get along great. We could have an awesome marriage.'

I blurt a thin laugh. 'We really could.'

Except getting married would mean we'd have to . . .

With a will of their own, my eyes travel to Zac's lips, which are plump against the beer glass he's gulping from. Kissing Zac is almost too weird to even imagine, but if I closed my eyes and just went with the sensation, I'm sure it could feel amazing. I wonder if he's the slow, savouring kind of guy who likes to brush lips in a soft, silky kiss, or if he's the type who grabs a girl's jaw and crushes his mouth to hers, capturing her tongue and biting at her bottom lip. With lips like his, neither option would suck.

'Why are you staring at my mouth?' Zac says throatily.

I almost tip back on my stool. 'I'm *not*. I'm just . . . I was wondering what your beer is like. Is it really hoppy?'

'Try it.' He holds out the schooner glass, and I take it and throw back a sip, even though I hate hoppy beers.

'It's all right,' I say, trying not to gag. When I pass the glass back to him, the tips of our fingers rub together, and Zac's cheeks darken a little.

'So does this mean we're engaged now?' he asks. He's back to smirking, but his voice sounds breathless.

'Not yet, Romeo. When we're thirty.' I fling a hand up. 'Actually, no. When we're twenty-eight.'

'Twenty-eight? Nine years is too long to wait to get into my pants, huh?' The suggestive gleam in his eyes sends a flush of heat to my cheeks.

Now I'm the one who sounds a touch winded. 'It's because I want to be married for at least two years before having a baby, and I'm not having my first baby any later than thirty.'

Zac's smile deepens. 'You've really thought this through.'

I make a definite nod. 'But only if we're both still single. We can call it "The Back-Up Plan".' I lift my beer and tilt it out to him. 'Deal?'

He clinks our glasses. 'To "The Back-Up Plan".'

I squirm through the nervous feeling spreading through my belly while Zac's eyes graze over his phone, the corners of his mouth slightly turned up.

'Oh, shit, someone just texted me about that costume party on Sunday,' he says. 'I still don't have anything to wear.'

'Want me to take you to the op shop tomorrow where I found my Cleopatra costume?' I offer while performing the 'Walk Like an Egyptian' dance.

He smiles. 'Thanks, future bride.'

CHAPTER 28

Today

I'm stress-sweating inside a Sydney taxi, twenty minutes late for my interview with a construction CEO thanks to the world's most confused taxi driver, when my phone jingles in my bag.

My nervousness spikes while I dig it out, still waiting for a call from Zac, but it's Doctor Ellison's office. My stomach nosedives and I consider throwing my phone out the window, but I swallow my terror and answer it.

'Everything came back normal,' is the first thing out of the doctor's mouth.

My forehead drops to my knees and my chest breaks open, air gushing into my lungs. She says a run of other things I only half-hear about my cough being post-viral and the intermittent bleeding being likely hormonal.

'Josie, might I also suggest we set up an appointment to talk a bit more about this health anxiety,' she adds in her lulling tone. 'There are lots of things we can do, like psychology sessions, and even medication to break that cycle of irrational thoughts and give the counselling a chance to work. Have a think about it, OK?'

I repeat my thanks on loop, gushing like she's literally saved my life, and make a mental note to set up that appointment. Whatever this is that's feeding on my brain and turning me into an emotional wreck, I want it gone. It's time to get my life back.

I tip the taxi driver who can't follow a simple GPS and ace the interview about major job cuts in the building industry. Back in the chaotic Sydney newsroom, I manage to focus enough to write up a story that lands in the opening segment of the evening news.

My car's crawling through traffic on my way to Christina's, who's been putting me up in her guest room, when a familiar feeling of dread slinks into my abdomen. What if something was missed in those test results? My left underarm was oddly itchy last night. Could that be a sign that something still isn't right?

After running my fingers over my underarm, I wrestle my mind off my health and back onto what Christina told me last night. She said that Oliver Novak's decision about her newsreading replacement is imminent, so if there's ever a time for me to shine at work, it's this coming week. I need to reset my head and *focus*.

My sense of being off balance hasn't been helped by the fact that I haven't heard anything from Zac since the wedding. *Ouch*. Fleeing the reception and driving to Sydney feels like an overreaction in hindsight, but

I don't want to text him to explain—it's probably something best dealt with in person.

I'm swirling my fork through a banoffee pie I bought to share with Christina when Natasha Harrington texts me. It's been a big news week in Newcastle, and she wants me to report back first thing tomorrow morning. *Argh*. It's also Zac's birthday tomorrow, so if I want to keep hiding from him, I'm out of luck.

The butterfly storm in my stomach upgrades to a cyclone at the thought of seeing him. But maybe his birthday is the perfect excuse to go back to what we do best: hanging out, being asshats, and absolutely *not* kissing each other's faces off while I grind against his erection. *Christ*.

After hugging Christina goodbye, I make a pit stop at her local liquor store to buy a bottle of whisky recommended by the salesman. It's not the most personal gift I've ever given Zac, but under the circumstances, it's all my panicking heart can manage.

I stick a silver bow on the bottle's neck and pull out my phone, deciding that a break-the-ice text might take the edge off our reunion.

> **ME:** Hey. Just wanted to let you know I'm heading back up north tonight. Hopefully it's still OK to crash at yours for a few more days?
> P.S. I got my test results back, and everything was normal. 😊 Hopefully the docs didn't miss anything! 🦴

He's probably at work, so I fire up my car, but a speech bubble pops up right away.

> **ZAC:** Amazing news! So happy to hear that. I'm sure the results were accurate.
> Sorry I've been quiet, it's been a hectic few days at work. Of course, it's fine for you to stay here. I'm on night shift tonight, just FYI, so might not see you.

I slump in my seat, rereading the message in search of clues that he's been thinking about that kiss as much as I have. But I don't pick up on anything other than the friend zone.

Which is where you need to be, Josie Larsen. You are moving back to Sydney in a couple of months. Don't screw up fourteen years of friendship over a moment of repressed sexual attraction rising to the surface.

Slapping myself into BFF mode, I head for the highway out of Sydney, making one more stop at Christina's favourite op shop in North Sydney after spotting its late-night 'open' sign. The clothing racks fail to impress me this time, but a book on display catches my eye. It's a large hardback titled: *Why Does My Poop Smell Like Food I Didn't Eat? 200 Questions You're Too Embarrassed to Ask Your Doctor.* A laugh sneaks out of me, and I buy it to go with Zac's birthday whisky.

The rest of the way to Newcastle, I remind myself that this is the safe space I need to stay in: gag gifts, friendly texts and zero romance. I can do this.

Zac must've got home from night shift before my morning alarm because when I do my zombie-walk towards the coffee machine, I notice his bedroom door is shut. The poor thing's going to sleep the day away on his birthday, but I'm pretty sure he's now starting his run of days off, so we can celebrate tonight and get our chance to talk. Nerves whip up my stomach, and I do my best to drown them in dark-roast coffee.

Before leaving for work, I set out Zac's favourite coffee mug beside the birthday whisky bottle and book. On a piece of paper, I scribble:

> *Happy birthday, favourite.*
> *I'm taking you out tonight, no excuses.*
> *Dress to impress and be ready at 6.*

Work plays out smoothly, and Lola and Isabella help me choose the perfect place for tonight: a live music bar called Nightjar that also does whisky tastings. I text Zac the address, offering to drive us home if he can Uber there. I need to stay sober tonight so I don't screw this up and try to kiss him or—worse—ask him again why he didn't pick me over his ex, who has since *died*.

I cringe in absolute horror and shame every time I think about it.

The moment I'm done at work, I zip across town to Nightjar, wanting to scope out the perfect spot for us to sit before Mr Punctuality arrives.

The bar is a dimly lit speakeasy hiding in the basement of a luxury hotel, the snug space packed with round tables topped with flickering candles in glass jars. The one table that's vacant sits in a particularly dark corner opposite the stage.

That table does not look at all like the perfect place to kiss the life out of someone until you get kicked out for indecency.

Tossing slightly annoyed glances at the other patrons taking up the less romantic spots, I order a lemon, lime and bitters and settle into the corner table, keeping an eye on the door and a hand on my stomach to stop it from collapsing.

Five minutes after six, Zac pushes through the door, and an instant rush of affection tightens my throat. A woman goes to exit just after he steps in, and he lurches back to hold the door open for her, giving my eyes a chance to soak him in. He's in charcoal slacks that sit somewhere between smart and casual, and his light-blue button-down shirt is rolled up at the sleeves. As he approaches me with a slightly flushed smirk, he runs a hand through the curls that flop handsomely over his head.

I am so totally fucked.

'Happy birthday,' I say with a strained smile, rising to wrap an arm around his neck, inhaling mint, body wash, and a touch of heaven.

'Thank you.' He slides in beside me on the couch, his heavy thigh skimming mine. 'How did you know I had that poop book on pre-order?'

A laugh rumbles out of me as I hand him the menu. 'And here I was worrying you'd think it was crap,' I say with an added *boom-tish*. 'Have a look at what you want to eat, but for drinks, I already ordered you the whisky-tasting package.'

'Oh wow, thank you. Just me?'

I mime driving a car, and he nods.

'You could leave the car overnight, and I can drop you off in the morning,' he offers, tapping the menu against the full bottom lip that I sucked on three days ago.

What's my name again?

'Thanks, but it's OK,' I manage through my scrambled brain. 'Some of us actually have to work tomorrow.'

I notice he seems more interested in my face than the menu. 'How was Sydney?'

The tremble in his voice echoes mine as we catch up over some awkward small talk about work, ignoring the eight-tonne gorilla in the room that looks a lot like the fact that, a few days ago, our tongues were wrapped around each other's.

A waiter glides over with a tray of whisky tasters, and we each order a plate of buffalo wings off the snack menu. We chat a little more about everything other than *that wedding,* and *that kiss*, and when the indie-rock trio kicks into their first set, I mentally thank the universe for giving us a reprieve. But I can't let Zac leave this bar without us talking about what happened. Not if we want to stay friends.

The band tears up the stage, and we relax into the couch seat, watching everything but each other.

When the musicians announce a break, the space floods with light chatter and background music, and I turn to look at Zac with an inferno in my chest.

'So, Zac Jameson,' I dangle, not playing this cool *at all*. 'You and I kissed the other day.'

He coughs, nearly spitting whisky back into his glass.

I smile and chew my straw at him like a bloody psycho, briefly losing my courage as I consider making a run for it.

Zac's startled gaze drops to the coaster he's fingering. 'We did.'

When the next thing to come out of his mouth is a jittery exhale, I jump in to save him—and myself—from the excruciating intermission we've been in for the past few days.

'So, what are your thoughts about it?' I ask, pleased with how mature I'm sounding; how I'm taking the reins. This is what we need to do. Just talk it out.

He stares at his drink for a long moment, and my stomach clenches with anticipation. When his gaze returns to mine, there's a look in his eyes that makes my cheeks flush.

'If you really want to know, Josie, in the past few weeks, I've spent what's probably an unhealthy amount of time thinking about you. Every time I get a text, I hope it's from you. Every time I get home, I want you to be there, and when you are, my heart starts racing. The reason I left in the middle of the night after the house fire was because I woke up next to you on the couch and wanted to kiss you so badly that I couldn't see straight.' His soft eyes graze over mine. 'Every time you look at me, I feel like there's no breath left in my body. It's like you've completely filled my head, and there's no room for anything else. And to be honest, I don't know what to do about it.' He lifts a shoulder, his expression caught somewhere between embarrassed and helpless.

I can't find air in my lungs. I need to speak, but I can't make any words, and my heart is punching my rib cage.

'Zac, I . . .'

'I know,' he says. 'This is heavy shit for us. Serious danger zone.'

'I don't want to ruin our friendship,' I admit, although the humming deep inside my body that feels a lot like joy says *to hell with that*.

My comment blows disappointment across his face, and I quickly cup my hand over his.

'I'm not saying that I don't want things to change,' I clarify, thinking this out as I go. 'But I'm so scared of losing you again. I only just got you back.'

He turns his hand in mine, and our fingers lace tightly together like we both need this. We shift to face each other and rest our shoulders against the couch, our gazes locking.

'I feel like I've been blind,' is all I can think to say.

He strokes the back of my hand with this thumb. 'I don't. To be honest, I've been looking for a really long time now.'

'You have?'

His cheeks stain red. 'When I just said I'd been thinking about you a lot for the past few weeks? That may have been a lie. It's been going on for a lot longer than that.'

My breath snags in my throat as I wait for him to say more.

When he eventually speaks, his voice comes out thick. 'I did choose you. Two days before the accident, Tara broke off our engagement.'

My lips fall open. '*What?*'

A guilty look floods his face. 'I loved Tara. I did. But these feelings for you just crept up on me out of nowhere. Or, at least, they came back. I first noticed them a few months after Tara and I got engaged. You threw us that amazing Gatsby party, and you were sitting with one of her cousins, who had his hand on your leg. The thought of you going home with him gave me this really strong urge to kick his ass. Which I now know was stupid, because I never saw you with Amin again.' Zac lets go of my hand and scrapes his fingers through his hair, sighing heavily. 'But I don't know; it just fucking woke something up in me that I couldn't switch off after that. Sure, I liked you for a bit in high school, and there was always that undertone of possibility. But after I met Tara, I came to see you only as my best friend.

Then, one day, you turned my head again, and I haven't been able to look away from you ever since.'

I'm melting. And my mind is reaching for the memories of those days, but they're mostly a blur.

'You didn't know I felt that way,' Zac confirms, searching my face.

'I had no idea,' I reply, wondering how I could have missed this from someone I know so well.

He swallows tightly. 'Well, it didn't go unnoticed by Tara. She flat-out asked me one day if I had romantic feelings for you. And if she hadn't put me on the spot like that, I might've thought through whether it was better just to lie and hope the feelings would go away. But I didn't, and you can imagine how spectacularly unimpressed she was to hear the truth. So, she gave me an ultimatum: her or you. She said if I wanted to stay with her, I could never see you again.'

'Jesus,' I say quietly, even though I probably would've done the same thing had I been in Tara's position.

'And even though I thought about it,' Zac adds, 'I couldn't do it. I couldn't pick Tara over you. Because as much as I cared about her, the thought of losing you was unimaginable to me.'

A tear slips down my cheek as I grapple with the searing lightness his words have unleashed in my heart, matched only by the crippling guilt of knowing what came next for Tara.

Zac catches my tear with his knuckle. 'I don't want you to feel bad,' he says softly. 'I want this to be a good thing.' His warm hands cup my cheeks, lifting my gaze to his. 'I mean, when I picked you up at that train station after not seeing you for so long.' Emotion crowds his features. 'I can't believe you didn't see it written all over my face.'

'Why didn't you tell me?' I breathe. 'Why didn't you tell me back then?'

A sad smile barely lifts his mouth. 'Because you want to marry Todd, the investment banker from Bronte.'

I frown. 'Who?'

'Yeah, my thoughts exactly,' he mutters. 'Or should I say *Lindsay*, the business analyst from Newcastle.'

I tilt my cheek into his fingers. 'You know I wasn't into him. It was pretty hard to be when I couldn't stop thinking about you.'

A soft line appears between Zac's brows, his expression caught between happy and sad. 'You have no idea how hard it was for me to see you with him.'

'Actually, I do,' I reply. 'Watching you and Meghan together . . .' I let out a coarse breath. 'At first, it was strange. Then, kind of uncomfortable. But towards the end of you and her being together, I honestly couldn't stand it. Now I know why.'

The warmth filling Zac's eyes floods my chest with a tingling heat. But there's so much heaviness tied up in the things he's said tonight.

His hand finally drops to rest back against the table. 'I'm so sorry I didn't tell you more about Lindsay and his drunk driving. I should have done more than hint at it, but, well, for one, I never saw him as bad as he was the night of your accident. I didn't think he'd ever go that far—especially with someone in the car. But also . . .' Zac glances away as he sighs.

'Also what?'

'I was worried you'd think I was just trying to keep you away from Lindsay. For *other* reasons.'

'Reasons like me thinking you were jealous?'

He nods with a guilty blush. 'I was terrified of you figuring out how I felt about you. But it was a huge mistake. Lindsay could've . . .' Imagined horror fills his gaze.

'Don't think like that,' I say. 'It all turned out OK.'

Zac just shakes his head at himself and reaches for his drink while my mind shifts to another question that I still need the answer to.

'Why were you even in that car with Tara that night?' I ask softly. 'If she'd broken up with you?'

He puffs a weary exhale. 'You knew Tara. She was kind of a ball-breaker, and she insisted that I be the one to tell her parents the engagement was off. She didn't want me to go into detail about why, of course, but she asked me to tell them to their faces, and how could I say no? That's why we were driving down to Mittagong.'

'Zac, how could you not have told me *any* of this?'

A soft sadness coats his eyes. 'Jose, the girl I was meant to marry broke up with me because I wanted to be with someone else. Two days later, she died on a trip that wouldn't have happened if I'd just loved her the way I'd promised to. It's been hard enough to live through my shame without seeing you every day. Just being with you here now like this . . . I feel like I'm betraying Tara all over again. Killing Tara all over again.'

It's my turn to catch his face between my hands and look right into his eyes. 'You did *not* kill Tara. What happened was a terrible accident. The only person at fault is that bastard drunk driver who's rotting in prison right now.'

Zac presses his lips together like he's not quite sure he believes me, but he rests his cheek against my palm. My heart rate skyrockets again, and for several endless minutes, we sit and silently stare at each other, fighting off the guilt infecting the happiness between us.

'I don't know what to do,' I eventually say, my hand slipping off his cheek and falling into his grasp.

He pulls my fingers possessively into his lap. 'Me either.'

'This is . . .' A deep sigh blows through my lips. 'It's a lot.'

Zac just nods. There really is no other way to put it.

He shifts in his seat. 'Maybe we should cool things down a bit until we've had a chance to think everything through. Before we jump off this cliff . . . decide if it's really the right thing.'

I nod my agreement, but half of me doesn't want that at all, and that half is caressing every one of Zac's fingers.

I must look disappointed, because he shifts forward and brings his mouth close to my ear. 'Don't think I don't want you,' he says, his voice a little rough. 'Being with you is all I can think about. I don't think you realise what you do to me. It's taking all the self-control I have not to kiss you right now.'

My cheeks catch fire, and my grip on him tightens. This is a form of torture I just can't take.

'I think we should go home,' I eventually murmur through the lump of glue in my throat, making sure my voice doesn't carry any suggestion one way or the other.

Because Zac is right. As much as we want each other right now, we need to be sure about what we're doing so we don't screw up what's left of this friendship. There's already enough baggage between us to take on a round-the-world holiday.

But questions have begun ringing in my mind at a volume I can't ignore.

Why have I spent most of my adult life single?

Why did I make that back-up plan with Zac to get married when we were twenty-eight?

Why have I been chasing after men who represent a set of ideals admired by others but not, in reality, by me?

Why didn't I want to take things further with Lindsay, even before the accident that revealed his true colours?

And why does this quiet, unassuming man sitting across from me make my heart pound out of rhythm and my throat constrict with longing?

This isn't a moment of repressed sexual attraction rising to the surface.

This is something much more complicated.

My thoughts scatter when Zac gets up. He steps aside so I can go first, his palm catching the small of my back as I brush past the heat of his body.

I'm not sure how much willpower I, of all people, will be able to muster. Because this man has become my castle in the sky, and he just admitted he's had a crush on me for years. So really, what am I supposed to do with that?

With my back to Zac, I rub the confusing ache in my chest before I suck it up and lead him out of the bar.

CHAPTER 29

Eight years ago

While Zac's attention is fixated on a funny-shaped bird digging through the roots of a tree, I toss a twig at him, which lands on the shell of his ear. His hand slaps the spot and he jerks up, frisking his thick curls for what I guess he thinks is a bug.

I burst out laughing. 'It was just a stick, fraidy-cat. I'm pretty sure it won't bite.'

With narrowed eyes, he turns to face me on the wiry grass blanketing the Bathurst park, lifting his palm over my thigh like he's gonna slap it.

I squeal and curl up my legs, clutching my shins. 'Don't you dare!'

His hand draws closer, my legs squeeze tighter, my shriek gets louder, and this performance continues until Zac eventually flops down onto his back.

'Coward,' I tease while shifting onto my stomach,

and three full seconds pass before Zac spins and cracks his huge palm right down on my ass.

'Owww,' I moan, but it's hard to sound angry when I can't stop laughing.

He's giggling too, but his laughter quickly blends into an 'Aww'. His remorseful eyes graze over the butt I'm covering with both hands.

'You gonna rub it better?' I tease, arching my back a touch.

Zac draws a quick breath, then shakes his head, blinking hard.

I stay on my front and pick at the grass while Zac stares up at the uninterrupted blue sky. When a woman strolls past tugging on the lead of a black dachshund, he beams at the adorable little dog until its flapping ears disappear around the bend.

'So, I kind of have some news,' I announce.

'What is it?'

I roll onto my back, a smirk tugging at my lips. 'I had my first orgasm last night.'

His jaw falls open. '*What?*'

'Not my first one ever,' I hurriedly explain. 'But my first one without the guy *or* me touching my, you know . . .'

Every inch of Zac's skin colours red.

When he doesn't reply, I moan, 'God, you're gonna make me say it, aren't you?' I gaze up at the blue universe. 'I had my first vaginal orgasm.'

'Oh, Jesus, fuck,' he mutters with a bewildered laugh, splaying a hand over his face.

'What?' I squint at him, stifling a smile. 'Don't be such a prude. You're my best friend; I need to be able to tell you this stuff, even if you don't have a—'

He flings out a hand. 'Don't say it.' He then drapes an arm over his eyes. I marvel, with adoration and wonder, at how easy it is for me to make Zac Jameson blush and squirm. It might be my superpower.

One of his eyes peeks out at me from beneath his bicep. 'So, *Felix* had the honour, huh?'

'Why do you have to say his name like that? It's not *Felix,* it's . . . Felix.' The second time I say the name, I mimic the breathy sound of a woman on heat.

Zac jabs his forefinger into his mouth, pretending to gag. I toss another stick at him, and it bounces off his springy hair.

'I guess "Felix" and I have something in common then,' he murmurs without looking at me.

'You've both given me a vaginal orgasm?' I deadpan.

Zac groans. 'Not *you*. Women.'

'Women?' I sit up on my elbow and offer him a super-impressed brow raise at his use of the plural.

'Yup.' The confidence in his tone makes me realise he's being serious.

Whoa. OK.

I glance away, trying to get the unwanted image out of my head of Zac making a woman come with just his—

'All right, we're done here,' I blurt, climbing to my feet.

'We are?' he replies as I scrape twigs and blades of grass off my jeans.

'I've got a date with Felix.'

I totally made that up because this conversation got awkward *fast*.

But Zac doesn't even reply. He just silently trails me out of the park with his hands stuffed into his pockets while I try to calculate exactly when talking to my best friend about sex became weird. And what the hell I can do to change that.

CHAPTER 30

Today

The entire drive home, all I can think about is how Zac's hand is resting on his thigh beside mine, and if I reached for his fingers and brought them to my lips, what would he do? Would he shrink away and stick with the established course of *let's think this through*? Or would he ask me to pull over on the side of the road and tug me onto his lap, closing this unbearable distance between us?

After we've parked, he trails me up the path to his front door and reaches past my shoulder to push his key into the lock, the ridges of his chest brushing against my upper back. I cough to hide my shaky breaths as he waits like a gentleman for me to enter the house first.

OK, what now? We go to our respective beds and try to ignore the fact that, twenty minutes ago, you told me that all you can think about is being with me?

'You're working tomorrow, right?' he asks, kicking off his shoes at the door.

'Right.'

I bound over to the sink and gulp down a glass of water, occupying my mouth so I don't have to think of something to say.

'Damn,' he says lightly. 'Thought that maybe, now we're home, you could help me drink some of this whisky that a cute girl bought me for my birthday.'

A delighted chuckle bubbles out of me as I twist to face him, leaning against the counter. *God, Josie, be more obvious.*

'I can do a whisky,' I say, settling onto a stool with my hands clasped like I'm waiting for my bar order. I really need to stop staying up late drinking on school nights, but this is absolutely not going to be that night. *No force on this planet could drag me away from this guy right now.*

'Sweet,' Zac replies, grabbing the whisky tumblers and pouring two nips. We haven't shared more than a flicker of eye contact since we walked in the door.

I clink our glasses and brave a direct look at his eyes. 'Cheers.'

Tenderness swims in his gaze as he smiles at me. I have to look away, or I can't be held responsible for what I'll do next.

'Wow, this is good,' he says, his tongue sweeping over his bottom lip like he's purposefully trying to torment me.

'It is,' I parrot, screaming silently at myself. *You are a smart woman, Josie. Think of something interesting to say!* 'So,' I add in a dramatic voice, 'I started taking the pill recently.'

Oh my god, woman.

Zac's brows fly up, but this train has already left the station, and there is no going back.

'Doctor Ellison prescribed it for the bleeding I've been having. It's going to help balance my hormones.'

He blushes through another sip, and I assure myself this was a good track to take. What better way to cool down a surplus of heat between two best friends than a bit of intermenstrual bleeding chat?

'When did you start taking it?' he asks, leaning onto his forearms across from me, his pale-blue shirt tightening over his shoulders.

Eyes up here, Josie.

'A couple of months ago. So, you officially won't get an SOS text from me in the next few weeks, saying: "Send thoughts and prayers, I've been knocked up by a biker called Shotgun!"'

He laughs lightly as I swallow a bigger gulp of whisky, hissing when it burns the back of my throat.

'You OK there, sunbeam?' Zac swirls his glass with a smirk. 'You don't have to drink that if it's too strong for your delicate little body.'

'Shut *up*. Let the record show that I'm the last person who'd ever be described as delicate.' I down the remainder of my glass in one go to prove my point.

Oh shit, bad idea.

A line of fire sears up my oesophagus, burning through my breath and threatening to make my mouth explode. I clutch my neck and cough so violently that it throws my shoulders forward. By the time I've caught my breath, Zac's moved beside me, his eyes wide and his hand running up and down my back.

'You OK?' he asks, scanning my face. 'See? This is why you can't have nice things.'

I cough out a laugh. And while I adore all the different sides of my best friend, sweetheart-Zac is the most irresistible. He's looking at me like he's the one who injured me.

'Seriously, are you OK?' He catches a tiny droplet of whisky off my bottom lip with his thumb before sucking the tip into his mouth.

Fuck it, I tried.

The tightrope inside me snaps, and I catch Zac's face between my palms and drag his lips down to mine. His spine stiffens as I brush my mouth over his, tasting whisky and something much more delicious. I want him so badly that my insides clench, but he's not responding. I kiss both corners of his mouth before pressing my lips to the sweet centre again, begging for entry that he doesn't give me, and my head jerks back.

'Sorry,' I say quickly, embarrassment flaming up my face as I step backwards. 'I shouldn't have done that. We said we wouldn't. I'm sorry.'

Oh my god, I just pushed him off the cliff before he was ready. No, I jumped off it like a lunatic and wrenched him down with me.

297

I turn away from him with my chest burning, but he catches the loop of my black pants in his finger and tugs me back around. His mouth slams against mine, a moan erupting out of me as our tongues wind together. He grips my shoulders and presses me against the counter, pinning me with the full weight of his body as he captures me in a deep, lush kiss that makes my knees buckle. His mouth breaks from mine only to glide his tongue over my neck before he returns his lips to my own, branding me with another kiss that leaves me breathless. His arms wrap around my lower back, and for what feels like eternities of bliss, we make out, totally lost in each other's mouths.

When his pelvis rolls against mine, I sigh and grind my body against his, wringing a groan from his throat as he cups my breasts through my silk shirt.

'Fuck,' he pants, stroking his thumbs over my nipples through the fabric. 'Should we be doing this?'

I nod firmly. 'Yes. We should definitely be doing this.' To underline my answer, I drop my elbows against the counter and tilt my chest upwards in invitation.

Desire flashes in Zac's eyes as he undoes the buttons of my shirt, pushing the fabric open to reveal my satin bra. He grunts with need and runs his knuckles over the bra's inner edges, the tips of his fingers sinking beneath the fabric, making heat pool between my legs. I'm already so turned on that I can't see a metre in front of me, and god help me when he touches me bare.

He returns his lips to my neck, and I fold my arms around him, turning my face to catch his mouth with mine again.

'I thought only in my dreams would I ever get to touch you like this,' he breathes against my lips. 'I think about this all the time. I'm like a teenager again, losing my fucking mind over you.'

'Again?' I tease.

'You know I had it bad for you back then,' he rumbles into my mouth, and our tongues return to doing something way more fun than talking. My hands roam down the muscular planes of his back before landing on the firm mounds of his ass, which I grab and squeeze like I'm claiming ownership. *Finally. Mine.*

He guides my shirt off my shoulders before lowering his mouth to lick a hot, wet stripe up my cleavage. *Oh my.*

'Fuck, I need to see you so badly,' he says in a rasp.

He slips his hands behind my back and unhooks my bra, tugging it down as his heavy gaze lands on my breasts.

'So fucking perfect,' he says huskily, capturing the soft swells in his hands and feeling his way around while I palm his ass harder.

I need to touch the thick length straining the fabric of his trousers, but Zac sinks down and pulls one of my breasts into his mouth. My head lolls back, and my legs turn to water as he drags his tongue over me on both sides while his fingers bite into my waist.

'God, Zac,' I moan like this is already too much, and he stands back up to kiss me again.

'We should go to the bedroom,' he whispers against my mouth. When I nod, he slides his arms around my back and turns us around, walking me backwards while kissing me senseless.

I don't even know what direction we're facing, but when my back collides with the cushioned backrest of the couch, instead of resetting our course for the bedroom, Zac drops to his knees and closes his mouth over one of my nipples again. I moan and claw at the messy curls of his hair before my fingers slip inside the neck of his shirt. When I grip the muscles bunching in his shoulders, I lose all patience with the fact that this man is still clothed. I give him a tiny shove so that his lips detach from my breast, twist his shirt collar in my fist, and use it to yank him back to his feet.

A sexy laugh slips out of him as I hook my fingers inside the front of his shirt and rip it open, sending buttons flying.

'I've always wanted to do that,' I say without apology. I slide the busted shirt off his shoulders and drink in the sight of his toned chest.

'You're so yummy,' I say as I glide my fingers over the ripples of his abs. 'It's not fair to the other boys.'

He just smirks and blushes, and our hands begin exploring each other's chests like we've been waiting for this moment for years.

Transfixed by the sight of him shirtless in a pair of pants that stretch tightly at the fly, I consider snapping a photo so that I'll have wanking-off material for life, but quickly dismiss the thought. I have more important things to do right now.

My hand departs from his stomach to trail down to his hardness, and a little sigh of lust rolls out of me as I grip him tightly through his slacks. His forehead falls into my neck, and he groans as I run my palm up and down.

With a shuddery breath, he suddenly drops back to his knees, and I lose my grip on him. He blinks up at me, pupils blown, cheeks flushed—a gift from my dreams—before he unbuttons my pants and tugs them down my thighs. I kick out of them, and he pushes one of my legs up and to the side. He braces his palm against my thigh, keeping me balanced, then runs his nose up the length of my core through my satin panties. *Holy shit*. He presses the pad of his thumb to that perfect spot between my thighs and circles it, and my fingers sink into his hair as I close my eyes and try to burn this moment into my brain so I never forget it.

Then, swearing under his breath, he hikes down my panties and looks at me bare before murmuring a sound of hunger. With a slow but firm glide, he runs his tongue up and down my wetness, swirling and sucking while my aching moans fill the air. He digs his fingers into my flesh and spreads me open, burrowing his tongue inside me before replacing it with his fingers.

'*God*, I can't get enough of you,' he breathes as he sinks two fingers inside me, and I become a completely dazed version of myself who's incapable of anything. His tongue swirls and sucks and his fingers thrust and twist until a volcano of heat bubbles up within me, the tension making me see double until it suddenly explodes, raining pleasure down on every cell in my body.

Zac hums a sound of approval and stands back up, his mouth swollen and edible. I kiss him while my hand returns to the rock-solid length in his trousers. I am so done with waiting. I unzip his fly and haul his slacks and boxer briefs down his thighs, wetness throbbing in me at the sight of his arousal. *Of course, he's perfect.* He drags his fingers through my hair while I wrap my hand around him and just feel him. Little moans tumble out of me as I stroke him, loving how it makes his brow crease and his chest heave. I want more, so I brush my thumb over his tip and begin pumping him harder and faster.

His fingers tighten around the back of my neck. 'Whoa, beautiful. Slow down. You're gonna make me come.'

The thought of watching that is an encouragement, not a deterrent, but I can see in his eyes that he doesn't want to, not yet.

I swallow a shaky breath. 'Do you think we should use a condom?'

His brow pinches as he tucks a lock of hair behind my ear. 'Why wouldn't we?'

'I'm on the pill, remember? And the doctor just did a check-up, and I was clean for everything. I don't know; I'm just wondering.'

His eyes flicker back and forth between mine. 'I'm clean too.'

'OK, then.'

My heart pounds as his affection glimmers in his eyes. 'I just want to feel *you*,' he says. 'All of you.'

Emotion throbs through me. 'Same.'

We really should move to his king-sized bed, but it feels much too far away when Zac clutches my backside and pulls my pelvis to his, dragging his length up and down my wetness. He curses under his breath and watches where our flesh rubs together before hooking his arms around me and lifting me into the air. I fold my legs around him and sink my tongue into his mouth, swallowing his moan as I feel myself being carried.

Somewhere on the way to the bedroom, the friction becomes too much, and he suddenly pushes inside me, breathtaking pleasure bursting through me like a dam breaking. We both groan and collapse to the floor, and I register the jigsaw-covered dining table at the corner of my vision as he sinks all the way inside until our pelvises are pressed tightly together.

My face contorts as I gaze up at him. 'You feel too good,' I gasp.

He drops his face into my neck, humming a deep sound of pleasure before lifting his head back up. 'You want me to stop?' he teases.

I smack his ass, then pull him harder against me.

A groan wells up in his throat. '*Fuck*, I don't know what to do with you. I'm so hard.'

He braces his palms against the floor, giving me the perfect view to watch his face change and his muscles tighten as he drags himself out of me before pushing back inside. He bites down on his bottom lip and hisses, and my eyes droop at the pleasure flooding my core as he begins driving himself in and out of me with deeper, harder thrusts.

'I feel like your body was made to fit mine,' he rasps as he increases his pace, the euphoria overwhelming: too much and yet not enough.

'I just want to do this until I die,' I moan, digging my nails into his back. A husky laugh rumbles out of him as he smacks himself into me again and again, each thrust filling me with more pleasure than I've ever experienced.

He slows, and we hug tightly and gyrate together like we're rolling atop an ocean of ecstasy, unsure of the direction the next wave will take us. Zac's fingers knot in my hair and we moan into each other's mouths before he flips us both over until he's beneath me. He pulls me over his lap so I'm straddling him and guides me to slide up and down his full length.

'That's it, beautiful,' he encourages roughly, gripping my ass and using it to push me down harder onto him. He swears and pants and sucks his bottom lip as he gazes up at me. Watching someone I already love so much coming undone for me this way feels like glimpsing a dream.

There are so many things I want to do to him, but he's so hard in me, his brow is so clenched with desire, and he's making me feel so unbelievably good that my mind empties of everything. Within minutes, the ecstasy inside me swells in a sudden, upward surge, setting fire to every part of my body and spilling white-hot pleasure through me until I'm left shuddering.

'Oh god, feeling you come on me ... *fuck*.' Zac tightens his hold on my lower back. I have just enough energy left to meet his hard thrusts with rocks of my hips until pleasure splashes through his features and he collapses against me, moaning out a broken sound. *So freaking hot.*

His arms wrap me up in a tight squeeze as we pant against the floorboards, my mind already in overdrive.

Well, that escalated quickly.

'What the hell?' Zac says, swiping a hand over his backside. His fingers produce a little cardboard square that was glued to his ass. A puzzle piece. Our eyes meet, and we break into laughter.

Oh, my goodness.

I just had sex with Zac.

I just screwed my best friend.

And I really hope I haven't screwed everything else up too.

CHAPTER 31

Six years ago

ZAC: Hey, any news?

You have 1 missed call from Zac Jameson.

ZAC: How is it going there? Are you OK? Tried to ring you before my tutorial. Call anytime, I'm heading home to study until after lunch.

ME: Hi, sorry I missed your call. My grandma died this morning. 😞😞😞 I can't talk on the phone right now because I'm in the car with my parents and Mum's really upset.

ZAC: Oh, Jose . . . I'm so, so, so, so sorry. Are you OK? 🙁

ME: We knew it was coming, but it's still really hard. I'm glad I was here, though. Thanks for pushing me to come home.

ZAC: No need to thank me. I'm really sorry that I couldn't come back with you. 😰

ME: Don't worry, you've got uni and the big birthday. I called Tara yesterday. Did you give her my gift?

ZAC: Yeah, she loved it. How long do you think you'll be in Sydney?

ME: Until after the funeral next week, then I'll get the train back.

ZAC: OK. Let me know when. I'll find a car to borrow and meet you at the station.

ME: Thanks so much, but I have my bike there, remember? Hopefully no one's cut the chain and taken it. 😬

ZAC: Jose, that bike is a fucking death trap, and you couldn't pay someone to steal it.

ZAC: Oh my god, I can't believe I just said death trap. I am so fucking sorry. 😩

ME: Lol, you actually said it twice. 😂 But thanks for the laugh, I needed it. 💜

ZAC: Wish I could give you a huge hug, sunbeam.

ME: Me too 💚

ZAC: 💚

CHAPTER 32

Today

I wake up in Zac's arms, his fluffy quilt wrapped around us like a cocoon. My gaze swallows up every part of his serene face while he snoozes, a question ripping through me.

How do I feel this morning? Was this the biggest mistake ever made?

As I listen to the hum of his breathing, a throb of want flares in my chest, making the answer to that question undeniable.

But then my mind shifts from wondering what I think to worrying how Zac will feel about it. With a flash of fear, I lean forward and touch my lips to his, stealing a soft kiss in case it's the last one I ever get.

His eyes flutter open and blink hazily into mine before he reaches to cup the back of my neck and pull my lips harder into his. *Gah.*

All I taste are traces of whisky and the same sweetness I sampled last night. If I'd known how delicious Zac Jameson is—how *fantastic* he is at kissing—I would've done this years ago.

When we break apart, he sits up on one elbow and gazes down at me, a disbelieving smile edging his mouth. 'I feel like I have contraband in my room.'

I lace my fingers behind my head. 'Oh yeah? Josie Larsen's on the banned substances list, is she?'

'I don't know, is she?' He reaches beneath the quilt to run his warm palm up my thigh, the sigh drifting through my lips giving him permission to move higher.

'You know I've slept in this bed before,' I remind him. 'Many times.'

'Did you ever touch yourself in this bed?' he asks, gently guiding my legs apart. My eyes are already glazing over.

His smirk makes it clear he's not being serious, but I answer honestly. 'Yes. Thinking about you.'

Heat flares in his eyes as they search my face. 'You're lying,' he decides.

I shake my head. 'Not lying.'

'*Fuck*. When?' His brow dips with desire like he's imagining it.

My cheeks colour. 'The night of the house fire. After we woke up on the couch together and I went to bed. Afterwards, I tried to pretend I wasn't imagining you when I did it, but I totally was.'

'You mean the night I broke up with Meghan because I couldn't stop thinking about you?'

His eyes flicker across my face before I lean forward and catch his mouth with mine. A moan winds through him as my tongue brushes his, our fingers weaving tightly together when he shifts closer to kiss me deeper. His free hand clutches my jaw as our lips mould together, and a question steamrolls into my brain that I can't kick out.

I pull back to look into Zac's eyes. 'Have you ever touched yourself thinking about me? Actually, don't answer that. If you say no, I—'

'Yes,' he cuts in. 'Many times.'

That mental image makes me drop my forehead into his shoulder like I can't handle it. When I lift my face again, a soft smile is playing around Zac's lips.

'I want to ask you something,' he says, his fingertips tracing patterns over my skin. 'When did things change for you? When did you start thinking about me as something more than a friend?'

My gaze shifts to the wall behind him as I search for the answer. 'I'm not entirely sure. I know I felt something that night we made The Back-Up Plan agreement, but there were probably times before and after that, too, which I just refused to acknowledge. We were such good friends, and you always had one girlfriend or another. You were off-limits.' I decide not to single out Tara. 'But I guess things changed when I didn't see you for a long time. I think it allowed me to step far enough away to be able to come back and see you for what you really are to me.'

The happiness swimming in his eyes makes me want to slap myself out of my own giddy stupor. It's enough to make anyone sick.

'What time is it?' I ask, a familiar ache building between my legs as I glide my hand over the dips and swells of his chest.

He winces. 'Nooo, don't ask that question.'

'Why?' I twist to glance at the clock on the bedside table. 'Shit!"

Zac groans and buries his face in the pillow as I lurch off him and scramble out of bed.

'I am so late,' I say in a panic, scanning for something resembling underwear, but they must still be in the living room.

'God, don't stand there like that, looking good enough to eat, then tell me you have to go,' he says behind me.

I snatch up one of his T-shirts and shrug it over my head, making an exaggerated inhale of its scent.

'Sorry,' I say, biting away the yearning spurred by the sight of him half-naked and twisted up in sheets. 'But the Sydney bigwigs are getting close to deciding on Christina's newsreader replacement. I *cannot* afford to mess up this week.'

Something shifts in Zac's eyes before he glances down, and I realise I've probably said the wrong thing. Why did I need to mention my imminent return to Sydney?

I hunch forward to stamp my lips to his. 'I know. You and I have got some talking to do. We'll do that soon.'

Slight alarm sparks in his gaze as I draw back, wanting to kick myself for being so indelicate, but right now, I have to get going. I dig out some clean clothes from my stash before slipping into the shower. The steam is billowing around me when a sharp twinge of itchiness strikes my left underarm. My eyes flash open and my fingers reach to scratch the spot, a warning bell ringing in my ear.

You're still itchy under there. Something's not right.

As my breaths begin to quicken, I remind myself that the doctor said I was fine.

I am fine.

Everything is going to be OK.

Deep breath.

By the time I've made it out of the shower, I'm even more late. When I hurry into the kitchen, tucking my vintage mint-green blouse into white slacks, Zac's waiting with a thermos of coffee and toast in a brown paper bag. The adorableness of this settles the jittery feeling still bouncing around my chest.

'Aww, thanks, Dad,' I say, collecting them from his fingers.

A playful frown tightens his brow as he clasps the back of my neck. 'I am *not* your dad,' he says firmly. He then presses his mouth to mine, his kiss sucking all the strength from my legs before he lowers his lips to my neck. My fingers sink into the back of his hair as he swirls his tongue over the skin beneath my ear, and I beg him to stop before I lose my self-control. He pulls back and presses his lips to my forehead so I can leave, which I reassure him is the last thing I feel like doing.

'Yum,' I say, giving his jaw a needy squeeze and pressing several more kisses to his lips before I push out the door with an overplayed groan of frustration that makes him laugh.

Once I'm alone in the car, anxiety over the conversation that Zac and I obviously need to have claws its way into my bloodstream.

What on earth are we going to do?

Is this just a bit of fun for him—an itch he's always wanted to scratch—and once I return to Sydney, we go back to being distant friends? Is that what he wants?

Would he consider moving back? If I really let my mind go there, would *I* want that?

I'm nearly an hour late for work, so I sneak into the quiet newsroom, grateful to find most of the reporters have already left to cover stories. I dump my bag beside a free computer, clicking open the day's rundown.

'There you are!' Man-Bun-Colin booms from across the room, and I want to shrink into myself as he strides over to me.

'I'm *so* sorry, my car wouldn't start this morning,' I lie.

'Natasha's been looking for you. You better get into her office before she changes her mind.'

'About what?' My heart falls out of my chest at his *I know something you don't* stare, but when he smirks like the news is good, I jump up and stride towards Natasha Harrington's office as if lions are on my tail.

She's murmuring into the phone, so I hover outside until I hear her hang up.

'Get in here, Josie,' she calls out, and I scamper inside the plush haven of her office.

I sink into the chair opposite hers, wondering if she can tell that I stayed up late screwing my best friend on the kitchen floor. *Josie, stay on subject.*

Natasha threads her manicured fingers over her crisp shirt. 'How would you feel about presenting the evening news this week?'

My lips pop open.

'Yvette's been called down to Sydney to fill in temporarily for Christina Rice.'

A dart of fear strikes my chest. *It's too early for the baby. What's wrong with Christina?*

'Think you can handle it?' Natasha asks.

'Absolutely,' I reply in the calmest voice I can manage. 'I'd *love* to. Thank you.'

'Good. You start today. The producers will talk you through it. You'll need to write up the weather and be ready to record updates. Speak to hair and make-up about what time they want you in the chair.'

It takes a second for reality to sink in. *Oh my GOD.* A fireworks display erupts behind my sternum, spraying my insides with shimmering lights. *I'm going to read the evening news. Actual dreams are coming true!*

After thanking Natasha repeatedly, I return to the newsroom and exchange a grin with Colin. I have no idea why Natasha asked me to fill in instead of Meghan Mackay, but there's no way I'm bringing up Meghan's name. Lately, Meghan's been giving me nothing but icy side-eyes every time I pass by her workstation.

The moment I'm back at my desk, I pull out my phone and text Zac.

> **ME:** Guess who's going to be reading the news tonight and all this week? 😂😂😄😄

> **ZAC:** Are you joking with me right now?

> **ME:** No way, Jose (See what I did there?)

> **ZAC:** Ahhh, congratulations, beautiful. 😍 No one deserves this more than you. You're going to be amazing. My TV might explode from the cute and the sexy.

> **ME:** Thank you 😊 Hope I do OK, eeeeek. P.S. 'Cute and sexy' applies only to you.

> **ZAC:** No chance. My body's being pretty clear about that right now.

I let the image roll around my head for a moment of Zac being hard, overheating at the thought.

> **ME:** Stop. You're teasing me now.

> **ZAC:** I can't help how my body reacts when I think about you.
> But my hand just doesn't feel the same as yours.

My head drops forward as heat licks up my spine. I should be familiarising myself with the stories and scripts for tonight, but I can't tear my eyes away from my phone.

> **ME:** Seriously, Zac. I should be working on my most important week ever, and now all I can think about is you touching yourself.
> Don't be playing with me.

> **ZAC:** I'm not. And I can't help it. You make me too hard.
> p.s. I would very much like to play with you.

I hunch over the phone screen just in case anyone's walking past. What would Natasha Harrington say? She'd probably take my presenting shifts off me.

> **ME:** Gaaah. You need to stop.
> I'm putting my phone away now.

> **ZAC:** I need to be on my knees beneath your desk right now.
> Then maybe I'll stop

> **ME:** I literally just considered how I might be able to escape work for an hour.
> You're making me insane.
> Going now

> **ZAC:** Coming now
> While imagining doing something filthy with my tongue

Argh. I shove my phone into my bag, which is where it stays for all of thirty seconds until my mind shoots to the reason I'm reading the news in the first place. Christina answers my call right away.

'Are your ears burning?' she asks sunnily. 'I was just about to call you with news. I had dinner with Oliver Novak last night.'

I grin into the phone, happy to hear that nothing's wrong. 'As you do when you're Christina-freaking-Rice. Elon next week.'

She shushes me with a chuckle. 'He convinced me to take my maternity leave early so he can get someone new trained in the job. I'm officially a lady of leisure, and I have no idea what to do with myself.'

'That's awesome! You deserve to do a whole lot of nothing for a while.' I swallow a pinch of disappointment.

'That means Oliver has already chosen your replacement. Yvette Sinclair's been sent down there to cover you.'

'Wait, I didn't finish my story. I fed Oliver an entire bottle of wine while singing your praises. Because he hasn't seen you read before, it was my idea to bring Yvette down for one week, so you could read the news up there. Darling, I orchestrated the whole thing. Oliver is going to be watching you this week!'

'Oh my *god*!'

'I know!' Her smile practically shines through the phone. 'If you read as beautifully this week as I know you can, I think you can expect a call from Oliver.'

Excitement churns up my stomach. *This is it . . . my shot! If I don't screw this up, I could become Sydney's next prime-time newsreader.*

I thank her at least a thousand times before my mind returns to the same place it's been glued lately.

'You OK?' Christina asks as I stare at the half-written weather report in front of me. 'You've gone quiet.'

I suck in a jittery breath. 'Something kind of happened up here last night.'

'What something?'

My teeth clamp down on my bottom lip. 'I slept with Zac.'

She gasps. 'You *did*? My gosh, you baddie! How was it?'

I close my eyes, flashing back. 'It was . . . incredible.'

She squeals. 'Well, that's great! Isn't it?'

'If you take away the fact that he's already told me he'll never move back to Sydney. And you know I can't stay up here, especially if Oliver is considering me for that job.' I clutch my forehead.

'What about long distance?'

The question makes me slump. 'I don't know. Does that ever really work out for anyone? Plus, I feel like I'm getting ahead of myself with this conversation. It might have just been a bit of fun for him.' A sharp pain pierces my chest.

I catch sight of Natasha Harrington crossing the newsroom and quickly say goodbye, focusing my mind back on work.

After I write up the weather reports and spend an hour in the hair and make-up chair, I take a few deep breaths and head into the studio to pre-record updates. My earpiece connects me to the control room in Sydney where everything's managed remotely, including the robotic cameras. When the light above the centre camera flashes red, and the director in my ear cues me to go, I begin reading the words on the screen the way I was taught to at university: with energy, but not hyper, and with careful enunciation of each word, but in a way that sounds natural. I keep my expression serious but warm, and make sure I don't slip into a singsong speech pattern.

'Good job,' the director says in my ear, and a rush of air escapes my body. *I really can do this.*

My butt stays glued to the chair for most of the afternoon, the hot lights burning down on my hair and the make-up artist fussing over me. At one stage, Lola slips in to give me a congratulatory hug and a caramel hot chocolate. She jokes about wanting to pour a shot of whisky inside it for Dutch courage, and I tell her not to make promises she doesn't intend to keep. Robert Knight wanders in just after two and maintains a patient smile while I fumble my way through everything. I pick up on how he sorts his printed scripts in front of him and angles the monitor just so, taking mental notes.

By the time I've finished nibbling on a roast beef sandwich from the downstairs café on my dinner break, I'm as ready as I'll ever be.

With the director's countdown in my ear and lights pointing at me from all directions, I begin presenting the evening news. Robert and I smoothly switch between stories, and when I make a tiny stumble during an intro, a face fills my vision. Zac is gazing at me through the black barrel of the camera lens with a steady, you've-got-this smile. I recover and deliver the rest of the bulletin without a mistake, trying not to beat myself up over that one slip-up.

'You did good, my friend,' Robert says as he taps his scripts in a pile against the desk.

I thank him and exhale what feels like a lifetime of pent-up air.

I switch my phone back on as I head out of the studio, a series of pings lighting up my screen. Lola is insisting that a few of us go for drinks after work to celebrate, and even Man-Bun-Colin says he's in! Isabella's already made a booking at my favourite bar. I type back that I wouldn't miss it for the world.

Christina has texted a long string of firework emojis followed by a meme about kicking butt at work. I reply with a series of kiss faces before tapping on the message I want to read the most.

> **ZAC:** Shit-hot. Smoothest, most stunning newsreader ever.
> You've probably got events to attend and autographs to sign, but I'm cooking svio if you're hungry.

His next message is an image of the Icelandic dish with the cooked sheep's head, and I huff out a laugh. *Noooo . . . he didn't.*

I text him back that I already promised a drink with my colleagues in Honeysuckle to celebrate and ask if he can join us, but he's already started prep for the svio. *Gag.* Shaking my head with a grin, I let him know that I won't stay out too long and can't wait to see him. He replies with a blushing smile emoji, and my stomach flutters.

When I reach the newsroom, I find Natasha Harrington leaning against my desk with a glint in her eye.

'That was excellent,' she says. 'Lovely gravitas, but still warm and open. You did great, Josie.'

I smile so big that my cheeks threaten to explode off my face. 'Thank you.' After a moment, I add, 'Natasha, would you be interested in coming out for a drink tonight? A few of us are going to one of the bars in Honeysuckle.'

Her face tilts with consideration. 'Why not,' she decides. 'I could use a vesper.'

I assume she's talking about some sort of chic Natasha Harrington drink rather than a mini motorcycle, so I smile and tell her that we plan to leave in a few minutes.

Best day of all time.

I arrive home just after eight, my nerves back at their peak over the talk I still need to have with Zac. He glances over at me from the stove.

'There's the superstar,' he says, tossing a tea towel over his shoulder and striding towards me, his olive eyes sparkling. He hooks an arm around my waist and drags me against him, and I collapse into his chest, still thrown by how my best friend can make me feel. I lift my face and our lips collide, his mouthwatering kiss burning through me as my hands clasp the back of his neck.

Talking, Josie, talking!

I break free and step back, taking a moment to appreciate how good he looks in his well-loved jeans and white 'Sold Out' T-shirt.

'How are the lamb's brains coming along?' I ask, and he breathes a laugh.

'Sheep's head. Come and see. I'm pretty sure my butcher thinks I'm on LSD.' He laces his fingers through mine, and I trail him into the kitchen like a doe-eyed schoolgirl.

I brave a peek inside the gigantic pot bubbling on the stove. Zac drags a fork through the steaming water, and the tip of a sheep's skull surfaces.

My hand flies to my mouth. 'You're not really going to make me eat that, are you?'

'But I worked so hard on it,' he says with a pout.

I pinch his T-shirt in my fingers and tug him back towards me, landing another kiss on his lips that makes me think there's only one thing I want to be consuming tonight.

How's the talking going, Josie?

He cups my face in his hands, looking like I've melted him as much as he has me. 'I'm kidding. I got it at the fancy pet shop in town where I buy Trouble her high-maintenance treats, and I've been waiting to get you back for the mushroom burger.' He laughs. 'I've got steaks marinating if you're hungry, or your favourite ice cream is in the freezer.'

'Mmm, ice cream for dinner, *please*,' I beg, pulling his mouth to mine for a few more delicious kisses. He exhales a sound like he's also struggling to stop before bending to fish out two ice cream bowls.

'You really were so amazing tonight,' he says.

I kick out of my shoes and turn around to pour myself a glass of water. 'Thank you. It's kind of embarrassing thinking about you watching me.'

'What do you mean?' he replies, tinkering behind me. 'You'd better get used to it. Want to bet they offer you a presenting job up here? You're way more compelling to watch than that Yvette Sinclair woman.'

My fingers freeze around the water glass. Does Zac not know that I'm still one hundred per cent set on moving back to Sydney soon?

'That's sweet of you to say,' is all I manage before tossing back the rest of my water.

Zac's chest suddenly presses against my back, his breath warming the side of my face.

'Close your eyes,' he says before the cold tip of a spoon brushes my lips. Just as my mouth opens and a whisper-soft, freezing sensation swipes over my tongue, he says, 'I put the lamb's brain into the freezer—'

I gag and spit, and Zac's soft curls fall into my shoulder as he laughs. 'Just kidding, it's ice cream,' he says while my tastebuds register the heavenly flavour of salted caramel. With a murmur of appreciation, I go to take the spoon, but he swings it out of my reach before pinning me against the counter with his hips. *Oh boy.*

I turn my head and let him feed me another rounded spoon of ice cream, moaning at the icy sweetness.

'I've been waiting all day for you to make that sound,' Zac says needily.

I want to turn around and face him, but he digs his pelvis harder into my backside, trapping me there while the length of him thickens.

Need. To. Talk.

He pushes another spoonful of ice cream into my mouth, and I let out a groan from deeper inside my throat, giving Zac what he wants. He sinks the spoon into the bowl again, but this time, after he slips the ice cream past my lips, I clutch the back of his neck and drag his mouth to mine.

Creamy ice cream bleeds between our mouths, but it's his tongue I'm chasing, and our lips twist in a messy kiss that's burning hot and ice-cold. He grips my jaw and holds me in place, sucking all the ice cream off my tongue until my eyes practically roll into the back of my head.

'*Fuck*, Josie,' he says, grinding his swollen length up and down my ass as I push back against him.

'I want you,' I grit out, an ache throbbing between my legs.

'How do you want me?' he asks. 'Would you rather . . .' I hum a laugh at the reference of the game we used to play on the train. 'Would you rather I carry you to the bed and make love to you gently and tenderly?' he says near my ear. 'Because I could totally do that with you, *easily*.' He then presses himself so firmly against me that I gasp. 'Or would you rather I fuck you inside out right here on this counter?'

Ohmygod. I reach back and grip his hard-on through his jeans, rubbing my hand up and down him as he groans into my neck. Without turning around, I unzip his fly and sink my hand inside his boxer briefs, gripping and stroking him as he palms my breasts through my shirt. When he pushes my chest down until it's pressed against the counter, my hand slips out of his boxers, and I breathe a moan as he rubs his thickness up and down me a few times through our clothes. *God, will we ever make it to the bedroom?*

Zac wraps my hair around his fist and steers me to turn around, driving my back against the countertop as he crushes his lips to mine. I shove down his jeans and boxers, and he kicks out of them while grabbing his shirt at the back of the neck and hooking it over his head.

He tugs down my slacks and wrenches my panties to the side, groaning as he takes a long look at me. He then buries two fingers inside me to the base of his knuckles, the burn in his eyes nearly sending me over the edge.

'Fuck, you're so wet for me,' he says roughly. 'I need to take care of this.'

Just as my knees turn weak from the weight of the ecstasy, he lifts me onto the counter, pushes my thighs apart, and sinks his arousal deep inside my core.

I writhe and moan as he takes me hard and deep, the sound of wet smacks filling the room as I lose all sense of where and who I am. There's only the all-consuming bliss as Zac drives himself into me with such force that I know I'll be sore tomorrow. I cup my hand over his and stare up at him—a messy-haired, glassy-eyed, sexy-as-hell version of my best friend. Then, he slows his pace and leans down to bring our mouths together.

'How did I get so lucky?' he asks against my lips.

Hot liquid swirls through my chest, and for a few endless breaths, we stare into each other's eyes and bathe in the intense connection buzzing between us. I lift my shoulders to taste his mouth again and he unbuttons my shirt and hauls down my bra cups, murmuring a needful sound before running his tongue over my nipples.

'You're so fucking perfect,' he rasps against my skin, picking up the pace of his thrusts until I cry out. 'I want you to come on me. Come on my cock, Josie.'

His words push the pleasure button, and my fingers clench around his biceps as he pounds into me, tightening the coil of tension until it snaps free, tipping me into an abyss of mind-bending ecstasy. He thrusts into me through my climax and then erupts inside me, the pleasure washing over his face stealing all my attention.

As we catch our breath, he strokes his fingers affectionally over my left breast and a line appears in his brow.

'What is it?' I ask throatily, but his fingers drop and he silences me with another drugging kiss.

I lay panting and smiling until I catch him eyeing off my left breast as he tugs his T-shirt back over his head.

'What do you keep looking at?' I ask, glancing down.

He tugs up his jeans, the look on his face sending a bolt of alarm through my chest.

'Zac, speak.'

He looks at me for half a second before stepping forward and gently cupping my breast in his hand, his brow wrinkling. 'I just felt something that I didn't notice last night.'

'Felt what?' My hand scrambles to join his as I grope around the soft mound.

'Here.' Zac guides my fingers to a small but firm lump lodged inside my breast tissue.

My stomach pitches and a rasp of shock flees my throat.

'What is that?' I say, madly feeling around the lump.

'I don't know, but you should probably get it looked at.'

For a moment, I can't feel anything at all in my body. Then, my heart begins ramming my chest wall. My skin catches fire, and I feel like I could burn through my clothes.

'How did you not notice that last night?' I gasp.

'I was . . . distracted.'

'*No*,' I mutter in a voice thick with horror as I slip off the counter and turn away from him, my breaths becoming shallow and my mouth drying up. 'See?' I cry hoarsely. 'Everyone keeps telling me I'm fine, but I'm *not*. I *knew* something was still wrong!'

'It's OK,' Zac says softly from somewhere, his voice fading as my vision narrows to an echoey funnel.

This isn't happening. They said I was fine. This isn't happening!

'Sweetheart, it's OK,' Zac repeats in my ear, wrapping his arms around me from behind. 'It's probably just a cyst. They're common.'

But the voice inside my head rings louder.

Your instincts were right. You're dying. All that hope and happiness you've had in your heart for the past few days? It's gone. And it's never coming back.

'Breathe with me,' Zac says against my ear, his inhales and exhales matching the steady thud of his heartbeat against my back. 'Follow my breaths. I'm here.'

I try to, but my chest is too tight and my head too heavy with the blood rushing to it. My vision flashes white, and a sudden wave of intense nausea crests over me, buckling my knees and turning my skin clammy before the world around me is sucked underwater.

CHAPTER 33

Six months ago

The studio director's voice in my earpiece cues me to stand by. I tell the visibly nervous doctor fidgeting beside me that we're about to go live before relaxing my face into a smile and staring down the black circle of the camera lens.

In the tiny speaker pushed inside my ear, Channel One's breakfast show anchor, Juanita Caro, says, 'As we continue our coverage of Pink Ribbon Day this morning, we've got our reporter Josie Larsen attending a beautiful fundraising breakfast at Centennial Park.'

Shit, someone screwed up. The breakfast cross isn't until after the eight o'clock news!

The presenter pauses, which means I'm on, regardless of the error. 'Good morning, Juanita,' I say to the camera. 'That's right, I am here at this beautiful location to celebrate breast cancer awareness month with some wonderful women, but before we get to the breakfast, I'm honoured to have here with me Doctor Mary Glover—a senior breast surgeon from the New South Wales Breast Clinic.' The camera pans to Doctor Glover, who gulps through a terrified smile.

'Doctor Glover, at what age should women begin screening for breast cancer?'

'Thank you for having me on, Josie,' the doctor replies shakily. 'The recommended age to begin screening depends on several factors, but what is true in *all* cases is that early detection saves lives. But in general terms, women over fifty should be screened at least once a year, but women over forty are also entitled to one free breast screening every two years.'

The knot that's embedded in my gut loosens a little at the specialist's recommendation.

Phew. I'm not even thirty yet.

I flick away a fly and move to the next question that I memorised on the drive here. 'Many of us know to do our own breast checks at home and go to the doctor right away if we find a lump. But what other, perhaps lesser-known symptoms should we be aware of?'

Doctor Glover nods through my words, some of her initial jitters easing out of her expression. 'Great question, Josie. There are a number of symptoms that can be indicative of breast cancer when there isn't a lump, and I'll run you through some of them. Any changes to your nipple, including any discharge, should always be mentioned to your doctor. Another concern would be if an area of skin on your breast begins to thicken or dimple, like the skin of an orange. Unexplained breast pain or tenderness is also worth talking to your doctor about. A swollen lymph node in your armpit can be a sign of breast cancer spreading to the lymphatic system, and believe it or not, even a cough that won't go away can mean that breast cancer has advanced—'

My entire body stiffens, and all my focus on Doctor Glover drains out of me before fixating on the dry cough that I've been battling for the past few months.

Oh my god.

What if I have breast cancer that's already spreading through my system?

The doctor's deep-set eyes and bobbed black hair distort in my view, then disappear inside a dark funnel, her voice thinning to a faint echo beneath the rush of blood to my ears. My chest rises and falls with sharp, shallow breaths that I can't seem to catch. I think I hear my name, but the accelerating pounding of my heart drowns out the sound. I clutch my chest and dig my palm into the point of pressure.

What is happening to me?? Is this a heart attack?

Feet shuffle before me, and a delicate hand lightly curls around my other wrist. I reach out to take the doctor's hand, but my palm is so sweaty that my fingers slip off hers.

'Josie!' a jarring voice snaps in my left ear, like there's a man crouched inside my eardrum. 'What is going on— you're still live!'

I can't breathe.

I can't breathe.

I can't breathe.

CHAPTER 34

Today

I don't know how Zac has this pull with Doctor Ellison, but at ten minutes past nine the following morning, we're sitting in her waiting room and his steady hand is cupping my bouncing knee.

From the moment I passed out in his arms last night, he's been by my side like the role model of a best friend, a boyfriend—I don't know what. A lump in my breast is my worst-case scenario, and my anxiety's wiping the floor with me . . . turning me into a petrified, furious, hollow shell of my former self.

The doctor calls my name, and Zac turns to me with a question in his eyes.

'I'll be OK,' I say numbly, giving his fingers a quick squeeze.

As I walk away from him and into Doctor Ellison's office, a bleak feeling sinks over me. I missed a chance to treat Zac like we're more than friends and invite him to remain by my side, but this is my fucking misery in life. He's had so much to deal with in his past; I don't want to bring him in on this too.

Doctor Ellison's already handing me a tissue when I slump into the chair. I can't believe I'm back in this stark room so soon.

'I found a lump in my breast,' I blurt before she even speaks.

The faintest line finds her brow. 'OK. Come and lie down, and I'll have a feel of it.'

I drag my lead-filled legs over to the narrow bed and stretch out on the crumpled paper covering it. Doctor Ellison snaps on a pair of gloves while I lift my shirt, my heart bunching in my throat. I scour her face while she feels around both breasts and gently presses the lump, but her expression gives nothing away. I climb off the bed and return to the chair, swallowing bile.

'OK.' She takes a moment, collecting her words. 'The lump feels small, and I'm not marking this as urgent, but it would be silly of me not to recommend an ultrasound to have a look at what's going on. I'm sorry, Josie; I know this isn't what you wanted to hear.'

I silently nod, the truth thundering through my head as I bite back tears. *This is really it. No more false alarms. This is the beginning of the end—right here, right now.*

An awful tapping noise takes over the room as the doctor types out my referral, while my thoughts shift to desperate.

What if I just tell her I don't want the test and go home? What if I move down to Sydney today, where no one knows anything about this? What if I pretend none of this ever happened and hope the lump goes away?

'I had an enlarged lymph node in my armpit about a year ago,' I remind her in a small voice. 'But it went away on its own. Could this be the same thing?'

Doctor Ellison passes me a small, sympathetic smile as she shakes her head. 'I'm afraid not.'

I lumber back into the waiting room, approaching Zac from behind. He's sitting beside a head of thick dark hair that's instantly familiar.

'Ross?' I say faintly as I round on them. 'What are you doing here?'

They both lurch to their feet. Zac's gaze sweeps over my face while his cousin kisses my cheek. 'I'm getting the flu vaccine and spotted my boy over here,' he says, giving Zac a playful nudge.

'Ross was the one who told me about Doctor Ellison,' Zac explains.

'Best doc in the city,' Ross adds, smiling.

For that few-seconds-long interaction, the lump in my breast leaves my mind, but the feeling of dread crashes back into my stomach when I catch Zac eyeing off the referral in my hand. His gaze flickers to mine, and he slides his arm around my waist, pulling me close.

Ross's brows slide up before a look of realisation washes over his face. Zac brushes our foreheads together for a split second that I know Ross doesn't miss. Ross's chocolate eyes snag on my own and hold there for a moment before a nurse calls out his name.

On the windy street outside the surgery, I fill Zac in on what happened with the doctor. He hugs me tightly, then steps back while gripping my waist, his body lowered so he can look me right in the eyes. I fight tears as he says sweet things to comfort me, but the look on his face only makes me feel worse, like he already thinks I'm going to die.

He's scheduled to stay with his parents overnight in Port Stephens to celebrate his birthday, and he offers again to pull out, but I tell him it's OK. He hasn't seen his folks in ages, and there's a painful pressure building behind my eyes that needs to be let out. Once I'm done at work, I need to go home and sob uncontrollably, and I don't want Zac to see me like that. As big-hearted as he is, I'm not sure he'll understand why I'm so horror-stricken over a tiny lump that might turn out to be nothing. He has no idea how truly screwed up my head is, how I'm already silently saying my goodbyes.

Through heavy breaths, I thank him over and over for being so supportive, and we kiss softly and part ways so that I can go to work.

Man-Bun-Colin's away today, and his replacement is an older woman I barely know, her shrill voice and direct tone doing nothing to relieve the tornado in my chest. She keeps changing the rundown, and I give up trying to learn it in advance, turning my focus to writing up the weather reports. Reading the news tonight is almost too much for my anxiety to take, but I have no other choice, because apparently one week of doing my dream job without this health shit hanging over my head was too much to ask. It doesn't help that Lola is about to be off work for two weeks; she's heading to Hawaii with her boyfriend. Not that I'm close enough to Lola to want to open up to her about this anyway. It's hard enough talking to Zac or Christina about it. *Maybe if I say I'm OK enough times, it'll become true.*

I'm in the make-up chair with half my hair in rollers when my phone lights up with a text from Ross.

> **ROSS:** Hey, lovely girl. So funny to run into you guys this morning. I'm just wondering if you have time for a coffee or a drink after work today?
> No worries if not, I just wanted to chat about something.
> P.S. Forgot to mention earlier that I caught you on TV last night – you were brilliant!

My brow pinches as I reread the message and compose a reply. I've known Ross through Zac for over a decade, but I don't think he's ever asked me to meet up one-on-one. I'm already in half a panic about what he wants to talk about, but we make a plan to meet at a late-night café in Honeysuckle.

The first part of the news bulletin goes off without a hitch, but during the third commercial break, the director barks into my earpiece.

'The news wires are reporting that Alexa Hamilton just died. Hunter is typing something up now, so your autocue's going to refresh. Josie, you read, and stand by for a possible phoner if we can get someone on the line.'

My heart jumps into my throat as I scramble to refresh the screen, skimming the new text before the director begins a countdown out of the commercial break. *Shit. I haven't had enough time to pre-read the story.* I glance at Robert Knight, but he's calmly scrolling through his laptop, off the hook for this one.

The camera light clicks to red, and the director cues me to go. I begin reading the words on my screen.

'And now to some breaking news. Much-loved Australian actress Alexa Hamilton has died following a short battle with breast cancer.' My breath catches in my lungs, making me stumble over the next sentence. 'The thirty-one-year-old passed away at St Vincent's Hospital in Sydney shortly after noon today with her family by her side. Hamilton was diagnosed with breast cancer in August last year, and her family has asked for privacy at this time.'

I break out in a cold sweat.

Stay calm, stay calm.

Breathe in, breathe out.

'Two seconds, Josie,' the director says, and the script flashes with another reset. I have no idea what's happening, but I keep reading.

'Joining me now on the line is iconic Australian actor Jeremy Lavigne, who worked with Alexa Hamilton on her last film, *The Beginning of Everything*. Jeremy, the entire nation is feeling this loss today. How will you remember Alexa?'

The studio around me darkens until all that's left is that piercing camera light and Jeremy Lavigne's husky voice in my ear as he talks about a thirty-one-year-old woman who will never open her eyes again, never feel her sweetheart's arms around her, never step onto any more film sets, never hold her first-born child.

Just like Aunt Susie.

Just like Tara.

'Josie!' the director hisses in my ear. I gape into the black barrel of the camera lens, totally lost as to where I am.

The red light switches off, and the camera facing Robert Knight flicks to red as he begins speaking, thanking Jeremy Lavigne for his time before reading the intro to the next news story.

'What the hell, Josie?' the director's voice crackles in my ear in an angry tone. My heart pounds in a frantic rhythm.

Oh my god. I just went dead on air. Again!

I draw in a shaky breath and fix my attention on the next story, presenting it smoothly before closing out the bulletin with only a couple more slips. Still, Robert Knight shoots me a look like I embarrassed him. When I leave the studio with a dead weight in my chest, I find Natasha Harrington waiting for me with sharp disapproval scrawled over her face.

'I'm sorry,' I say in a rush. 'I zoned out for just a moment, but that is *never* going to happen again.'

'It was a lot longer than a moment, and zoning out is not acceptable, Josie. It makes us all look like idiots who don't know what we're doing.'

I nod and chew my bottom lip, ready to be sick all over the floor. I consider telling her about the lump in my breast—how it triggered my reaction to Alexa's passing—but the words die in my throat. Not only is there no excuse for spacing out, but the last thing I want is for Natasha to bench me because she thinks I'm going to end up like Alexa Hamilton.

Her brow is a mess of lines. 'I chose to put you on air over Meghan and Genevieve because I thought you had something really special.' My chest clamps up at her use of the past tense. 'But you're clearly not ready. So, I'm pulling you off presenting duties, and you can go back to reporting tomorrow.'

I throw a hand out. 'Please, no—I promise you it's not going to happen again. I can do this. I can be good at this.'

The begging only makes me sound pathetic, and Natasha steps back like she doesn't want to be near me. 'See you on Monday, Josie.'

The thought of being put back on reporting rounds while Meghan points her smug smile at me on her way into the presenters' studio makes me want to scream.

With my eyes stinging, I grab my bag and escape downstairs to where no one can see me spilling tears. I pick up my phone to cancel on Ross, but he's already texted me.

ROSS: I'm already here in case you finish early. Sitting inside. x

Shit. I can still pull out, but I wipe my eyes and steady my pulse with a few deep breaths. What if Ross has some really big news to tell me? What if it's about Zac?

Fighting off flashes of Natasha's displeased face, I drag myself up the street towards the harbourside café, spotting Ross waiting at a corner table. Nerves ripple through my stomach as I approach him. I can't take another drop of bad news today.

'Hey, you,' he says, getting up to give me a one-armed hug. When he pulls back, he frowns at my red-rimmed eyes. 'Are you OK?'

I flop into the chair. 'Work dramas. Honestly, I'd rather not talk about it.'

He nods, and I order a caramel hot chocolate and a Caesar salad, even though my appetite has vanished. Ross insists on paying, which makes my curiosity alarm ring louder.

After a couple of minutes of painful small talk, I cut to the chase. 'You said there was something you want to talk about?'

The atmosphere shifts as Ross picks at the edge of the menu, his gaze falling there. 'Yeah, so, this morning, when I ran into you and Zac, I couldn't help but notice that something has . . . changed?'

The back of my neck heats up while Ross continues quickly.

'It's not my business, and believe me, I know how out of line I am here. But I also know you so well that I feel like I can say this to you. I *need* to say this to you.'

'Say what?' My gut draws tight.

Ross's face empties of colour. 'I don't know how much Zac's told you about the last couple of years, but he hasn't been himself, Jose. I know he seems OK now, and he puts on a really brave face, but he's been to *hell* and back, believe me. The accident with Tara screwed him up big time. Worse than you can even imagine. Worse than he's probably told you about, because I know how he is with you. He always wants you to see the best side of him. But at one point, after he moved up here, I thought . . . I thought I was going to lose him.' Ross's voice splinters, and the sunny-faced guy I know fades away as tears coat his eyes.

I reach out and clutch the back of his hand, my heart drumming in my chest.

He gulps back water. 'Fuck me, sorry. I didn't realise how much I'd been holding in about this.' After a moment, his voice thickens again. 'Zac never said he wanted to hurt himself or anything, but I've never seen him like that. It was as if he'd died inside. He was just going through the motions of life, but it was so obvious he didn't want to be here. And I'm sure a lot of that was because of his guilt over the accident.'

My heart wrenches up. 'He thought it should've been him who was driving. He told me.'

Ross's fingers close around my hand. 'What else did he tell you?'

'He told me that Tara broke off the engagement just before the accident,' I add with a tremble.

His eyes search mine. 'And did he tell you the reason for that?'

My throat bobs as I nod.

A sad smile tugs at Ross's cheeks. 'I'm honestly happy for you guys. I feel like this has been a really long time coming. For Zac, at least. But there's one thing I need to say, even though it's going to make me feel like a total asshole. After everything I've seen Zac go through in the past couple of years, I feel like I *have* to say this. He's more than family to me.'

'Please just say it,' I cut in tightly.

Ross lets go of my hand and releases a long breath. 'You need to be sure, Josie. You need to be *really* fucking sure.'

My brows shoot up. 'What?'

He presses his lips together. 'He can't lose someone else. Especially not you. And I know it's not my business, so you do whatever you want, honestly. But if I don't say something, I'm worried I'll regret it. Because this isn't two years ago when Zac was that happy, carefree guy you went to uni with. He's been through something life-changing, which you're also directly tangled up in. And it's only been in the last few months that I've seen him come back into himself, picking up surfing, going to the gym, adopting a dog—even being able to return to his normal job is a huge sign that he's in a much better place. So, all I want to say is, if this is just a temporary thing for you, it won't be for him. I'm sure of that. And I don't think that guy can take any more heartache. I also don't know if you realise quite how much you mean to him.'

My brow creases as I sit and stare at Ross, unsure what to say or how to feel about the fact that he obviously doesn't trust me with Zac's heart.

'I have no intention of hurting Zac,' I say, but my head's already flying through possible scenarios.

'What about your plans to move back to Sydney?' he asks gently.

'Jesus, Ross, you're getting a bit ahead of things, aren't you? Plus, this is really a conversation I should be having with Zac.'

'I know.' He leans back so the waitress can deposit our drinks onto the table. Ross empties a sugar packet into his coffee, fixing his gaze on it. '*Fuck*, I probably shouldn't have said anything. I've majorly overstepped. I can be like that. I'm sorry.'

'It's OK,' I mumble through the burn in my throat. 'Your heart's in the right place.'

He brings his coffee to his lips, staring at me. When he eventually speaks, the affection in his tone catches me by surprise. 'You're an angel. You never hold a grudge against anyone, do you?'

I lift a shoulder. 'I don't think so. I don't know.' I certainly don't feel like much of an angel—especially right now.

Ross thankfully changes the subject to a lighter topic that has nothing to do with Zac, but our conversation has opened up a cavern in the pit of my stomach.

Ross's warning whirls in my mind all the way home.

'He can't lose someone else. Especially not you.'

'You need to be sure, Josie. You need to be really fucking sure.'

With Zac away for the night, I'm left to curl up under his quilt with nothing but my warped thoughts for company. I fight off a sick feeling that I shouldn't even be here—in his room, in his bed. We were supposed to think things through before making this leap. That plan lasted less than an hour because I threw myself at him like a wild animal. *Why am I always so freaking impulsive?*

And as intrusive as Ross's words were, I can't deny their truth. Zac isn't the laid-back guy I went to high school with. Not anymore. He's emotionally scarred for life . . . a survivor of the worst kind of trauma. And I'm not some girl he picked up on the beach like Meghan Mackay.

I'm the girl he's called his best friend for fourteen years. Someone who's supposed to be there for him through thick and thin. A one-person support system that never wavers. Someone he can completely trust his heart with.

I roll onto my side, clutching the pillow like it might relieve some of the ache growing in my chest.

I can't stay in Newcastle forever. Sydney is where my life is, all my plans. But when my fingers trace over the lump in my breast and my face crumples in the dark, I know that moving to Sydney isn't really the biggest issue.

I might actually have breast cancer—a disease that's already snatched away two women in my family.

What on earth would I do if I was diagnosed with an illness that became terminal, and Zac had to watch someone else he loves die? *My god, it's unthinkable.*

The hole in my stomach expands as I lie in the dark and attempt to make bargain after bargain with fate.

If I could just get rid of this lump, Zac and I could talk about Sydney and see what happens, like a normal couple.

If I could just go back to that wedding and resist the urge to kiss him, putting our friendship before everything else, then at least if I do have cancer, there's still some safe emotional distance there.

If I could just be a normal, healthy person instead of an anxious bundle of misery who can't even do a live interview on air without screwing up, then maybe I could be with Zac without worrying about destroying him.

If I could.

If I could.

I frantically feel my breast again, the firm lump rolling against my fingers like a physical barrier sitting between me and everything I want. My jaw clamps up with anger, and I twist to bury my face in the pillow and scream at the top of my lungs.

Then, I shudder silent sobs into the sheets belonging to the man I couldn't ever imagine hurting and cry until my tears run out.

CHAPTER 35

Four years ago

'Their faces are too cute,' Tara coos, one of her arms draped around my shoulder as we face the new sloth exhibit at Sydney's Taronga Zoo.

'Are you kidding? They're creepy as fuck,' Zac comments on Tara's other side. I instantly turn to them and impersonate the sloth, curving my closed lips into a tight, dead-eyed smile. Tara chuckles, but I get a bigger laugh from Zac.

'By the way, I'm pretty sure they're not actually smiling,' I say. 'That's just the way their faces look. They're quite unfriendly and hate being touched. They can also turn their heads almost all the way around.'

Zac grimaces at the coarse-haired mammal hanging from a tree by its king-size claws.

'How do you know so much about sloths?' Tara asks me, turning to rest her back against Zac's chest. He slides his arms around her waist and drifts his nose over her sheen of ebony hair. I don't blame him; Tara always looks and smells like she just wrapped up a photo shoot for a hair commercial.

'I did a story on them for our web channel's mis-understood animals series,' I explain.

'Sounds riveting,' Zac replies, smiling coyly as he rests his chin on Tara's shoulder. 'How many sloth action shots did you get?'

I make a face at him. 'They're amazing animals. Their species dates back to prehistoric times. And did you know it's the female who decides when it's time for sex? When she's feeling randy, she does this really loud scream, and the males hear it and run towards it.'

Zac snort-laughs. 'But by the time they arrive, she's died of old age. Or at least, she's definitely not in the mood anymore.'

Tara elbows him. 'They should do a doco series about all the ways different animals have sex,' she says to me. 'You should pitch that to your boss.'

'Ooh, I'd watch that,' Zac chimes in racy tone.

I shoot him a brow-raised look of *ew* while Tara skates a hand up the back of his neck and tilts her face around, her lips seeking his.

Feeling like I'm already watching a mating process, I turn to give the lovebirds a moment of privacy and amble over to the wooden platform leading out of the exhibit.

I hear Zac call out, 'So why are sloths so damn slow, David Attenborough? Are they all high as kites like koalas?'

'There's no way a science nerd like you believes that about koalas,' I reply over my shoulder as he and Tara catch up to me. 'And sloths just have an extremely slow metabolism. They only go to the toilet once a week.' Zac and Tara burst out laughing. 'Actually, the "poo dance" was what made them my favourite animal,' I add. 'They do this cute twerking move at the base of a tree before they poo.'

The platform reaches a crossroads sign leading to different exhibits. But instead of studying the sign, Zac's eyes make a quick slide down and up my body. 'Go on then, sunbeam. Show us your best twerking impersonation.'

My gaze darts to Tara, whose expression pinches a touch when she glances up at Zac.

Zachary—no. You can't ask a woman to jiggle her butt in front of your girlfriend, even if it's me.

'Let's not scare the sloths,' I say with a scoff. 'Or trigger any sudden bowel movements.'

My arm links through Tara's. 'Come on, babe; we've seen my slothies. Let's go find you some elephants.' Her lips split into a grin as I tug her forward.

When I glance back at Zac, I find him smiling at Tara's back. But then his soft gaze cuts to mine, and I quickly turn away.

CHAPTER 36

Today

I wake at the buttcrack of dawn to Trouble scratching at the front door to be let out. Before I've even lifted my head, the thought tsunami crashes into me.

'You're clearly not ready, so I'm pulling you off presenting duties.'

'It would be silly of me not to recommend an ultrasound.'

'I don't think that guy can take any more heartache.'

Too wired to fall back asleep, I throw on a coat and take Trouble for a stroll around the block before defrosting on the couch with a mug of coffee.

I've got a dentist appointment this morning, but when Zac and I were texting last night, he said he'd be home before breakfast. My heart bunches up in anticipation of seeing him, my head still on a merry-go-round over what to do about The Zac Situation. Calling the whole thing off feels over the top—and is the opposite of what I want—but we do need to talk about where this is going. Whatever happens, I have to make sure that I don't flip his settled life up here upside down.

Dark-roasted coffee rolls over my tongue as I pick up my phone, finding a message from Lola.

> **LOLA:** Oh my god, I'm at the airport and just saw the article!
> I'm so, so sorry. I hope you're OK. I can't believe I'm going away today! What shit timing. 😖
> I'll text you from Hawaii, OK? I promise it'll blow over. 💬

What'll blow over? What article? My gut tightens as I open my social media feed to see if there are any more messages or clues there, finding myself tagged in a video by a gossipy news account. *OK, that's weird.* I play the video, nearly spitting out my coffee.

It's a clip of me gazing at the camera like a deer in headlights, the accompanying headline reading: '"Josie, We Are Live!": Excruciating On-Air Gaffe Goes Viral'.

'Oh my god, it's got eight thousand bloody views!' I cry to the empty air. Any hope that Oliver Novak might have missed my blunder disintegrates as I scroll through the comments, braving a read of the first four before hurriedly swiping out of the story.

My fingers sink into my hair as I stare open-mouthed into space. *I'm viral. I'm viral for all the wrong reasons. I'm a laughing-stock!*

I need to peel my mind off the look that will be on Natasha Harrington's face when she sees this by busying my mind and hands, so I scurry into the kitchen and fling open the fridge, scanning the contents. For months, I've wanted to repay Zac for the countless meals he's made for me, and breakfast feels like a safer bet than dinner. I google 'easy international breakfast dishes' until I hit one that matches our pantry ingredients.

My fingers shake as I move about the kitchen, frenetically frying chopped onion, garlic and capsicum before tossing in a diced tomato. I crack eggs over the top, and they're simmering away when my self-control plummets and I check the gaffe video. It's reached nine thousand views, and I clench away the urge to toss the phone at the wall.

My culinary effort goes surprisingly well under the circumstances, and when Zac steps through the door, two bowls of pretty-damn-edible-looking shakshouka are staring up at me.

'Perfect timing,' I say to him, working hard to sound light.

'What's going on?' He heads into the kitchen with a curious smile, but instead of inspecting the bowls, he comes straight to me. He cups the back of my neck and pulls my lips to his, an urge to deepen the kiss firing a heated dart through me. But I shuffle back a step, knowing that if I take a piece of him now, I'll want more, and there's too much I want to say first.

A trace of alarm flickers in his eyes before he peers closer at the steaming bowls. 'What are you making? Is this shakshouka?'

I manage a small smile, impressed. 'Bullseye. I decided it was time to cook for you for a change. I make no guarantees about the taste.'

His eyes lift back to mine, and a rush of longing fills my chest. I'm back in dangerous I-wanna-kiss-him-so-bad territory, so I hand him a fork and pull out a bar stool. 'Eat.'

Zac settles beside me, biting into the eggs. 'Holy shit, this is good. Better burn my chef's apron.'

My laugh comes out strained. 'On a cold day in hell.'

We chat about his parents for a bit before his cheeks tint pink. 'I actually have some news. I got a phone call when I was up there. I'm going to be the next critical care paramedic for the Hunter region.'

'Oh my gosh! Are you serious?' I leap up and wrap my arms around his back, intending only to squeeze my congratulations into him, but the press of his firm chest against mine and the divine smell of his hair make me hold on tighter. My lips turn into his neck before I regain my resolve and pull away.

'That's bloody brilliant, Zac,' I say, sitting back down. 'You're going to nail it.'

He blushes. 'Thank you. I'm fucking nervous, but whatever. I'll figure it out. I'm just so relieved that I finally feel strong enough to be able to do a job like that. Talk about a milestone.'

'I'm so proud of you,' I say as a thought crashes into my mind.

Zac can't move to Sydney now. That's it—he's staying up here, no matter what. And after that viral video, I might not even have a job anymore at NRN News. I could be sent home tomorrow.

My shoulders tense, and Zac glances at me with a trace of a frown. 'What is it?'

With a long sigh, I open the gaffe video, sliding my phone towards him.

'What's this?' he asks as he presses play. I hold my head in my hands while he watches the embarrassing clip.

'Oh no, Jose . . .' He traps me in his soft gaze. 'What happened?'

I shrug helplessly. 'It was because of the topic, the cancer thing. After my appointment, talking about someone not much older than me who'd just died of breast cancer freaked me the hell out. I went dead; I was like a bloody corpse. Just like that time on Pink Ribbon Day, except this time it was even worse because I was the news anchor.'

He tuts a sound of sympathy and leans closer to pull me into his arms. I clutch on to his back, nuzzling into him like a safe space.

'I'm so sorry,' he says into my hair. 'But this kind of thing happens, right? It's live TV.'

'This kind of thing should definitely *not* happen. Not at this level. I could get fired for this now that it's become so public.'

We separate, but he reaches out to tangle our fingers together.

'I guess I'll find out soon,' I add, checking the time on my phone. I have to leave in an hour. I force myself to grow a spine and slap on the bravest face I can muster.

'Zac, we need to talk,' I say, my hand turning clammy inside his.

He stiffens at my change in tone, even though this can't be a surprise to him. 'Yeah?'

I inhale a quivery breath, feeling like I'm driving my car along the edge of a deep ravine in pitch-black darkness. One wrong turn, and I'll plummet to my death.

'Obviously, things have taken a turn here,' I begin carefully. 'And I am happy about that.' Warmth sparks in his eyes as I squeeze his fingers. '*But* I think it's probably a good idea if we talk about where we're both at with this thing and set some boundaries.' *Fuck, I wish I'd planned this out better.*

'Boundaries?' Zac leans back a little, although he doesn't let go of my hand.

I swallow past the razor in my throat. 'I don't want to get all *serious* on you right away, but this isn't exactly a normal situation where we just met and are getting to know each other. There's a lot at stake here already, and the most important thing to me is that I don't lose your friendship. Or should I say that you don't lose *my* friendship and support in your life.'

He blinks at me for a long moment. 'Are you saying you just want to be friends?' he eventually asks, his grip on my hand loosening.

'No,' I reply quickly. 'But I think we need to have a serious think about where this is going and whether it's really the right thing for you.'

'For *me*?'

His hand slowly slides out of mine, and my heart thumps harder as I figure out what I'm trying to say. 'Zac, you just got an amazing job up here. And you seem really happy in Newcastle. You've got a lovely home . . . a dog.' He gives me a what-the-hell look, but I keep going. 'You know I'm not an easy person to be with. You've seen that already. And I don't even know if I'm healthy or how long I'm going to be around.' He frowns, but I barrel on through my muddled thoughts. 'I've pretty much screwed up my chances at NRN News, and I'm not sure how that's going to go down in Sydney, but you already know that I'm moving back there soon.'

Silence stretches between us. I reach my hand out, but the expression on Zac's face stops me from connecting our fingers again.

'I'm not saying I don't want this,' I clarify, trembling. 'But I don't want to hurt you, either. Do you understand that? I *never* want to hurt you. You've been through so much already and have worked so hard to feel settled again. And yes, this new thing between us feels good, but so does the friendship. Our friendship is very important to me. So, for once, I'm trying to think things through.'

He shakes his head a little and looks down. When his gaze lifts back to mine, emotion builds in his eyes. 'We jumped off the cliff, Josie. We did that. We can't climb back up and pretend it didn't happen.'

'It's just sex,' I say in a small voice. 'Why does it have to change everything? I've loved you for half my life. I refuse to believe that a few hook-ups mean more than all the years we've spent together.'

'*Hook-ups?*' He gapes at me before his face tilts up to the ceiling. 'Is that what this was to you?'

I mutter a sound of frustration. 'Of course not. But we have to think about this like grown-ups. I'm moving back to Sydney soon. You're about to start a new job in Newcastle. What exactly are we meant to do with that?'

Every part of him tightens, and the excruciating silence rolls back in.

When he speaks, his voice comes out throttled. 'You can't just take my love and play with it. I'm not a toy to have a bit of fun with, then stick back on the shelf.'

A long, thick breath leaves my throat. 'You're taking me all wrong. I'm only trying to talk this out and be realistic. Like I said, we're not two people who just met. There are big feelings involved here, which is part of the problem. When you already love someone so much, it can become . . . confusing. That's what got us into this situation. I love you, you love me; I find you attractive, you find me attractive, but does that mean we should be putting that before fourteen years of friendship? When we already know we're going to be living in different cities soon?'

'I'm not confused, Josie.' His eyes sting with hurt. 'But you clearly are. And I don't want you to feel like you have to push so hard.' He heaves a sigh and rakes his fingers through his hair. 'You know what? It's all good. You can consider yourself off the hook.'

My brow rumples as I give him a hard stare. 'Off the hook?'

He gazes at me, his eyes watering. 'You're right. There *are* big feelings involved here. At least for me. So, if you're not one hundred per cent sure about me in that way, then we're better off stopping right now. I know I've never been your idea of the perfect guy, or the right marriage material, or whatever the hell. But I need to be enough. I deserve to be enough. And right now, you're clearly not sure about this, so I'm sorry, but I can't be here.'

His stool scrapes the floorboards as he gets up, and my heart pushes painfully against my ribs. *Good fucking work, Josie.*

'I'm so sorry,' I say in a choked voice.

'It's OK,' he says, brushing the heel of his hand over his eyes. 'I'm sorry, too. I've probably said too much. And I really do want to be your friend right now, especially with the health stuff you've got going on.' His voice slips. 'But I need a bit of time, OK?'

Tears wobble in my vision as a feeling of loss upon loss washes over me. I don't want to upset Zac. I don't want to go through my tests alone. I don't want to have breast cancer. I don't want to lose my job. I don't want my parents to be in Thailand. I don't want any of this. I don't even know how I got here.

He sighs at the look on my face. 'I'm sorry. You're right; we shouldn't have jumped off the cliff. Not without thinking it through properly first. I can see that now.' I just nod at him through my sniffles until he backs up a step. 'I'm going to go stay at Ross's place for a bit.'

My face falls.

'It's OK,' he says softly. 'He's got a spare room, and he loves the dog, and I know he and Holly won't mind. I'll stay there until you go back to Sydney, OK?' A sheen of tears glimmers in his eyes. 'I'm so sorry, but I just can't be around you right now. I want more, and that's not good for me. You're right that I've just started feeling okay again in my life, and . . . I think it's a good idea that we both take some time to think.'

My tears swell up. 'But this is *your* house; there's no way.' If only I could ask Lola if I could stay at her place while she's away, but her brother's already house-sitting. 'I'll go back to the serviced apartment,' I say.

Zac shakes his head. 'That'll be way too expensive. No, it's fine. I'll go to Ross's. Please don't feel bad.'

I turn my tear-stained face away from him, my mind flying back to when Zac picked me up at that train station in Hamilton. He looked so well, so settled. He'd been dating a local girl and was finally on track to rebuilding a contented life. Then Josie the Bulldozer arrived, messing it all up.

'I don't know what to say,' I murmur, my palms pressed to the ache in my chest. 'I'll do whatever you want me to do. I just want you to be happy. I love you so much.'

Zac rushes forward, folding his arms around me and pulling me into him. I cry into his chest, making silent pleas to go back in time so that none of this ever happened. How far back would I go? To before I arrived in Newcastle? To before the car accident? To that university bar where we'd struck that marriage deal right before he met Tara? To the day he stood over me on a train station bench outside our high school and asked me to be his girl?

I lift my face, finding his eyes brimming with emotion, before his gaze dips to my mouth. He slowly lowers his face, the sweet heat of his breath fanning over my lips, and I breathe out a sigh. But then he presses his lips tightly together and steps back from me.

'I'll see you later, sunbeam,' he says, and my eyes fill up again.

I want to beg him to stay, but I can't. Taking time to think is clearly the right decision. This is the smart thing to do.

'I'll see you soon,' I force out.

He drills one last look into my eyes before turning towards his bedroom, the truth punching me in the gut.

When I get home, Zac will be gone.

CHAPTER 37

Two years ago

ME: Hey, how's it going? I've tried calling you a few times, but you haven't answered. ♡

ZAC: Hey. Sorry I haven't been in touch, I've been really busy with the move.

ME: Has it gone OK? Are you still staying with Ross? I'd love to come up and see you both when you've settled into Newcastle.

ME: Just checking in because I haven't heard back from you . . . How are you? X

ZAC: Sorry, thought I replied, but it mustn't have sent.
I'm going OK, thanks
Coming up here has been a good change I think. Mum and Dad also told me they're moving up to Port Stephens, which isn't far away.
Yeah, I'm still at Ross's.

ME: That's great to hear that you like it up there! And wow, big news about your parents. Got time for a phone chat? Say hi to Ross from me.

ZAC: Will do

ME: Happy birthday to you! 🎂
I just tried calling, but no joy . . . I'm around all day, if you have time to give me a ring back?

ZAC: Thanks so much for the b'day message. I hope things are good with you? Can't chat today as I'm working, but will try to call soon.

ME: Poor thing, having to work on your birthday. Sorry I'm not up there to celebrate with you . . .
I'd love to come up for a visit if there's a weekend that works?
Or let me know if you're planning a trip down here. Would love to catch up. X

ME: Hey, stranger, how are you feeling? Whenever I call, you don't seem to pick up. 😔

ZAC: Hey, sorry I've been MIA. I've started a new role up here in the ambo offices, and I'm back on crazy shifts. It's probably easier to reach me via text these days. How are you?

ME: I'm going OK, thanks. I've got a job interview with Channel One News on Friday. 😄

ZAC: Oh wow, that's amazing. Good luck

ME: Thank you

ME: Can I call you?

ME: Guess what—I just found out I got the job!! I'm gonna be a reporter for Channel One 🥹 🥹 🥹

ZAC: Sorry, meant to reply to this yesterday 🙈 That's incredible! Really well deserved. I'm happy for you.

ME: Thanks! How are you, favourite? I miss you.
Wish you'd give me a ring? Or let me know when I can call you. I'd love to come up and visit too. I assume you've found a place by now?

ZAC: Yeah, in Hamilton. It's a great spot.

ME: Wish I knew where Hamilton was!

ME: Hi favourite, how are you? ♡

ME: Tried calling again but can't seem to reach you. I miss you.
I hope you're OK.

ME: Hi Zac, I'm just checking in again as I haven't heard from you. How are you?

ME: Hey Zac, is this still your number?

CHAPTER 38

Today

I'm two minutes from Honeysuckle—barely seeing the road in front of me—when my phone blasts, sending me out of my skin. My whole body turns rigid when I see the name 'Natasha Harrington' flashing on the screen. I answer the call on speaker.

'Have you seen that the video has hit the comedy talk show circuit?' are the first words out of her mouth.

The awful feeling in my stomach grows. 'Yes.'

She sighs deeply. 'I was hoping it would be missed, but it's out there now.' I can feel her shaking her head. 'It will all blow over, but right now, I need you to lie low.'

'Lie low?'

'You've still got a month left on your contract, so take the next two weeks off, starting today. We'll manage, and I cannot risk another one of these clips right now.'

'Natasha, I promise you, it will not—'

'I've made my decision, Josie.'

A moments of tense silence passes between us before her tone softens a touch. 'Look, if there's anything you want to talk to me about, you can give me a call, OK? Otherwise, I'll see you in two weeks.'

'OK,' I mumble. 'Thank you.' *She sounds like she can't get rid of me fast enough.*

After we hang up, I pull into a driveway and sit with my forehead against the wheel, reliving that disastrous on-air moment. A desperate need to call Zac surges up my spine and takes hold of my throat. But when his stricken face from the other day slides into my vision, I force away the impulse.

I kick on the engine and drive towards Nobbys Beach, where I sit on the damp sand in the wintry wind with my arms curled around my knees.

Breathe in, breathe out.

Stay calm, stay calm.

Then I catch my face in my hands and cry.

I last for two more days moping around Zac's house before I crack and begin stuffing random bits of clothing into my suitcase. It makes no sense that Zac's crashing at his cousin's while I'm swanning around the house he pays for. But it's more than that. Everything that surrounds me here belongs to him and reminds me of him. Trouble's empty dog bed is enough to stir up my stomach, let alone the sight of Zac's untouched sheets. *I can't be here.*

My mind is also on a mission to torture me, constantly picking apart our last conversation and recalling the gutted look on Zac's face when he left. If only I could reverse time and fix things and feel less hideous than I do right now. But as much as it hurts, I refrain from calling him. We both need time in our respective corners, like we agreed. Impulsive-Josie needs to take a damn breath.

I call Christina and put the phone on speaker while scrubbing the guest bathroom, determined to leave this place as clean as I found it.

'Hey, you,' she sings.

'Hey.'

She gasps at my broken tone. 'What's wrong?'

'Can I come and stay with you for a few days? I need to get out of Newcastle.'

'Of course. What's happened? Is this about the video?'

My throat constricts on the words I haven't been able to say aloud until now. 'I've been put on forced leave for two weeks. The news director up here wants the dead-air story to die down before I'm allowed back at work.'

'Oh, darling. I'm so sorry.'

I scrape the sponge across the granite countertop. 'Thanks. I'm lucky I didn't lose my job entirely. But I can kiss goodbye the idea that Oliver Novak is going to call, begging me to be your replacement.'

A deep sigh leaves her lungs. 'He hasn't said anything to me. But never say never; it's possible he hasn't heard about it.'

I snort a mirthless laugh. 'Keep dreaming, my friend. Even my parents saw it on the internet in *Thailand*.' When Mum and Dad called about my on-air break-down, I told them I hadn't been feeling well and spaced out, which was at least partly the truth.

'Well, I'd love you to come down and stay,' Christina says gently. 'Pete's actually in Melbourne for work this week, so you can keep me company. I'm in the middle of setting up the nursery. I'd love your input.'

I catch my reflection in the mirror, my haunted expression and puffy eyes proving that there's more to my Sydney escape than my work suspension. But Christina assumes that's all there is to it, and if I bring up Zac's name right now, I'll probably burst into tears.

I finish packing and slide my suitcase into the back of my car. My chest twists sharply as I tap out a message to him.

> **ME:** Hey. I'm officially off work for two weeks, so I'm heading to Sydney today. I can't put you out of your house, it's not fair. Please move back home. I'll find somewhere to stay temporarily when I get back, and I'll get the rest of my stuff then if that's OK. Thank you so much for offering your home to me.

I add the words 'Miss you' at the end before deleting them, my stomach shrinking into itself. I can't play with Zac's feelings right now—or my own. I have to keep things simple and civil.

When he replies while I'm flying down the motorway, I pull over at a rest stop just so I can read his message.

ZAC: OK

My heart crawls into my throat as I spin the wheel back towards the motorway.

Simple and civil. That's how things need to be right now. But the problem is that the first person I want to call and moan to about my sore heart is the same person who's causing it. Not that any of this is Zac's fault. He's done nothing wrong, whereas I can't seem to make a right decision to save myself.

A second message from him pings five minutes later. Waiting until I reach Sydney to read it feels torturous, so I find another rest stop.

ZAC: What about your test? Isn't that tomorrow? I was going to ask if you still wanted me to go with you.

A wave of nausea throbs through my body. I don't know how to tell him that I cancelled my breast ultrasound this morning. He'll never understand that I just don't have the mental strength to face the possibility of bad news right now, and I don't want him to blame himself. I'm planning to rebook the test as soon as I feel capable of handling the possible results, but that's one hundred per cent not going to be this week.

371

At a loss for what to say, I swipe out of the message and resume my drive to Sydney, trying to keep my zombie eyes from glazing over and causing an accident. The traffic gridlock sets in the minute I reach the city's outskirts, and it takes just as long to crawl to Christina's terrace in Kirribilli as it did to drive more than one hundred kilometres down the motorway.

Christina greets me with a gorgeous baby bump and a comforting hug, and we carry mugs of hot chocolate outside to her courtyard garden. We chat about her baby, Pete's work stint in Melbourne, a new historical bestseller we both loved—everything other than the lump growing in my breast and the fact that I had sex with my best friend and damaged both our hearts in the process. I know I need to get better at opening up to people about my issues, but giving those words airtime will trigger my anxiety. I'm starting to realise I keep my lips sealed for the same reason I run in the opposite direction from medical tests: if I pretend bad things aren't happening, maybe they'll just disappear.

Christina has to say my name twice to get my attention back.

'Are you OK?' she asks with a pout.

'Yeah. Sorry. What was it you just said?'

She swallows tightly. 'I got a call while you were on the way down here. Do you remember Dev Parvin, the chief Melbourne reporter for Channel One? He's moving to Sydney, and I'm wondering if it has something to do with my maternity leave. I can't think of why else Oliver would move him up here.'

I nod sadly, still coming to terms with the fact that I screwed up my one shot at my dream job. But if I can't even face an ultrasound, what chance do I have of being trusted to read the nation's most watched news bulletin? I don't deserve the promotion.

'That makes sense,' I finally say, inhaling a calming waft of milky chocolate before taking a sip.

'To be honest, I'll be ticked off if they replace me with a man,' Christina adds, and I hold up my mug in a 'cheers to that' salute.

'Do you want to talk about what else is bothering you, my love?' she asks. 'You seem so unhappy. And while I know this job means a lot to you, I'm wondering if there's another reason you've run out of Newcastle so suddenly.'

I absently turn my gaze to the tendrils of vines coiling up the trellis.

'There's been a lot going on,' I murmur, wondering where to begin.

Stop avoiding everything, Josie. Try telling the truth for a change to someone who cares about you.

'You already know that Zac and I hooked up,' I say with a sigh. 'More than once. And I was really hoping it was the right thing, but it's already screwed everything up between us.'

'In what way?' she asks softly.

When I struggle to answer, she hazards a guess.

'One of you wants it to continue, and the other one doesn't?'

I slowly shake my head, digging for the truth, but I can't seem to find it. 'I think we both want it. But he lives up there, I'm moving down here, and I don't see either of us budging on that. I have no interest in doing long distance, and I don't think he does either.'

'But if you have feelings for each other,' she says, leaning forward, 'shouldn't there be a way to figure something out?'

A slow, shuddery breath leaves my lungs. 'I think because we're already so close, this feels much bigger than it would if we'd just met. I don't want to hurt him. I've told you what he's been through in his life.'

'But why would you hurt him? I can see how much you care about him.'

My fingers make an instinctive shift closer to the left side of my chest. 'Zac can't lose another girlfriend,' I say in a strained voice. 'I won't do that to him. And the truth is I'm not sure how long I'm going to be around.'

Even to me, the words sound exceedingly premature, but I can't take risks with Zac's heart. I won't.

Christina's face has tightened up. 'What are you talking about?'

A tear slips down my cheek as I open up to her about the breast lump. Her eyes widen when I remind her of my family history and bring her up to speed on what the doctor said—including the test I was meant to have tomorrow.

She gets up and reaches for me, pulling me into as best a hug as we can manage over her swollen belly.

When her worried eyes rake over me like I'm already on my deathbed, I ask if it's OK if we drop the health topic for now. More than anything, I want to help her as much as I can while I'm here. Christina's family all live up in north Queensland, and while they are planning a visit, it won't be until the baby's born.

We agree to drive into the city to take my mind off things and shop for some nursery furniture that Christina and Pete still need. Her caring eyes keep landing on me as we browse the department store's baby section, but she doesn't push me to talk further. I'm sure she's ready to drag me to that ultrasound clinic with her bare hands, but she keeps silent.

We stroll along George Street, my arms loaded with Christina's bags, the smell of exhaust fumes and suits hurrying in all directions making me pine for the slow, easy hum of Newcastle. A few metres ahead of us, an approaching flash of neat blonde hair stops me in my tracks.

'Is that Meghan Mackay?' I say, my mouth open.

Christina slows beside me. 'Who?'

'Zac's ex from Newcastle. The one I work with.'

Christina holds a hand to her brow in search of a face that would be vaguely familiar to her at best. But to me, the tall, willowy figure and sleek blonde hair are unmistakeably Meghan's. She crosses the road up ahead, then disappears into a clothing store.

'I thought she was reading the news up in Newcastle this week,' I say to Christina. *Looks like I'm not the only one who's been pulled off presenting duties.*

If Meghan had been nicer these past few months, I'd probably send her a message to ask if everything was OK. But ever since Zac broke things off with her, her iciness towards me has become outright glacial.

After we arrive back at Christina's place with an early takeaway dinner that I don't really feel like eating, she disappears into her room for a lie-down. I stretch out on her guest bed and flip on the TV to distract myself from anxious thoughts before pulling out my phone. I jerk up against the pillows. I've got two missed calls from Zac and three texts.

ZAC: You didn't answer my question about the test tomorrow . . . is it on? Pls let me know, because I can take the day off if you want me to come with you.

ZAC: Jose, please reply, I'm getting a bit worried.

You have 1 missed call from Zac Jameson.

ZAC: Is there a reason you're not talking to me? Because the last I heard, you were driving down to Sydney, and right now, I'm freaking the hell out that something happened. Please reply or call me.

I hurriedly tap his number, my heart racing. I hadn't even considered that he might believe I was in a car accident when I didn't respond to his text. He's likely on shift, and the phone rings out, so I type out a message.

> **ME:** I'm so sorry. I'm absolutely fine. I was at the shops with Christina and didn't check my phone until now. I'm sorry I scared you.

I leave my phone out where I can hear it and rest my head against the pillow, a little buoyed by the fact that he was so concerned about me, even though I hate that I did that to him.

My exhausted eyes sink shut, and when they drift open again, the sky is a curtain of black through the window and the credits are rolling on the evening news. I scoop up my phone, my heart skittering at the new message notification.

> **ZAC:** Phew. You still haven't answered me about the test?

> **ME:** Thank you so much for offering to take time off and come with me, but it's not needed. Please don't freak out, but I cancelled the test. I will go, but I need to work up the confidence first.

A speech bubble appears before disappearing and reappearing like he's figuring out how to respond to my lunacy.

> **ZAC:** I'm sorry to hear that, but of course it's your decision.
> Just know I'm still happy to come with you when you decide to go (which I hope will be soon).

> **ME:** Thank you.

> **ME:** How are you doing?

I stalk my phone, but this time he takes ten minutes to reply.

> **ZAC:** I've seen better days.

> **ME:** Me too.

When he goes silent, I send another message.

> **ME:** I miss you.

My stomach dips and dives while I wait for his reply. Several painfully long minutes pass before an alert pings that he's 'liked' the message, but nothing else follows.

After overanalysing that in my head for a good fifteen minutes, I mope out to the living room, finding Christina watching a documentary about the French Revolution.

'Hey,' she says with a smile.

'Hey.' I flop beside her and hand her my phone, the message chat with Zac still open. 'So, I told him I missed him, and he just "liked" the message instead of replying. What do you think that means?'

She reads through the messages before her eyes widen a fraction.

I snatch the phone back. 'It's the kiss of death, isn't it?'

'He probably doesn't know what to say back,' she offers. 'It doesn't mean he doesn't feel the same way.'

But as I stare at Zac's lack of response to my message, a horrible feeling grips my lungs, suffocating me.

'I don't know what I'm doing,' I say, catching my head in my hands.

Christina reaches out to stroke my arm. 'Nobody does who's in love.'

I keep my palm pressed to my forehead as I look back at her. 'In love?'

One side of her mouth slants up. 'I can see it in your eyes, Josie. You're mad about him.'

I blink at her. 'I feel hideous. Like I could actually vomit. I've never felt this way about a guy.'

She chuckles softly. 'The classic symptoms of love. And I don't mean friendship love, not even best friend love. This is romantic love.'

I sigh into my hands. 'I can't believe this is happening. Out of all the men I pictured myself feeling this way about, none of them was anything like Zac.'

She shifts to face me. 'And what were they like?'

The words fill my head instantly. *Corporate, fancy, wealthy.* God, yuck. How unforgivably superficial. No wonder I've been locked up in singledom prison forever—it's what I've deserved.

I try to make sense of it all to Christina. 'I guess the men I'd imagined being with were more like my sister's husband or your husband—and don't take that the wrong way. What I mean is, I've always felt like I have to have "the perfect job" and "the perfect man". Someone successful and distinguished. Someone who lives in a big city and works in the corporate world and fits into this life.' I wave a hand at her priceless Sydney home.

A laugh sneaks out of her, and I narrow my eyes.

She lays a hand on my knee. 'Darling, I'm not making fun of you. But I am thinking that you might be confused about why Pete and I are together. It's got nothing to do with our jobs, our lifestyle or our home. Yes, I love living here, but you also know I buy most of my clothes from op shops. Pete and I aren't together for money or status; it's because we love each other. Because we couldn't bear to be apart. Because we make each other feel wonderful and supported. We could be living on the street and we'd still be together. In fact, we became a couple long before all this.' It's her turn to wave a hand at the room. 'So, instead of this checklist you've had in your head, why don't you tell me a little more about Zac?'

The question wraps me in a warm blanket, and my lips twist up. 'He's a hard person to describe. He's really not what you'd call "fancy", but just for the record, I'm hugely proud of what he does for a living—I think it's amazing. His medical knowledge is incredible.' She smiles as I continue. 'He's very real, very unpretentious, very smart, very thoughtful and *very* kind.' I could go on for hours, but I spare Christina and stop there.

Her eyes sparkle. 'Maybe love is a checklist, after all. Just not the list you thought it was.' She flips the volume down on the TV and rests her hands on her baby bump. 'OK. You already know what I think about this, but I'm going to ask you this question. You love Zac, there's no doubt. He is a very special person in your life, and he means a lot to you. But are you *in love* with him, Josie?'

There's still a part of me that wishes I could say no— or even hesitate. But the answer already lives deep inside me, where it's tattooed over my heart.

'Yes,' I say with a heavy sigh. 'Yes, I'm in love with him. Maybe I have been the entire time and I've been in extreme denial—I don't know.' I clutch my stomach, trying to settle the nerves swirling there. 'All I know is that I feel like driving up there right now and telling him how much I want him. But I'm so scared of something going wrong. It's the weirdest situation. I'm caught between wanting to protect him fiercely *and* being the one who could hurt him.'

'Love *is* scary,' Christina replies. 'And I bet it's even scarier when it's with someone who's been your best friend until now. But, darling, these aren't feelings you can just switch off. If you're in love with him, and he's in love with you, I don't think either of you has a choice. You're going to have to take the risk. Either that, or stay completely away from each other, which sounds painful and unnecessary.'

I bite down on one of my fingernails. 'I don't know if he's in love with me.' Just saying those words crowds my chest with longing.

'Well, there's only one way to find out. You have to tell him how you feel, Josie. You have to roll the dice. Just remember that when you're afraid, the fear is often worse than the danger itself.'

A heavy fog drifts over me as my thoughts travel from my heart to another part of my chest.

Not when it's cancer.

The sky is barely lit when Christina yanks open the guest-room curtains. I cry out in protest before pulling a pillow over my head.

'I have an idea,' she says with a zing in her voice that no one should have at this time of day.

I open one eye. 'It better involve me going back to sleep for a year.'

The bed dips with the weight of two people when she sits beside me. 'I'm having breakfast with Oliver Novak this morning.'

'What?' I gasp, sitting up on my elbows. 'You didn't tell me that.'

'He only texted this morning—just before six am, mind you—saying he has a meeting in Kirribilli at nine, and do I want to meet for breakfast. So very Oliver.'

She laughs knowingly, like it's normal to have the CEO of Channel One News think of you as an ideal break-fast date.

'Anyway,' Christina continues, 'you're going to come along and convince him to give you a screen test for my maternity gig.'

My lungs fly into my throat. 'Oh god, no. *No.*'

'Why not?'

'Because the reason I'm even down here is that a gaffe I made on live TV went *viral,* and there's no way Oliver doesn't know about that. I do have some dignity, believe it or not.'

'Yesterday's news,' she scoffs, knowing full well that's a load of crap. She flings the striped quilt off me. 'Now get up. This opportunity has dropped out of the sky like it's meant to be, and you're not missing it. The worst that can happen is you get to know Oliver a little better, which is a great thing for your career. And you just never know, darling. If he likes you, he will consider you, I guarantee it. Oliver does what he wants; always has.'

It's painfully clear that she's not going to back down, so with a terrified sigh, I crawl out of bed and head into the shower to get cleaned up.

My stomach turns into a washing machine on spin cycle during our short stroll to Christina's favourite café. When Oliver strides in ten minutes late, I nearly throw up into my coffee, but at least I made Christina text him to give him a heads-up that I was coming.

She plants an air kiss on his cheek, and I mirror the move, my lips landing on the edge of his ear as he turns his head. *Oh, Jesus.*

Oliver brushes it off with a gruff chuckle and orders himself a double espresso, speaking at a million miles per hour and freaking out the waiter with his authoritative tone. He's so ripe for one of my impersonations that I have to school my features not to slip into one by accident.

For the first ten minutes, Oliver angles his designer jacket towards Christina and chats with her like I'm not even here. She keeps trying to bring me into the conversation, but it's evident that Oliver couldn't care less what I have to say, and I work hard to not let the disappointment show on my face.

'Have you given more thought to who you'll get to replace me?' Christina asks him boldly, and I nearly make a run for it.

Oliver dabs his mouth with his napkin. 'I'm considering options. Dev's coming up from Melbourne to screen test, but I don't know. I'd like someone with a bit more pop. You know you are a hard act to follow, my dear.'

She smiles, blushing. 'Thank you. But I know someone who would be excellent. Smooth delivery, beautiful voice, lovely face. Plus, she has gravitas *and* empathy.'

He twists his blindingly expensive watch. 'And that would be?'

'Josie Larsen,' she blurts through an awkward half-laugh before lifting her mug to her lips.

I want to slide right through the floor, fall through the centre of the earth, and into the pits of hell where no one can find me.

Oliver glances at me through ice-cold eyes, then back at Christina. 'Ah. I'd figured that's why you brought company.' *Why does he keep talking like I'm not even here?*

I need to say something, but Christina cuts back in. 'Just think about it,' she says to Oliver. 'I'm not saying this because Josie's my friend. I have a lot of friends who are reporters, and I'm not here to do them professional favours. Josie is young, yes, but she's got *it*. She's been doing an incredible job up at NRN News for the past few months, and the audience loves her up there.'

'It's OK,' I burst out in a nervous breath, grateful for Christina's kind words but too aware that Oliver is looking more irritated than impressed. 'You're so sweet,' I add to her, but when Oliver leans back in his chair and gives me an up-and-down look, I realise this is my opportunity to pounce. Yet, for some reason, my sales pitch comes out a little half-hearted.

'I didn't come here to railroad you about this,' I say to Oliver. 'But I've been reporting for a number of years now, and while I won't deny that I love being out in the community and telling people's stories, I believe I have what it takes to present. I'm comfortable on camera, and I've been told that I read well—'

A waiter swoops in with our breakfasts before I can finish. Oliver sprinkles pepper over his poached eggs and speaks without looking at me. 'Look, I appreciate you saying that, Elsie, but it's not a decision I can make right now.'

'Of course,' I reply quickly, shrinking into my seat as I fumble whether to correct him about my mistaken name. When I catch Christina's eye, I find a flicker of sympathy in her gaze.

'I heard about the slip-up last week,' Oliver adds between bites. 'And then there was that hiccup last year, too. Or that time you misnamed the Minister for Housing on live TV.'

Actually, it was the Minister for Lands and Property, I think, but I keep that to myself. Looks like I'm not the only one who slips up now and then.

'To be honest, any one of my reporters can read an autocue,' Oliver continues gruffly. 'What I need is someone who can present the news when there is no script, or when the lights blow, or when there's breaking news with no warning.'

My cheeks catch fire. 'That's not going to happen again,' I say, faking the assurance in my tone. There's still a lump in my breast that I've done nothing about, and if I think I have a handle on this situation, I'm living in a fantasy world.

'We'll see how things go,' he mutters before switching the topic to Christina's baby plans.

Oliver doesn't pay me an ounce of attention for the rest of our breakfast. The guy doesn't even know my bloody name. When his colleague strides in ahead of their meeting, Oliver introduces the smiley-faced guy to Christina but not me. That's when my slightly awed stare at Oliver morphs into a thinly veiled glare. Why am I trying so hard to impress this rude man who remembers every mistake I've made, but not my name? Why am I so desperate to be back under his watch in the frightening pressure cooker of his newsroom, which feels more ruthlessly competitive than the Olympics, and where I'd probably have to work until I die if I ever want to afford to buy my own place in Sydney? Why am I putting such high expectations on myself about something I'm not even sure I want anymore?

And if my life is going to end prematurely, does any of this really matter?

After Oliver pays for our meals on his platinum credit card and dashes away with his colleague, I turn and look at Christina. 'That was the sweetest thing you've ever done for me, and I love you to death. But I'm not getting that gig. There's no way in hell he's going to hire me as your replacement.'

She makes a big sigh of empathy, but the strangest thing is, all I feel is relief.

*

> *You have 1 new message.*

> **ZAC:** I'm in Sydney. A work thing.
> You still here?

I lurch up in the bed, which I've barely left, apart from the horrible meet-up with Oliver that I've since dubbed breakfast-gate. My fingers can't type fast enough.

> **ME:** Seriously? Yes, I'm still here. Do you have time to meet up?

He doesn't reply right away. I pace Christina's house like a caged animal, giving the place a clean for her and wondering how the hell this is even happening. I used to share all my most embarrassing secrets with Zac. Now I'm losing my stomach over the prospect of even seeing him.

My next thought strikes without warning. What if I saw Meghan in Sydney because she's here with Zac? What if they're together again? *Oh my god, I'd cry a fucking river.*

My phone pings again, and I scramble to open the message with my stomach in my throat.

> **ZAC:** Sorry, I was in a meeting. And sure, given I'm here.
> Drink or a bite after I'm done at work? I'm staying in Circular Quay and should be done around 5.

> **ME:** Perfect. I can meet you at the Opera Bar? 6 pm?

> **ZAC:** See you there, sunbeam.

CHAPTER 39

Three years ago

'*Hello?*' crackles a voice that sounds a million miles away, like it's trapped inside a 1980s Commodore 64 computer.

'Zac?' I say because it's his number showing on my phone.

I think I hear my name, but it's hard to make out through the ear-piercing popping and humming.

'I can't hear you—you may have regenerated into a psychotic robot with a stuttering disorder,' I reply at the top of my voice. Simon, who runs our internet news channel, shoots me a disapproving glower from across the room, which is quite the event given he has resting-bitch-face ninety-nine per cent of the time. Simon prefers our newsroom to be quieter than a grave-yard, which is an unending hardship for the rest of us reporters.

With an apologetic glance, I inch past Simon's meticulously tidy desk and out into the hallway with my phone held to my ear.

'Zac?' I say again.

'. . . *you hear me?*'

'I can hear you, but not well. There's a lot of static. Is everything OK?' My stomach contracts a little. I've been texting back and forth with Zac and Tara since they left for their backpacking month in South America, but a phone call is out of the norm.

'. . . *gaged!*'

'Sorry, can you speak a bit slower?' I squint like that'll miraculously sharpen my hearing.

'*We're . . . engaged!*'

'What?' I reply loudly, cupping my other ear with my palm. 'It sounds like you just said you're engaged.' I snort half a chuckle.

'. . . *are!*'

'What?'

A buzzing noise overtakes the crackling before Zac's cyber voice switches to a robot version of Tara.

'. . . *asked him to marry me . . . Machu Picchu . . . engaged!*'

My breath stalls inside my lungs, and I twist to stare at the tiny white bumps of painted concrete on the wall, trying to unscramble those words in my brain. *Did Tara just say . . .*

'*Josie?*' Zac's voice is back on the line.

'I'm here. Wait . . . what? You guys are *engaged*?'

'Yes! . . . *wanted to ring and tell you.*'

'Oh my god—*wow.* Wow, wow, wow!'

Want to say 'wow' for the seventeenth time, Josie?

I clutch one side of my face, my lips frozen into an 'O' shape like one of those clown heads at a fair.

What the hell?

Zac is getting *married*!?

A confused, delighted, stunned smile begins to grow across my cheeks as the reality of this jaw-dropping, *wonderful* news sinks in.

Yet, somewhere, too deep inside for me to reach or even feel sure it's there, is a twinge of something disorienting—and almost painful—that I can't quite name.

CHAPTER 40

Today

Christina drops me outside the Sydney Opera House in her silver Audi convertible, promising to pick me up after she's finished her late-night shopping. I really want her to meet Zac, so we hatch a plan for me to keep him there until she arrives.

My eyes make a sweep of the waterfront bar, but I'm fifteen minutes early and there's no sign of him. I order a glass of rosé and settle into a table facing the lit-up arch of the Sydney Harbour Bridge, grateful for the relatively warm temperature for this time of year. As smartly dressed urbanites stroll along the promenade in thick clusters, I get a pang for the low-key vibe of Newcastle and its mellow cafés, sleepy beaches and quiet, leafy walks.

A hand lands on my shoulder, and I twist to meet Zac's slightly flushed face. I lurch out of my seat to hug him, his arm sliding around to cup my lower back.

I've missed everything about him—his touch, his smell, his presence—but when I press a little closer, he gently untangles himself from me.

'You OK for a drink?' he offers, even though my wine's barely been touched.

'I'm good, thanks.'

When he returns from the bar gripping a foamy beer, I suck in his handsome features and black T-shirt that says 'Cute But Crazy' as he sinks into a chair across from me.

'How are you?' I ask.

He taps his fingers on the table, and I have to make a fist in my lap to stop myself from reaching for him.

'I'm OK,' he replies with an exhale. 'It's been a long day. We're doing a wellbeing week for new critical care hires. It's basically a big love-in where we all talk about our feelings.' One side of his mouth quirks up.

'Oh, in that case,' I say over the tug in my throat, 'you probably didn't need to bother coming because you're a guy and, therefore, will have absolutely nothing to say about feelings.'

A light laugh bubbles out of him. 'That's a bit of a sexist comment, isn't it?'

I smile, and we manage to relax enough to chat more about his short Sydney stay and how my visit's been going with Christina. It still feels like the strangest thing that the two of them have never met—like a left shoe without a right—but I assure him that'll be rectified tonight if he's happy to stay until she gets here.

'You mean I have to wait until a woman's done shopping?' he asks with a grimace that's all show.

I exaggerate my frown. 'That's a bit of a sexist comment, isn't it?'

His gaze falls as he smiles, and a long moment of silence chews up the air. It hits me now that, in the past few weeks, I've gone from feeling stupidly happy to unbearably lost.

The question throbbing in my chest comes out faintly. 'You're not here with Meghan, are you?'

Zac's frown is instant. 'What? No, why would I be?'

I almost collapse with relief. 'Thank god. I saw her here in Sydney, and I just thought—'

'Of course not.' When his soft eyes hold mine, I just about lose my breath.

'I'm really glad you said yes to meeting up,' I venture with a slight tremble. 'I wasn't sure if you'd want to.'

Emotion deepens in his eyes. 'I always *want* to. That's never been the problem.' He blinks away from me. 'Or maybe that is the problem. I want to a little too much.'

A feeling of hopeful excitement blows through my stomach.

'Zac.' I reach out and lay my hand over his forearm.

He doesn't respond to the touch, but he doesn't shift away from me either. 'Jose, the reason I agreed to meet is because I wanted to talk to you about something.'

My heart kicks into a gallop. 'Yes?'

'Why didn't you go for your test?'

My stomach curdles at the mention of the lump in my breast that I've been fighting like hell not to think about, and my palm slips off his arm. *So, that's what he wants to talk about. Not us.*

'I'm really worried it's because of me,' Zac adds, his expression turning serious. 'Because I upset you and scared you down here.'

'It wasn't because of you,' I mumble.

'Then why?'

I shrug my shoulders, tears threatening my eyes. 'Because I'm fucked up, Zac. I'm not a normal person; I'm not a sane person. I'm someone who, because of this anxiety, screwed up the best chance I had to become a TV newsreader, which you know has been my dream since high school. And that's fine, because I don't deserve that job if I can't handle myself on air.'

He blinks at me through pained eyes. 'I didn't know it was this bad. That you would be too scared to even go for a test. I'm so sorry.'

'Don't be sorry. You're someone who's been through real, actual horror. And here's me in a soul-destroying, career-killing panic over something that hasn't even happened yet.'

It's the first time I've admitted that my anxiety is leapfrogging every random health symptom I have into a death sentence, but Zac shakes his head with a crease in his brow. 'Stop doing that.'

'Doing what?'

'Acting like I'm the only one who's allowed to be scared. Your problems matter just as much as mine, OK? Having lost a girlfriend doesn't give me the world exclusive on fear and sadness. Nor does it mean I'm the only one allowed to be affected by what happened.'

I bite away tears as I nod.

He tuts like he's breaking his will and leans across the table to collect my fingers in his. The action sends tears spilling down my cheeks.

'I'm just so tired of this,' I cry as he strokes my fingers. 'I don't know how to fix it. I know I need to go to that test, but what happens if they tell me I have cancer?' My voice breaks, and I hide my face in the crook of my arm, wishing we weren't in such a public place.

Zac's hand stays tight in mine. 'How many medical tests have you had in your life? How many of those came back with bad news?'

His words bounce off my ears, making sense to someone else but not me. A heavy sigh drags through my lips as I gaze around the bar scattered with girls in stylish winter dresses and guys sharing belly laughs, seeing nothing but bleakness and despair.

'I'm scared that this test is going to be the one,' I finally admit. 'I'm scared that I'm going to die. I'm scared that I'm going to die young and alone.'

'Look at me,' Zac demands softly, and I raise my tear-filled eyes to him. 'You will never be alone,' he says. 'Not as long as I'm here. And I'm not going to sit here and tell you it's wrong to be scared. I'm not going to tell you that everything's always going to be fine, and that bad stuff doesn't happen to good people. I am, however, going to hold your hand for as long as you need me to.'

I twist my palm in his and weave our fingers together, electricity burning a trail from his hand into my heart.

Zac swallows thickly. 'As a friend,' he clarifies.

A terrible, helpless feeling pushes against my sternum. 'Can we talk about that?' I ask in a whisper.

He reaches for his beer with his free hand and tosses back a gulp, tension filling his face. 'Not now, Josie, OK? I just need a bit more time to think. To get my head right.'

Unease rips through me, and he squeezes my fingers, looking right into my eyes. 'We'll talk, OK? But right now, more important than anything is that I need you to promise me you'll rebook that test. And I can come with you when you take it. Whatever day it is, I'll get it off work, I swear. Please.' His brow tightens with desperation, and I find myself nodding. I'm tired of running. I'm just so fucking tired.

'Is this the famous Zac Jameson?' asks a voice made for television, and my head snaps up to meet Christina's smile.

'I don't know; who's asking? Certainly not the famous newsreader Christina Rice,' he replies, crossing his broad arms with a smirk, and her face lights up.

I warned you. He's adorable.

'Nice to meet you,' she says with a laugh, and he rises to kiss her cheek while I unhook a shopping bag from her arm. Zac drags over a chair, and I ask Christina if she wants something to drink, but she declines.

'You were quick,' I say, happy to see her but also a touch gutted that my conversation with Zac has been cut short.

She runs a hand over her lower stomach. 'Yes, I'm not feeling too well.'

Alarm shoots through me. 'Are you OK?'

'I think so. I think I'm having those false contractions you get before you go into labour.'

'Braxton Hicks,' Zac comments as she winces. 'How far along are you?'

'Thirty-six weeks.'

'How bad are the pains?' he asks. 'Scale of one to ten?'

She lets out a long breath. 'They're mild. I'd say about a two.'

'Yeah, it does sound like Braxton Hicks. As long as the pains don't get any worse or fall into a rhythm, your body's just practising for labour.' His lips tug up. 'Congratulations, by the way.'

'Thank you.' Her eyes flicker back to mine. 'I'm so sorry to have interrupted your night, darling, but I think I need to lie down. Would you prefer to get an Uber home?'

'No, don't be silly. I'll come with you.' I gently rub her sleeve. 'I can drive if you like.'

'All right.'

I feel Zac's gaze on me as I scoop up all our bags and hang them off my wrist.

'It was nice to see you,' I say as he gets up. He wraps an arm around my back, drawing me close.

'I'll see you up north,' he replies into my neck, the gentle heat of his breath setting my skin alight.

'And I'll let you know about the test,' I say as I pry myself off him. 'Promise.'

His eyes roam all over my face. 'Do you want me to walk you both to your car? I can carry the bags.'

'No, that's OK. We're big girls, aren't we?' I give Christina a tiny nudge.

The three of us stroll towards the road, where I say one more reluctant goodbye to Zac before Christina and I head into the Opera House carpark.

The moment we're out of his view, she catches my arm and squeezes it.

'Oh my gosh, darling, that boy is so lovesick for you.'

'What?' My pulse jumps.

'Oh, come on. He looked like he was going to cry when you walked away.'

If she wasn't pregnant, I'd give her a playful shove. 'You're just trying to make me feel better.'

'Am not. And you didn't tell me he looks like a heart-throb.'

I sigh. 'Yes. While the rest of us are coping with the ageing process, that guy just gets prettier every year.'

She snorts. 'How old are you again? Don't forget you're talking to a dinosaur.'

I shush her as we step into the carpark lift. When I catch her suggestive smirk in the mirrored walls,

I break the bad news. 'He told me tonight that we're friends and that's it.' I slump against the wall as those words settle into my head.

Her lips part. 'He said that?'

I nod. 'I don't think he wants me. At least not right now.'

Her mouth twists down, and I reach out to drape a lock of her hair over her shoulder.

'Don't ever kiss your best friend,' I say like I'm giving her important life advice.

'You're my best friend, darling. And I'll try not to.'

I laugh, but inside, my heart sinks so deep in my chest that I'm not sure I'll ever be able to get it out.

I'm fast asleep in Christina's guest bed when a sharp cry jolts me awake. Disoriented, I blink hazily at the ceiling until a groan sounds from the other side of the wall. I kick myself out of bed and dash into the hallway, where Christina is standing with both hands braced against the wall.

'I think I might be in labour,' she grits out.

My hand flies to my chest. '*What?*'

This can't be happening. This can't be happening! Her husband isn't even here!

I race towards her and help her back into her room, sitting her on the edge of the bed. She talks me through the pains in her lower stomach, which are now more intense and coming several minutes apart.

'Do you think you could call Zac?' she asks, her features pulled tight. 'He seems to know about this.'

'I'm sure he'll just say to call an ambulance,' I reply breathlessly.

'But it could still be the false labour pains. My water hasn't broken, and isn't it still too early? The doctor said just last week that everything looked on track.'

'I'll try him quickly first,' I decide, running back into the guest room to grab my phone.

Zac picks up after four rings, sounding groggy and a little panicked. 'What's wrong?'

'I think Christina might be in labour. But we're not sure.'

His voice springs to life. 'Tell me what's happening.'

I dart back into Christina's room, finding her hunched over. With Zac on speaker, I hurriedly catch him up on her symptoms, and he instructs me to call an ambulance right away.

Christina points at her phone on the bedside table. 'Use that one. I'd feel better if you kept him on the other line.'

I use Christina's phone to call an ambulance, then Pete in Melbourne, before slipping into the hallway to give her and her husband some privacy.

Zac's voice in my ear tries to soothe and distract me with an anecdote about the time he was transporting a woman in labour to hospital, and she began reciting romantic sonnets to keep herself calm. He said he spent the entire drive trying not to swoon.

A short scream sounds from Christina's room, and my heart nearly falls out of my chest as I dash back in. She's lying on the bed with a puddle of water seeping through the sheets, her brow clenched.

'Zac,' I choke into the phone. 'Her water just broke.'

'God, I feel like I really need to go to the toilet,' Christina bites out.

'She needs to go to the toilet!'

'OK, the baby might be coming sooner than expected,' Zac says calmly.

'Oh my god! Have you ever delivered a baby?' I gasp at him.

'I have never delivered a baby, but I have helped many mothers deliver their babies. And that's what you're going to do right now. How's Mum doing?'

I glance at Christina, devastated that her husband's going to miss this. Bloody Sydney mortgages and the constant pressure to work yourself into the ground at any cost!

I rest my hand on her forearm, and she gazes up at me with a slightly panicked smile.

'She's OK,' I tell Zac.

'Good. Now, the first thing you should do is be really calm in front of Christina, OK? Tell her she's doing great.'

I smile at her, tears springing to my eyes. 'You're doing great.'

Zac begins the next instruction, which is to make sure that Christina's well away from the edges of the bed.

While I help her shift up the mattress, she blinks up at me, her newsreader voice turning stern. 'Josie, I want you to promise me right now that you're going to get that ultrasound you need, so we can all put this behind us.'

My jaw hangs. 'You're having a baby! Don't worry about that now!'

She levels a look at me. 'If I can do this, then you can do that. Deal?'

I press my lips together to stave off the tears burning in my eyes. 'Deal.'

'OK, I love Christina already,' Zac says in my ear. 'Now, let's help her meet her baby.'

CHAPTER 41

Three years ago

'Wow, that glitter wall—Jose, you're amazing!'
Tara's hand slips inside mine, tugging me
towards the curtain of shimmering gold strands that
I carefully pinned to the wall inside the Sydney hotel bar
this morning. 'Come on, let's all get a photo.' Her other
hand pulls on Zac's, and the three of us shuffle in front
of the glittery display, with Tara standing in the middle.

'Just one with me, then the two of you,' I say,
feeling like the hanger-on who's photobombing their
engagement party pics. The three of us make sassy,
serious-browed, Gatsby-style poses for the clicking
photographer before I blurt, 'Now you two,' and leap
out of the spotlight.

Zac slides his arms beneath Tara's hips, and she
squeals as he scoops her off the floor, her fringed dress
swinging around her thighs. While the photographer
peers through the camera lens, Tara kicks one leg

straight out and the other back while Zac's fedora sits adorably askew on his head.

Smiling, I watch for a few more snaps, then turn my gaze to the gradually filling bar, spotting Zac's cousin Ross sitting on a corner couch beside a guy in a black shirt and red braces. My feather boa tickles my shoulders as I weave my way through to Ross and practically launch myself at him. Now that he's moved to Newcastle, I hardly ever see him.

'Josie-girl,' he greets, lifting off the couch to wrap me in a hug. My three-inch heels are already chewing through my toes, so I drop onto the emerald-green couch between Ross and Red Braces. I thought he might be a friend of Ross's, but he introduces himself as one of Tara's cousins, Amin. The guy smells incredible, and when he offers me a warm smile through his fake moustache, I become a little caught up in his dark, soulful eyes.

After a catch-up with Ross that Amin joins in on, I climb back up and begin making rounds of the room, mingling with old uni friends, tossing back pink champagnes, and dancing as much as my weeping feet will allow.

Every so often, I wander back to the couch corner for a rest, where Amin spends most of the evening chatting with a few of Tara's family members. At some point, Amin and I end up alone and engaged in a deep discussion about his intense work as an industrial relations lawyer. While I soon figure out, with some disappointment, that he's not really my type after all—the story of my life—the champers has made me buzzy enough not to want to squirm away when Amin lightly rests his palm on my thigh while speaking into my ear.

My face snaps up when a voice that sounds indisputably drunk and ridiculously happy cries out my name. I grin over at Tara, who's waving me back onto the dance floor.

Beside her stands Zac, one of the best dancers I know, but he's hardly moving. With his shirt sleeves rolled up and his fingers tightly clutching a whisky glass, his gaze is resting on the spot where Amin's hand sits splayed on my thigh. Zac's eyes spring to my face, back to Amin's hand, then away from us both, a little line drawn between his brows.

Something about Zac's expression makes me realise that I'm probably leading Amin on, and he doesn't deserve that.

I twist to smile at my new friend. 'I'm gonna go dance with your gorgeous cousin.' Giving his arm a little squeeze, I climb up off the couch, and his fingers slide off my bare leg.

I don't return to the couch for the rest of the night.

CHAPTER 42

Today

Sweat slips down the back of my T-shirt as I scan the faces in the radiology waiting room, unable to tell who's here routinely and who's sweating bullets like me.

I reset my gaze on my phone screen that's filled with images of Christina's baby's smooshed-up face caught between her and her husband's glowing smiles. A glimmer of calm loosens my lungs.

Give him ALL THE KISSES from me, I type out.

'Hey.' Zac drops into the seat beside mine, his concerned eyes exploring my face. 'Sorry I'm a few minutes late. Traffic.'

'In Newcastle?' I joke, and he glides his hand up my back before giving my shoulder a light squeeze.

'How are you doing?' he asks.

'As expected. Bricking it.' The shudder in my voice nearly makes my teeth chatter.

He gives a sympathetic murmur, and for a moment, I lose myself in his golden-syrup eyes before turning away. It still hurts to look at him.

'Want to see what the baby looks like?' I ask.

He nods, a smile cutting into his cheeks. I scroll back past the last few memes that Christina and I shared before I reach the baby pictures. Thinking of the night Ashton was born still makes me misty-eyed. Zac stayed on the phone until the ambulance came, helping me guide Christina through her contractions while I came up with corny dad jokes to keep her calm. I never let go of her hand—not in the ambulance nor in the delivery room, where Pete stayed close on speakerphone, and I sobbed when Ashton was placed on Christina's chest.

It was the first time I ever walked out of a hospital smiling, and the bubble of joy didn't burst until I arrived back in Newcastle a few days later to face this dreaded test.

'He's a cutie,' Zac says, chuckling as he swipes through the photos. And now I'm imagining dad-Zac. *God.*

I slide my phone into my bag. 'Her husband quit his job. He was so pissed off over missing the birth that he quit. Wants a lifestyle change.'

'That's understandable. It's one of the reasons I left Sydney.'

I inhale deeply through my nose but can't seem to catch my breath. Zac's hand finds my knee, his thumb grazing my bare skin through the rip in my jeans.

'So, did you hear about the dung beetle who walked into a bar?' he asks. I roll my eyes at him. 'He said to the bartender: Is this stool taken?'

I just stare at him before a laugh flies out of my chest, catching a few glances from those in the waiting room. I hook my arm around Zac's and lean into him.

A nurse strides in clutching a clipboard, and bile shoots up into my throat. But the name she calls out isn't mine.

Zac moves his lips to my ear. 'Listen to me,' he says softly. 'There is a monster in your head right now whispering a whole bunch of bullshit. It's trying to scare you with made-up stories. Don't listen to it, OK? Listen to me.' He gently holds my jaw and guides me to look him in the eyes. 'I know you,' he says. 'I love you. You are not alone. You're not getting tested today, *we* are. And whatever happens, we're going to figure it out together.'

My entire body buzzes with warmth. His face is so close to mine that he'd only need to tilt forward a touch for our mouths to collide. But instead, he raises his lips to my forehead. 'I've got you, sunbeam,' he says into my skin.

My drained eyes fall closed. 'I'm not a sunbeam. I'm a cloud. One of those horrible, purple ones you see right before a storm that looks like the harbinger of Armageddon.'

He pulls back with an amused smile. 'Nope. I've told you before. Looking at you is like staring right into the sun . . . so bright, it's blinding.'

Our gazes bind together, a soft feeling expanding in my chest. As much as I know I should look away from him, I can't.

'I love you too,' I say in a breath, and his cheeks flush.

Are we talking friendship love? I want to ask before a voice booms from across the room.

'Josephine Larsen!'

I gasp as Zac lurches to his feet, pulling me up with clammy fingers. The fact that his nerves are spiking nearly as much as my own should make me feel worse, but for some reason, his outbreak of the jitters makes me feel like less of a freak.

'I'll see you back out here?' he guesses.

I clutch him with both hands. 'Can you come in with me?'

'Of course.'

Holding on to Zac like a lifeline, I brave a smile at the waiting nurse and follow her into the examination room. Zac turns his back while I change into the gown, and when I stretch out on the treatment bed, he drags a chair close.

The radiographer paces back in with my file, checking my details and explaining what will happen during the scan.

My arm instinctively falls towards Zac, and his fingers cover mine as the nurse squeezes warmed gel over my chest. Her ultrasound wand finds the lump immediately, and my eyes lock on her expression, my heart drumming against my throat as I wait for her reaction. But as she presses, tilts and glides the wand over the lump, I can't get a read on what she's thinking.

'Do you think it's cancer?' I utter, and Zac squeezes my hand.

An apologetic look eclipses her face. 'Unfortunately, I'm not qualified to answer that, nor am I allowed to. A doctor needs to look closely at the scans and measurements. But I can make sure you get your results by tomorrow afternoon, OK? One thing I can say is that this lump is small.'

A whisper of hope flurries through me, and I thank her and lie in silence while she continues gliding, clicking and measuring, my gaze drifting to Zac's. He winks at me, still holding my hand, and I tighten my fingers around his.

'I love you,' he mouths at me, and hot liquid gushes into my chest, filling it up.

I smile and mouth the same words back, but in my head, there's an edit that I keep to myself.

I'm in love *with you*.

My eyes sink shut, my mind finally able to prepare for the next step in my health journey. Because one thing I'd never considered when I started believing I was going to get cancer was that Zac Jameson would be holding my hand.

I keep my phone beside me in the serviced apartment bathroom while I get ready for work, the ringer turned all the way up. The debate I had with Zac yesterday over staying at his place lasted nearly thirty minutes, but I held my ground. Despite what happened at the clinic, he hasn't said anything to indicate he wants something more than friendship right now, and my heart can only take so much.

He also tried to convince me to take today off, but I'd go out of my mind sitting around waiting for the doctor to call. Plus, it's my second-last week at NRN News, and I must have some seriously good karma in my spiritual bank because Natasha Harrington actually wants me in the newsroom. I also can't wait to see Lola when she gets back tomorrow—she'll no doubt have a big hug ready for me after the viral video debacle.

Christina calls me on my short walk to work, restoring my smile.

'Hey, baby mumma,' I say.

'Hey, baby daddy.'

I laugh. 'Poor Pete,' I moan for the zillionth time. 'How's Ashton?'

'He's divine,' she coos, and I can tell she's gazing at him. Her voice drops in tone. 'But darling, I'm afraid I'm calling with some not-so-great news.'

Oh god, what now, I think, but I remain peppy for Christina. She's in new-baby heaven, and I'll do nothing to ruin it.

'Oliver has hired someone to cover me,' she says with a sigh. 'It's Meghan Mackay from NRN. That's why you spotted her in Sydney recently. She was there for a meeting with Oliver, and she's already started the role.'

'Oh my god, you're kidding me!'

'I know, I'm ticked off about it,' she replies with more frustration in her tone than I've ever heard. 'You're much better than her. To be honest, I don't understand it at all. But upside: it's a woman.'

'I know why,' I say as I turn onto the promenade, shivering in the wind gust. 'It's because Meghan can handle herself through anything on air, and I can't. It's as simple as that. And it's the way it should be. I had my chance, and I blew it. I can own that.'

Silence falls between us. 'Did you hear from the doctor yet?' Christina asks.

All the blood in my face drains away. 'Not yet. It's supposed to be today, though.'

'OK. Well, when you want to, you tell me how it went, OK? I'm thinking of you, darling.'

'Thank you, my friend.'

We hang up, and I drop my phone into my bag before turning to face a sandstone wall and screaming into my arm.

Meghan Mackay, really??

After a few deep breaths, I suck it up and head upstairs to work. It's the first time I've shown my face since my viral gaffe, so I inch into the newsroom with my head ducked, but Man-Bun-Colin greets me with a grin, and was that an actual wave?

'Good timing,' he says as I pass by his desk. 'Remember the West Wallsend baby woman who was charged with murder? Her husband's just been charged with being an accessory after the fact. He's facing court today. Can you head out there with Gus?'

I swallow a chuckle at being paired with Mr Unmotivated for one of my last reporting shifts up here. But at least Colin's kindly ignoring the humiliating on-air blunder that's now up to forty-seven thousand views on YouTube.

The shoot at the courthouse goes smoothly, apart from nearly missing the accused man's departure because Gus was having a natter with a security guard. I still manage to secure a comment from the accused man through some clever questioning, and my story ends up leading the afternoon news bulletin.

It's all been the perfect distraction from the relentless silence of my phone, and I'm giving it another check to make sure I haven't missed a call from the doctor's office when Natasha Harrington sidles up to my desk.

'It's good to have you back,' she says, handing me my favourite afternoon drink—a caramel hot chocolate—from the downstairs café. *Wow, OK. Why is she giving me treats instead of murdering me in my sleep?*

'Thank you so much,' I reply, open-mouthed.

She leans against my desk and crosses her arms. 'You've heard about Meghan?'

'I have.' I force out a smile that I intend to turn into something genuine as soon as I've gotten over my disappointment in myself. I also remind myself how much of an ass Oliver Novak was towards me and that I'd rather pluck out my own fingernails than work for him directly again. I'm planning to contact another news network about job openings when I get back to Sydney.

'I was surprised,' Natasha says carefully, the look in her eye delivering a message that she doesn't think Meghan was the right pick. Her voice then lowers. 'But, Josie, what I came here to say is that I'm sorry for reacting so strongly to the blunder you made on air. There is a lot of pressure on me in this role, and I've been given free rein to choose my own presenters. So, when something like that happens, it makes me look like I can't do my job.'

I stare at her, trying to stop my jaw from hanging. I've never had a TV executive be this honest and vulnerable with me. Natasha then shifts like she's about to scamper, so I blurt her name.

'Have you got five minutes?' I ask, standing up. 'There's something I'd like to talk to you about.'

She checks her watch. 'Why don't you come into my office?'

My heart inches into my throat as I trail her up the hallway, taking my phone in case the doctor calls. I settle into the chair that has, strangely, become a familiar place of comfort.

Natasha sits opposite me with her full attention, and I draw in a deep breath and admit everything about my health anxiety. I tell her how long it's been going on, how severe it is, how terrifying I find certain topics, and how much I want to get better. I don't tell her about the breast lump because, if it does turn out to be cancer, I need to think through how I want to handle work before beginning that conversation.

Her surprised eyes move over me like she's seeing me for the first time. 'Thank you for telling me, Josie. And I really hope you are getting the support you need. Will you let me know if there's anything I can do to help?'

'Of course. Thank you.'

Her gaze then clouds over with a look that's classic in our industry. 'I have an idea,' she says, tapping her chin. 'But I don't want you to feel pressured about it. What would you think of—'

My phone chimes from my lap, sending my stomach into freefall. I snatch up the handset, recognising the number.

'I'm so sorry, but this is the doctor calling, and I have to take it,' I say in a rush.

'Of course.' Natasha gets up and steps out of her own office as I press the phone to my ear, my entire life flashing before my eyes.

My voice locks in my throat. 'Josie Larsen speaking.'

'Hi, Josie; it's Doctor Ellison. I've got your ultrasound results—it's just a cyst. Nothing to be concerned about.'

My entire body splits open. 'Are you serious?' It takes everything I have not to collapse onto the floor.

'Very,' she says in a warm voice. '*But* the test did show that you have what we call fibrocystic breasts.

Which means you have a high number of cysts, and your breast tissue is quite dense. None of that has anything to do with cancer, but it can make screening for cancer trickier because it's harder to see what's going on in there. So, I am going to recommend that you get an ultrasound every year—purely as a precaution. And I want you to know, Josie, this also means we are likely to find more lumps like these, and each one will need to be screened just to be safe. With that in mind, I think we should make that appointment we talked about for your health anxiety. I know you've been suffering in the lead-up to this test. So, I'd really like for us to be better prepared for the next one. Sound OK?'

I wipe my eyes and nod. 'Yes, please. One hundred per cent. I don't want to live like this anymore.'

'Great. If you hold now, I'll transfer you to the receptionist to make an appointment.'

'Thank you, Doctor Ellison. Thank you so much.'

'Are we good to go?'

'Rolling,' Gus grunts behind my shoulder. *Wonders never cease.*

I smile at the kind-faced psychiatrist who came highly recommended by my contact at the John Hunter Hospital. 'Thank you for your time, Professor. I'd like to begin with a simple question: what is health anxiety?'

Professor Singh gives me a soft smile. 'Well, almost all of us worry about our health at times, which is perfectly natural. But when we begin to worry *constantly* that we are unwell and begin interpreting our changing bodily sensations as dangerous, then we start to have a problem. If we develop a preoccupation with the belief that we have—or will have—a serious illness, and that gets in the way of our ability to enjoy life, *that* is health anxiety.'

The spot-on description of me makes my cheeks heat, but Professor Singh's gentle tone keeps me grounded. The interview continues for nearly an hour, and by the time I get up and shake his hand tightly, I not only have reams of material to use, but I understand for the first time that I'm not a screw-up. I have a condition that's diagnosable and treatable.

Gus and I head outside to record my piece to camera, my mouth drying up at this point of no return. But I'm so tired of the fake smiles and the pretend laughs and acting like I'm OK when I'm not.

Words I once said to Zac linger in my head. *It's just as brave to say you're not OK.*

I inhale a deep breath and stare down the barrel of the camera. 'A few weeks ago, I suffered a panic attack on live television while I was presenting the news. I was interviewing an actor about the passing of an Australian icon when I began to shake and sweat. My heart was racing, my vision narrowed, and I lost track of where I was. While the terrifying experience made me the subject of a viral video and led me to question my ability to do my job, it also had a life-changing impact on my understanding of mental health. It made me realise that anxiety can affect anyone, anywhere—even when you're doing something you love. And I'm sharing this with you because I believe that telling *my* story will help me do a better job of telling yours.' In the corner of my eye, I catch grumpy Gus's mouth slant up, even though I keep my gaze fixed on the camera. 'Josie Larsen, NRN News.'

Foamy waves spill over the glistening sand of Nobbys Beach in the peach light of early evening. I spot Zac sitting on the short brick wall overlooking the vista, his hair twisting up in the gentle wind. It's the first time we've seen each other since the ultrasound, and I stand back for a moment, collecting myself, before I move to sit beside him.

'Hey, Shirley Temple,' I say, giving his soft curls a light pat.

'Sunbeam.' He smiles and presses his full lips to my cheek, and my eyes close at the torture. 'I'm so happy for you,' he says. 'I didn't think it would be the best idea to say this before the test, but *I knew* it would be fine. I just knew it.'

'You had a lucky guess,' I tease through a wry smile before we turn our gazes to the glimmering strip of blue bridging the sand and the horizon.

'Thank you so much for being there for it all,' I say for the hundredth time.

'Of course. And I saw the news story last night about your anxiety. It was absolutely fucking amazing. I'm so proud of you, Josie.'

I smile into his gleaming eyes. 'Thank you. All of our affiliate news channels around the world have picked it up, and some even want to interview me. I only agreed to do it because I didn't want to say no to Natasha, to be honest. But after working on the story and talking to Professor Singh, all I really want out of this is for people like me to feel less alone.'

His eyes soften. 'Well, you've definitely done that—even for me. You know, ever since the accident, if I come across an article about a car crash, the first thing I do is scan it to see if anyone died. It's like I've become obsessed with motor vehicle mortality. The same way I've seen you look at those articles about cancer deaths.' He leans forward, pinning me in his gaze. 'And you're a reporter—you know that people only tend to post online when something bad or unusual happens. You're reading about a tiny percentage of people and are being tricked into believing it's the standard. You're also probably ignoring most of the positive things you read. It's called confirmation bias.'

'I know,' I murmur, still wishing that Zac and I had been there more for each other over the past two years. 'I'm actually seeing Doctor Ellison about it tomorrow before I go.'

Something shifts in his eyes before he forces a tight-lipped smile. 'That's great. Hopefully, she can hook you up with a doc in Sydney who can continue helping you with it.'

My chest splinters. Zac isn't exactly throwing a party over my imminent departure, but it seems that he's resigned to it.

I have to do something, and I have to do it now. Or I'm going to regret it for the rest of my life.

I gently lay my hand over Zac's thigh where it pokes out from his athletic shorts, stroking his bare skin with my thumb. His gaze flies to mine, and for a few endless breaths, I stare into his eyes, begging him to see what I want. But when he doesn't do anything to close the distance between us, I charge. I clutch the back of his neck and pull him towards me, but his spine straightens, and his eyes dart away.

'Zac,' I plead.

He sucks in a quivery breath. 'I'm so sorry, Jose. I can't.'

A deep, wrenching pain grips my heart. 'Why?'

'Don't get me wrong.' His brow lines as he looks down. 'Every time I'm around you, all I can think about is kissing you. That's the problem. You make my head spin.'

I lean into his view, feeling the lost look in my eyes. '*Why* is that a problem? You want to kiss me; I want to kiss you . . . What could be less of a problem than that?'

His jaw grinds like he's at war with himself. 'You're totally ignoring everything you brought up last month. You're moving to Sydney in a few days. And you know I can't move back there. Every time I drive past the highway there that leads to Mittagong, I'm going to relive that fucking awful thing all over again. It's bad enough having to go down for work now and then.'

'But we can figure it out,' I beg. 'Sydney's just two hours away. People have relationships on different sides of the world.'

'It's not only that, though.' He stares out at the sea with weary eyes. 'I can't go through a big hurt again. You were right about that. I'm finally on my feet, and I can't feel a loss like that again; I *can't*. I've worked too hard to get better.'

'But, Zac, my test was fine.'

He blows a mirthless chuckle through his lips. 'I'm not talking about you dying, Josie. I know you. You like guys with beach houses who can mingle with TV executives at parties and fit into your fancy Sydney world.'

He's wrong—we've both been so terribly wrong about that—but when I shake my head, Zac looks away.

'I know there's attraction between us,' he admits throatily. 'But if we go our separate ways for a while, we'll get past it and realise we live in two different worlds now and are better off the way we've always been. As friends. Because if we start something up, I know you'll get sick of being in a long-distance relationship. Before long, you'll be going on dates with corporate guys down there again, and I'll be sitting up here fucking dying from heartbreak.'

My throat is so full I can hardly speak. 'There are no other guys, Zac. I want *you*. *You* are the reason that

I've been single for so long and never wanted any other man when he was put in front of me. *You* are the person I compare everyone to, and no one ever measures up. All my life, I feel like I've been making one wrong decision after the next—chasing after things I thought I wanted. But those were other people's ideals, other people's dreams. *This* is what I want. *This* is the right decision.'

Turmoil swirls in his gaze as he looks back and forth between my eyes. But then he drops his face with a pained sigh. 'I'm so sorry, sunbeam. It took me two years to get my life back on track, and I can't risk my heart like that again. The fucking devastation I felt after our conversation that day in the kitchen made me realise I just can't do it. But I don't want you to ever feel alone, OK? I'm still your friend.'

I turn my head and blink rapidly through my tears, feeling like my heart's being torn out of my chest. But then a hopeless realisation sinks over me that I've done all I can here. If Zac doesn't want to pursue this, I can't make him, and I don't want to. I would never try to force him to put his heart on the line if he's not ready— not even for me. His happiness is too important.

The words leave my lips in a whisper. 'OK. If that's what you want.' I offer him a shaky hand. 'Friends.'

His forlorn gaze locks with mine as his fingers close around my own, a silent explosion shattering my chest.

'Best friends,' Zac says.

CHAPTER 43

Fourteen years ago

The moment Mrs Waldon turns to face the white-board, I twist in my seat and find Zac pouting at me from two rows over, three seats back.

I perform an exaggerated eye-roll, because he and I were having too much fun whispering our plans to go to Luna Park this Saturday for my birthday before our bossy maths teacher separated us.

Zac's eyes flicker in the direction of her floral dress before he holds up a scrunched ball of paper and tosses it towards me. The note lands near my shoe, and I surreptitiously snatch it up and unfold it.

Check your locker after class for a b'day surprise

From Zac

I curl back around to shoot him a quizzical grin, but he pretends to focus hard on his work, a smile hinting at his mouth.

As soon as the bell rings, Zac jumps up and sails out the door with Cody and Hayden crowding behind him, so I head in the opposite direction, towards my locker, curious and giddy over this birthday surprise. How would Zac have even got something inside my locker without knowing the combination?

I hastily unlock the stiff door and yank it open, finding another note dropped onto my stack of tattered textbooks. Zac must've pushed the note through the door vents.

Look under the poo table in art class

I snicker into the back of my hand. Zac's got geography on his timetable now while I have art, so I hurry across the quadrangle to the art rooms to get to what I guess is going to be another note. In the rear corner of the art studio, one of the high wooden desks is permanently stained with an unfortunate splatter of orangey-brown paint that looks like a diarrhoea explosion. Chewing my bottom lip as I smile, I unstick the note from beneath the table.

Check under the guide dog coin tin at the canteen

That note, which I quickly retrieve between art and history, turns into two more.

Look inside Mr Roland's ugly vase that's always empty because living things die around Mr Roland

Something special awaits you inside your favourite library book

With no sign of Zac anywhere at recess, I practically run to the library, saying a quick hi to Amy and Emily who are lounging on the inside couches, escaping the summer heat, before heading right for *The Book Thief* by Markus Zusak. It strikes me that Zac could've gotten mixed up over which book is my favourite, but pressed between two pages is a small, thin packet of wrapped pink paper. My lips part, and my heart swells in my chest.

I peel back the tape and fold open the paper, a delicate silver bracelet tumbling into my palm.

'Oh my gosh,' I whisper as I brush my fingertips over the bracelet, finding a little charm of a sun dangling from one of the links.

'That's for "sunbeam",' murmurs a familiar voice, and I spin to find Zac leaning against the shelves, his arms crossed, and a trace of a smile on his lips.

'Zac.'

Lost for words, I stare at his flushed face because I hadn't expected him to get me a birthday present at all, let alone something so . . .

'It's beautiful,' I say, my throat closing up. 'I *love* it. Thank you.'

'You don't have to wear it if you don't want to,' he mumbles, but relief warms his eyes.

'*Of course* I'm going to wear it. I'm gonna wear it right now.'

I drape the cold chain around my wrist while Zac pushes off the shelf and says, 'Spoiler alert, but I'm gonna get you a charm for it every year on your birthday. At least, that's the plan.'

I'm struggling to close the clasp, so he takes over with his long, deft fingers and clips the bracelet on for me.

A deep wash of affection warms me up inside as I stand on my toes and loop my arms around Zac's neck before he can escape. He smells like boys' deodorant and mint chewing gum.

'Thank you, favourite,' I say against his shoulder. 'The best present of all is having met you.'

He drops his chin into the nape of my neck, squeezing me a little tighter. 'I hope we're friends forever, sunbeam.'

CHAPTER 44

Today

I rest my shoulder against the apartment window that faces Hunter Street while staring at my phone's live-stream of Mum and Dad's distressed faces. My admission that I've just had a health scare *and* been diagnosed with severe anxiety seems to have stolen all the words from their throats.

'I'm going to be fine,' I say, aware that I'm at risk of falling back into my usual pattern of pretending I'm A-OK and that my life is a Hallmark movie. But I'm done 'faking it until I make it' to my own family. Last night, I unloaded to Lola about my severe anxiety over dinner, and she burst into tears in the middle of the sushi bar, then hugged the breath out of me. How can I open up to someone I've only known for a few months and not to my parents? It's time to admit that my life isn't made up of a series of adorable little ducks sitting in a perfect row. My ducks are injured and losing feathers, and one has a bung eye, but that's OK. That's me, stumbling through life.

'Actually, no,' I correct to Mum and Dad, 'I *don't* know that everything's going to be fine. I actually think I have quite a long road to recovery ahead of me, if Doctor Singh's advice is anything to go by. But I'm going to work really hard to give it my best shot.'

'Oh, Josie,' Mum says tearfully. 'We had no idea. I'm so sorry.'

'It's not your fault. It's mine for not telling you. I didn't want to worry you or upset your beautiful retirement life over there.'

'Don't you ever worry about that.' Mum peers closer at the screen while Dad's pained frown behind her pierces my heart. 'You are more important to us than *anything*, Josie,' Mum says. 'And I'm so sorry we haven't been back recently to visit.' She exchanges a regretful glance with Dad.

'It's OK,' I reply. 'It makes me happy to see you guys having such a good time over there; it really does. The medication I've just started should settle my catastrophic thought spirals, and I've got the phone numbers of some recommended counsellors in Sydney. I'm working on it. And I'm really, really sorry that I haven't been more honest with you.'

While talking openly about what I've been through with my health anxiety has lifted a dead weight off my shoulders, I choose to leave out what happened with Zac for now. Once I can talk about him without the contents of my stomach lining my throat, I'll break it to Mum and Dad that he and I will probably never be best friends again, despite what we said to each other at the beach.

Even though I'm still not quite sure what went wrong with Zac, I believe that if I'd been in a stronger state of mind through it all, I would have been better equipped to deal with that complicated situation. Ross has also been torturing himself and called me yesterday, beating himself up over what he'd said in the café. But I know it came from a place of love. I'd wanted to ask him how Zac was doing, but I chickened out.

After my parents and I hang up, I rest against the serviced apartment's kitchen counter and reopen last night's text chat with Zac.

> **ZAC:** Please let me take you to the train station on Monday. Your train leaves at 10:10 am, right? I've got the day off, so it's fine.

> **ME:** Thanks again, but the apartments here have a shuttle, which will be too easy.

> **ZAC:** But Trouble wants to say goodbye.

He'd added an image of himself holding up Trouble's rust-coloured paw, her tangled fur hiding half of his smiling face and shining hazel eyes. I hadn't replied after that.

Gazing at that picture now, and for far too long, I know I can't be anywhere near Zac for a very long time. With every part of my body sagging, I type my response.

> **ME:** Give her the biggest kiss from me.
> But I'm sorry, I can't.
> I'm the one who needs time now.

Given that I sent my reply more than twelve hours after Zac's message, I don't wait to hear back from him right away. He may not even reply at all after what I just said.

With a nervous churn in my stomach, I dial a number that I've been meaning to call for days now but have kept putting off. I don't expect Meghan to answer, but after a few rings, her silky voice filters through the line, albeit with a scratchy edge.

'Josie?'

'Hi, I'm not interrupting you, am I?'

A yawn escapes Meghan's throat. 'No. I was just grabbing a nap. It's been busy down here.'

'Oh shit, sorry.'

'It's fine. I needed to get up anyway. I have to be at Channel One in an hour.'

Another nervous breath pulls through my lips. 'I won't keep you long, but I wanted to call and give you my congratulations about the Sydney job. Actually, I'd love to do it in person when I move back soon. Maybe we can grab a coffee if you're free one morning?'

Meghan's stunned pause is hardly a surprise. But I recognise that I've been projecting a tonne of my own insecurities onto Meghan since I got here, and that's not the kind of person I want to be. Plus, if there's anything

I've learned in the past few months, it's that there's more to life than a big shiny promotion.

'Thank you,' Meghan eventually replies, her tone softer but still cautious. 'I was actually planning to message you.'

'You were?'

'I saw your health anxiety story, and I wanted to let you know that I thought it was excellent. I'm sure you already know this, but we ran it down here in Sydney in a couple of different bulletins. Lots of viewers emailed in saying how much they loved it. It was honestly out-standing.'

My smile widens. 'Thanks so much.'

'I've gotta run, Josie, but maybe I'll see you down in Sydney for that coffee.'

'Hope so.'

After grabbing a bite from the sushi bar down the street, I catch an Uber to Nobbys Beach since I've already returned my car to NRN News. The warm sheen of spring is peeking through the last week of winter, and I may as well breathe in as much of the salty ocean air as I can get before Sydney's carpark battles turn me off beach visits for life.

My arms are crossed behind my head when the name 'Natasha Harrington' flashes on my phone screen. I lurch forward.

Shit, what have I done wrong this time?

'Natasha, hi.'

'Hi, Josie. I'm sorry to call you on a Sunday.'

'That's fine. I'm just down at the beach, enjoying the quiet, especially knowing what's ahead of me at Bondi.'

She chuckles politely. 'It's certainly the day for it. But that's actually what I'm calling about. It would be much better to say this in person, but I know you're set to leave tomorrow, and—put that down! Sorry Josie, I'm at the movies with my kids.'

What the hell? Natasha Harrington has kids? Who knew?

'Sure, what's up?' I reply.

She clears her throat. 'I know this puts you on the spot, but I'm sure you realise by now that things move pretty fast in our world. Genevieve Meleska has been poached by Melbourne,' she huffs. 'And I've been looking through a stack of CVs this weekend, but it just hit me that it's been staring me in the face this entire time.' I sit up higher, my breath catching. 'I know you had that slip-up, Josie, but the way you followed through with that brave report on anxiety was, frankly, spectacular journalism. In fact, that story got more eyes on NRN News around the world than we've ever had. And you already know that I think you're a lovely newsreader. So, take the afternoon to think about it, but if you're interested, I'd be willing to give you another go on the presenting desk. You would be replacing Genevieve as the weekend newsreader on a trial basis— if you can promise to continue getting the support you need with your health. And, if I'm honest, I can't think of anyone else I'd want more in that seat. You've truly got something special.'

My heart thrashes in tandem with the waves lashing the shoreline, an entire future that I've never imagined exploding across my vision.

'Short notice, I know,' Natasha adds when I'm too gobsmacked to reply. 'But I wanted to talk to you about it before you left for Sydney. If you choose to accept, you wouldn't need to start right away. You could still go down and sort out your things and head back up here in a couple of weeks. I can have a contract drawn up for a three-month trial, but if all goes well, of course, I'd be happy to keep you indefinitely. You're a real asset to us. In fact, I *know* the Sydney team will want you eventually, so I'll need to work hard to make sure you're happier here with us.'

I'm trying to make words, but all my breath is trapped in my lungs. 'Thank you so much,' I gasp. 'I'm blown away and thrilled and am kind of having trouble speaking right now.'

'Ha, that's understandable. As long as it doesn't happen on air again.'

'It won't,' I add quickly, wanting to slap myself for reminding Natasha of that, but her tone stays light.

'It's all good, Josie. But I've got to run; I'm going into a bloody Minions movie.'

I snicker, and we end the call as a dazed grin spreads across my cheeks.

'Oh, my fucking god!' I cry out, and a mother clutching a toddler's hand frowns while they totter past me.

I clamp a hand over my apologetic face that can't stop smiling and shakily dial Christina's number.

When she answers with her baby cooing in the background, I spill the news about the job offer in a breathless gush.

'Darling! That's fantastic!'

'I can't believe it,' I reply, still reeling, still figuring out what this means.

'It *is* in Newcastle, though. I guess you have to ask yourself if you want to live there for the foreseeable future.'

I glance at the uncrowded ribbon of sand bleeding into an aqua-blue ocean; this whole place looks like it's snatched off the cover of a luxury travel magazine. 'I freaking *love* it up here,' I say honestly. 'It's got everything I like about Sydney, but with no traffic and a ten-times-easier lifestyle. In fact, apart from seeing you, I was kind of dreading going back to Sydney.'

She squeals. 'Oh, I'm so happy for you! But I will miss you so much.'

'I'll miss you too. And I'm still coming down tomorrow for a couple of weeks to tie up loose ends and give Ashton *all* the snugs.'

She murmurs cute sounds at her little boy as it dawns on me that I'm going to say yes to this job. I'm going to be a newsreader, and I'm going to be doing it in a city in which I can genuinely imagine building a life. Plus, after years of getting nowhere with Oliver Novak, I made the biggest screw-up of my career with Natasha

Harrington, and she not only forgave me for it, but she promoted me. I can't promise Natasha or myself that I won't ever drop the ball like that again, but she trusts me enough to let me try. That's the kind of person I want to work for.'

Christina's voice shifts tone. 'Darling, I have to ask: is this about Zac? Is he the reason you want this job? Because there would be nothing wrong with that. Work is important, of course, but so is love. If Pete needed to move to East Timor tomorrow, there's no question I'd go with him.'

An uncomfortable flutter takes possession of my stomach. 'No, he's not the reason. In fact, I'm not even going to tell him about this right away. I don't know when I'll tell him. I just . . . I don't want him to think I'm stalking him by moving up here, and I'm also not ready to be around him yet. It hurts too much.'

'I understand.'

My head flops against the beach chair, and I let the soothing breeze caress my face while Christina fills me in on Ashton's intense feeding schedule and her severe lack of sleep. She wants me to feel sorry for her, but all I do is smile into the phone with a silent hope that, one day, I'll find my Pete and my Ashton. And I don't care what my man does for a living, or what social circles he moves in, or if he has a beach house. There's only one criterion now.

He has to make me feel the way Zac Jameson does.

*

The lead-footed shuttle driver drops me off forty minutes early for my train, so I settle on one of the benches with my to-do list to keep me occupied. Every few minutes, an arriving train blasts its horn, awakening the sleepy platform with a flurry of activity before the air deadens again.

After messaging my sister to ask when she can catch up over a video chat, I email the removalist company, telling them I'm going to need all my stuff that they picked up from Zac's place turned around and sent right back up again. *Classic.* There are plenty of messages I still need to send, but I switch to browsing a real estate website for a place to rent in Newcastle. Natasha hasn't mentioned salary yet, but I'm confident she'll offer me an increase that reflects my promotion, and excitement fizzes inside me as I click through images of a cute little weatherboard home in Merewether. Although, I think, I wouldn't mind being closer to Nobbys.

'Josie.'

My face flings up, my stomach hitting the concrete. At first, I see Zac in silhouette, the sun's shadows hiding the expression on his face. Trouble's hovering at his feet, sniffing some old food caked into the ground. He gives her little lead a tug.

'What are you doing here?' I ask in a breath.

He steps forward, looking so good it hurts in grey jeans and a navy T-shirt that says 'My Eyes Are Up Here'. The words are unnecessary, though: his honey-green eyes are all I'm looking at.

He exhales and sits beside me, his hair releasing the faintest waft of mint shampoo. Trouble flops down at his feet.

'I know you didn't want me to come,' Zac says, his voice deep and nervous. 'And I don't want to upset you. I'm sorry. But there's something I really wanted to give you. I hope that's OK.'

It's the perfect opportunity to break it to him that I'm not moving to Sydney anymore, but the words hover in the back of my throat.

He digs inside the pocket of his jeans and reaches for my hand, miniature fireworks bursting between our fingers as he presses something cold into my palm.

I gasp at the small silver charm bracelet he gave me for my fourteenth birthday. 'What? How did you—'

'I swiped it from your jewellery shoebox just after you moved in.' His lips quirk up. 'You didn't notice?'

I shake my head, and he carefully clips the bracelet around my wrist, a string of new charms brushing against my skin.

'*No*,' I say in a stunned breath. 'You added these?'

He rakes a hand through his hair. 'I've added a charm for every year that's passed since I gave you the last one, just like I said I would. Better late than never, right?' He smiles through his blush.

'Oh my gosh, *Zac*.'

His soft fingers gently pull my hand into his lap so that he can explain each charm. 'The bicycle is for your first year at uni when you insisted on riding that shitty bike all over Bathurst. The graduation hat is for the year you finished, the microphone is for the year you started your first reporting job, the sea turtle is for that year you became obsessed with scuba diving and didn't want to do anything else.' Tears spring to my eyes as he talks me through the rest of the charms—a puzzle piece, a sloth, a coffee cup, a musical note—each one capturing favourite things and moments that I thought only I'd remember. When his fingers pause at two identical charms of broken hearts, sitting side by side, his voice tightens.

'And those represent the two years we spent apart after I moved up to Newcastle.'

My abdomen clenches as my eyes lift to Zac's. Our gazes cling together for a few heart-stopping breaths before my fingertips nudge the last charm on the bracelet—a tiny silver door.

'Which year is this one for?'

Pink spreads over his cheeks. 'That one isn't just for one year; it's for fourteen. All the years we've spent together. Because the truth is, Josie, since the day I met you, I feel like all I've been doing is fumbling around in the dark, trying to find the door to your heart.'

My lips fall open and emotion clogs my throat.

He sighs heavily, his gaze falling to his lap. 'I know I haven't been the greatest friend to you in the past couple of years. Two broken heart charms aren't nearly enough to express how hard it was to not have you in my life. And I know I've been running away for a very long time. Running from the accident, from the memories of it, from the images I can't get out of my head. But mostly,

I've been running from you. Because of my guilt over what happened with Tara after she found out about my feelings for you. But sunbeam, something's dawned on me in the past few days.' He sucks in a long, deep breath. 'I need to stop thinking about what I've lost and start thinking about what I've found.'

He reaches out to pull my fingers into his lap, squeezing them as he traps me in his gaze.

'I've been so fucking wrecked these past few weeks, you have no idea,' he says thickly. 'Seeing you in Sydney was *so* hard. You've turned me inside out.'

I do know, I want to say, but I'm too choked up to speak.

He glides his hand down my cheek, his eyes travelling over my face. 'Next to you, every other girl is a blur. When you're in the room, I feel like there's no one else in the world but us. And I've been so worried about losing you and going through the worst kind of grief all over again. But the problem is that I feel even more lost when you're not there. And if there is one person in the world I would risk my heart for, it's you.'

An overwhelming feeling of longing bursts through me, spilling warmth into every corner of my body. I cup the back of his neck with both hands, bringing our foreheads together.

'There's something about you, Josie Larsen, that I don't want to live without,' Zac says against my lips. 'And I've told you a thousand times before that I love you. But what I've never told you is that I'm hopelessly in love with you. It's always been you.'

A tear rolls down my cheek. 'I'm so in love with you, too,' I whisper. 'Zac, I've been so lost and alone without you.'

He sighs as he presses his mouth to mine, and for a moment, we breathe each other in before our tongues catch and slide together in a dizzying kiss that leaves me panting. I grip the back of his neck again and push against him, kissing him deeply and thoroughly, claiming him for eternity. I want to hear one of his moans that drive me crazy, so I scrape my fingernails down the ridges of muscle through his T-shirt and sweep my tongue hard against his until I catch the sound I'd been hoping for.

When we break for air, Zac brushes his thumb over my bottom lip, his eyes foggy and his cheeks flushed.

'I don't want to do long distance,' he says. 'So, if it's OK with you, I'm going to ask for a transfer to Sydney. Even with this new role; I'm going to have to figure something out.'

A smile breaks out across my face. 'There's nothing to figure out. I've actually got some pretty huge news that I haven't told you about. Yesterday, my news director up here offered me a job. I'm the new weekend news presenter for NRN News!'

Zac's lips pop open.

'I'm moving to Newcastle,' I add. 'Hopefully permanently. And I love this city—I mean, why didn't you tell me it was this freaking good?'

Zac gapes at me before hooking an arm around my shoulder and dragging me close. 'Oh my god,' he says into my hair, his bewildered laugh making clear he's as happy about this news as I am. 'Oh my god, *yes*! I told you that you were fucking brilliant, and they'd be lucky to have you.'

The fact that he was prepared to move to Sydney—risking his new critical care job and putting himself back in the city that caused him so much suffering—almost makes me want to sob.

I clutch his back and bury my face in his neck. 'I love you so much. And I'm going to be saying it *a lot*—just a word of warning. I'm officially doe-eyed. I'm a doe with eyes.'

A warm laugh oozes out of him as he pulls back, and a memory shifts inside me.

'What was that question you once asked me on a train station bench?' I say, pinching my brow like I'm having a hard time remembering, even though I could never forget it.

And *boom*. Zac's adorable laugh hits me right in the chest.

He gets up on his feet and turns around to look down at me with a fierce blush, so very beautiful. So very kind. So very *Zac*. And so very mine.

'What do you say, Josie Larsen?' he murmurs, the happiness in his gaze reflecting my own. 'Will you go out with me?'

I smile up at him, fourteen years of love passing before my eyes.

'I thought you'd never ask.' I pause. 'Again.'

Then, we burst out laughing.

EPILOGUE

Today

ZAC

My palm grips Josie's thigh as our car inches along Victoria Road, my pulse nicely settled now that we're basically going ten kilometres per hour. She had to ply me with whisky, impersonate me until I nearly fucking died laughing, then undress me to get me to agree to let her drive on this road trip to Sydney. I hate saying no to her and always have, but this was a massive, heart-pounding step for me. It took six months of us being together for me to work up the courage to drive four hours to Bellingen for our half-year anniversary and another nine months for me to come around to being in the passenger seat on this Sydney trip.

It's another first that Josie's given me without really realising it. Just like I'm pretty sure she's still clueless that she was my first crush, my first heartbreak, my first love. My first everything.

Those ocean-blue eyes that I don't have a hope of resisting glance at me for half a second. 'Come on, admit you miss this traffic,' she says. 'You have wet dreams about it.' Then she throws her hands up at the windscreen. 'Honestly, it's not even two pm on a Thursday. What the hell, Sydney!'

One side of my mouth pulls up. 'Feeling a little stressed there, sunbeam? Want me to drive?'

'Hell no. We had a deal. You do what you do best—sit and look pretty.'

I let out half a laugh. 'She only wants me for my body,' I pretend-grumble. My gaze then veers to the strip of tanned thigh that I've been reaching over the console and grasping for most of the way here, but I force my eyes off it. No time for that right now.

'*Finally*,' Josie moans as the GPS leads us off the main road and onto a side street, the gridlocked traffic slowly disappearing in the rear-view mirror. 'Oh my god, there it is.' She snorts a laugh.

I peer through the windscreen at the approaching slab of burgundy brick wall and share her grin. We must be the only humans on earth this excited over a decaying high school that holds as many bad memories as good, but it's a key stop in our little nostalgia tour around Sydney. Since leaving Christina's baby shower this morning, we've already driven around the sleepy suburban streets that we used to race bikes down as kids, gawked at our humble, tan-brick childhood homes from the footpath, and are now pulling up outside this shitty old school that I love because it gave me Josie.

We park across the road and step out of the car, gazing up at the silent, weathered building coated in street art that's been left alone for the school holidays.

'It's so small,' I say, my eyes trailing over the main complex, which used to feel like an entire planet.

'I know, right?' Josie leans so close to me that our thighs rub, and I fold an arm around her back. I turn my head and brush my nose over the wild waves of blonde hair that will be the death of me, inhaling deeply because I need a little hit. That's all it takes for her to twist and lift her mouth to mine, and my stomach dips hard when our lips connect. I cradle her face and do a thorough job of kissing her until she's gorgeously delirious, her eyes blinking dizzily into my own.

'I love you,' she says, and I fucking kiss her like crazy again.

'I love *you*,' I eventually get out, wrapping my arms around her lower back and just holding her for a while.

'Do you want to go inside and walk around?' she suggests into my shoulder. 'That could be a head-trip.'

Nerves grab my stomach and I shake my head. 'We don't have much time.'

We've still got a couple of stops left on this little trip down memory lane, and it all has to be done today because Josie's now reading the news four days a week and is back on air tomorrow. With my critical care shifts all over the place, it hasn't been easy for us to find a window to make it down to Sydney at the same time. Christina even picked her baby shower date around us, and with her second little guy due in four weeks, we were cutting it fine.

Josie gazes up at me with her you're-my-favourite-thing-in-the-world face that always makes my heart pick up its pace. 'Should we head off then?' she asks.

I jerk my head at the train station beside the school. 'I just want to have a quick look and see if my graffiti's still there.'

'Graffiti?' Her eyes expand. 'You bad bitch!'

I chuckle and link my fingers with hers. Hand in hand, we head up the stairs to the station overpass and down the other side until we're standing on the dusty platform that was once our favourite hang-out place. I almost snicker at that memory—this noisy pile of concrete sucks, but back then, it felt like our little sanctuary. It was the place where I first fell in love with this beautiful creature holding my hand. So how can I turn my nose up at it?

'I just need to remember which bench it was,' I say, twisting around. It's been over a decade, so it takes me a few seconds, but I step towards what I'm pretty sure is the right one. I'd thought for sure it would've been replaced with a newer one by now, but there it is, the sun-bleached strips of wood marred by globs of blackened chewing gum, sparking a rush of memories.

'Looks like they scrubbed your vandalism away,' Jose says with a snort, nodding at the otherwise clean bench.

'Hold on.' I crouch down and crawl beneath the seat before shifting onto my back to gaze up at the underside.

'What are you doing?' Josie says above me.

Holy shit, it's still here. My eyes roam over the strip of faded black letters scrawled into a spot where I knew no one would find it. I pull my phone out of my pocket and snap a couple of pics because I'm sure this bench's days are numbered.

'Come and see this,' I say to Josie's legs, and a second later, her head pops into view. She's got an unsure look painted on her face, but I grab her wrist and whip her towards me, loving the little squeal she makes. *Come to me, beautiful.*

'Check this out,' I say with a smirk as she crawls beside me and looks up at where I'm pointing. Her lips fall open at the words: 'ZAC LOVES JOSIE FOREVER'.

'Oh my god, *what*?' she practically screeches.

'Told you I had it bad for you.' Our eyes catch in the shadows, and a little bolt of electricity flashes between us. Just as I peel my gaze off her to look at the graffiti again, she rolls to face me, grabs my T-shirt, and pulls me against her, my shoulder knocking the underside of the bench.

'What are you doing?' I laugh against her lips, knowing how this must look—two sets of tangled legs sticking out horizontally from beneath a bench. The sun beats down on my calves through my jeans, and our groins knock together as Josie reaches around my hip to cup my ass. She gives me that hungry, needy look that instantly wakes up my dick.

'*Fuck*, don't look at me like that,' I say, wrenching myself off her. I wouldn't put public sex past Josie, but I'm not about to get us both arrested for indecency. Plus, there's a bigger reason than graffiti that I wanted to bring her to this spot, and if she keeps rubbing her body against mine, she's going to feel two things sticking out of my jeans.

Still, I make out with her under there for way longer than I should, then shift to get up, whacking my head on the edge of the bench. 'Ouch.' I wince and rub my forehead while Josie crawls out beside me.

'Oh no,' she says, nearly laughing because she's always been ten per cent sadist. 'Are you OK? Aww.' She clutches my head and kisses the sore spot on my brow.

'Probably concussed, but don't worry, I still mean everything I'm about to say.'

She tilts her head. 'What?'

I blow out a jittery breath, trying to expel some of these out-of-control butterflies. But at least the train station's pretty dead, so we don't have an audience. *Hurry the fuck up, Zac, before an army of office workers descends. This isn't Newcastle.*

I steady myself in the comfort of my girlfriend's eyes and reach for her hands, my fingers wrapping around hers.

'Josie,' I begin in that tone that says something big is coming, and her eyes flash wide. 'I know this is literally the most unromantic place in the world to do this, but as my exceptional graffiti masterpiece has just shown you, this spot has sentimental value to me. I don't know if you remember, but this is the exact bench you were sitting at when I asked you out when we were fourteen.'

Her eyes soften as they sweep over my face. 'Of course I remember. You were perfect, and I was an idiot.'

I chuckle through my thick throat. 'No, you were perfect then, and you are perfect now, and you will be perfect tomorrow. But even so, the fourteen-year-old guy in me got pretty badly burned that day, and he's never really gotten over it, to tell you the truth. So, I wanted to bring him back here and give him a second shot at becoming the happiest man in the world.'

My fingers shake with nerves as I stick them inside my pocket, and Josie gasps. I know she must be expecting me to produce a velvet box, but what I place into her palm is much smaller and made entirely of silver. It's not a diamond ring, but it looks exactly like one.

A sound of shock flees her lips as she lifts her hand to her eyes, the tiny charm of an engagement ring glimmering in the afternoon sun.

'Josie Larsen,' I say, my voice cracking and my heart racing. 'I knew it then, and I know it now. And I tried to ignore it for *so* long. I didn't think you'd ever want me like that, and I didn't want you to feel uncomfortable or scared, so I never talked about it. I kept it buried deep inside my heart, and I tried so hard to love someone else. And you know I got close.' Tara's serene face slides into my vision, but I push it back out. 'But close wasn't good enough,' I say into Josie's eyes as they gleam with a film of tears. 'Close wasn't you.'

Her face scrunches like she's fighting not to cry, and the sight makes me bite away my own tears. 'All my happiest memories are with you, beautiful. You're not my "close"; you're not even my enough—you're my everything.' I inhale a deep breath and sink to one knee, even though I didn't really think through the concrete. Thank god I'm wearing jeans. But the second I look up and meet Josie's watery gaze, everything else melts away, and my own eyes fill up. 'You are the brightest thing in my world, Josie Larsen. I can't imagine a life without your light. So, I'm asking you, sunbeam, please. Will you marry me?'

A sharp cry bursts from her lips, and she flings her arms around my neck, clutching the back of my shirt and dragging me to my feet.

'God yes, hell yes—*yes*!' she says into my hair, and I don't know if I'm laughing or crying more as I squeeze her so hard that I'm worried I'll hurt her. And she's holding me just as tightly, every part of her gorgeous body trembling.

When we let go, I wipe my eyes and dig inside the other pocket of my jeans. 'I was hoping you'd say yes, so there is this one other little thing I got.' When I produce the black velvet box, Josie shrieks and tackles me so hard again that I nearly trip.

'*Zac*,' she says achingly as I slide the sparkling solitaire diamond ring down her fourth finger. She gasps and holds it up to the sunlight, and it's so blindingly beautiful that we both stare at it for a little bit. Josie's mum and I looked at a whole bunch of rings in secret during her parents' last visit to Newcastle before deciding on this one. It's perfect.

'Oh my god, I *love* it,' Josie says, her beaming smile making my heart run a marathon. Tears slip past the corners of her eyes. 'I don't know what I did to deserve you,' she says. 'I'm such an idiot for not just saying yes back then.' She drops into a crouch and her head disappears beneath the graffiti bench. 'Do you hear me, childhood-Josie-Larsen?' she scolds in her angry-school-principal voice. 'You are an idiot!'

That cracks me up, then her face reappears, her eyes doing that soft thing they do whenever I laugh too hard. She gets back up and curls her fingers around my wrists, gazing up at me with the heart-eyed look that always reassures me that she feels the same way I do. Like all the fears and anxieties that we're going to keep battling in our lives will be OK. Because when we're together, we're always OK.

I comb my fingers through her wild waves of honey-blonde hair. 'I kind of like that you said no to me back then,' I admit. 'You made me work hard for it, you little shit.' She blurts a laugh, looking utterly delighted at that comment. 'And you were an awesome best friend,' I add for the record, resting my forehead against hers.

'You're still my best friend,' she replies immediately.

'With benefits?' I lift a brow and bite down on my bottom lip.

Her eyes darken as though she likes that, but then they reset to something heartfelt, a world of emotion shining through. 'With everything, favourite. I can't wait to marry you.'

AUTHOR NOTE

Please be aware that the following note
contains a major plot spoiler.

I wrestled with the idea of writing a story that involved a woman finding a lump in her breast and that lump turning out to be benign. I certainly didn't write that from a fairytale 'and they all lived happily ever after' point of view. My deeply loved father passed away following a gruelling battle with cancer, so I am painfully aware of the grim reality of this disease.

I also know, however, that I didn't set out to write a book about living with cancer. This is a story about living with health anxiety—a lonely, obsessive disorder that I personally battle every day and have been medicated for at times. While I certainly don't intend for this book to represent what health anxiety looks like for everyone, if any of Josie's story resonates with you,

I hope it helps you realise that you are not alone, you are not losing your mind, and that your condition is important and treatable.

Also, stay off Google because I'm pretty sure that not all the five billion people on the internet went to medical school.

With much love,

Natalie x

ACKNOWLEDGEMENTS

Of course, my dream-come-true book almost became a nightmare because the universe has a cheeky sense of humour. After sending this manuscript to my dream publisher, I constantly hit refresh on my email like a maniac but got nothing back. Until the day I decided on a whim to check my spam folder, which I hardly ever did because I have no need for a $CashApp$ or to enlarge my penis. The day I did, however, I stumbled upon a reply from Allen & Unwin saying how much they loved this book and asking if it was available for acquisition. Must I say the words—always check your spam folder, regardless of how big your penis is!

Since that glorious day, I have loved every single moment of working with the publishing dream team, including Annette Barlow, Greer Gamble, Samantha Mansell, Shannon Edwards, Rosie Scanlan, Isabelle O'Brien, Sandra Buol, Hilary Reynolds and the rest of the fantastic crew who helped bring this book to life. Thank you so much for trusting me and for allowing me inside your beautiful world of books.

Kelly Fagan, thank you endlessly for believing in this story and for choosing me. This all began with you. My thanks also go to the whip-smart editor Abigail Nathan, and the talented Christa Moffitt for designing such a stunning cover.

To Penny Carroll, you were the first person to read this book after me, and I don't think I took a full breath until I got your message saying how much you loved it. Thank you for helping me figure out this story that you know I found exceptionally tricky to write, but look—we did it! I must throw in a bear-hug for the fabulous author Karina May for not only introducing me to Penny, but for being a hilarious and supportive friend. The 'delayed roll-in' is now legendary. Thanks also go to the fantastic author Maya Linnell for your patient advice during this exciting but bewildering time.

Thank you to my favourite Australian romance authors for your beautiful words about this story, including Ali Berg and Michelle Kalus, Amy Hutton, Clare Fletcher, Karina May, Penelope Janu and Steph Vizard. You put the biggest smile on my face (as have your swoonworthy books).

I could not have told Zac's story without the help of seasoned paramedics Nikki Hammer and Philip Walker. Thank you both for giving up your time to answer my endless questions about a job I greatly respect. To the inspiring journalist Jane Goldsmith—thank you for letting me turn the tables and interview you about the world of TV news reporting and anchoring. You are a gem, and Newcastle is so lucky to have you. Dr Elizabeth McKensey, thank you for taking on my embarrassingly long list of questions about health and health anxiety and for being so kind. Any mistakes or inaccuracies in this story are entirely my own.

I feel like I should apologise to my beta readers for asking them to read a much rougher version of this story than this one! So, a big thank you to Kathleen, Jenny, Marcia and Kerry for putting up with my drivel.

I owe a great deal of appreciation to Elise, Seb, Georgia and Kas for keeping me sufficiently caffeinated while I wrote this book and for installing a 'Nat' button in your amazing café that instantly brings up my coffee request. I promise to never change my order.

Thank you to my lovely friend Linda for letting me borrow the name 'Trouble' for Zac's fur-baby and pay tribute to the real Trouble. (Plot twist: the real Trouble is a cat, and the best one I have ever known. Rest in peace, sweetheart.)

I'm sending out masses of virtual hugs to the Bookstagram community for being my people and for making me feel less alone in this solitary job. Special thanks to Jenny Hickman/Fyfe, my brilliant co-writer and treasured friend. I'm still laughing about the balls. Also, a shout-out to Ashley Mills-Thomson for suggesting the perfect wedding song for when Zac and Josie begin losing their battle against romantic love.

Speaking of love, to my mum, Eva, and stepdad, Thom—just skip past the naughty parts, 'kay? Lol. Seriously, though, without your unwavering support, I wouldn't be writing these words. Thank you for always cheering me on and for being my breath of fresh air when I'm feeling trapped.

To my deeply missed and late father, Les: life will never feel whole again without your soothing voice, but I will keep listening for it. I love you.

My dear sister and unofficial twin, Tania, to whom this book is dedicated: no one deserves absolute and complete love more than you, and that is something you will always have from me.

To my gorgeous husband, Brent: thank you for your tireless care and understanding throughout not only my topsy-turvy creative career but also through my relentless health anxiety. There is so much of Zac Jameson in you. You are my everything. And of course, smothering kisses go to our precious babies.

Finally, a huge thank you to *you* for taking a chance on this story and for (hopefully) reading it all the way through. Friends-to-lovers is the best trope, yeah? That *I've been waiting for this for so long* moment . . . gah. Gets me every time.